DAN FESPERMAN

# THE WARLORD'S SON

Dan Fesperman is a former foreign correspondent who worked in *The Baltimore Sun*'s Berlin bureau during the years of civil war in the former Yugoslavia, as well as in Afghanistan during the recent conflict. *Lie in the Dark* won the Crime Writers Association of Britain's John Creasey Memorial Dagger Award for best first crime novel, and *The Small Boat of Great Sorrows* won its Ian Fleming Steel Dagger Award for best thriller. His Web site is www.danfesperman.com.

AUG

2012

ALSO BY DAN FESPERMAN

*The Small Boat of Great Sorrows*

*Lie in the Dark*

# THE
# WARLORD'S
# SON

# THE
# WARLORD'S
# SON

## DAN FESPERMAN

VINTAGE CRIME/BLACK LIZARD
*Vintage Books*
*A Division of Random House, Inc.*
*New York*

FIRST VINTAGE CRIME/BLACK LIZARD EDITION, SEPTEMBER 2005

*Copyright © 2004 by Dan Fesperman*

All rights reserved. Published in the United States by Vintage Books,
a division of Random House, Inc., New York, and in Canada by Random
House of Canada Limited, Toronto. Originally published in hardcover in the
United States by Alfred A. Knopf, a division of Random House, Inc.,
New York, in 2004.

Vintage is a registered trademark and Vintage Crime/Black Lizard
and colophon are trademarks of Random House, Inc.

This is a work of fiction. Names, characters, places, and incidents
either are the product of the author's imagination or are used fictitiously.
Any resemblance to actual persons, living or dead, events,
or locales is entirely coincidental.

The Library of Congress has cataloged the Knopf edition as follows:
Fesperman, Dan.
The warlord's son : a novel / by Dan Fesperman.
p. cm.
1. Americans—Afghanistan—Fiction. 2. Pakistanis—Afghanistan—Fiction.
3. Afghanistan—Fiction. 4. Translators—Fiction. 5. Journalists—Fiction.
I. Title.
PS3556.E778W37 2004
813'.54—dc22
2004011841

**Vintage ISBN-10: 1-4000-3048-X**
**Vintage ISBN-13: 978-1-4000-3048-4**

*Book design by Virginia Tan*

www.vintagebooks.com

Printed in the United States of America
10  9  8  7  6  5  4  3  2

*To the memory of fallen colleagues*

The eye of the dove is lovely, my son, but the sky is made for the hawk. So cover your dovelike eyes and grow claws.

*—Pashtun proverb*

# THE
# WARLORD'S
# SON

## CHAPTER ONE

T HE SUN does not rise in Peshawar.

It seeps—an egg-white smear that brightens the eastern horizon behind a veil of smoke, exhaust and dust. The smoke rises from burning wood, cow patties and old tires, meager flames of commerce for kebab shops and bakers, metalsmiths and brick kilns. The worst of the exhaust sputters from buzzing blue swarms of motor rickshaws, three-wheeled terrors that careen between horse carts and overloaded buses.

But it was the dust that Najeeb Azam knew best. Like him, it had swirled down from the arid lands of the Khyber and never settled, prowling restlessly in the streets and bazaars as if awaiting a fresh breeze to carry it to some farther, better destination.

In the morning it coated his pillow, a faint powder flecked with soot. In the evening he wiped it from his face and coughed cinders into a handkerchief, never quite able to flush it from either pores or lungs. Wherever he traveled it went along for the ride, a parasite, a little gift from his adopted home. He was respectful of its mysterious cloaking powers, because things had a way of disappearing in Peshawar—people, ideas, entire political movements. They would be loud and noticeable one day, only to vanish without a trace the next, and with each new day someone or something else always seemed to have gone missing.

A Peshawar dawn nonetheless had its charms, and Najeeb liked to rise early to savor them. So, on a warm morning in mid-October he stood in the darkness of his small kitchen a half hour before sunrise, brewing tea while listening to Mansour's horse cart leaving for the

bazaar. He knew without looking that the old man stood like a charioteer on a narrow wooden flatbed, reins in hand, pomegranates and tomatoes piled behind him, the baggy folds of his *shalwar kameez* flowing ghostlike in the pale light. The lonely *clip-clop* was soothing, yet also a sort of warning, like the ticking of a bomb. It was part of Peshawar's daily countdown to chaos. Soon enough the narrow streets would explode with vehicles, animals and people, beggars and merchants elbow to elbow as both cried out for rupees.

The loudspeaker of a nearby mosque crackled to life. Najeeb strolled to the living room, setting his teacup on a shelf and kneeling, lowering his forehead to the rug in prayer. This, too, was a ritual of tranquillity, yet it never seemed quite peaceful enough here.

In the tribal lands of his boyhood the muezzin's cry had been a solitary call, haunting and lovely. He used to pretend the message was for him alone, and to Najeeb there was still no grander expression of power than the words *Allahu akbar,* "God is great," when carried on a morning breeze across empty countryside. But in Peshawar there were more muezzins than he could count, and their calls became an unruly conversation—one voice trumping another in a war above the rooftops. Cats yowling over turf. Or perhaps Najeeb was turning into an infidel, a worldly backslider. A Kafir, as his father's Pashtun tribesmen would have said. Life never seemed half so holy now as it once had, and in a country where not only a man's calling but also his marriage was generally set in stone by age eighteen, Najeeb was still a work in progress at twenty-seven.

As a boy he'd roamed a wonderland of extremes, a rural princeling at play among bearded, turbaned men with rifles slung on their backs, all of whom owed their allegiance to his father. After breakfast he might sprint barefoot through the dew of waist-high poppies, dodging marauding boys from the village with slingshots round their necks. As the sun climbed higher he sought the refuge of high defiles to watch smuggler parades of camels and horses, teatime caravans swaying and clanking through the passes. Then, off to bed on the verandah of his father's *hujera,* the men's guest house, where he gazed up at stars so icy bright that it seemed they might pierce his skull. Pleasantly weary, he stretched out on a rope bed, eavesdropping on his father's guests and supplicants—smoky, piratical gatherings in the *hujera's* great room, with hubble-bubble hookahs and high-caliber bandoleers, lulling him to sleep with the streamside murmur of their mutter and growl, and

the whine and hum of their radio, beaming news from the great beyond. Occasionally a burst of laughter or an angry shout shouldered into his dreams, but by morning there were only him and the muezzin beneath another clear sky.

Yet that world also had its special cloaking magic. It was a place where he learned quickly to conceal his thoughts and dreams, and from his earliest years Najeeb's elders taught him to hold in his emotions, sheathing them like a weapon.

At the age of eighteen he abruptly left that world behind, dispatched across the seas to a university in the United States. It was his father's idea, a vain stab at worldliness to impress a few haughty ministers in the government corridors of Islamabad. Najeeb went reluctantly, and for months he held himself sternly under wraps, bookish and brooding through a North Carolina winter amid airless dreams of home.

Then came the spring, and Najeeb emerged timidly from underground, sampling the bounty of bright new places that began to make home seem small, plain and crude. There were supermarkets as big as his village, libraries the size of canyons, lush trees alive with blossoms and songbirds. Then there were the women, practically naked compared to the ones he'd grown up with. They were a temptation, he knew, yet there was a holiness about them, too—as if heaven and hell had been rolled into one amazing creation of bare arms, exposed legs and lustrous heads of hair, their animated faces open to the world and all its possibilities. They soon became responsible for an altogether new kind of training in Najeeb's life. Tell us your feelings, they demanded. Share your thoughts. Having been exposed to Shakespeare in the same heady spring, Najeeb found himself torn in ways he had never anticipated. To feel or not to feel, that was the question.

And now, years after his homecoming, he was not only restless but trapped—banished from tribal lands by his father, barred from America by consular officials.

His father's action had followed a betrayal that Najeeb no longer cared to revisit. The consular ban was of a more recent vintage. The United States had decided the previous month that it no longer wanted his company, after his two worlds had collided in ways previously unimaginable in the burning skies of lower Manhattan.

So he soldiered on in Peshawar, feeling as if he'd snagged a little of himself in each place he'd departed. And as each morning's peace dis-

solved he often found himself brooding over what was missing, sometimes believing that he, too, was disappearing into the Peshawar haze,
as indistinct as the horizon. In a country where most people defined
themselves by family or faith, Najeeb found himself resorting to a
more American approach, seeking identity from his various occupa-
tions. For the moment, then, he was a translator and guide, a painter of
birds, an unemployed computer engineer, and, most recently, a journalist of sorts, reporting for a rambling English daily called the *Frontier Report.*

The few people in Peshawar who knew Najeeb well could have
added further labels—disowned son, enthusiastic fornicator, occasional imbiber of forbidden beverage, habitual consorter with foreigners—tireless seeker of any path, in other words, that might lead
beyond Pakistan. And at this precarious moment in the city's history,
when choosing sides was the order of the day, Najeeb remained dan-
gerously neutral.

One thing no one ever called him was lazy, and today's schedule was
particularly industrious. First on the agenda: a ride on his motor
scooter to the humble offices of the *Frontier Report,* where, as always,
there would be plenty to write about. His daily task was to fashion a
digest of news briefs from the tribal hinterlands of the North-West
Frontier Province. It always made for strange reading—rustic feuds
and oddball robberies, villages convulsed over the tiniest of matters.
Perhaps someday he would collect them in a volume of curios for his
friends in the United States, a Pakistani gothic that would finally help
them understand what made this place tick.

The most important business of the day was scheduled for late
afternoon, when Najeeb would meet yet another foreign journalist
who wanted to hire him for guiding and interpreting. A fixer, the job
was called, and today's client was American.

With most of the journalists so far the routine had been pretty standard. They spent their first few days doing interviews in the streets,
liking the lilt of the word "bazaar" in their copy and enjoying the way
every merchant invited them inside for tea. Najeeb translated while
fending off hordes of curious barefoot boys and legless beggars.

If there happened to be a demonstration that day, they covered it,
taking care to stay upwind from the tear gas. Then came the obligatory
visit to a madrassah, one of the religious schools that supplied the Taliban with so many foot soldiers. Black-haired boys kneeling in straight

lines on scrubbed marble floors, heads bobbing as they recited the Koran. Then perhaps a chant or two of "Death to America," before collecting quotes from the resident Holy Scholar.

Najeeb and his clients always shared an awkward laugh in the taxi afterward, the reporter never quite sure where Najeeb stood on these matters, and Najeeb never eager to say, not when every cabbie was a potential informant.

Then, unless there was some new wave of refugees to badger, Najeeb would escort his client east, three hours down the bouncing highway to the calm green sterility of Islamabad, to seek out bureaucrats and diplomats who might grant travel papers for the Afghan border—because Afghanistan was the ultimate goal of every client, even if the border had been closed for weeks and would likely stay that way awhile longer.

If it ever opened, Najeeb would probably cross it as well. Not that he enjoyed gunfire. But at a pay rate of a hundred fifty dollars a day he couldn't afford to say no, because the one thing that might yet get him out of this place was cash.

Yet even as his supply of cash reached three thousand dollars and counting, the American embassy grew ever more remote. A hasty security cordon that had gone into place after September 11 had crept ever farther down the surrounding boulevards. Now, a mere five weeks later, you couldn't get within blocks of the place, and for the moment a visa was out of the question. Not only had most of the embassy staff left the country, but there was now a waiting list, a clerk told him by telephone. It might take weeks, even months. Meanwhile, reports filtered back from the United States of young Pakistani men disappearing into jails by the hundreds, gone without a word of explanation. So Najeeb bided his time and stacked his crisp fifties and hundreds, stockpiling ammunition for a battle that might never come.

Such was the drift of Najeeb's thinking that morning when, still on his knees, he was startled by a whisking sound from over by the door. Had he completed his prayers? He wasn't sure. The loudspeakers of the mosques were silent. A rickshaw whined past outside, scouting for the day's first fare. He checked his watch—still time for another cup of tea—but his eyes were drawn to a spinning white object on the floor tiles. It was an envelope, just coming to rest. Someone had shoved it beneath the door. He listened for departing footsteps, but there was only the clopping of another horse, so he rose stiffly and crossed the

room, throwing open the door in expectation of discovering the crouching messenger, caught in the act.

But there was no one. Nothing. And the stairwell was silent. It was as if the envelope had fallen from the sky with the first shaft of sunlight. Shutting the door, he picked it up. Whoever had sealed the cream-colored envelope had done so without a single smudge, meaning he was either clean or careful.

Najeeb tore it open at the top and pulled out a folded sheet of paper of the same creamy complexion. There was no letterhead or official markings, only a handwritten message in black ink, neat and cramped, giving the impression of someone not accustomed to writing. At the top were the numbers "24:30," and the writing below was in Arabic. It was a passage from the Koran. With no one there to watch, Najeeb allowed himself an irreverent smile. No doubt he was about to receive a scolding from a neighbor, some lesson in morals from a well-meaning meddler.

"Enjoin believing men to turn their eyes away from temptation and to restrain their carnal desires," the first line said. "This will make their lives purer."

His smile widened. Someone must have seen Daliya exiting a few nights ago, and it probably wasn't the first time. The memory brightened his mood. Whereas he thought of himself as wispy and insubstantial, she was full and complicated, a soul worth clinging to. He continued reading.

"Enjoin believing women to turn their eyes away from temptation and to preserve their chastity; not to display their adornments."

Oh, but such adornments. If this writer only knew. Another set of numbers followed, 24:39, meaning the writer had skipped ahead. The next passage took his smile away.

"As for the unbelievers, their works are like a mirage in a desert. The thirsty traveler thinks it is water, but when he comes near he finds that it is nothing. He finds God there, who pays him back in full. Swift is God's reckoning."

Najeeb wondered angrily what sort of "reckoning" the writer had in mind. Did God's self-appointed scold also intend to be His avenger? He crumpled the page, then reconsidered, smoothing it out and reaching for a pen. This demanded a reply. He pulled his own copy of the Koran from between English editions of Philip Roth and Paul Auster, thumbing the pages. Where was that verse that had recently caught his

eye? There. Just as he remembered. He'd be quoting it out of context, of course. In fact, he was likely misinterpreting it altogether, a thought that returned his smile with a gleam of mischief.

"2:79," he wrote. Then he scribbled in rusty Arabic: "Woe betide those that write the scriptures with their own hands and then declare: 'This is from God,' in order to gain some paltry end."

He stuffed the page into the messenger's own envelope and resealed it with tape, then wrote on the outside in Urdu, "A reply to this morning's visitor to apartment 12." After a second cup of tea he grabbed his satchel and the keys to his scooter, taking care to lock the door before rushing down the stairwell. He posted the envelope by the mailboxes at the entrance, wondering how long it would be before someone took the bait. For a moment he had misgivings—why stir the pot?—and his stomach rumbled, as queasy as if he'd just eaten too much *chapal kebab*. He'd have to remind Daliya to take more care in her comings and goings. The city grew more dangerous and irrational by the day.

"Meddlesome fanatics," Najeeb muttered on his way into the streets. "They'll be the death of us all."

## CHAPTER TWO

A s the second Molotov cocktail exploded into flame a mere twenty feet to his left, it occurred to Skelly that he was paying the price for having forgotten an old but important lesson: Choosing the wrong fixer can get you killed.

It was not supposed to have been a problem, this demo—five hundred hotheads with a scratchy bullhorn mounting an hour-long rant against America and Musharraf, Pakistan's latest president for life, followed by the roughing up of a straw-filled effigy. The effigy, a sort of all-purpose Ugly American painted red, white and blue, was to have been set alight for the cameras. Then everyone was supposed to break for lunch and call it a day.

But halfway through the festivities the policemen waded in, and when the crowd shoved back they began swatting at skulls and rib cages with long wooden batons, flailing like enraged schoolmasters. Things got ugly in a hurry. Had Skelly stationed himself a hundred yards farther down the block everything would have been fine. He would have had a nice seat, in fact, a vantage point with easy escape and a cozy teahouse at hand, somewhere to relax afterward and put his notes in order while the smoke cleared. Mopping up would have required nothing more than a few interviews with shopkeepers—a spice merchant, perhaps, they were always good for a little sensory detail. Though God knows you wouldn't want to convey the smell of this place, with its open-air toilets and slicks of donkey shit.

It would have been an easy first byline on this, Skelly's first full day in Pakistan, leaving him the afternoon to shower, get his stomach

under control, crank up the airco and slide under the hotel sheets for a real night's rest. Then he would get going in earnest tomorrow, having held jet lag and microbes at bay.

Instead he found himself at the epicenter of an angry mob, backed against a filthy stone wall while the firebombs exploded. And it was all the fault of his idiot fixer, Babar, same name as the elephant. Just look at him, Skelly thought. The man's wide eyes and strangled look of panic bespoke his lack of qualifications far more eloquently than his broken English.

Skelly had known Babar for all of thirty-seven minutes, having chosen him hastily from a crowd in the hotel lobby. Picking an interpreter that way was breaking a rule right off the bat, but Skelly had been in a hurry. There had been a dozen or more to choose from, lingering by some couches near the front desk. Each had been dressed in a *shalwar kameez*—a loose-fitting shirt drooping to the knees, with matching baggy pants cinched by a drawstring. Skelly was already accustomed to seeing this traditional costume in the streets, but it looked incongruous in the lobby of the Pearl Continental, what with the smartly clad desk clerks, the handsome wood paneling, the wall-mounted televisions blaring CNN and the well-appointed breakfast buffet, complete with a man in a white chef's hat who fried omelets to order. Or maybe it was lack of sleep that made them seem such a spectral bunch—dark faces hovering above billowy pastels, like a gospel choir waiting to sing at a funeral. It was an appropriate enough image, Skelly supposed, because these men were definitely hoping to perform, and it was death that had put them in business. Journalists were besieged by such characters at the fringes of every war and insurrection, and their eager come-ons were virtually the same from country to country: "How are *you*, sir? You need a translator?" They were the lounge lizards of the trade, and usually only one in ten knew what he was doing, so you hired instead from the staffs of local newspapers or on the recommendations of colleagues.

But three years in the suburbs of the Midwest had left Skelly forgetful of past lessons. He'd grown used to being spoon-fed quotes by publicists and spokespersons, heading back to the newsroom with a press release, a few handouts and a Styrofoam cup of overbaked coffee.

In Pakistan he felt as if he were starting over, and he clumsily tried to pick a winner from among the lobby long shots. Babar had stood out as the friskiest in the paddock, aggressive yet well organized, reeling

off a patter that made his English seem passable. Spoke Pashto as well, Babar said, along with Urdu, the standard tongue of Pakistan. In fact, Babar had claimed to speak all the languages of the Afghan exile community, a population that in Peshawar numbered in the hundreds of thousands. Fluent in Dari, middling in Balti. Even knew a touch of Baluch in case Skelly was interested in heading south into the desert. And he had a driver. His cousin, of course. *Everything that you need, sir.* A sweeping gesture. *The car is waiting.*

But did Babar know the borderland tribal areas, and how one acquired the proper passes and permissions to visit them? Skelly had felt he ought to ask *something*, and this question had struck him as suitably difficult.

*Oh, yes, Mr. Skelly.* A dismissive wave. *It is not a problem.*

No problem. *Aucun problème. Nema problema.* From West Africa to the Balkans, it was the litany of can-do fixers the world over, and somehow Babar's words had reassured him.

But it was all a sham, of course—the sales patter rehearsed, every boast empty. Skelly had suspected as much when he saw the cousin's car, a rusting '83 Toyota with cracked windows and holes in the floorboard, the rushing pavement visible below.

His fears were confirmed by Babar's performance during their first interview, just before the demo began. They'd flagged down a weathered old man in a turban who had gone off on a lengthy tirade in Pashto in response to Skelly's first question, jabbing his finger and bobbing his head.

"He says he is angry," Babar offered in translation. "Angry at America."

"Yes?" Skelly prompted, waiting for the rest.

"Because of the planes bombing Afghanistan. He is angry. Angry at . . ."

"America. I know. But what else did he say? He went on for five minutes."

"You want with him five more minutes?" Furrowed brow. Utter incomprehension.

"No. I just want . . ." It was hopeless. Why bother? "Never mind."

"You mind him?"

"No."

"You want that we should . . . ?"

"*No.* Just forget it."

"Okay, Mr. Skelly. We forget him. It is not a problem."

Babar had then led them straight to their present precarious location, the only block of the bazaar where the level of risk now extended above and beyond the call of duty. Skelly had sensed the miscalculation as soon as he saw that the only other Westerner within sight was a young French photographer, a lean T-shirted daredevil in an Afghan scarf and a six-pocket vest, hair in a ponytail. His type was like the needle of a compass in these situations, pointing straight toward the places you least wanted to be. Twenty-five years ago—could it really have been that long?—an old foreign editor had advised Skelly to "stay away from the bang-bang and don't get yourself killed. That's for young French photographers."

Yet here was Skelly, shoulder to shoulder with Agence France-Presse, the man's motor drive whirring, Domke bag slung like an ammunition belt as he crouched for a low-angle shot of a fallen policeman, not even flinching as half a cinder block landed beside him with an alarming *thunk*.

Skelly felt tired just watching, if only because it reminded him of every other capital of world misery he'd visited—Managua, Baghdad, and the deserts of Kuwait. Sarajevo and Pristina. Mogadishu and Goma. Port-au-Prince and Panama City. Hebron and Gaza. Khartoum and, then, there at the last, Monrovia, deep in the anarchy of Liberia—the very capital of random death. Malice and cunning had grinned from thin faces and deep-socketed eyes, every gun barrel following him like a stare. But the worst of it had been the armed tyranny of twelve-year-olds, vacant-eyed boys who had lost all sense of fear, order and limits. He wasn't sure what it was about them that scared him most—the bored way in which they shot holes in people or their eerie resemblance to his own sons, like some foreign X-Games version equipped with a Kalashnikov, ruled by hormones, every parent's worst nightmare. Those horrors, plus the gastrointestinal bile that left him writhing on a dirty cot for two weeks, out of touch and out of money, had convinced Skelly that he would never again see home. Thus had his eventual escape seemed like divine deliverance, a stay of execution, some last-minute pardon from the Creator. Skelly took it as a sign that it was time to get out of the game, even if it meant the newspaper might put him out to pasture.

Which is exactly what happened, of course. Because what could be more worthless to an aspiring young editor than a weary scribbler

home from the wars, trailing a third wife, a fifth child and the correspondent's de rigueur collection of Oriental rugs and international folk art. Any fool could have seen that Skelly was a burnout, saddle sore from too many long rides with each of the Four Horsemen.

So he became the chattel of the suburban editor, a chirping young product of good schooling and a sheltered upbringing, thoroughly workshopped in people skills and every sort of ethnic and gender sensitivity. The man knew everything, in fact, except how to cover breaking news on a deadline, or the difference between Appalachia and Asia Minor, and he exhibited no desire whatsoever to approach Skelly, much less prod for signs of life. Instead he chose the easy way out, dispatching Skelly to the local version of Siberia, forty miles up Route 19 to Warren County, with its Wal-Marts, belt roads and Assemblies of God. Skelly wound up covering store openings, school openings, park openings and weather stories, filling in for whichever twenty-three-year-old had just pulled up stakes for the metro desk, that faraway place downtown that everyone but he aspired to.

After so many years abroad, he found himself struggling to make sense of his homeland. America, it seemed, had turned into a land of big-box stores and hundred-channel cable. On half the channels, grown men in suits argued with each other. On the other half, shapely blondes offered the latest numbers from Wall Street. The heavy, uncomfortable vehicles he'd once rented to cross deserts and minefields had become the transportation of choice for commuters and soccer moms, and nearly everyone over the age of thirty seemed to have either just scored big in the stock market or become the host of a new talk show. Skelly had never beheld so much prosperity, yet to a man his neighbors complained about money, and their lack of it, or of the faceless bureaucrats who were supposedly "on their backs," trying to take it all away.

Then, on a sunny September morning, the dirtier, hungrier world that Skelly knew better shouldered its way back into the public's view. He was at the Warren Mall doing man-in-the-street interviews about shark phobia when the first jet crashed, and then the second. He watched the twin towers crumble on a TV screen at Radio Shack, staring in rapt disbelief while young clerks from the food court sobbed on either side, his sense of dislocation growing by the minute. An hour later he returned to the office to find that his skills were suddenly back in demand.

"Help us understand them," his editors pleaded. "Why do they hate us?"

So he got a visa, went to a doctor for a few shots, and hopped on a plane. And, barely a month later, here he was—Stanford J. Kelly, if you're wondering about bylines, a.k.a. Stan Kelly, a.k.a. Skelly to just about everyone in the business except the new foreign editor, who insisted on calling him Stan. He was back in the game in yet another location, parachuted from the heavens after scarcely as much preparation as you might make for a weekend at the beach.

Still blinking against the glare, he felt rusty and uncertain. And he was downright ashamed of having made a blunder as egregious as hiring the wrong fixer. Because if war journalism in a foreign land is a sort of glorified tourism—overland adventure holiday, as the Brits might say, combined with geopolitical peep show—then the fixer is both travel agent and tout, one part hustler and another part sage. They are the first line of defense against cheaters and ne'er-do-wells, and the best-known weapon (apart from Marlboros and American dollars) against obstructive officials and checkpoint trolls. The best ones know who to talk to and where to find them, and can decipher the Sanskrit of local politics and all its petty grudges. But mostly what a fixer does is keep you alive and functioning, right down to knowing where to buy phone adapter plugs, the cheapest rugs and the cleanest food.

Skelly had already made up his mind to undo the damage of his current choice as quickly as possible. He would pay off Babar and head back to the hotel, and at four he'd keep the tentative appointment that a colleague had made for him with a fixer who came highly recommended. Najeeb something or other. Perfect English, supposedly, and his Pashto was as good as his Urdu. He even had a dash of Western sophistication in the bargain, it was said. He was pricey—Babar, at least, came cheap at sixty dollars per day—but a good fixer was worth every penny. Let the bean counters worry about the money. This was no place to cut corners.

For the moment, his more pressing worry was getting out of the demonstration alive. He grabbed hold of Babar, who, God help him, was following in the wake of the photographer, angling deeper into the maelstrom.

"Not there!" Skelly shouted. "This way."

Babar turned, following mutely, stunned livestock on a tether, and Skelly shoved him toward an alley that looked reasonably safe, the

noise of the crowd ringing in his ears, a buzz of anger and panic that seemed to ionize the dust. Other bodies jostled his, warm and damp against his shirtfront. People always smelled different in other countries, and their scent now was close and unmistakable. Not unpleasant, just different, a bouquet of sweat, spice and sandalwood that from now on would always remind him of this moment, this street. The wooden stock of a policeman's carbine bumped his hip bone. Babar's pale clothing loomed just ahead, flowing like something out of the *Arabian Nights.*

"Come on," he shouted, as Babar again threatened to veer astray.

"But my cousin's car, it is this way." Wild-eyed now, in need of a jolt.

"Fuck your cousin," Skelly shouted.

This was the sort of English even Babar could understand, and he followed without further resistance. A third Molotov cocktail released an orange genie of heat and flame, but it was well behind them, over by the photographer. Good. Skelly's instincts had been correct. It was like being tossed into a rip current but finding you could still do the strokes, if barely. Just keep paddling sideways until the current released its grip.

"Move it, Babar. C'mon!"

By now the police were gaining the upper hand, and Skelly managed to squeeze behind the cordon, the uniformed phalanx moving onward. Several policemen toward the rear had unholstered their pistols. Others were raising carbines to their shoulders, taking aim. But so far, no shots. That would burst the dam for sure.

Skelly reached into his pocket for his cell phone. Unless shots were fired, he and Babar would be safe now, having made it to a narrow empty street where every shop was locked and shuttered. He'd better call this fellow Najeeb to confirm their appointment. But what if somebody else had already hired him? Skelly swallowed a bubble of panic. There were certainly enough new journalists arriving for it to be possible.

In fact, Skelly was part of the media's second wave. The shock troops of mid-September had come mostly from bureaus in Europe and the Far East, plus the usual wire services and network crews. By now, a month later, many of the initial arrivals were already grumbling, convinced that either they or the story had gone stale. But one and all took comfort that at least they weren't among the unfortunates

marooned in the upper reaches of Afghanistan with the Northern Alliance. By now everyone had heard the horror stories—correspondents sleeping twelve to a room on the floors of dirty teahouses for fifty dollars a night, bathing outdoors from buckets of cold water, no doubt loaded with microbes. Working off portable generators and typing by headlamp while their breath frosted the keyboard. Rice and bread for breakfast, rice and bread for dinner. And there was nothing like a little shelling to kick-start your diarrhea first thing in the morning.

So far on the Pakistan front the only apparent hazard besides food and the occasional mob was ignorance. Most of the world's press had been caught well behind the learning curve, and on slow afternoons now in Islamabad you saw the latest arrivals from Washington, London, Paris, Frankfurt, Rome and Tokyo lounging by the pool of the Marriott, poring over shiny new books on the Taliban and Bin Laden, or digging into a Lonely Planet travel guide—the next best thing to interviewing your cab driver.

For all of Skelly's experience in poking and prodding at the world's oozing sores, his travels had never taken him either here or Afghanistan, a gap he'd always regretted, even if he was well past the age when it would have thrilled him most. He had long read of the region's intrigues, its violent patchwork history as a land of adventurers and warlords, whether they were tradesmen on the Silk Road or imperial chessmen in Kipling's Great Game. He knew also that it was a land that punished the timid and the naive, and, more to the point, anyone who had lost a step. But it was soldiers and spies who usually filled the casualty lists, and he was merely a hack. He'd be fine.

His introduction to Pakistan had come only eight hours earlier. He'd arrived at 3 a.m., stepping into the humid night air from a 757 out of Dubai following a twenty-six-hour journey that had begun on a crisp fall afternoon in the American heartland. He'd walked stiffly down the metal steps to the darkness of the warm tarmac, strolling past a silent line of military police in blue berets. The crowd of arrivals funneled through glass doors toward the fluorescent glare of the passport line. A mute gang of jumpsuited baggage handlers stood just beyond, waiting for something to do. He easily spotted the print journalists among the crowd. They were the cheapskates who insisted on manhandling their own battered trolleys into position by the squealing carousel. No one spoke, everyone too stunned by the hour and the air

miles to say a word. Trolley loaded, he moved onward past sullen customs agents, out a swinging door into a waiting crowd of hundreds who stood behind a rope—all those dusky faces staring at Skelly in the middle of the night, everyone in robes and veils but nary a word from any until the gypsy cabbies lunged to the fore, reaching for Skelly's bags and asking his destination as he muttered a terse "No, no," over and over, scanning the sidewalk ahead for the real taxi stand. He'd forgotten how he would need to be a hard bargainer, haggling with drivers and shopkeepers who would be trying to charge double or triple the local rate. It was all part of the game, even though the hundred rupees at issue might be worth only a buck and a half, and even though the driver might have eleven mouths to feed.

There was only enough time in Islamabad for a few hours of restless sleep, followed by a hazardous breakfast of runny eggs. Then he caught a hired car to Peshawar, leaving just before dawn, because his marching orders couldn't have been clearer: Get yourself to the Khyber Pass, and see how close you can creep to the Afghan border. If you can get across, do it. If not, see what else you can come up with.

Easy enough, Skelly supposed, except a thousand others already had the same idea.

But something about the brightening of the horizon had roused him from his stupor during the ride from Islamabad. He rolled down the taxi window to breathe in the day's last wisp of cool air, watching the countryside's slide show of minor wonders, stunning scenes of exotica beneath aromatic droops of dusty eucalyptus. He pulled a notebook from a rear pocket, suddenly determined to record everything he could while it was still fresh and new.

The first sight to catch his eye was an old man already at work in the half-light, sweeping the curbs of the four-lane road to Islamabad with a crude rush broom, harvesting a bottomless crop of dust. Then he saw two more, doing the same. Did someone actually pay them for this? They might as well try shoveling all the sand off a beach.

The sights multiplied as they eased into the countryside, Skelly's right hand hurrying across the narrow page with a tiny scratching sound:

> *rough wooden beds on rooftops of low homes, and in cane fields,*
> *w/people still asleep. thin blankets & sheets, same gray as their*
> *clothes. river crossing at Attock where alexander the great once*

*crossed, ancient fort on bluff. small stream in muddy ravine w/tent
pitched next to goat herd. 3 water buffaloes knee-deep in irrig ditch
& one grazing in tall grass. dung patties (cows?) pressed onto plaster
walls of houses, drying for fuel. camel on haunches in cane field.
bikes loaded with everything—sticks, burlap sacks, milk pails, boxed
TVs. tall mud chimney belching heavy black smoke, terrible
smell . . .*

"What's the smoke from?" he asked the driver, pencil pausing.
"Brick kilns."
Of course. Bricks were stacked all around them.
"They burn old tires to bake the bricks," the driver added. Skelly
wrote it down, all of it.

Passing them on the left, loud and jangling, a cargo truck. Like all
the others it was ornately painted, a thousand different colors and
designs from stem to stern, the cab lit by a red dome light that made it
glow like a bordello. The front of the trailer jutted over the cab, angled
like the transom of a galleon on the high seas. Magnificent. An earlier
one had been so overloaded with hay, every bulge swaddled in a white
sheet, that from behind the truck it had looked as if it were wearing a
giant turban, making Skelly laugh.

Then, off to the left, a high formation of bare stone, opening
deeply onto a quarry. There were dwellings up there, he saw, small
caves hacked into the side of the limestone bluff. Chairs and beds facing outward from the openings. A boy no older than three stared back
from the precipice, lit by the rising sun. Skelly waved. The boy didn't.

Every few miles there was some sort of military installation. A barracks, followed by an engineering unit, followed by the School for
Armor and Mechanized Warfare, its parking lot full of tanks. So incongruous, with their modern look and the sense of money being spent, as
if the government had decided to ignore all other points on the map
except these.

There were mosques, too, some of them large and grand but most
of them tiny and every bit as humble and grimy as their surroundings.

The driver turned on the radio for news on the hour, finding a version in English: American aircraft had mistakenly bombed a hospital.
The Taliban were claiming a hundred more civilian casualties. The
Northern Alliance offensive was stalled. In American sports, the Yan-
kees were back in the World Series.

None of it told Skelly a thing he hadn't known. Nor could he likely add much, even after a full day of reporting. Why not give them this instead, he thought, watching the landscape roll by. Give them this whole damned drive with its sights and sounds, even the smells. Because here on the ground, without the benefit of a single interview, you could already see how easily the anger might stir, build and grow in a place like this, finding both its solace and its outlet at those little mosques, the imams issuing marching orders in holy screeds, the Arabic verses charging the air like bolts of lightning.

But at best, Skelly knew, he'd only have room for a paragraph or two of descriptive detail, and that would likely have to wait for his weekend story. Even supposing he could supply everything, could somehow distill this journey into twenty column inches of deathless prose, who would read it? Some Midwestern housewife, perhaps, over her second cup of coffee after carpooling to grade school in her combat vehicle. Or some bored accountant, yawning through a lunch break. Most everybody else would skip it, content to get their daily feed from television or, for those who wanted more, from a national paper like the *Times*, or from the Internet.

As a correspondent from a mid-sized daily, in other words, Skelly was obsolete, as quaintly useless as a typewriter in a roomful of laptops, dispensing information that would be stale hours before it ever saw print. He knew as well that this initial rush of enthusiasm and insight would subside, overwhelmed by repeated exposure and his own limitations. Try as he might, his prose would never be supple enough to stretch to the heart of the matter.

So he would have to settle for the usual rewards, not that those were insignificant. In the weeks to come, Skelly knew, he would enter realms of old codes and unbreakable taboos. His hosts would be men wondering one minute how they might cut his throat while in the next they'd offer tea and refreshment, breaking bread pulled from a smoking ceramic hole in the ground, just as they would have done it five hundred years earlier.

Yes, he was back in the Third World, all right, with its taste upon his tongue and the stench high in his nostrils. And now, standing in a cobbled alley of a Peshawar bazaar, he was doing what so many Third World people do, at least in Pakistan. He was punching in numbers on a cell phone. He wanted to reach Najeeb, but on this block, at least, the signal was too weak, so they kept walking, Babar still nervously prattling on about his cousin.

When they reached the top of a rise, Skelly tried again. Glancing back toward the demonstration, he saw that the mob was receding, a storm tide heading meekly back to sea. Utterly ridiculous that it had ever been such a close call. But it would be something to tell Janine tonight on the phone. She was the latest of his wives. *Three of them.* The number still a marvel to him, as if he were a Hollywood playboy. Sometimes he mused that if he lived in one of the Persian Gulf States he'd still have all of them, each living on her own floor in a house that would have grown higher with every marriage. Might as well do it that way, at the rate he was paying the first two. And Janine was already in a pout over this trip. The thought of their late-arriving son, Brian, was like a stab of guilt in Skelly's chest, not so much because he missed the boy (after four previous children he'd experienced quite enough of the routines of infancy) but because in Brian he recognized yet another face that would grow disaffected and bored with him, no more inter-ested in Skelly's strange experiences than he would be in the tax code. Brian, like his predecessors, would grow up affixed to MTV and the Internet, saying "like" and "you know" and doing kick flips on a skate-board before he was old enough to wear a helmet. The Nation of Off-spring remained the one country Skelly was reluctant to enter, and he now feared he'd waited too late to request a visa.

Enough of these thoughts of home. The jet lag must be getting to him. Pay this fellow Babar a crisp fifty, plus a tip for the equally useless cousin. Then grab a cab back to the hotel, and with any luck his fixer problems would soon be solved. But first he'd try the number again.

He punched it. Waited. Finally it began to ring.

This fellow Najeeb had better be good.

## CHAPTER THREE

### Regional Briefs

By Najeeb Azam

**TWO KILLED:** Two women were killed in a clash between factions of the Hafizi tribe at a village near Khairpur yesterday. The warring groups resorted to free use of clubs and axes. The dead were identified as Ms. Akhtar and Ms. Jatoi. Five unidentified were taken to hospital. According to reports, an old enmity existed between the groups over the theft of a cow last year, a dispute that has claimed several lives. Last Wednesday several armed men from one group attacked a rival village with grenade launchers. Police rushed to the fighting today and controlled the situation, but both groups are said to have taken up positions in the area.

**WEDDING MURDER:** A man shot his daughter dead on her wedding day in the village of Karwanzai in the Mohmand Tribal Agency yesterday. According to police, Shahid Khan, whose daughter was to marry his daughter-in-law's brother, was unhappy with the *wata-sata* arrangement, whereby a brother and sister of one family marry the sister and brother of another. Shahid visited his daughter, Sakeena, on the morning of the wedding, then shot her in the chest and fled. She was rushed to hospital, where she succumbed to her injuries.

T HERE WAS SOMETHING WORRISOME about this fellow Skelly. But what, exactly?

Najeeb took the man's measure from across a table at the Pearl Continental, after both men had piled their plates with the bounty of the

afternoon buffet. At nine dollars a plate it was criminally expensive, enough to support a family of beggars for weeks. But why complain when someone else was picking up the tab? So Najeeb had attacked the steaming silver vats with relish, ladling out chunks of chicken and lamb, drenched in curries and heavy sauces. He moved on to the sliced tomatoes and cucumbers, mounds of steamed vegetables, and big scoops of yellow rice. Lastly he plucked a few samples from what seemed to be every sort of bread from East and West, making a note to leave room for a visit to the dessert table, where honeyed pastries and frosted cakes sat regally on silver platters, barely touched even at this late hour of the afternoon. He wondered if the staff took home the leftovers.

"Been doing this long?" Skelly asked, mouth full, eyebrows cocked.

Presumably he meant interpreting, not freeloading, although there was enough of the rake in his expression to suggest both.

"A month," Najeeb said. "Strictly Europeans and Americans so far." Najeeb spoke as precisely as possible when meeting prospective clients. Journalists were notoriously hard to disabuse of first impressions. He was also trying to get a fix on Skelly, and what he had detected so far made him wary, although he couldn't yet say why.

The man was in his early fifties, by the look of it. Full head of wavy hair going silver. His clothes were faded, rumpled and looked as if they'd already picked up a week's worth of dust, although he had apparently just arrived. Decent shape. An extra pound or two around the middle, but moved as if he'd be quick on his feet when necessary. But his most striking trait was his gray-blue eyes, animated yet beaming a sense of calm and resolution that seemed at odds with the circumstances. Skelly wasn't goggle-eyed the way most first-timers were in Pakistan. Although, like everyone else, he was already complaining about Peshawar's soupy air.

"How can you stand it?" Skelly asked, mopping a puddle of orange sauce with a flap of local bread. "I thought you'd at least be able to see the mountains from here."

"When I was a boy you could see all the way to Afghanistan. On some days now the smog even blows up into the Khyber Pass, although usually it is clear up there."

"Another good reason to head for the border."

So he, too, wanted to go to Afghanistan. Hardly a surprise.

"By the way," Skelly said. "If I ever suggest anything foolhardy, I hope you'll have the good sense to let me know. So don't be shy."

Najeeb nodded, wondering if the man had recently had a close call.

"On the other hand, if you ever see the slightest chance for getting us off the beaten path, away from the hordes"—he spread his hands to encompass the cafe, where his colleagues of all nations filled the air with multilingual chatter—"then let me know right away, even if a little hazard and hardship might be involved. Am I making sense?"

"You don't wish to be killed. But you will take a few risks for a story the others do not have."

"Exactly." He smiled broadly, although Najeeb knew better than to be flattered by mere smiles. He'd found them to be cheap currency in America, doled out by shop clerks and fast-food cashiers.

"But I guess you get the same request from everybody."

Najeeb supposed he did, although none of his clients to date had been quite so up front about their ignorance of local affairs. His previous client had also been a first-timer from America, but he'd been neat and organized, pants creased and collars pressed. At their first meeting he had handed Najeeb a typewritten list of story ideas and people he wished to meet, and he had never wasted a chance to show off his knowledge of Peshawar, making it awkward for Najeeb to correct him on the numerous occasions when he was wrong. The man had apparently read somewhere that the best first question to ask a Pakistani man was how many children he had, so he'd done so at every opportunity and was crestfallen to find that Najeeb was not only childless but unmarried, as if there were no category for that response on his chart of Peshawar demographics.

Skelly, on the other hand, was almost blithe in his ignorance.

"So what should I be asking you about this place? Went to a demo this morning, but it was nothing special. Hardly seemed like the whole city was up in arms. Just a few hundred idiots who let the police push them around. What's everybody think of the war?"

"They hope it will not last long. The longer it goes on, the more likely the hotheads will take power. And no one wants them getting hold of the bombs."

"The nukes?"

"Yes."

"Reasonable enough. You're Pashtun, right? Seems like I heard you grew up in the tribal areas."

"Yes." No sense leading him further in this direction.

"Are you Afridi? Your tribe, I mean. Isn't that one of the biggest, with all sorts of clans and subclans?"

"Yes." Stony expression, which he could pull with the best of them. "Is that a problem for you?"

"Well, no. I just . . . no. No problem at all."

Skelly seemed flustered, as if worried he'd just made a cultural gaffe. Good. Let him think so, if that was what it took to prevent further prying. Theirs would be a business relationship only, seller to customer, and under those terms Najeeb would shape the role however Skelly wished. A Swiss television crew a few weeks ago had fancied him as the Pakistani party boy, so that's what he'd become, letting them coax him into drinking a few beers up in their suite. He'd slurred his words and gotten obligingly giddy, playing the exotic fool to their knowing nods. The previous American, on the other hand, had pegged Najeeb as the stone-faced sage, and maybe that's the role Skelly would choose—Najeeb the Inscrutable.

It would at least be in keeping with his training as a boy, when it was considered an advantage to hold your face rigid through both anger and elation. As his father had always said, "It is all right to boil. Just don't show them any bubbles or steam." He remembered a wedding celebration where the men of the village had easily spotted an outsider from Punjab only because the man had dared to tap his feet to the music. Now, with four years of America under his belt, he was somewhere between the two extremes, and perhaps it was his more Western side that suddenly felt a little sorry for Skelly's discomfiture. To undo the damage, he found himself asking, of all things, "How many children do you have?"

"Five."

"Boys?"

"Two of them."

Most clients would have then been off to the races, chatting with abandon about their families. In America perfect strangers had opened themselves to him like books aboard buses and trains, or in restaurants and bars, telling him everything from their annual salary to the details of their divorce. Skelly was another matter. He shifted in his chair and grinned, or was it a grimace?

"My daughter Carol is the oldest. The youngest isn't even two. But they're spread all over creation. Three wives, you see."

"Yes. Of course."

No snapshots followed. Nor did Skelly take the occasion to say how much he missed them. Perhaps he was the sort of man who was more comfortable in the world at large.

"Do you travel much?" Najeeb asked, his curiosity piqued.

"Used to. Gotten rusty the past couple years. I've mostly been stranded in the Midwest, doing next to nothing. So it's good to be out and about again."

Stranded. An interesting way to refer to home. But it was how Najeeb felt about Peshawar, and maybe that was what unsettled him about Skelly. It was almost as if he were speaking to some latter-day version of himself, a bit heavier and grayer, yet still straining at his tether, still looking for somewhere to take root.

A sudden commotion by the hotel entrance turned their heads. A young man who had just entered the revolving door was being greeted warmly in an outburst of hugs, salaams and joyous shouts. Even the ridiculous doorman, decked out as if he were still an imperial servant of Queen Victoria, smiled appreciatively, something he almost never did for a local.

"What's going on?" Skelly asked. "Recognize any of them?"

It was partly a test. Show me your stuff, Skelly was saying, and Najeeb realized with relief that he did know the young man, although not well.

"It is Haji din Razaq, the youngest son of Mahmood Razaq."

"The Afghan warlord?"

"Yes. Mahmood Razaq was a Mujahedeen commander. He fought the Russians for years, but when the Taliban took power they kicked him out. Now he is rich. Made all his money in Dubai and Saudi. But he has returned, waiting like all the others to get back in the door. If it ever opens."

"Seems like I read where he was thinking about making a forced entry. Wanting to lead his own insurrection. Or had been, until the air strikes started."

"The word on the street is that he still is. He is supposedly going to lead a hundred men into Afghanistan."

"When?" A quickened response with an edge to it. Najeeb should have kept it vague. Razaq's departure was expected any day, but that sort of news would probably get Skelly up out of his chair, heading straight for Haji din Razaq.

"No one knows for sure. This week, perhaps."

"Interesting."

You could see the wheels turning, the man weighing risk and chance, wondering if he might get himself across the border even sooner than expected.

"Could you introduce me to the son? Before he leaves the hotel, I mean. You did say you know him."

"I think he will recognize me." He hoped it was true. Haji din Razaq was usually agreeable enough, if a bit impulsive like his father. For people who were about to embark on such a sensitive mission, the family was certainly spreading the word all over town. But that was in keeping with the Razaq way, which on the whole was boastful and arrogant.

"Would you like me to ask him if we could arrange a meeting with his father?"

"Yes. That would be great."

Najeeb put down his napkin, glancing forlornly at his food. By the time he returned it would be cold. On the other hand, with a little luck he might now merit half a day's pay.

"Wait here. I will go and see."

Skelly watched Najeeb make his way across the lobby floor. Interesting fellow, and his English was perfect. Bit of a cold fish, but after the glibness of Babar, circumspection seemed like a virtue. Besides, Skelly had never believed it was necessary to become your fixer's best pal, unlike some reporters who took it to extremes, even buying gifts for their children.

He did believe it was important to build trust and good chemistry. Nor was he above a few transactions in the barter of small favors—putting in a word with some consular official in exchange for a job well done. And the cold ones, he had found, almost always warmed up. But there was nothing cold or aloof about the man's deep brown eyes, which seemed to take in everything. Guarded—maybe that was the better word. And the fellow had certainly gotten prickly about his tribal heritage. Maybe he was simply a snob. Well, even that might prove useful. Skelly would love to sneak a peek inside Pakistan's tribal aristocracy, especially if they couldn't find a way across the border.

And maybe this Razaq fellow would lead somewhere, although Skelly figured he was at least the hundredth reporter in line. Both *Time* and *Newsweek* had already written of the old warlord's intentions.

By now Najeeb had reached Razaq's son, and they were shaking hands. Good. A breath of fresh air after that dolt Babar, who was again lurking near the lobby couches, looking sheepishly in another direction whenever Skelly glanced his way. The long hours without sleep were beginning to catch up to Skelly, and the heavy meal was already making him drowsy. But he knew better than to take a nap. Probably

best to stay up as late as possible if he wanted a good night's sleep, so he poured another cup of coffee in hopes of recalibrating his spinning inner clock. He decided not to venture out for any further interviews today, lest some merchant ply him with more green tea, which would keep him from ever sleeping.

He looked again toward Najeeb, watching the man nod at the young Razaq. A good face, lean and handsome. Black hair angled lankly across the forehead, beard neatly trimmed. Physically the man reminded him of a favorite fixer from Gaza, years ago. Ahmed something or other. But Ahmed had been a chatterbox, full of gossip, hands always moving, a windup toy that never ran down. This one seemed to hold his energy in reserve, which he supposed would serve them well if they ended up traveling rough.

So how much would he have to pay for today's services? Up to now he'd only counted on buying the man's lunch. But if Najeeb arranged an interview with Mahmood Razaq, that would merit something extra. Shelling out for half a day would mean he'd already spent $135 on interpreters, with nothing to show for it but a brief on the demo. Not his money, though, so why worry. The worst the paper could do was call him home early, and that wouldn't be the end of the world. Although he found himself warming to the chase. Meeting Razaq might lead to something more. Or perhaps he could take a closer look at the local exile community with its layers and its fissures. They were the ones vying to rule the new Afghanistan, already auditioning for the West even as the Taliban held fast, five weeks and counting and still in their trenches. All of which meant no hacks would be getting into Afghanistan from Peshawar anytime soon, unless you could latch on to someone like Mahmood Razaq.

But even from here Razaq's son looked too soft and well groomed for such rough business. And who was that other man, hovering nearby, a step or so apart from the crowd? He was turning away now, heading for the elevators as if going up to his room. But when the doors opened the man didn't board. Instead he took a cell phone from his pocket, punching it only twice—meaning a programmed number, someone he called frequently. He spoke a few words, leaning low, then pocketed the phone and sauntered back toward the door, milling with a few people who had just gotten off the second elevator. Then he placed himself back within earshot of the celebrated Haji din Razaq, who was still talking with Najeeb, neither of them heedful of the eaves-

dropper. Perhaps it was a bodyguard. Interesting nonetheless. Skelly was reminded of all the history he had read during the long flight overseas. Peshawar was quite a place for intrigue, a listening post and trip wire for every stripe of empire and invader, as well as a prime staging ground for smugglers and agitators. Chart the world's various spheres of influence and they all seemed to cross here, no matter what the era. So maybe he could scare up some decent copy even if he never set foot across the border. Just look at them over there, up to God knows what. Snoops, lurkers and pretenders, milling and babbling as one but probably with a dozen conflicting agendas. This was far preferable to Islamabad, with its ministerial briefings and bland flock of diplomats, not to mention the TV crews that paid a thousand dollars a day just to do stand-ups on the Marriott rooftop.

Yes, Skelly decided, he was going to like it here just fine.

## CHAPTER FOUR

NAJEEB NODDED to the armed guard outside the hotel as he swerved his motor scooter into late afternoon traffic, tucking between a minibus with three men hanging off the back and a pickup overloaded with logs, probably the latest haul of the timber mafia that was stripping the countryside clean.

All in all, he'd had a successful meeting, pocketing seventy-five dollars after finagling an interview for the following morning at Mahmood Razaq's house.

That, of course, raised the possibility that he and Skelly might join an overland expedition into Afghanistan. Hard living and gunfire were two things he'd rather avoid, but their chances of being invited along were almost nil. Others had already asked and been turned down. Razaq was vain but not foolish, and the last thing any guerrilla force needed was an advance guard of camera crews and scribblers, lighting the night with klieg lamps and shouting into satellite phones from the mountaintops. It would be the one sure way for Razaq to alienate the locals he needed to win over. His only hope of success would be to assert enough Pashtun tribal authority to trump any lingering fealty to the Taliban. If the bearded elders who ran the show up there were known for anything, it was pragmatism, and this wouldn't be the first time they had changed mounts at the first sign of a lagging gait.

Even at that, Razaq's enterprise struck Najeeb as foolhardy. His enemies would be forewarned and waiting, and it might take only a few days for some local band of enforcers to rudely shove him back into Pakistan. Not that they'd do him any harm. Razaq was still a figure to

be reckoned with among the tribes astride the border. Kill him and you'd have a blood feud on your hands. So they would shoo him like a fly, him and his so-called warriors, a band of money changers and office boys if you believed what you heard in the streets.

Razaq wasn't exactly in his prime, either. A dozen years earlier he'd fought the Russians with energy and cunning, living off the land and sometimes escaping on horseback, and it was widely reported that he carried an old British saber that his great-great-grandfather had liberated from a dead redcoat at Jalalabad a century earlier. Now he was plump as a Buddha, rarely stirring from the embroidered cushions of his parlor, more attuned to interest rates and import quotas than to the small-bore tactics of leading scared young men across hostile ground.

But even failure might serve its purpose, marking Razaq as a leader willing to risk his life for his country's future, just in time for the changing of the guard. Or maybe he would be lucky enough to cross the border just as the Taliban crumbled. Then his rivals-in-exile would be left stewing over their teacups, from Quetta to Peshawar, jealously watching the whole thing unfold on the BBC while Razaq galloped gloriously into Kabul. So give the man three points for guts while deducting two for hubris.

The traffic stalled as Najeeb neared his turnoff, but he spotted a narrow opening to the right. Another two blocks and he would be home free. But as he got under way, a jeep loaded with military police pinched in front, forcing him wide, squeezing the hand brake. There was an incoherent shout from the jeep as Najeeb eased past, left foot grazing the pavement for balance.

Scream all you want, Najeeb thought. I can make it and you can't. Then there was another shout, the word "Halt!" unmistakable. He considered gassing it on through, but a glance over his shoulder revealed four staring policemen, hands at their holsters. He stopped, and an officer stepped down, gesturing angrily. What law could Najeeb possibly have broken? As if there were any laws in this motorized scrum.

The officer stepped closer, and Najeeb finally heard his words above the roar of revving engines and musical bus horns.

"Come with us, please."

"What have I done?"

"Come with us."

The officer locked his hands across the handlebars—large hands,

capable of plenty of damage, especially if wielding the baton strapped to his belt.

"Get in the jeep. I'll take your bike."

"But what have I done?"

"Just come with us."

A second policeman approached, pistol unholstered. Najeeb raised his hands and climbed from the saddle. They rolled his scooter to the rear of the jeep through a cloud of blue exhaust. Traffic passed on either side, brown eyes staring curiously from open windows at the young man being taken into custody.

Najeeb fleetingly thought of the note he'd posted that morning, his reply with the verse from the Koran. Was he now facing some sort of blasphemy charge? Impossible. If anything the government was headed in the opposite direction, rounding up the more vocal religious fanatics.

"What have I done?" he asked again, shouting above the sputter of a rickshaw. No one said a word. They strapped his scooter to a metal frame on the back of the jeep, then hustled Najeeb aboard.

"It will all be explained," the officer deadpanned. "No more questions."

They headed into the city's ancient center, Najeeb fidgeting under the stare of every passing driver. A young woman riding sidesaddle behind her father on a motor scooter peered through a slit in her white head scarf. Her eyes were astonished. "What foolish thing have you done?" they inquired. "You're lost to us now."

She probably assumed he was a terrorist, some rogue arrival from India, or perhaps a hothead who'd been waving the black flag of Jamaat-i-Islami, although Najeeb's beard was too trim for that bunch. Everywhere these days there seemed to be some sort of security crackdown, and it would be natural to conclude that Najeeb was another fallen leaf swept into the stream toward jail. Heart fluttering, he opened his mouth, but all he could think of to say was another "What have I done?" so he held his tongue. Within an hour it would be dark. Najeeb wondered how long it would be before he was back on the streets.

They turned left toward the cantonment, the greenest part of the city, home to former imperial barracks and officers' clubs, low-slung buildings with long white verandahs built by the British. Most of them now housed the Pakistani army and security forces, and these police-

men were presumably stationed along one of the groomed lawns. But they drove on, into the chockablock haze of the Old City, its narrow and twisting lanes clogged with rickshaws and microvans, the market stalls already stoking their fires for the evening crowds.

The jeep braked to let a horse cart clop past, the nickering beast rolling its eyes. A sugarcane vendor eyed Najeeb suspiciously from a curbside table where he wielded a machete, methodically chopping the long green stalks into stubby treats. Other merchants ignored him, too busy shouting prices and wares. The odor of hot grease drifted past like a humid cloud foretelling rain.

Just before the end of the block the jeep pulled left at the mouth of a narrow alley. The officer grabbed Najeeb by the arm, and they stepped awkwardly in tandem to the cobbles, a second policeman falling in behind. Did that one have his gun out? Hard to say from the reaction of the parting crowd, which seemed to have already written him off. He wanted to shout that he didn't even know what he had done, but they'd probably heard that before.

The alley was in shadow, cooler and quieter. They descended four steps and continued another twenty yards before stopping at a recessed entrance on the left, at a gray steel door marked only by deep scratches and faded graffiti. The officer knocked politely, as if it were a private club where they would need a password. A tiny tapping answered from within, presumably someone punching in a security code. Then the door opened with a metallic shriek, just wide enough to reveal a short, plump man in a pale blue *kameez*. His face was bland and unsmiling, that of a clerk used to taking orders. He didn't appear the least bit surprised by Najeeb's arrival, and he opened the door wider for the policeman, who instead of stepping inside merely offered up Najeeb, releasing his grip.

"Thank you, sir," said the man at the door, who Najeeb already thought of as the Clerk. "Wait a minute or two, in case he gets frisky. Then you can be on your way. He won't be needing any further escort."

Pondering the import of that remark, Najeeb crossed the threshold into a shock wave of air-conditioning, a sour, unfiltered chill. As the door shut behind him he felt as if he had entered a cave, a dim labyrinth where new arrivals habitually lost their way.

The office was windowless, a pallor of gray desks on a crowded plain of black linoleum. Three other heads were bent to their work,

one wearing headphones. No one bothered to look up. Large maps covered every wall. In a rear corner was an impressive tower of electronic equipment, lights blinking, as if at this very moment voices were being received and calls intercepted from all points of the city. That, plus an utter lack of identifying logos, placards, labels or nameplates told Najeeb that this could only be a field office of the ISI—not that anyone here would likely admit it. The hair on his arms rose beneath his sleeves. He hoped it was only a reaction to the chill.

The ISI was Inter-Services Intelligence, and as did any national bureau of spymasters it had become the popular subject of legend and folklore. Local conspiracy theorists would have you believe the ISI was behind every major disturbance and upheaval on the Indian subcontinent for the past fifty years, but even the most conservative guesses credited the agency with mysterious powers, citing a well-documented ability to command billions of dollars in foreign assistance despite a reputation for working both sides against the middle. The agency might inflame a popular movement one week and extinguish it the next, then select a new set of prospects to begin the cycle anew.

Years earlier, when a military dictator named Zia had became troublesome to the ISI, the dictator's plane conveniently blew up, disposing of Zia along with five of his generals and, less conveniently, the U.S. ambassador. The ISI offered a few vague explanations of mechanical failure and moved on.

But the agency's most notable recent adventure was its role as midwife to the Taliban. Now there was an odd feat, Najeeb thought—a coldly secular bureaucracy assisting at the birth of an impassioned army of religious scholars, supplying twenty-first-century savvy and firepower to keepers of fourteenth-century ideas.

With an Afghan war now on and U.S. Marines on the doorstep, the ISI was on its best behavior, operating under a new set of marching orders. Or so everyone said. Now the Taliban was the enemy, and the agency was supposed to be cutting all ties to its pious and prodigal offspring. But by reading between the lines of official pronouncements from Islamabad and news items in the daily papers, it was clear that the agency was finding the going rough, the terrain uncertain. One sensed the grinding of bureaucratic gears as first one and then another key man was sacked or transferred. Priorities were being redrawn, mandates rewritten. All that remained certain was that India was still Public Enemy No. 1, and Kashmir the top prize, even if for the moment

the rest of the world was fixated on Afghanistan, and the wavering mirage of security and order along Pakistan's nine-hundred-mile Afghan border.

"The border is now sealed," the government regularly proclaimed, while those in the know suppressed laughter, certain that the long-standing ebb and flow of humans and weapons would continue as it had for centuries, as undisturbed by the bombing as it was by the border police. The tribes, which preferred to see no border at all, had their own agendas, and always would.

But the ISI was still masterful at bending and refracting that mirage to its own devices. And if some foreign power wanted to gaze into the shimmer and see a stone wall where there was actually a sieve, then so be it.

All the same, Najeeb was surprised to think that such work would be left in the hands of men like these, stooped and studious, not resembling magicians in the least. Men such as the Clerk, who was now leading him past the gray desks to an opaque glass door, also unmarked, in the rear corner opposite the high bank of blinking equipment.

"Come in," a gruff voice said before the Clerk could even knock.

The door opened on a man seated behind another larger, gray desk. He was bent over a stack of papers with pen in hand, the front of his round bald head wrinkled with effort, eyes crinkling as if he were either in pain or on the verge of solving a vexing riddle. Najeeb recognized him immediately, and his apprehension turned to anger. The recognition was mutual, and the man smiled slightly before quickly shaking his head, as if to say, "Why am I not surprised?"

His name was Tariq. Or so he had said the first time they met, seven years ago in the sunny offices of a far less notable agency along the marbled boulevards of Islamabad. Najeeb wondered now if the ISI had been the man's employer all along. He tried to recall Tariq's last name, then remembered that he had never stated one, and it was doubtful he would now.

Najeeb's most vivid memory of that day was Tariq's maddening patience, waiting calmly even as Najeeb had refused to answer questions, hands folded on the desk while a clock hummed on the wall, precious seconds ticking away. There had been a flight waiting. Najeeb had been due back in the United States for his senior year in college, but security forces had pulled him from the check-in line and hauled him into the city, ignoring his angry protests and parking behind the

white walls of the ministry. It was after hours, and Tariq had seemingly been the only one left in the building. He had greeted the fuming Najeeb by placing a hand consolingly on his shoulder—"Don't worry. We'll have you back in plenty of time. As soon as you've answered a few questions."

It sounded reassuring enough until Najeeb heard the questions, the last of which had been the most alarming of all:

"Tell me what's going on in the cave. The one in the bluff near your father's house. Then tell me, in as much detail as possible, how to find it. Do that and you may go. Don't do that and, frankly, I think we may have some problems with granting your exit."

Tariq hadn't seemed to mind when Najeeb didn't respond. He'd stared down at his papers while the sun traveled lower, until the sky darkened and the office was a tiny pool of fluorescent light in a hushed and empty building, the traffic outside dwindling to almost nothing.

The flight's scheduled hour of departure came and went. Tariq pulled a sandwich and a water bottle from a drawer, chewing slowly. Najeeb stood once to leave and Tariq merely pushed a desktop button, producing a guard with a truncheon. Najeeb sat down.

An hour later, between bites of an apple, Tariq said offhandedly, "We're still holding the plane, you know. All those people, sweating and angry on board. Nice to know there are some advantages of a state-run airline. But we won't hold it forever. And it's this flight or nothing. So make up your mind."

Yet, Najeeb still held his tongue, so Tariq began to prod. He said little, but his few thrusts were deft, as if he'd known just where to aim after hours of study. The line that finally worked followed a full five minutes of silence.

"What must your father think of you by now?" Tariq had asked. "I know it was his idea to send you away to school, but look at you. Hardly the sort to be either feared or respected, at least not where you come from. Or maybe that's why he sends you away?"

It was the same thought Najeeb had always tried to avoid, and he flashed back to one of the more awful moments in his life, his father roaring and ranting, having discovered that his boy—his only boy, no less—had been sketching birds, painting them when he should have been shooting them. Not only that, but the boy had actually saved the colorful drawings, rolling them up as a woman might do with her embroidery and placing them beneath his bed. The Pashtun had

always honored their poets, their singers and, of course, their warriors, but painters simply didn't exist, at least not among the male of the species. So his father, sputtering and swearing, had torn up the sheets one by one, while attributing Najeeb's urges to every sort of vile motive he could think of, although the one he eventually settled on was quite predictable. "So what do I have for a son, then?" he'd said. "Some kind of *bedagh*, out servicing the local elders like the village whore? Is that what you've become behind my back?"

So, prodded by Tariq, Najeeb began to talk. The words came slowly at first, then in a torrent, until even Tariq was rubbing his eyes and flexing his cramped hand, having heard vivid descriptions of mountain pathways down to the last boulder, places where Najeeb had once frolicked and scrambled, and, yes, had taken his drawing pad and his colored pencils, clandestinely, with the great thrill of the forbidden.

After an hour or so they whisked him back to the airport without a further word, hustling him straight through security as if he were a diplomat or a celebrity. Najeeb boarded the sweltering plane before a sea of glaring faces, but at least Tariq had upgraded his seat to business class. Najeeb tried to calm down, telling himself that the worst of the experience was behind him. But in the brief time that it took for the big plane to taxi to the head of the runway his relief turned to shame and confusion, and as the wheels left the ground he vomited furiously into a bag, his shrunken stomach offering up the little that remained from a farewell lunch, lovingly served by his mother eight hours earlier. After clearing customs the next morning at JFK he tried phoning home, either in warning or in penance, he wasn't sure which, leaving messages of every sort at the tiny public telephone office in his home village. But the authorities must have acted quickly, because by the following day when he tried again his father had already left word for him to cease calling. And his mother, an unfamiliar voice warned, "will be unable to call you anytime soon."

It was months before he heard the further consequences of his betrayal, and then only in vague reports of arrests and government raids, although his father rode out the storm with the usual bribes and accommodations. But it wasn't until the following May, the end of the academic year and graduation, that Najeeb faced the full realization of what he'd forfeited. The tip-off came when no one showed up at the airport to meet him. No driver or cousin or uncle. He hired a cab and made the lonely ride west with a creeping sense of desolation, hoping

vainly that his diploma might soften the blow, a conquest abroad that would allow for atonement.

It was not to be.

At the edge of his father's lands the taxi came upon a red Toyota Land Cruiser parked astride the pavement. A distant cousin, Riaz, stepped from the truck, rifle in hand. Riaz said little, apart from telling Najeeb that he must turn back. Then he handed over a small bag of Najeeb's belongings, plus a letter from his mother and a sealed envelope of cash. The taxi turned around without a further word, and Najeeb got off in Peshawar, stepping into the haze that had never seemed to abate in all the days since.

And now he was again face-to-face with the man who had made it all possible.

"Congratulations on your promotion," Najeeb said disdainfully, still standing. "Or was it just a relocation?"

"I'm not sure either word is correct." Tariq set down his pen and folded his hands, squinting upward in appraisal. Satisfied that Najeeb had nothing further to say, he gestured to an undersized wooden chair.

"Be seated."

The chair was hard and uncomfortable, probably by design.

"You finished your university years successfully, I trust?"

"I have a degree, if that's what you mean."

"The University of . . . North Carolina? If memory serves."

Najeeb nodded, flashing on a wispy vision of vast green lawns between colonnaded brick buildings. Tanned young women gliding beneath yellow pin oaks with books in hand, slim thighs scissoring in dappled sunlight. A bell tower tolling on a fall Saturday with golden leaves fluttering heavenward in a breezy blue sky.

"Tell me about your meeting this afternoon with Haji din Razaq."

Najeeb was amazed, then decided he shouldn't be. Of course they'd be watching Mahmood Razaq, plus everyone in his family. A son's visit to the Pearl Continental, the very center of activity for foreigners, would be too enticing to pass up. The question was whether they were working for Razaq or against him, and why.

Najeeb, if anything, was relieved. At least this time the questions weren't about him or his family. It emboldened him to be a little resistant.

"Who wants to know?"

"I do."

"Because you're ISI now? Or have been all along?"

A theatrical frown. Here came the standard disclaimer, Najeeb supposed, or some lecture about how all of us were only doing our duty, and you had best do yours. But Tariq surprised him.

"Think whatever you want. There are at least a thousand rumors in the streets, but I don't think I've heard a single one that's true. The only important thing is that you tell me what you know. You're hardly in a position to be uncooperative. It's not like you can just run back home."

"Thanks to you."

"It's not my job to anticipate repercussions, merely to get information. Mahmood Razaq is the subject. But I can always move on to other matters. Your newspaper. Your girlfriend. Daliya, is it? Or maybe Razaq, if you prefer."

"You probably know more about his plans than I do. Anything I can tell you has already been in the papers. His son was in the hotel lobby and my client wanted an introduction."

"Stanford Kelly. An American." Tariq glanced at a paper on the desk. "Just arrived this morning."

"Your people obviously don't have enough to keep you busy."

"We've far too much. You just happened to have stumbled onto two of the people we're interested in."

"Skelly? What's he done?"

"See? As always you have no idea what or who you're dealing with. Do you know where he's been?" Tariq consulted the paper. "Somalia, Bosnia, Panama, other places. Wherever U.S. forces go, he goes."

"In America that's called covering the news."

"You can think of it however you want, as long as you keep us posted on his movements. Who he sees. What kinds of questions he asks. Where he wants to go next."

"He wants to go to Afghanistan, just like all the others."

"Yes. But *where* in Afghanistan?"

"I'm not sure even he knows. He just wants a dateline from across the border. The sooner he gets it the sooner he can go home."

"And he's hoping to tag along with Mahmood Razaq."

Najeeb shook his head. "You know they won't let him."

"Maybe they will, but just don't know it yet."

It was an interesting remark, but Najeeb didn't rise to the bait.

"Then why did you need to talk to me?"

"Every bit helps. Have you ever heard of triangulation? Calculating your exact position by readings from at least three different points. The more sources, the better. So what did he say to you then, this son of Mahmood's? Is the great man going to see you later?"

Najeeb hesitated. No harm in telling the truth, he supposed. No doubt Tariq's people were already staking out Razaq's house.

"Tomorrow morning. Ten o'clock."

Tariq paused to write something down. If anything, Najeeb had probably just confirmed that Razaq's little war party wasn't setting out this evening. Unless Razaq's son had lied to him, of course.

"What do you do with all of this trivia, anyway?"

Tariq said nothing, continuing to write. Then he set down his pen.

"You may be receiving a visitor from time to time in the next few days. At your apartment, not your office. When you do, I urge you to be cooperative and answer all his questions."

"So it was your man who left the note, then?" Somehow it made Najeeb feel better. An official snoop was more predictable than a fanatic.

Tariq frowned. "The note?"

"Warning me to behave. Quoting the words of the Prophet."

"We've got enough religious nuts to worry about without creating any. Your contact's code name is Abdullah. He dresses like a phone man, partly because he *is* a phone man. It will all be very boring and businesslike. Unless you become uncooperative, in which case we'll make other arrangements. As I told you, I don't concern myself with repercussions, only with information."

Najeeb took that for what it was, while wondering again about the note under his door. He decided to retrieve his reply if it were still posted by the mailboxes. He began to stand, but Tariq motioned him back down.

"I'll say when you're done."

"Another goon outside?"

"No need. Not in here." He said it with some distaste, as if he, too, felt claustrophobic. "We don't always just use the stick, you know. There's a carrot, if you're interested. And if you really help us. You want to go back to America, I understand. Calling the consular section day and night."

"Not anymore. They've stopped answering and sent everyone home."

"But you'd leave tomorrow if you had a visa."

"Me and a million others."

"But a million others don't have the chance to accompany Mahmood Razaq."

"And I won't, either."

"An opportunity could present itself. And if it does, you should be prepared to take it."

"So I can get myself killed?"

"You know they won't touch a whisker on his beard. They just want to show him who's boss."

"And so do you."

"We have other reasons. And other clients."

"And if I'd rather not take advantage of this opportunity?"

"Then we'll find someone else, and go back to using the stick."

Najeeb said nothing. Tariq stood. The meeting must be over. "Someone will show you out. Your motorbike is in the alley."

The Clerk followed Najeeb to the door, punched in a few numbers while shielding the code with his other hand, then shut the door behind him with another screech of rusting steel. So much for the legendary ISI, Najeeb thought, strangely calmed by the experience. It reminded him of a movie he'd seen his freshman year, when he seemed to have done nothing but watch the free films showing on campus every night, as if he might ingest American culture from a spaghetti bowl of celluloid. The movie was *The Wizard of Oz*, and the humbug in the title role now struck him as being a lot like the ISI. Did all of Oz look so bland and harmless once you reached its core, he wondered— quiet, burrowing men in windowless cubicles where everyone watched the clock. Then he remembered what had happened after his previous appointment with Tariq, and his assessment darkened. You ignored these humbugs at your peril. At the moment neither the carrot nor the stick seemed to promise anything but pain.

It was dark now. His scooter was waiting as promised, and the military police were gone. The market crowds were reaching their peak and his eyes smarted from the wood smoke. But it was good to be out of the frigid office, which had numbed his fingertips. Casting a parting glance at the nondescript door, he wondered how late everyone inside would be working tonight. There was no keyhole or numbered pad outside to allow for independent entry, meaning that unless there was some other entrance at least one person must have to stay here round

the clock, babysitting all that equipment with the blinking lights. Would they have bothered to place some sort of listening device on his scooter? Doubtful. He was letting the legend work on his mind. Pay no attention to the man behind the curtain, he told himself. Just wait to hear from this fellow Abdullah, and take it from there.

He kick-started the scooter and eased into the crowd. It was less than a mile to his apartment, where he arrived to find that the lights in the stairwell were burned out once again. But he could see well enough to notice that his reply to this morning's messenger had already disappeared from the wall. Great. Another enemy cultivated. He climbed the echoing stairs while thinking ahead to the morning, wondering what had made Tariq believe that Razaq might actually invite Skelly and him along. And why would they suspect Skelly of being anything other than a typical scribbler?

Fumbling for his keys, he was alarmed to find his door ajar. He placed a hand on the knob, wondering if he should enter. Perhaps the ISI's man Abdullah was inside, already making a courtesy call, showing who was boss, or adding a few enhancements to the phone line. Then a voice called faintly from inside, sweet yet frightened.

"Najeeb? Is that you?"

"Daliya?"

"Someone attacked me. Someone on the stairs."

He pushed open the door, but the room was dark, and as he reached for the lights Daliya cried out, startled.

"No! Leave it off. He cut my face, just a few minutes ago. He might still be out there."

Najeeb glanced backward, seeing no one, then stared ahead into the darkness for Daliya, finally spotting her on the cushions against the far wall. As he drew nearer he saw tears on her cheeks, reflecting the glow of street lamps from the window. There was also something darker beneath her right eye, where she held a washcloth to her face.

He leaned down to touch her, console her, suddenly shaky himself. It was the most disturbing moment yet of an odd and disturbing day, but things were about to get worse. As his hands reached her quivering shoulders he saw a cream-colored envelope lying unopened on the cushion beside her.

It was just like the one he'd received that morning.

## CHAPTER FIVE

THE PEARL CONTINENTAL'S lunch buffet must have been just what the doctor ordered, because Skelly's stomach rallied throughout the late afternoon and on past dark. By eight-thirty he felt sufficiently recovered to try a platter of Szechuan chicken at the Pearl's Chinese restaurant, tweezering aside the hot peppers with his chopsticks as a precaution.

The dinner cried out for a beer, but of course there wasn't any, not there or at any other restaurant in Pakistan. You could order a drink in your room by calling a special number, but how much fun was that? So Skelly took the elevator to Peshawar's one and only bar, a windowless room with a speakeasy atmosphere tucked away on the top floor.

An armed guard stood at the entrance by a small sign: "The Gulbar. Non-Muslim Foreigners Only." Skelly nodded and pushed through, nearly choking on cigarette smoke. The place was tiny, with a dozen small round tables of brown Formica. The bartender, a local in a red vest, was watching a cricket match on an overhead TV, muttering with disapproval as a tiny white ball skipped toward a yellow mesh fence.

The tables weren't even half filled, and Skelly surveyed the landscape for a familiar face. Two Japanese women were in the corner, probably TV hacks judging from the makeup. A pair of scraggly, chain-smoking Nordics in multipocket vests sat by the door. Then, from a table in the back, a fleshy American face smiled pinkly and called out his name.

"Skelly! So the rumors of your resurrection were true. Come on over!"

It was Sam Hartley, which didn't surprise him a bit.

Hartley was a businessman, or that's what he'd called himself since leaving the diplomatic corps twenty years earlier. Even in his government days he'd been something of a puzzle, a gregarious roustabout of dubious portfolio—economic liaison one year, cultural attaché the next. Now he was a glorified corporate advance man, going everywhere the multinationals wanted to set up shop but were still too timid to send in the regulars. If journalists were the Greek chorus for world strife, Hartley's ilk were the talent scouts and stage mothers, impresarios of every subplot involving money or corporate influence. But his knowledge and connections made him the perfect source for gossip and rumor, and he was always eager to share as long as you never quoted him by name, perhaps because he often picked up more information than he imparted.

"Jesus, you old warhorse," Hartley said. "How the hell are you?"

"Tolerable. And more than a little jet-lagged. Yourself?"

"Reasonable enough, considering. Shipped over last month on a day's notice. Been waiting for the bad guys to blow town, just like everybody else. Jesus, Skelly, when was the last time? Manila? That botched coup?"

"I skipped that. Jerusalem, I think. Somebody had just blown up somebody else."

"Well, that narrows it down. No, wasn't it the assassination? The nut who shot Rabin?"

"Yes. Lobby of the American Colony. You were drunk, telling Kuwait war stories."

"Yes. That awful Hilton the Iraqis trashed. No electricity or food. Had to walk fourteen flights of stairs. Jesus. Hack hotels I have known."

But Sam Hartley had never been a hack, of course. He only slept in all the same beds, out on the leading edge of American private interest.

"Let me buy you a round, Skelly."

"What's the beer?"

"Murree. And only Murree. Local, believe it or not. Special brewing permit from the mullahs. Gives you quite a headache if you're not careful. I'm sticking to Scotch. No ice, even though they claim the water's bottled."

"Make it a Murree, then."

Hartley signaled the bartender, tipping an imaginary mug.

"So whose vital interests are you representing now?" Skelly asked. "Some arms dealer with a heart of gold? Or are you here to open Kabul's first Toys R Us?"

"Actually, a combination of those two would be just the ticket. Grand opening with Geoffrey the Giraffe in a turban. Free Stinger missiles to the first hundred children."

"Limit one per customer."

"That would be a first!" Hartley roared with laughter. "No. Just more of the usual. Trying to get my foot in the door but stuck on the porch like the rest. What about you?"

"Looking for any warlord who'll take me across. I hear Mahmood Razaq may be going." Might as well bounce it off Hartley, who would probably know the latest.

"Yes. Unfortunate. We've advised him against it."

"We?"

"Transgas. My current employer. They want to build an oil and gas pipeline through Afghanistan."

"Didn't know they had any oil and gas."

"They don't. But it's a prime shipping route. There's a load of the stuff by the Caspian Sea, but the most direct route cuts through Iran, which leaves a bunch of ayatollahs holding the Off switch. Transgas wants to build an alternate route. Unfortunately, so does Petrotek, and they've been lobbying over here since Alexander the Great."

"And now you've got Mahmood Razaq on your team."

"Possibly. Lately he's been on the fence."

"Then I hope you're hedging your bets."

"We always do. We even found a way to cozy up to the Taliban. At least until public opinion shamed us out of it."

"The Taliban?" Skelly was incredulous. "When was this?"

"Back in '97. Flew four of them into Houston. Damnedest thing you ever saw. Those long beards with suits and ties. Like touring with ZZ Top. Bunch of muttering scolds right there in the penthouse of the Petroleum Club."

"Ply them with drink?"

"Bottomless Evian. I lived like a monk for a week. And all the secretaries wore long skirts so the guests wouldn't be offended. Two days of biting our tongues and nodding our heads, and you know what impressed them most? A tour of a beef slaughterhouse. Big beasts lining up to take it between the eyes really got them going."

Skelly laughed. "I'm surprised the State Department let them in."

"Oh, the diplos are on our side. Petrotek's Brazilian. Transgas is the home team. But we're on our own here, of course. Uncle Sam's too busy chasing terrorists."

Skelly doubted it, but didn't care to argue the point, so he signaled for another beer.

"Careful with that. You'll feel it in the morning."

"I'll be all right. I'm sure Razaq will offer plenty of strong tea. I'm heading out to his place for a morning audience, if he's still in town. For all I know he's leaving tonight."

Skelly watched Hartley for a reaction, but the man offered nothing.

"So he's really on your payroll, then?" Skelly asked.

"I believe all I said was that he might be on our team. We talk from time to time. And other people talk to us about him."

"And what do those other people tell you?"

"Between you and me?"

Skelly nodded. He knew the drill. This was for insight, not for quotes. Burn Sam Hartley and entire realms of sources would dry up. But if the tip was good, others might confirm it.

"I'm hearing Razaq wasn't such a good investment. Not that we're paying him, of course." Big wink. Vintage Hartley. "High probability for short-term losses."

"You don't think he'll make it?"

"Not if the fix is in."

"From where? Washington?"

Hartley shook his head. "I was thinking closer to home."

"Islamabad? The, what's it called, the SII?"

"I-S-I, Skelly. You haven't done enough reading by the pool."

"So they've still got a soft spot for the Taliban?"

"Or for Petrotek's money. And if that's the problem, then I'm supposed to be able to do something about it."

And even if Petrotek money wasn't the problem, Skelly thought, Sam Hartley would hardly mind if a story leaked to the press suggesting that his main rival had sabotaged Mahmood Razaq, fallen warrior of the West. But Skelly would never be able to decipher that kind of a tale for his readers. Too many players with too many agendas. His editors wanted it simple: good versus bad, with an update of the latest score.

"So what's the story with you?" Hartley asked, having planted the

seed and moved on. "I'd heard you'd gotten out of the business, but here you are."

"I was the only one left who'd go. Nobody wants foreign postings anymore. Too worried about losing their stock options, or falling off the waiting list for private school."

"Even so. Hardly see any of the old crowd anymore. Not the hacks, anyway."

"What about non-hacks? Whatever happened to Thad Beeston?"

"Still with DEA. Over here, in fact. Roving around the desert in mufti, or so I'm told. Somewhere near Quetta."

"Arlen Pierce?"

"Ah, Arlen." Hartley paused reverentially. "The Dark Lord. Mysterious as ever and still without official portfolio. Knocking around the embassy in Cairo, last I heard, in rooms no one else is allowed to visit. Surprised I haven't seen him here."

"Weren't the two of you involved in something once? Back when you were still on Uncle Sam's payroll?"

"God, those days are too far back to even remember," Hartley said.

But Skelly certainly remembered tales of Pierce's Cairo days—working hand in glove with the regime during a crackdown on Islamic militants, and not in a way that would have made the homefolks proud. Although none of it showed up in the press, of course.

"Last time I saw Arlen was at the Intercon in Amman," Skelly said. "Trying to pick up Susie Kellman of the *Times* at the hotel bar."

"He always did have a thing for Susie. Who quit, by the way, and is now living in rustic paradise in Tuscany. Little villa with an olive grove and her own private gigolo."

"Don't any of these people ever go home?"

"Well, you did. But I suppose that's attributable to the rare charms of Larissa."

"Actually it's Janine now. And Larissa was Belgian."

"Sorry. And Janine would be number . . . ?"

"Three. But who's counting?"

"Goodness, time flies. So how old is your oldest, then? Carol, was it?"

"Yes, Carol." Skelly was shocked Hartley remembered. "She's . . ." A pause. Do the math, Skelly. The oldest of his five children, born in . . . '75? No, '76, right after Mao died. He'd had to cover it, even though the Chinese never granted a visa. Stuck in New Delhi for a

week while Susan fumed, but he made it home just in time for the birth. Susan was his first wife. She lived in Toledo now. Ohio, not Spain.

"She's twenty-five," Skelly said.

"She was always a smart one. What's she up to?"

Skelly wished he knew. Carol was pregnant, big as a house. Three years ago she'd dropped out of law school to get married. Broke Skelly's heart, but maybe she would yet finish her degree. Or maybe he only felt bad because she'd ditched school for the one thing she'd always wanted more, a father figure who wouldn't leave her behind for months at a time. Pop psychology, but it worked for Skelly.

"She's about to become a mother, actually. Due in January.

"So tell me," Skelly said, wanting to change the subject. "If Razaq goes down the tubes, where does that leave Transgas? Sounds like the main man."

"Oh, there are a lot more warlords where that one came from. Sounds so . . . unseemly, doesn't it?" Hartley chortled like a dirty old man who'd just peeped down a blouse. "But it's the new Great Game, Skelly, just like in Kipling, only now it's America and the multinationals fighting over the scraps, instead of the Queen and the Czar."

"I'm beginning to see what keeps you busy."

"Busy and worried. But as long as the Marines get their man, things shouldn't get too complicated. Still, if they don't . . ." He shrugged, his voice trailing off.

"Bin Laden, you mean?"

"Who else? Imagine the embarrassment if one of our very own warlords ends up hiding him, rolling out the red carpet of Pashtun hospitality for the world's most hated man." He seemed to catch himself before saying something more. "Jesus, Skelly, I'd forgotten how you operate. Lube us up and let us rip. Not taping me, are you?"

"Hell, I don't even have a notebook on me. And after a few more of these"—he lofted his Murree—"I won't remember a word anyway. All I'm after is an Afghan dateline. One last merit badge, then back to the 'burbs."

There was a huge groan from across the room. The bartender was shaking his head at the TV screen, where the white ball again rolled toward the low fence.

"Tell you what, Skelly." Hartley dropped his voice and leaned forward. "If crossing the border is all you're after, I may know a way in.

Another fellow you can visit after Razaq says no. I'll write the name on a business card. Your fixer will know where to find him."

Skelly waited, took the card. He turned it over, pronouncing the name slowly.

"Muhammad Fawad. He's going in, too?"

"Not as a fighter. He's taking a few truckloads of humanitarian aid. Strictly symbolic and all very private, and that's how he wants to keep it until he's inside. Then, of course, he'll want to make a big deal out of it. He wants to be seen as a moderating force who can work with everyone. Supposedly the skids are greased for safe passage via Torkham, right through the Khyber Pass. One or two hacks know, but you should be in pretty select company. Who's your fixer, by the way?"

"Najeeb Azam. Just met him, but he seems pretty good."

"Azam . . . of course."

"You know him?"

"I know *of* him. Or of his father, who's a bit of a player out in Afridi country. Injun territory, completely lawless. Him heap big chief with heap big wampum."

"A player how?"

"The usual warlord stuff. Smuggling. Transport and timber. Maybe some other interests."

"Like Transgas?"

"Or like Petrotek. We'll find out when it matters."

Skelly wondered if this was why Najeeb had bristled when he'd brought up the subject of his tribal roots. Was the son embarrassed? Impatient for his inheritance? And if his dad was so well connected, why was Najeeb working here?

"When's Fawad leaving?"

"Day after tomorrow. Probably won't stay inside for more than a week, so he'd be perfect for your purposes. And feel free to mention my name."

"So he's another of yours, then."

"Frankly, Fawad is one of the few who's still on the fence, and he seems inclined to stay there. And that being the case . . ." Hartley leaned forward, dropping his voice again. "There's a small favor I'd like to ask, if you don't mind. But only if you get in, of course."

So here was the price, the proffered quid pro quo.

"Go ahead."

"It would be helpful if we could have another chat once you're

back." Skelly wondered if that was where Hartley had been headed all along. "After you've filed your stories, of course. And I certainly wouldn't ask for anything you wouldn't give your paper."

"In that case, you can read my stories. They'll be online, I'm sure."

Hartley laughed, not as jolly this time.

"Oh, I will. But I know how it goes. You always pick up more than you can use. Impressionistic stuff. Gut feelings about people or places. Just a short debriefing over lunch, really, or a drink." He paused, as if trying to gauge Skelly. "I could even pay a small retainer if that made you feel better."

"Actually, that would make me feel worse."

"Oh, yes. Journalistic ethics, the great oxymoron. I was hoping maybe you'd outgrown that. It always mystifies me the way you fellows are so eager to swap information—the one thing you have that's of value—yet the minute someone wants to pay you for it you raise the hideous cross and back away. Just as well for my budget, I suppose. We'll do lunch, then, and you can pick up the tab."

Skelly had to admire the way Hartley made a further meeting seem inevitable, so he nodded, figuring he could blow it off later. Hartley knew that as well, and perhaps that explained his next overture.

"So, tell me. When this is all over, what do you think you'll be doing at the paper? Seriously."

Skelly shrugged. "If I've been a good boy maybe they'll let me out of the county bureau. But I expect I'll be too busy for a while covering this mess. Foreign news is finally a growth industry again."

Hartley snorted. "Hell, give 'em another month and they'll be tired of reading about bearded fanatics. They'll need another war to hold their interest."

"Jesus, Sam, even I'm not that cynical, not after 9/11. But if you're right I guess I can always write editorials."

"The ivory tower? Not your style. Believe me, you'd miss the road."

"And all the lovely places like the Gulbar?"

"You know what I mean."

"I'm too old for another posting. Even I think so."

"Unless you changed employers, found a more rewarding line of work." He paused for dramatic effect. "Transgas, for example. Always looking for more eyes and ears. Doing what I do."

"Whatever that is."

Hartley smiled.

"A lot of schmoozing, really. Same as you, only no demos to cover, and with a bigger expense account. And sometimes people actually tell you the truth, because they know it won't be plastered on tomorrow's front page."

"Or in my case, 12-A."

But the idea had its charms, something Skelly never would have admitted even a month ago. Unless he broke some sort of huge story, Pakistan would be his last hurrah, and within a year his editors would be pushing him to take a buyout. And after that? Working PR for some utility company, perhaps, explaining away rate hikes and industrial accidents. Or worse, flacking for a local politician. At least out here he'd be moving in familiar circles, jazzed by the travel.

"Let me think about it," he said, surprising himself. "As long as you're serious."

"Dead serious. I can even start putting in a word for you. When the door finally opens they're going to want as many troops on the ground as possible."

"Keep it to yourself for now. Probably not good form."

"Yes, I can understand that." Hartley still seemed to be recovering from the shock of Skelly's interest. Of course, now Skelly would really have to give Hartley a debriefing. He began to feel queasy about the whole thing. Years of indoctrination to overcome. Leaving the newspaper business could be as hard as leaving a cult. But Hartley's offer, if you could call it that, had hooked him at some deep level. Janine would be against it, but he'd cross that bridge later.

"I'd say this calls for another round, plus a toast," Hartley announced. "To the future."

Skelly raised his glass. "The future," he replied weakly.

AN HOUR LATER Skelly was in his room, seated on the edge of the bed with the lights out, reeling slightly from four beers. So many of his colleagues hated hotel living—the disorienting sameness of the rooms, the sad clutter of damp towels and room service trays, chrome lids crashing like cymbals. But Skelly found it liberating. You left your room a shambles every morning and returned to impeccable order. Your laundry went out in big plastic bags and returned pressed and stacked, tagged with those stickers that at first seemed annoying—

clinging like leeches—but later were like badges of worldliness. He'd accumulated five on one set of briefs, and whenever he wore them at home they were like a reminder of his wanderings, little dueling scars of the initiated.

Skelly leaned woozily toward the pillow, where the spread was turned back and a foil wafer of chocolate sat neatly on the starched sheets. He unwrapped it, popped it into his mouth, a minty chill oozing down the back of his throat. Tossing the foil to the floor, he picked up the phone and punched in the international access code, then the full number for a call to the States. He had to try six times before it went through, listening to all the clicking and whooshing on the line after fighting his way through a series of rapid busy signals. Was someone listening in? Doubtful, but you never knew in places like this, especially in a hack hotel. But who cared. He was just boozed enough to feel nostalgia at its keenest, a genuine stab of homesickness. But for where, exactly? His wives and children were strung out like a chain of islands, places that he usually visited on a single sweep, in the manner of an aging monarch touring former colonies.

But his oldest daughter, Carol, had fought hardest to maintain the tie. She was the only one among them who made him feel that the connection still mattered.

Her phone was ringing now, that stateside flutter that sounded like no other nation's—Ma Bell welcoming him into her kitchen. Now if only Carol's husband didn't answer.

"Hello?"

"Carol? It's me."

"Daddy? The line's all funny." Then, with suspicion, "Where are you calling from?"

"Pakistan. Off near the Afghan border. Khyber Pass, gateway to the stars."

"You're drunk."

"Just a few beers, nothing serious. But how can you always tell?"

"When else do you call? From overseas, anyway."

"That's hardly fair. I just wanted to hear your voice."

"Well, you're hearing it. But I thought you'd sworn off wars. Whatever happened to the great Liberian epiphany?"

"Superseded by the great suburban epiphany. That and the editors don't have anybody over twenty-one who can walk and chew gum at the same time. Or not in a place like this."

"Well, where are all the future Skellys? Weren't you like that once?"

"Doubtless. Especially when I was trying to do something like change a diaper. Which reminds me—how's it coming along?"

"Pretty well. No more morning sickness. All systems go."

He imagined her patting her tummy in response, gazing down at the big hump below the breastbone, another little Kelly on its way. Though of course this one would be a Lindeman. Terrible name to give a child.

"The doctor says he's going to be a big one."

"He?"

"Yes. Minus his grandfather's wandering gene, I hope."

"Hmph."

Only Carol could have said that and made it sound affectionate. Or was he imagining it? He waited for a second, listening to the static.

"You always do this, Daddy. Run out of things to say about halfway in."

"I'm just enjoying the moment. With your brothers and sisters I always feel like I have to keep talking. With you I can actually enjoy the silence. Your pauses were the only ones I felt like I could translate."

"At ten dollars a minute I hope you're getting something out of it."

"Not my dime. Don't worry about it."

"You're going to be careful this time, aren't you?"

She said it with such concern that the lid on Skelly's tenderness opened like a trapdoor. His stomach plunged, and a sniffle bubbled up from deep in his chest.

"See? That's what I thought you were thinking." He strained to keep his voice from breaking. "But it's quite tame here, really." No sense mentioning the Molotov cocktails, or the possibility of catching a convoy into Afghanistan. "Probably be here a few weeks, then they'll get bored and bring me home."

"Well, as long as you're back by January."

"For New Year's?" Had she just invited him to a party?

"My due date! Remember? The twelfth."

"Of course. I'll be there. I won't miss it."

"How many of ours did you miss?"

She knew the answer, but he'd oblige her anyway.

"Three. Made yours. Made Brian's. *Saw* Brian's, even." Brian. A vision of a runny nose and blurred eyes, the boy years away from intel-

ligent conversation. Tiny hands and knees scuffing across an old rug Skelly had bought in Damascus. He felt weary just thinking about it.

"I'd almost forgotten Brian," Carol said. "Hard to think of him as a half brother. Maybe he'll be a playmate for Sidney."

"Sidney?"

"It's the name we've picked. Charlie's favorite uncle. I won't ask if you like it."

"Good. Then I won't tell you I don't."

She laughed, a piping, hollow sound, as if blown by a flute carved from the rarest tropical wood. For a few years of his life Skelly had lived for that laugh, and for his ability to conjure it out of tears when no one else could. He felt sated now, even if she suddenly were to hang up.

"How is Janine, anyway?" Carol asked. "She taking this okay?"

"Oh, you know Janine."

"Actually, I don't. Except for a few minutes at the wedding."

"Well, at least you came." Twenty guests beneath a leaky tent. Overcooked tenderloin and an embarrassing round of toasts from an old colleague he'd invited but had never expected to come. Carol had been the only sane guest, not to mention the only one of his four older children to respond to the invitation. Boycotts arranged by their moms, no doubt.

"I should go now," he said, weighted by regret. "Early day tomorrow."

"What time is it there now?"

"A little after ten. I'm sorry! Did I wake you?" Jesus. Out of practice for sure, forgetting to check the time difference before calling.

"No problem. It's one in the afternoon. Charlie just went back to the office after stopping by for lunch. I had put on a pot of coffee and was lying on the daybed. It's peaceful, really. Just me and Sidney, kicking around beneath a blanket."

"Sounds pleasant."

Skelly wished he could be there, could join her in time for the second cup of coffee. But he was sleepy, and she was a full day of airports away from here.

"Well, say hello to Charlie for me."

"I will. He envies all your adventures."

"And take care of yourself. You and Sidney both."

"You're the one who needs that advice. Be careful, Daddy."

"Don't worry. Get some rest now."

He hung up, finding himself back in a darkened room with the humid night air creeping in between the curtains of the balcony window. He'd planned to shut the windows and switch on the air, but the evening had cooled, even though it still reeked of exhaust and smoke. Sputtering motors streamed past along the boulevard.

He thought ahead to the morning. Prelude to a journey, perhaps. An adventure. What on earth would Carol think once she heard he had reached Afghanistan? He should have called Janine instead, but he was too tired now to do anything but crawl beneath the raspy sheets. Shut everything off and dream of redcoats and tribesmen, of brittle old empires shattering upon the stony floor of deep ravines. Of anything except home and family.

## CHAPTER SIX

DALIYA SAT in the darkness pressing a damp washcloth to her cheek as Najeeb hovered at her side. He lightly touched her shoulder, as if she might shatter, although she'd calmed since his arrival. How long ago had that been? Five minutes? Ten? Yet he'd been too preoccupied to even shut the door.

"He attacked me on the stairs." Daliya's voice barely exceeded a whisper. "I didn't see his face, but his hair was long. I heard a shout, then he was coming at me. I don't know if he'd followed me or was already here, waiting. Maybe he was just a thief and I caught him in the act. He smelled like hash, I know that."

But they both knew thieves didn't shout, "Cover yourself, infidel!" and disappear empty-handed. For Najeeb there was also the matter of the envelope, still unopened beside her on the cushions.

Fortunately the cut wasn't deep. Daliya had leaned away from the blow, and the attacker hadn't stayed for a second try. Almost equally disturbing was that none of the neighbors had come to her aid. Maybe it happened too quickly to catch anyone's attention. Or maybe they'd heard and approved, Najeeb thought, suddenly suspicious of everyone. He wondered why he hadn't seen the attacker leaving the building. Unless, of course, the man was still inside, a thought that prompted Najeeb to go shut the door.

He paused at the threshold, listening carefully. Nothing but the faint echo of a television downstairs, blaring a music video. They were beamed in from India via satellite dish, loud and rhythmic, with long, sinuous lines of dancing women, heads bare, hair lustrous, deep, mean-

ingful gazes into the camera. So much for the piety and patriotism of his neighbors.

"Good thing you had a key," Najeeb said, remembering how he'd hesitated to give her one.

Daliya shook her head. "I didn't need it. The door was unlocked."

"Then I must have forgotten to lock it this morning," he said weakly, glad it was too dark for her to see his surprise.

He inspected the doorframe. No sign of a break-in. It could have been the work of professionals, although the knife attack seemed sloppy. He shut the door and threw the bolt, for whatever that was worth anymore.

"Where was that envelope when you came in?" he asked, trying to keep his tone relaxed.

Daliya shrugged, leaning back with a sigh of exhaustion.

"I hadn't noticed it until now."

"It was there when you got here? On the cushions?"

She shrugged again, disinterested. Meaning the messenger must have entered the apartment. But for how long? And was he the attacker? Najeeb switched on a lamp, blinking against the glare.

"Second one today," he said, forcing a lighter tone as he picked up the envelope. "Got one this morning saying I was going to hell. Quoted the Koran. 'Women should cover their adornments,' that kind of thing."

He now had Daliya's attention, and felt her shiver as he settled next to her.

"Do you think it's the same person who . . . ?"

"I don't know. Maybe you surprised him."

Or maybe he'd been waiting for Najeeb, with a more decisive stroke in mind.

Inside was the same neat but cramped handwriting, again in the language of the Prophet. The numbers "41:26-28" were at the top. Daliya knew only a few rote prayers in Arabic, so Najeeb translated for her:

"The unbelievers say, 'Pay no heed to this Koran. Cut short its recital with booing and laughter, so that you may gain the upper hand.' We will sternly punish the unbelievers, and pay them back for the worst of their misdeeds. Thus shall the enemies of God be recompensed. The Fire shall forever be their home, because they have denied Our revelations."

"Very neighborly," she said mirthlessly. "Very Peshawar."

"So was this," he said, gently pulling back the washcloth. "The bleeding has stopped. We should wash it again. Make a bandage."

"We should call the police."

"And have them find you here? A single woman?" He shook his head. "Some of them would arrest you as a whore. This isn't Islamabad."

"No kidding."

"For all we know it *was* the police, or somebody working for them. Or maybe I'm paranoid because of where I've come from."

He told her about being hauled in by the ISI, about Tariq and his offer of a visa in exchange for information, provided Najeeb managed to hook up with Razaq's mission into Afghanistan, a long shot at best, not to mention dangerous. But Daliya, too, believed that a visa was worth a little danger these days. She sought escape almost as badly as he did, and she was also a self-made orphan of sorts, even if her estrangement from family was supposedly only temporary, an exile of one year. Mutual isolation had brought them together, you might say. They were like two castaways sharing a raft that suddenly seemed leaky and insubstantial.

Daliya had hated Peshawar from the first day, despising its small-town strictness and frontier mentality, the dirtiness and the refugee chaos. "The ocean of beards," she called it, feeling she'd been banished to the past, cast into a medieval sea of burqas and turbans and scowling holy men, a harsh colony of Pashtuns driven west by years of war. She was a Punjabi, a believer in the virtues of refinement, and for a week she'd been defiant, dressing as she pleased. But the leers and insults of the men in the streets soon wore her down, and she now kept a chador hanging next to her car keys, throwing it on to cover her head and most of her face whenever she went outdoors.

She'd grown up in Islamabad, the child of a civil servant in the Ministry of Finance. By Pakistani standards it was a privileged upbringing, rarely requiring her to venture beyond the asphalt belts that cordoned the city. It was an insular place, just as intended by the Greek architects who'd mapped it out forty years earlier. Each gridded sector had its own market, its own park, its own shops. There were no mule carts or rickshaws because the government had banned them, which was just as well, since only the poor needed them. In much of Islamabad, in fact, you could hardly tell you were in Pakistan at all. It was a freak

appendage in the jarring tradition of Brasilia and Ankara, other instantaneous national capitals that tried to deny their nationality. Thus, the long-standing joke about Islamabad's convenient location—"only ten miles from Pakistan."

At some of the city's better mini-malls you could shop for a dress and buy a slice of pizza and almost pretend you were in London or New York, or so it had seemed to a sheltered young girl who'd seen just enough of the chaos of neighboring Rawalpindi to know that she deserved a better, calmer existence. And when she began her college years, just across town at Quaid-i-Azam University, she took her seat alongside like-minded young men and women, speaking up when she pleased, egged on at times by female professors. Looking back now, those moments seemed the best of all, the last rays of light before the gathering darkness of perdition.

Then it came time to arrange her marriage. She knew the process had begun because she heard her parents on the telephone, fielding calls and asking questions when they thought she wasn't listening, swapping vital statistics as if preparing for a corporate merger, a transaction of livestock—not that she would have considered such analogies fitting at the time. At the time, in fact, she'd been excited, even eager. She had always known it would be this way and had assumed the arrangement wouldn't be so bad, if only because everyone else went along and seemed to survive, even prosper. Her parents had gotten married that way, and so had her older friends. Some had taken husbands in the States, or Great Britain, moving away and somehow making it work. It might not be love, but the lucky ones adjusted, and in any case you soon had children. Presumably it was the way things were meant to be, *inshallah*. Besides, she was twenty years old. It was time to face up to the sacrifices and responsibilities of adulthood. So, when her parents informed her one morning before classes that they had arranged a meeting with the first suitable candidate, she nodded and vowed to be on her best behavior.

The boy's mother arrived first, like a scouting party, to make sure that Daliya's bona fides matched the parental propaganda. Her name was Sultana, and she came knocking on a blistering Sunday afternoon in May, wrapped regally in a golden head scarf, somehow managing to look cool and composed in the heat. Daliya sat before a bountiful tea tray while her parents tiptoed out of the room. Then the conversation began—if one could call interrogation conversation.

The woman's tongue was sharp, and she wore an impatient frown that implied the clock was ticking and competition was stiff. She rattled off questions as if from a checklist: What kind of cook are you? Do you sew? Will you make your own clothes? Do you spend much money? How much? What kind of children do you want? How many? How should they be raised? Are you prepared to leave the university? Not a single query about what she was studying, what she'd learned, or her opinion on more worldly matters.

The prospective groom arrived shortly afterward. His mother made introductions, then retreated to a roost in the corner with a final sharp glance, as if warning that so far Daliya's answers had fallen short. But by then Daliya couldn't have told you a single word that had left her mouth, feeling she'd been parroting phrases that had been programmed into some other mind altogether. Could this be what was meant by the power of tradition, she wondered? Did your voice simply begin speaking from some buried channel to your family's past? But the young man himself was refreshing. His name was Pervez. A little plump, but he had a pleasant face and a gentle demeanor, especially in contrast to his mother, who glared from her corner like a caged owl, preening every few moments to remind them of her presence.

At first he was as shy as Daliya. Then they warmed to the moment, his deep-set eyes unafraid to hold her gaze, his questions gaining in assurance yet never prying or presumptuous. There was no further mention of sewing, or cooking, or children, or of dropping out of school, and by the time he departed Daliya had convinced herself she could live with this, and with him. She even felt a flush of excitement, wondering where it all might lead, and when word came a few days later that the arrangement had been accepted by both families, she felt a genuine sense of triumph.

A date was set. They would marry in the fall, and sometime soon the betrothed would be allowed to meet again—with chaperones, of course, although Daliya knew there were ways around this restriction with the help of friends and confederates—secret trysts where they might even touch, hold hands, exchange a caress or two, laying the groundwork for the further excitement of matrimony. Might they even kiss? Perhaps. Goose bumps rose on her arms. She hoped he was as gentle as he'd seemed.

Yet, as those first days passed, the match somehow failed to take root in her mind. One problem was the thought of having to quit the

university with only a year remaining before she earned a degree. She began regarding her classes with nostalgia, especially those moments when she had made her points forcefully, imposing the will of her opinion on her classmates, the boys included.

There was also the matter of Pervez's mother. The married couple would of course be expected to move in with his parents. And while their house was said to have ample space, Daliya knew it would be dominated by the birdlike mother, whose position would be high above her own.

So, one morning over breakfast a mere week after the betrothal, Daliya, certain that she would be understood, calmly announced to her parents that the marriage must be postponed, at least until the end of the academic year. The extra time for adjustment would serve the marriage well, she explained, not yet noticing their looks of horror. And it made no sense to waste her first three years of schooling. If the boy and his mother couldn't adjust, she continued, then this probably wasn't the right match, and there would undoubtedly be other suitors who were more flexible. She was sorry, of course, for any inconvenience or social awkwardness, but she was sure it was all for the best, which is why her decision was final.

It was exactly the sort of logical presentation that had always won the day in the classroom.

And that is how she ended up in Peshawar, summarily withdrawn from the university by her enraged and mortified parents. They farmed her out to an uncle's computer business, where it was hoped that a year of hard and menial work would teach her not only humility but the way her life would be forever if she continued to disregard her parents' wishes and decisions. It was a punishment detail, in other words, a one-year sentence to be served among sniping nephews and leering delivery boys in a low-ceilinged basement office with pallid fluorescent lighting, deep in the worst of the hurly-burly of Saddar Bazaar. Her living arrangements were only slightly more appealing. She had her own small room, but as a guest in her aunt's household nearly every waking moment was observed by her kin.

Yet so far the exile had produced the opposite effect of the one intended. Her resolve to finish her schooling and pick her own husband was now greater than ever, even if it meant she had to apply for a scholarship abroad, although that of course would mean she would also have to secure a visa.

She had taken her first step toward freedom in only her third day on the job, meeting a like-minded and equally restless young woman named Rukhsana, who worked next door as an accountant for her father. Rukhsana's own marriage was six months away, and her new alliance with Daliya gave both young women a pretext for leaving the house on their own, even if Daliya's frowning aunt tutted that *she* had never taken such liberties at that age.

But even with that escape hatch at her disposal, Daliya soon began to wonder if she might go crazy here in Peshawar. Her uncle's family was a cold and humorless bunch, speaking only of rules, and she dearly missed her own family's daily gatherings at the dinner table, where they had always chatted amiably of the events of the day. She missed even more her daily strolls with her friends, with their gossip and their exchange of ideas. Her father phoned once a week, but mostly just to check on her "progress"—his way of coaxing her toward reform.

It was in this state of solitary besiegement that she met Najeeb. He came by the office shopping for software, arriving just after Daliya's uncle and cousins had left for lunch. They'd ordered her to hold the fort, just as they did for an hour every afternoon, knowing there was scant likelihood of business at that lazy time of day. Most of their clients were small businesses that ordered by fax or e-mail, and their lack of a storefront meant a minimum of walk-in trade. But Najeeb had spotted their small sign down the alley as he emerged from a barbershop nearby, so on he came, the buzzing door making Daliya look up suddenly from her terminal in the back.

If Najeeb hadn't spent four years in America he never would have been open to the possibilities of their first brief encounter, would never have been able to read that look in Daliya's eyes that spoke so eloquently of loneliness and need. Such signals never appeared on the male-female radar screens of the Tribal Areas, where a virtual communications blackout was imposed once girls reached ten and the confinements of purdah. Young men of Najeeb's clan spoke only with their mothers, sisters and aunts, and even that occurred mostly within the high walls of the family compound, a claustrophobic realm where the rules of engagement were basic and blunt. He had been taught that the female tongue was a weapon, wielded without mercy, and that males who strayed within range of its fury were either torn to pieces or fought back with their fists. Those with no taste for combat, like Najeeb, could simply retreat out the door into the world at large,

knowing the women couldn't follow, and thus transforming defeat into a sort of automatic victory.

In America he had employed this strategy only once, walking out on an argument with a girlfriend his sophomore year, thinking that would put an end to it. Instead she had followed him three blocks across campus in her determination to have the last word, and their running battle on the sidewalk past hundreds of students mortified Najeeb enough to recalibrate everything he'd ever learned about how to deal with women. But, of course, there was a pleasurable upside to his reeducation, and he had returned home keenly attuned to the cues, signals and sweet possibilities of flirtation.

So, when the shy smiles and small talk commenced beneath the low ceiling of that dreary basement office in Peshawar, Najeeb knew right away what Daliya was up to, even before she did. And by the time her uncle and cousins returned through the buzzing door, when he deftly shifted the conversation back to invoices and diskettes, Najeeb was already composing a follow-up note in his head and contriving a means of slipping it to her along with one of his business cards, printed with his cell phone number and e-mail address. She responded in kind, all of this transpiring without a hint of suspicion among the grumbling cousins, drowsy from their heavy meal.

But the cell phone was the true hero early in their saga, a tool of subversion that had broken the iron grip of elders all across Pakistan. Daliya set hers to buzz, not ring, and found she could even speak to Najeeb from her aunt's house, provided she first slipped into a closet or bathroom. So this was how they began, chatting back and forth in a demure but very Western telephonic seduction, each as hungry as the other to finally share hopes and grievances with someone who understood.

For two weeks all they did was talk. Then Daliya boldly proposed using her girlfriend Rukhsana as an intermediary to help arrange a meeting. In defiance of every local custom they met in a local park, posing as brother and sister.

Up to then, Daliya's experience with Pashtun men had been limited to the few she'd met at the university, stern and brooding boys who were quick to anger even if loathe to express it. They were boys who kept to themselves in smoldering little knots of disapproval and exclusion. They'd had their own dormitory, their own student association, their own table in the dining hall, and the frictions

between them and the Punjabis, the Sindhis and the rest had been palpable.

Clearly, this one named Najeeb was different, stretched by his travels, more open to possibility. And even in their stilted first meetings he displayed a gentle wit and a lovely if subdued laugh, although at times she thought she detected a certain coolness in his eyes, an implicit warning that he might withdraw at any moment if necessary, to someplace so deeply chill and remote that he might never return.

By their third meeting they'd conquered most of their inhibitions, agreeing that further trysts were worth further trouble. After the fourth, with a growing sense that if they were going to break the rules they might as well break them all, they decided to meet at the one place promising true privacy. So, arriving after dark and feeling more scandalized with every quick, quiet step up the stairway, Daliya visited Najeeb's apartment, virtually holding her breath until she reached his door.

It would be difficult to overemphasize the seriousness of the risk Daliya took by carrying out this tryst. While most Westerners might wonder at all the fuss over a mere date, just about anyone from Peshawar would have considered her visit, to put it bluntly, a whore's errand, an assignation for the damned.

They both knew this, yet both also had agreed without even putting it into words that henceforth they would be operating by their own rules, and that in doing so they would walk their brave new path in tandem. The word "commitment" never once came up, as it inevitably would have in America, yet Najeeb knew as well as Daliya that each further step took them closer to something that was beginning to look a lot like Destiny.

They said a tremulous hello, then she removed her chador—a symbolic flourish that briefly took his breath away. At first their words were just as halting as on the park bench. Najeeb made tea, and conversation came easier. After a while, so did the little touches, and for all of Najeeb's experience abroad he knew to move slowly, letting the newness thrill without overwhelming. Their slow, gradual progress only seemed to heighten the sense of seduction. Fingertips brushing forearms. The light pause of her hand upon his knee. Then their hands clasping, squeezing, one pulse answering another. A stroke of his palm across her cheek and a slow movement forward, the rustle of garments in the stillness, the smell of his hair. And, finally, a kiss, lips softer than Daliya had imagined.

Events proceeded from there through three more such meetings until they reached the inevitable, both of them surprised at how easily and naturally they disrobed when the moment of truth arrived. Neither felt shamed or embarrassed afterward, and that, too, was a kind of victory, even if it took Daliya a full week to absorb the momentousness of what she had done. She had stepped past the point of no return.

Now, three months later, here was Daliya once again, seated on the cushions in Najeeb's living room. But instead of their usual oasis of solace and comfort, everything had changed, and for the moment there seemed to be nothing to do but huddle together and wait for the worst to pass. Without either saying a word, they also knew it was time to cross another frontier. This time, she would stay until morning, no matter how many lies and cover stories were necessary.

Lately they had tended to rush their passions, partly because she could stay for only a few hours. But in the wake of a knife attack and a detainment by the ISI, what could possibly feel dangerous about making love, about sleeping together? So they moved slowly, much as they had the first time, with open eyes and lingering touches. Najeeb skimmed his fingertips down her long, slender legs—a glide across velvet, the phrase lodging pleasurably in his mind as the bubble of anticipation expanded. Later, still trying to keep his mind off the evening's earlier events, he looked into her eyes, which stared back as steadily as ever.

"Another blow against the extremists," she said, smiling. "Doing our part for a more secular tomorrow."

Najeeb smiled.

"You think that's what this is? A political act?"

"I think it has been all along," she said, taking the idea to heart. "At some level, anyway. We're spitting in the face of everything we grew up with. Do you know what my mother did when I started growing breasts?"

He wasn't sure he wanted to. He was still on uncertain footing in this new territory. New in Peshawar, anyway. But he shook his head and waited for the answer.

"She used to make me stoop. After a lifetime of lectures about bad posture, she wanted me to stoop, so my breasts wouldn't show. Then she started dressing me in the baggiest clothes she could find. And she bound me up. Wrapped me around the top until it hurt. I tried to help her, of course, until I realized how stupid it all was. So, sure, part of this has to be political."

Najeeb wasn't sure whether to feel insulted or exalted. He wanted to believe that it was his rare appeal that had lured her across the threshold of taboo. Yet why not be part of something bigger, as long as it was this deeply pleasing. He felt the sweat drying on his back in a prickly band of salt. Daliya's eyes shone like those of a small nocturnal animal, flushed from its burrow into moonlight, and a wave of tenderness overcame him, this time cleansed of desire. He pulled her closer, cradling her face at his chest, and for several moments neither said a word. They listened to the night sounds of traffic, the sighs of their breathing.

Then he climbed from bed and stepped barefoot to the window, looking across the rooftops toward the few stars visible through the haze. Daliya soundlessly joined him, slipping a hand into his.

"Do you think they're out there now?" she asked calmly.

"The ISI? Or our friend with the knife?"

"Both."

"If they are, they're getting an eyeful." He recalled the text of the first note, about women and their adornments. He knew the ISI had special equipment, night vision surveillance and all sorts of tricks.

"Maybe you should put something on," he said, knowing the instant the words left his mouth that he'd ruined the moment. Daliya cocked her head, scrutinizing his face as if noticing certain traits for the first time.

"You're still one of them, aren't you? In some ways, at least."

"Them?"

"The Afridi. Your tribe and your clan. All those people up in the Khyber." Her tone was level, no hint of anger, but she hadn't budged from the window. "And in a few months, when you're tired of me and all the Americans and gentleman scribblers have gone home, you'll end it. You'll go crawling back to your father to beg forgiveness and claim your rightful place. Then he'll find you a nice Pashtun girl from some Afridi family he wants to connect with, and that will seal it. You and some dynasty for the ages, with me nowhere in it."

"You have no idea what you're talking about. Do you know how I'd be treating you if I was still really 'one of them'?"

She shook her head. "But I can guess. And I'm sure it wouldn't be pretty."

"Besides, even crawling back wouldn't be enough for my father. There are things I've done that will never be forgiven. Not even if I begged. I know. I've tried."

She waited for more—she had always waited for more on this topic—but Najeeb did as he always had, and changed the subject.

"If we could only get our visas, these problems wouldn't matter."

"That's your solution to everything. Getting to America. But it's not going to happen. Not now."

"Maybe." Then he told her more about the ISI meeting, and they talked again about Tariq's offer. Daliya cautioned him not to trust anyone who made a living from duplicity, and maybe she was right. And if Tariq failed them? Then there was only one other realistic option, although up to now neither of them had dared bring it up. But, this being an evening of firsts, Daliya got straight to the point.

"We could marry, if you really wanted to get to America. It's always easier for a woman to get a visa. Then, after I got a green card I could bring you over. It would still be an arranged marriage, of course, only on our own terms."

Najeeb nodded, saying nothing. If he was going to raise an objection, or back away, now was the time. But he let the moment pass, and by doing so realized he'd conceded the point, surrendered the territory. And was that so bad? Most any man he knew would say so, but he no longer knew whose rules mattered. He supposed that Daliya and he really were pioneers now, although they couldn't keep going the way they had, not in the fevered atmosphere of Peshawar. Between the demonstrations in town and the air attacks fewer than forty miles away, it was as if the city itself were part of the war zone. The anonymous notes and the slash on her cheek were confirmation.

So when Najeeb next spoke, his tone was softer, yielding, a tiny white flag that accepted her terms. "You know, if I really were 'one of them' I'd probably be quoting you poetry now. Some line from Sher Azim Khan, who believed that all women were nothing but temptresses, luring us into traps."

"Try me." She smiled, willing to be humored, knowing that though he hadn't exactly acknowledged her point he also hadn't shoved it aside. It was progress.

Najeeb searched his memory for the right stanza. All those smoky nights in his father's *hujera*, listening to the old men recite for hours on end.

" 'Your curls are a swing," he began, the words coming back.

" 'Your forelock a snare.

" 'Your face a lamp

" 'That draws the moth.' "

"Very romantic," Daliya sneered. "And very deft, the way you avoided my proposal entirely. Or seemed to, anyway."

Najeeb smiled, saying nothing.

"But what should I do tomorrow?" she asked. "I probably shouldn't be seen leaving in daylight. Not after what happened."

"Then you'll have to wait until dark. Stay here all day with the door bolted." Although he wondered if that would do any good at all, given the day's events. "If I'm not home in time, you'll have to call Rukhsana. She'll have to vouch for you anyway. You'll really have to come up with something good for your aunt and uncle."

Daliya shook her head.

"There's no way I'm staying here all day. Maybe Rukhsana can come get me. I should call her now, anyway, to set up my cover story. My aunt and uncle will be climbing the walls by now, wondering why I haven't come home."

So much planning and deception merely to spend the night with a lover, Najeeb thought, surprised that the word "lover" had even come to mind. In one context it was so Western, so casual in its assumptions. Or did he mean it in the deeper sense, one of "commitment," the unspoken word the American girls had bandied about more than all the others. He considered saying "lover" aloud—professing it, so to speak. But again he let the moment pass, and he looked up to see Daliya eyeing him watchfully, as if she knew that he had allowed some opportunity to slip away.

"You'll probably be okay staying here if you want," he said, with less certainty this time. "But I'll be out most of the day. And if we somehow get permission to go with Razaq, then we'll be busy rounding up supplies."

"You'll also have to update your little ISI friend, Tariq."

"He's not my friend. If you only knew."

"Maybe I would know, if you'd tell me. I've confessed every detail of my family's blowup. All about my exile and the boy I almost married. But you're hoarding your biggest mystery: the banished son who won't say why. Too much of your past is like a big blank space on a map, and now you're about to travel back into it. For all I know, you'll disappear altogether and I'll never have the slightest idea of why."

She was right, of course, and if there were anyone he would entrust with his secrets, it would be Daliya. And what if he did somehow disappear into the Khyber? Or into Afghanistan? Who would miss him but

her, yet she wouldn't even know where to inquire for him, or what to tell the authorities. So he at last told her of his betrayal, haltingly at first, then easily. It surprised him how quickly the words tumbled out once he finally unlocked the door that had remained closed for so many years.

When he finished, she was silent. She stroked his cheek, then pulled him close. He was relieved she didn't seem to think less of him for it. Indeed, she seemed grateful, if only for his trust, and he spoke before she could reply, the words again coming slowly.

"If I ever do just 'disappear,'" he said, holding her gaze. "Out there, I mean. Out in the Khyber, or across the border." She nodded gravely. "It won't be because I want to. Remember that, because you might be the only one who would ever want to find me."

"And where would I even look for you?"

"Bagwali. My home village. The one and only place to start. If I was to be taken in the Khyber, they would be the people who would claim me."

"And if you were to go missing in Afghanistan?"

"Still Bagwali. Unless I was dead. They'd be the only people with enough influence to make sure I was sent back."

"And they'd use that influence?" She seemed to flinch. "Even after what you've done?"

"It would be a matter of pride. Of blood. But having retrieved me, I doubt they'd be inclined to turn me loose."

"So I just catch a bus, then, and come take you away?"

Najeeb smiled grimly. Everyone knew how hard it was for outsiders to travel in the Tribal Areas, especially on your own. Even men found the going dangerous, and for women it was virtually impossible. Foreign aid workers didn't go without armed escorts. So Najeeb went to his desk and then returned with a scrap of paper. He had scribbled a name and a telephone number.

Daliya took the paper in hand as if it were a treasure map.

"It's a number for my mother, Shereen. You can't reach her directly. My father would never permit that. And there's no cell phone made that works out there. But this will get you to the PTT office in Bagwali, and you can leave her a message. The regular operator is a friend of my uncle's, and keeps her messages a secret."

This only raised more questions, and Daliya was quick to ask them.

"I thought that you were never in touch with your mother. And who is this uncle?"

Najeeb wearily shook his head.

"Not tonight. Too much ground to cover, and not enough time to cover it. Right now what we need is rest."

Daliya turned away from the window and began putting on her clothes.

"I guess you're right," she said with some bitterness. "I should cover myself, in case one of your admirers is out there watching. I don't feel like sleeping now, anyway."

He moved to follow as she headed for the bedroom door, but she dismissed him with a wave.

"Go back to bed. You've got a long day ahead. I need time to think. Besides, the way things are going I'll have plenty of time tomorrow for sleeping."

NAJEEB AWOKE to the sound of the loudspeakers, calling out the day's first prayers in the dark. Daliya was back next to him in the bed. He should rise, wash himself and pray. But it felt as if doing so would reveal them both to the outside, so he snuggled against her back, sacrament enough for the morning. He got up a few minutes later to brew a pot of tea, carrying the cups to the bedside table. Then he stood at the window to watch the horizon brighten, and as Daliya joined him it stirred memories of a time long ago in America, a morning in Chapel Hill when he had first experienced the pleasure of awakening next to a woman; a frosted winter sunrise and the excitement of heading out together to breakfast, warming his hands on a mug of coffee while she read the paper across the table of a cafe, conversations buzzing at nearby tables as if this were the most normal thing in the world. At the time he had wondered how such a deep feeling of calm and well-being could possibly result from an act of sin, an act against God. Now he pondered the question anew, here where the stakes were so much higher.

Mansour's horse cart clopped into motion below, a few minutes behind schedule this morning. Another day was coming to life, and out there somewhere among the groggy and the pious were all the people he now had to deal with, one way or another. There was the faceless messenger, perhaps with a knife stained by Daliya's blood. There was Tariq, who for all he knew was still in the windowless office, handing out new orders to the Clerk. And of course there was Skelly, the itiner-

ant scribbler, itching for a field trip into Afghanistan with Najeeb as his guide.

But it wasn't the prospect of a journey across the border that troubled Najeeb. It was the passage through the Khyber itself, six miles of it across land where his father's word was law. As long as they stuck to the main highway any such trip would almost certainly proceed without a hitch. No one but the frontier police would even know Najeeb was there, not until later anyway, when word might filter back from one source or another—his father had eyes and ears in every office of the provincial government.

It had been more than seven years since Najeeb had set foot on those lands, and he wondered if the place would still feel at all like home. And if so, what then? And if not, might that even be worse?

He sipped his tea, urging the day onward.

CHAPTER SEVEN

S KELLY HAD ARRANGED to meet Najeeb in the morning at the offices of the *Frontier Report*. The cab driver took twenty minutes to find the place, and there was of course no meter. When Skelly grumbled the man answered in Urdu, as if no longer able to comprehend English. A string of wooden worry beads clicked against the rearview mirror as they swerved and bounced, at last pulling into a dirt alley by a crumbling four-story building.

"Here you are, sir," the driver announced in perfect English. "The *Frontier Report*. Five hundred rupees."

"*One* hundred," Skelly huffed, flicking a folded bill onto the front seat and slamming the door. "I didn't ask for the tour." Aggrieved shouts pursued Skelly to the entrance, where a bored policeman inspected his satchel, then nodded him through.

The newspaper was on the fourth floor, up a dingy courtyard stairwell past the offices of insurance brokers, travel agents and money changers, none of which seemed to have any customers. He was five minutes late, but Najeeb hadn't arrived. Not a good sign, but hardly disastrous. While promptness was a virtue in a fixer, in some places it was a cultural impossibility. Perhaps Pakistan was one of those places.

The *Frontier Report*'s office looked like newsrooms everywhere—a proletarian jumble of scuffed, undersized desks piled with papers and obsolete computer terminals. The walls were covered with torn maps, and Skelly especially coveted one for the North-West Frontier Province, with its markings for dirt roads and obscure mountain

passes. The seven Federally Administered Tribal Areas, highlighted in yellow along the border, offered at least a dozen unpaved entries to Afghanistan. But of course you needed a pass just to enter the Tribal Areas.

Taped to desks and walls here and there were the usual cartoons and jokes. Someone had posted an oddsmaker's picks on upcoming cricket matches, and Skelly wondered if it was part of an office betting pool, just like the bracket competition for March Madness. He experienced a stab of nostalgia, not for the States but for his previous career on the road. For twenty-two years running Skelly had clipped NCAA tournament pairings from the *International Herald Tribune* and mailed his picks to the home office from whatever war or insurrection he'd been patrolling. The last two years it hadn't been half as much fun delivering the entry in person. By next March he supposed he'd be home again. Or maybe he'd be working for Transgas. To his continuing surprise the idea was still appealing.

"Sir?" A polite voice from behind. It was the clerk who'd ushered him in, who'd been answering the phone almost nonstop. "Some tea for you, sir?"

"Yes, please. Thank you." Skelly took the steaming cup, although there would probably be another gallon of the stuff to drink at Razaq's. But where the hell was Najeeb? Ten minutes and counting. At least Skelly's headache was fading. The Murree was to blame, and to make matters worse a blanket of smog had crawled in through his open window. When he'd emerged from his morning shower the room had smelled like a bus garage.

Skelly sipped tea as he continued exploring. They were short on resources here. A reporter on the phone took notes on torn copy paper. No spare pens or pencils lying around. Pens were always one of the first things children begged for in Third World countries, one of those odd shortages that probably had bigger repercussions than any dictator ever imagined.

He checked out the bulletin board. A memo from a deskman caught his eye: "'Osama Bin Laden' at first occurrence. 'Osama' subsequently. Never 'Bin Laden.'"

That made him smile. The next one wasn't so amusing: "The recent amendments to the anti-terrorism ordinance banning Lashkar-i-Jhangvi and Sipah-i-Muhammad prohibit publication of any press statement or public utterance of anyone speaking on behalf of those

organizations. Violation of this law is punishable by imprisonment up to six months."

Well, now. It never hurt to be reminded of the nature of your working environment. A misstep here could land you in jail, although he doubted they would arrest a Westerner.

"Anything interesting up there?"

It was Najeeb, who seemed harried and was fifteen minutes late.

"Ready to roll?" Skelly shouldered his bag, trying to convey impatience without scolding. "We'll go over what I want to ask on the way to Razaq's. How long's the ride?"

Najeeb looked as if he'd rather have a cup of tea first, but too bad.

"This time of day, maybe half an hour. I am sorry, it was a long evening, then a long morning. Personal complications. I will get us a taxi."

They said little along the way, Skelly too intent on bracing himself against collisions as the cabbie careened around rickshaws and buses. One woman darted barely out of harm's way as the fender flicked the trailing hem of her blue burqa. Skelly had been shocked to see so many women covered head to toe here, having assumed, like most Americans, that burqas were strictly a Taliban obsession. Instead it seemed to be a Pashtun thing, as were all the bushy beards. He wondered if Najeeb trimmed his as some form of rebellion.

At a stoplight they pulled alongside a motorcycle with a young woman riding sidesaddle behind an older man, probably her father. Her mouth was covered, and every strand of hair was tucked beneath a white chador, but you could see her eyes. She clutched three schoolbooks, holding herself regally amid the chaos of the traffic, then glanced his way, checking out the Westerner in the cab. Her eyes were a deep, moist brown, pools you could swim around in. Skelly tried out a smile—friendly, not leering, he hoped—and a sudden crinkling of her eyes told him she'd smiled back. Amazing. A good omen, perhaps. Or maybe he was being lured into some deep and troubling maze that only the locals understood. The light turned green and the motorcycle sped away.

"Little Kabul," Najeeb said, pointing to low-slung shops lining the four-lane road. "In this part of town almost everyone you see is Afghan."

As in town, the shops were grouped by specialty. First came the auto parts district—shiny rows of mufflers hanging from low corru-

gated rooftops, welders and grinders at work in showers of sparks. Next came the poulterers with their bent cages of filthy birds stacked five deep. Then the butchers—skinned sides of mutton hanging from hooks, collecting flies and soot. Then a block of sheds with construction materials heaped in great piles, followed by dress shops with plate-glass windows, giving way to two-story wedding palaces with theater-style marquees.

"What happens if all these people go back?" Skelly asked.

"Would you? All you need is one look at the real Kabul. Their nation isn't really Afghanistan, anyway. It's Pashtun, and this is their new capital."

Your capital as well? Skelly wondered. A few miles later the buildings gave way to a sprawl of low mud huts on their right. Rooftops were made of plywood, logs and sheet metal. Windows were square holes, and smoke poured from makeshift chimneys. Looking down narrow alleys as they passed, Skelly saw seemingly endless streams of people and herds of sheep on lanes of packed clay. They crossed a narrow stream where children waded knee-deep in green water next to women washing clothes or drawing water in plastic jugs and ceramic pots, cheek by jowl with half-submerged cattle. The stench of sewage and animals was almost unbearable, but the place went on and on, the low rooftops stretching as far as he could see. It was like a scene of biblical plague, worse than anything Skelly had encountered even on the West Bank or in the war zones of the Balkans, although several sites in West Africa would give this one a run for its money.

"Jesus," he muttered. "What the hell is that?"

"The Katchagarhi camp," Najeeb said. "More than a hundred thousand refugees. *These* are the ones who will go back. Whether they want to or not. The minute the war is over, the government will start loading them up."

"How long have they been here?"

"A lot of them since the Russians came. Early eighties."

The taxi slowed, and the driver signaled for a left turn, away from the camp and up a broad paved lane. A hundred yards ahead was a guardhouse. On a vast cratered mudflat to the right several skinny boys played cricket, running barefoot in their baggy *kameez*. Dust devils swirled past them in a blazing sun. They'd propped up a narrow stone for a wicket. A barbed-wire fence lined the edge of a field behind them, and beyond it—farther still from the highway—was a green

neighborhood of three-story homes built of brick and marble, all of them fairly new. After Katchagarhi it looked like paradise.

"Hayatabad," Najeeb said. "Home of the refugee aristocracy. It's where Razaq lives."

"It's a wonder the people from Katchagarhi don't just cross the highway and kill everyone in their sleep."

"That's why there's a guardhouse. In case the thought ever occurs to them. But it would be the same in Afghanistan. Or where I'm from. The Pashtun like to call it leadership." Then Najeeb stopped, as if he'd already said too much. Skelly got out his press card and passport for the gunman at the guardhouse, who waved them through. Two blocks later they turned right toward Razaq's place, a few hundred yards farther on the right. Every home was surrounded by high concrete walls, and considering that Razaq's eldest son had been killed by Taliban assassins two years earlier, it probably wasn't a bad idea. It was quiet here, the only sound coming from workmen hammering new tiles onto the rooftop next door. Skelly wondered if there were more than just roofers up there, considering the prime vantage point.

A tall man with an automatic weapon greeted them at a latticed iron gate, passing along their IDs to someone else, who motioned them inside. The place was busy. Five ancient fellows in full beards knelt on the clipped lawn on prayer rugs angled toward Mecca. One had unwrapped his turban and was carefully folding it beside him on the grass. A portable radio blared the news from the tiles of the front porch. Inside was just as crowded. The smell of cooking wafted from the kitchen on a cloud of steam. Two other older men eyed them suspiciously from the entrance hall, a clean bright place with thick carpet and expensive-looking paintings. A younger, bareheaded man entered and shook their hands before placing his hand on his heart in the local gesture of welcome.

"Razaq's younger brother, Salim," Najeeb said, making introductions.

"You will have tea?"

Skelly knew better than to refuse.

Salim led them down a hallway. More bustle. Younger men now, chattering loudly in Pashto. Skelly caught a glimpse of the kitchen, where there was a crowd around the stove, pots clanging. He had yet to see a female. Presumably the women had their own part of the house. The place had the feel of a way station, a caravansary along the

Silk Road. But who *were* all these people? One last gathering before the big expedition? Or was it always this busy?

Salim ushered them into a smaller room, where they sat on colorful embroidered cushions along a whitewashed wall, and momentarily a young boy entered balancing a brass tray with three china cups and a steaming teapot. He poured the milky brew, Najeeb gulping it as if his life depended on it. A rough morning, indeed, Skelly surmised.

"You're still willing to go if he'll have us, aren't you?" Skelly asked.

"Yes. But our chances are small."

"So I've heard. Ran into an old friend last night at the hotel. Works for one of the pipeline companies."

"Petrotek?"

"Transgas." Hartley would have been dismayed that Najeeb thought first of the competition. "He says there's another fellow going in tomorrow, if this doesn't work out. Muhammad Fawad."

Najeeb frowned. Obviously this was news to the fixer, and that was fine with Skelly. The fewer who knew, the better.

"He's taking in some food and medical supplies, just to put his name on the map. Supposedly the skids are greased for a crossing at Torkham, but keep it under your hat. Don't want a hundred other hacks hearing about it."

"You'd still need passes to get to the border."

"Maybe we can round them up this afternoon. Worth a try, anyway."

Razaq swept into the room, puffy as a summer cloud in loose white clothes, bald head gleaming. The boy followed closely in his wake with more refreshments.

"Asala'am aleikum," Razaq said, shaking hands with a firm grip, then placing his right hand on his heart. Skelly awkwardly returned the gesture, feeling as if he were about to spout the Pledge of Allegiance.

"Please. Be seated. We will speak English, as long as your interpreter doesn't mind."

Razaq's English was polished, almost formal, probably because he'd been educated in Europe. Recently he had made a fortune in import-export in the Gulf States, and Skelly figured he must have also cashed in on the arms trade during the fight against the Soviets. Between the Saudis and the CIA, Peshawar had been afloat in enough guns and money to build an army of millions. Not that Razaq hadn't paid a price, losing a son to assassination and his wife to a mysterious car crash in Dubai.

"Who are all of your visitors?" Skelly asked.

"My guests? They are mostly from Afghanistan. Elders and tribal leaders. Village chieftains. All of them are concerned about the situation, so we meet. We exchange the latest news, discuss the future. We talk about what we might do to improve the situation."

"Why not just wait for the bombing to do its work?"

Razaq shook his head.

"The bombing has only made my work more difficult. I could have given America what it wanted without anyone firing a shot. The people are hungry for new leaders, and weary of the Arab guests who have only created problems." Skelly noted the reference to Bin Laden and his private army, something that even his editors would understand. "But the bombing has made them angry. Now they're suspicious of everyone."

"Suspicious of you?"

Razaq smiled. "I am one of them. Why would they be suspicious of me?"

"And those people who live across the highway. In . . ."

"Katchagarhi?"

"Why would they support you when they can't even see you without getting past an armed guard? They seem hungrier for food than for new leaders."

Razaq wasn't flustered in the least. He seemed accustomed to Skelly's casual brand of disrespect, as if he would have expected no less from dogs or journalists.

"'Those people,' as you call them, share a very important interest of mine. We both wish to go home. Maybe I am more comfortable during the time of waiting, but neither of us wants to be here. And they know I am one of the few who can lead them back."

"But why risk it now? You said yourself the bombing had made the job tougher."

"Mr. Kelly, have you never felt the hand of fate across your brow?"

Skelly wondered for a moment if Razaq was joking, but his expression was serious.

"Can't say that I have. What's it feel like?"

But Razaq wasn't succumbing to flippancy.

"As if you've just awakened from a dream. The answer you've been seeking is suddenly clear in your mind, washed clean by the rain of your sleep. It is a very real moment, and for that instant the way ahead

seems clear, and unavoidable. If you let the moment pass without acting, fortune may never favor you again."

Skelly was too busy scribbling to react. Perfect stuff, really, just the sort of mystic bullshit his readers would expect. Link it to a description of the old men out front, bowing on their tiny rugs, and he'd have the perfect scene-setter.

"So you're certain of success?"

"That depends on what you mean by success."

"You're sure the people will rally to you. That you'll be triumphant. Smash your way to Kabul."

Razaq grabbed a handful of pistachios, prying a nut from its shell.

"I won't be smashing my way to anyplace. My aspirations aren't military. But I do think certain elements will find common cause. The people are weary of the last five years, and wearier still of war. With me they have a chance for something better. Otherwise all they're doing is waiting for Masud's men to sweep down from the north, or for the American Marines to land. And there are many who would still prefer the Taliban to either of those alternatives."

"So you'll leave when, then?"

"In the near future."

"And you will be accompanied by what? A hundred men?"

"I'm sure you can understand that I don't wish to share further details. Let's just say that many of the rumors one hears in the city are gross exaggerations. With a hundred men I'd be seen as a war party, and inviting disaster. All the necessary people have been told what to expect, but this won't be an invasion. There are simply some people I wish to meet with in some of the provinces. Logar, Nangarhār, Paktīā. To see if I can be of any help in the transition to a new order. Assuming that a new order is inevitable, of course."

"And no one will harm a hair on your head?"

This time he smiled slightly, with the air of indulging a fool.

"Are you familiar with the concept of the blood feud, Mr. Kelly?"

"Kill one of ours, we kill one of yours?"

"Except that it is rarely so neat, or limited, especially when betrayal is involved. If harm should come to me, everyone knows there will be blood to avenge. Anyone who assisted my enemies will be held accountable."

"You're saying they won't touch you, even if you fail."

"Failure is not an option, Mr. Kelly."

"Is that what the Americans have told you? Have you been promised help?" Sam Hartley hadn't seemed to think so. Or perhaps he, too, had something to hide. Razaq lowered his gaze. Skelly doubted he'd get an answer, but the man surprised him.

"'Help' would be too strong a word, with all the wrong implications for my people. But we have been in touch. We are both aware of each other's needs."

The man obviously thought he'd secured some sort of promise from Uncle Sam. Skelly hoped for Razaq's sake that Uncle Sam felt the same. Then Razaq stirred, as if about to rise and depart, alarming Skelly enough that he asked the first thing that popped into his head.

"You'll be going on horseback, I've read, the same way you traveled when you fought the Russians." He couldn't help but wonder how massive a beast it would take to heave this load over the mountains. A Budweiser Clydesdale might do it.

"Perhaps at some point. But for a while at least we'll travel in cars and trucks, like anyone else."

"And what about this sword I've read about. Some sort of family heirloom?"

"My grandfather's."

"You'll be taking it with you?"

"And why not?"

Why not indeed. "May I see it?"

Razaq again seemed amused by Skelly's brashness. He spoke rapidly to the boy, who disappeared, and a moment later the younger brother Salim entered holding a long bundle wrapped in white cloth. Razaq stood, more gracefully than Skelly would have expected.

"It is only a symbol, of course," he said, taking the parcel in hand. "Nothing to do with luck or superstition. A matter of mere tradition."

"Yes. Of course."

He withdrew the blade in a sweeping motion, deftly draping the cloth across his left arm. Skelly had expected something sleek or dashing, like a cavalry saber or a dueling sword. But if this had indeed been taken from a fallen redcoat, then it was like nothing Skelly had ever seen in depictions of British arms. This weapon looked more like an oversized cleaver—a two-foot blade, perfectly straight along the top and tapering across the bottom, from a three-inch width at the hilt—which was surprisingly delicate and stylish—to a sharp upward curve ending in a fine point. Surprisingly, it was deeply tarnished, as if Razaq

hadn't wanted to rub off the evidence of its age. But the cutting edge shone. Obviously he kept it sharpened.

"As you can see, merely symbolic. You can't fight Kalashnikovs with it."

Now there was a quote. Skelly quickly wrote it down.

"Your grandfather used it against the British?" Skelly asked.

Razaq shrugged, noncommittal. Thus were legends allowed to grow.

"And the design up near the hilt, is that writing? What does it say?"

"A few words added later by someone in my family," Razaq said. "Nothing of significance." He slipped the blade back beneath the cloth. Skelly hoped Najeeb had gotten a look at the inscription. Salim departed with the sword.

"I trust that will be all?" Razaq said, an order more than a question.

Skelly shut his notebook to signify compliance, but there was a final piece of business.

"One last thing. More of a request, really."

"Of course."

"We'd like to come with you. My interpreter and I. Providing our own food and equipment, of course. And if at any point we get in your way or become a hindrance, then obviously you can send us back. But when this is all over you'll doubtless want the world to know about it."

"And the world will learn it best from the pages of the . . . what was the name of your publication?"

Skelly acknowledged the put-down with a grim smile. He tried unsuccessfully to mirror Razaq's sardonic expression, but wound up with more of a sneer, a wiseass grimace that said, "Can't blame a guy for trying."

"I think you can understand why for now we prefer a lower profile. I've hidden my intentions from no one, of course. That is why I offer time to journalists such as yourself. I have turned away no callers and no questions, lest anyone believe me to be a tool of the Americans."

Or of a pipeline company, Skelly thought. Or of any number of other competing moneyed interests.

"But when the time comes to get down to business, as you Americans say, then I intend to be quite on my own. So I hope you will understand. Afterward? Who knows. I'm sure in a few weeks there will be plenty of time for more conversations like this, and you will of course be welcome in my new home."

"In Kabul?"

Razaq shrugged. "Kabul. Jalalabad. Maybe a village in Logar. But somewhere on the other side of the mountains, *inshallah*."

"*Inshallah*." Skelly genuinely hoped the man didn't come to a bad end. It was always unsettling hearing that someone you'd just interviewed had gotten his head blown off. You could never help feeling you'd been an instrument in his destruction, if only as a tiny wheel in the grand contraption of fate. Salim returned to show them out.

The old men out front had disappeared, but as Skelly and Najeeb neared the gate a younger man approached. He was wire thin, with an untrimmed beard and dirty nails. He said something to Najeeb, who tried to brush him off. But the man grabbed Najeeb's sleeve, speaking into his ear in a low voice. Probably begging for a job.

"What's he want?"

"He's saying he can take us with him. That he can get us in."

"Into Afghanistan?"

"Yes. But he's a liar. A jackal." Skelly hoped the man didn't understand English. "All he wants is your money."

"Probably. But how does he propose to get us invited?"

The man, noting Skelly's interest, had let go of Najeeb's sleeve. Skelly smelled onions on his breath.

"He claims to know the man who's leading Razaq's rear guard. But this man is in Katchagarhi, and that's where we'd have to meet him."

"Ah, so there's the catch."

"Yes. This one would cut our throats the minute we left the highway. I doubt he's even supposed to be here. Probably just a charity case."

Skelly couldn't help but agree. The man's eyes were red, as if he'd smoked something for breakfast.

"Tell him thanks but no thanks, and that we're in a hurry."

Hearing Najeeb's answer, the man shook his head vigorously, making some unreadable gesture with his hands and raising his voice.

"Christ. He's worse than a shopkeeper in Cairo. What's he saying?"

"That I'm a fool not to believe him. That I'm letting you down, wasting your money."

"Well, he's persistent, I'll give him that," Skelly said, quickening his pace as they passed through the gate, finally leaving the troublesome man behind. "Nice to see our cab's still here. Might as well start rounding up our passes for the border. Oh, and did you happen to get a look at that inscription, the one on Razaq's sword?"

"Yes," Najeeb said. "And I am not surprised he didn't tell you. It was only two words, and one can only presume they're supposed to refer to the fate of the enemy."

"Two words?"

"'No Return.'"

"Goodness," Skelly said, pulling out his notebook. "You're sure?"

"Positive."

"Perfect." He scribbled it down, already composing the story in his head. "Great closing line. Let's just hope it's not his epitaph."

CHAPTER EIGHT

I T WAS DARK by the time Najeeb returned to his apartment. He was anxious to make sure that Daliya was safe and sound. He was also exhausted. Skelly and he had spent the balance of the day tracking down travel documents, after a phone call to Muhammad Fawad quickly established that the minor player from the plains of Jalalabad would be all too happy to have them accompany his caravan.

So they had wandered a bureaucratic maze in the smog and heat in search of the proper papers. Skelly was able to secure the passes in a single day only by bribing a section officer at the Department of Home and Tribal Areas, where a pair of crisp fifties soon had them on their way, to the shocked dismay of a Dutch television crew that had been waiting for hours.

Normally they would have also needed to round up a military policeman to accompany them, with more paperwork and an additional fee. But Fawad was providing his own security, so they used the extra time to buy a week's worth of supplies. They easily found a generator, plus a jerry can for fuel. Skelly had brought a sleeping bag from America, and Najeeb could make do with a pair of heavy blankets. Sleeping in the cold hadn't been a problem since he was a boy. But their quest for a satellite phone came up empty. Skelly's newspaper owned only two, and one was in the snowy wilds of northern Afghanistan while the other was marooned in Jerusalem. Fortunately, Fawad assured them that they could use his, although exactly who provided Fawad's equipment was another matter. Perhaps Sam Hartley would be tuning in.

Twice during the day Najeeb tried without success to reach Daliya on her cell phone. Perhaps she'd turned it off to get some rest. Maybe she was still awaiting his arrival.

He and Skelly parted company well after dark at the offices of the *Frontier Report*, where they arranged to meet the following morning— "*promptly* at eight," Skelly stressed. Najeeb pocketed his pay and climbed aboard his scooter, eager to get home. Last night had changed things for Daliya and him—for the better, he thought—but he wasn't sure what that meant next. And now he was on the verge of a journey into Afghanistan where, aid mission or not, there was a war on. Missiles and bombs were hitting unintended targets, and practically everyone was armed and ready to shoot. All the more reason to speak with Daliya as soon as possible.

Rounding the last corner for home he saw a small crowd of men gathered in front of his building in the glow of the street lamp. It could only mean trouble. He came to a stop and slammed down the kickstand, not bothering to lock the scooter. There were about a dozen men, with more approaching, a tightening circle with everyone gazing down at something.

"I've called the police," one said as he approached. "Probably take at least twenty minutes, knowing them." The others nodded. Najeeb eased past a downstairs neighbor to see a body curled on the ground— a man's, thank God. He bent closer, unable to see much more in the shadow cast by the crowd. But where was Daliya? He stood, glancing toward his windows—dark, curtains drawn. Surely she would have phoned if something had gone wrong, or if she'd been frightened. Unless things had happened too quickly. He pulled out his cell phone, hemmed in as more men joined in the gawking.

"Was he shot?" someone asked. A dark liquid oozed from beneath the body. A leather satchel, still strapped to his shoulder, lay to one side.

"Do we even know he's dead?" someone asked. Another man knelt to check for a pulse, although the gesture struck Najeeb as futile. He punched in Daliya's number, and when the line rang he half expected to hear the melodic beep filtering down from his window. But there was nothing, and no one answered. He waited five rings and hung up. Then someone flicked a cigarette lighter, giving everyone a better look.

The first thing Najeeb noticed was the hair, a long, tangled mess. The man's face was stained with a deep grime that one found only

among the very poor or the very rural. His clothes were ragged, a patchwork garment Najeeb had seen only one other time, worn in the empty hills of home by a wandering *malang*. The realization chilled him. *Malangs* were the stuff of legend and myth—or had been when he was a boy. Mendicants and mystics, they claimed a personal relationship with God and spent their days trying to drum up followings, which sometimes grew into cults and, at still rarer times, bloomed into armed uprisings. Tribal chieftains, fearing their potential for instability, spread wild tales about them to keep their children at a distance. Najeeb had grown up believing that any *malang* would try to eat him, and even the sight of this dead one so close to home gave him the creeps.

The pressure of the growing crowd was almost unbearable now, and Najeeb decided to head indoors. But as he turned to leave, someone switched on a flashlight just as a person in the crowd jostled the dead man's shoulder bag. The upper corner of a cream-colored envelope poked out from the bag, just like the ones delivered to his apartment.

A police jeep approached, bathing the scene in a blue strobe keeping time with Najeeb's heartbeat. Doors slammed. An officer shouted for order. The flashlight went out, and for a moment the crowd's attention was diverted by a bullhorn voice calling for everyone to disperse. The crowd turned to see what the police would do next, and Najeeb took advantage of the moment to squeeze past two men and kneel quickly by the body as a knee bumped his back. He groped through the shadow and plucked the envelope from the bag, barely maintaining his balance as the onlookers jockeyed to hold their positions. Bent across the body, he caught a whiff of hashish from the man's clothes, then stood, elbowing his way back through the crowd as the first of the policemen brushed past him. He walked briskly toward his building, expecting a cry or a hand on his shoulder, certain that his theft would be unmasked. But it had apparently gone undetected, so he stuffed the envelope in his pocket. The paper felt just like the others, and he was visited by a fleeting but unshakable sense that Daliya and this messenger must somehow have crossed paths. The sensation was so vivid that he whirled around, scanning the dim ground for more blood, or further signs of struggle. Was Daliya watching from the edge of the crowd? She wouldn't have dared. There were only men here, and emotions were running high.

A second jeep arrived with reinforcements, and officers in berets backed the crowd away, billy clubs raised as a few foolhardy souls shoved back. Najeeb glanced again toward his darkened windows, suddenly fearful of what he would find upstairs. Someone turned on a bright light, and he glanced over his shoulder a final time to make sure no one was in pursuit. This time he saw the flash of a familiar face watching from the edge of the mob. The man quickly turned away, but couldn't resist another look, as if to see if he had been recognized. Then he nodded slightly, a sheepish hello.

It was Karim, a sight almost as astonishing as that of the dead *malang*. Najeeb shouted his name above the din, and Karim waved a hand, an emphatic gesture that seemed to plead with Najeeb not to risk attracting any further attention. They worked their way toward each other around the perimeter of the crowd as more policemen shoved toward the middle.

Karim clasped Najeeb's hand. Then they hugged, as men always did in greeting in the village of Bagwali, no matter what their class or status. Karim then bowed slightly, showing his respect. The man was very much off his turf, and looked it—the weathered face of the countryside, crooked yellow teeth and rheumy eyes. He was in his mid-forties but looked closer to sixty, another customary mark of the Pashtun hinterlands.

It was only the third time Najeeb had seen Karim during his seven years of exile, and on both previous occasions the man had been carrying messages from Najeeb's mother, Shereen, and also from his uncle, Azizullah Akbar Khan, who Najeeb had always known affectionately as Aziz. Uncle Aziz had dispatched Karim on those occasions, and he did so without the knowledge of Najeeb's father, meaning that everyone involved had been risking his neck, even Najeeb's mother.

A second envoy had also made contact over the years, a boy named Jameel. But Jameel brought messages only from Najeeb's mother, meaning that Karim was loyal first and foremost to Uncle Aziz.

Aziz was the youngest of four brothers, of whom Najeeb's father was the eldest and therefore the heir. The middle brothers died in their teens, ensuring plenty of rivalry between the two survivors, a rivalry that would have grown even more intense in later years if Aziz had ever fathered sons of his own. That's how brothers most often did battle in their adult years—through their sons. But Aziz's three wives bore him only daughters. Thus, deprived of a lineage, Aziz signaled his apparent

surrender in the fraternal wars by befriending Najeeb, becoming his boyhood guide across hunting paths and caravan routes, indulging him in ways that a father never would have dared. And so, when the great breach had occurred between Najeeb and his father, Aziz had resumed his rivalry in silence by opening the channels of communication to the banished son. What better way to undermine the father than to subvert the loyalty of the son—even a son in disgrace. And if the boy's mother also participated in this forbidden back channel, what did that say about her relationship with Aziz?

Or perhaps it had all been innocent, a pair of adults who simply believed that Najeeb's punishment was too harsh. That's what Najeeb preferred to think, if only because he knew that upheaval and scheming had long been the norm among his people. You only had to listen to the old songs and poems to know that, verses rife with themes of deceit.

"You are well?" Karim asked.

"Well enough. And how is my mother? And Aziz?"

"Well also. Both of them."

Najeeb waited for more, but Karim seemed hesitant.

"Have you brought a message?"

"No." Karim stared at the ground. "I was sent only to check on you. You weren't supposed to know I was here."

"Do you do this often?"

Karim seemed to consider the question for a moment, then shook his head.

"No. Not often. Only when your uncle is worried about you."

"What do you know about the *malang*?" Najeeb asked, choosing to ignore the implied warning. "Did you know him?'

"No," Karim said quickly, looking away. "I arrived when you did. When I saw you were okay I decided to come back later. Then you saw me." He shrugged, as if there were nothing further to say.

"Come inside. I'll make tea." Najeeb had at least a dozen more questions, not least because he wasn't buying Karim's version of events. But even the binding tie of offered hospitality wasn't enough to hold the edgy Karim.

"I am sorry, but I cannot stay. I have other business. And I have no message for you. I must go."

Karim quickly clasped Najeeb's hand, then touched his right hand to his heart.

"Wait." Najeeb grasped the man's arm in the nick of time. "One last question. When you arrived, did you see a woman here? Near the *malang*, or running from the building? Was there a woman?"

Karim's face was blank, noncommittal. "No. No woman. Until the next time, then, *inshallah*."

Najeeb released his grip, and Karim melted into the crowd.

By now a battered ambulance had pulled to the curb, and the crew was unloading a stretcher. Could Karim have killed the *malang*? If not, then what had he really been doing here, and what had triggered Uncle Aziz's concern?

Perhaps, despite Karim's denials, this visit was only one of many. Maybe Karim had been watching over him for years. It was a comforting thought, this idea of a guardian angel dispatched by Aziz, and it brought to mind a favorite sura from the Koran, the short one about "the nightly visitant . . . the star of piercing brightness. For every soul there is a guardian watching it."

Or maybe Karim had told the truth: This was a rare appearance, and he'd simply come along at the wrong time, knowing nothing about either the messenger or the killing. Which raised another possibility—that Abdullah, Najeeb's purported ISI contact, had crossed paths with the victim and had decided to get rid of one state security problem even as he kept tabs on another. No guardian angel at work, then, just a lethal government snoop. The possibilities seemed endless. Maybe the contents of the envelope would tell him more.

He turned toward his apartment, sprinting up the stairs, grateful that someone had replaced the burned-out bulb. Reaching the landing, he saw with a jolt that his door was again ajar, and he paused on the threshold, calling Daliya's name. There was no answer, so he pushed inside and switched on the light.

The place was a shambles. Books were pulled from the shelves in a scramble of splayed covers. Every drawer of his desk was open, and his cushions were slashed. Stepping into the bedroom, he saw that his mattress had been pulled to the floor. It, too, was slashed, the batting swelling whitely from the wound. Daliya was nowhere to be seen, thank God, nor was there any blood. Either she was long gone by the time this happened or the intruder had taken her with him. Might she have killed the *malang*? he wondered. Possible. If so, she might have fled anywhere.

Then he remembered his money, the stash of dollars that repre-

sented every hope of escaping Pakistan. Robbery suddenly seemed a plausible motive for this mess, and he rushed to the bathroom where he kept the folded bills in a bandage box, in the medicine cabinet above the sink. Someone had emptied the cabinet's contents into the sink, and he saw the box in the pile, its top open.

His heart sank, and he reached for the box, expecting the worst. But the bills were still inside, bundled tightly by a red rubber band, just as before. He leaned against the sink in relief, the only sound the dripping of the shower. Then he counted the money. It was all there, although whoever had tossed the place surely must have seen it. Not even the most diligent servant of state security could have resisted this much temptation, he thought, more puzzled than ever. A religious fanatic, he supposed, might have. But if the *malang* had made it all the way up here, then why had he still been carrying the envelope?

Najeeb picked up the phone, almost surprised to hear a dial tone. Then he tried Daliya's number, waiting in agitation as the ringing continued just as it had throughout the day. He counted the tones to calm himself, pulse slackening, and when he reached twenty he hung up.

Stepping back to the living room, he pawed through the wreckage of papers beneath his desk, finding Rukhsana's number scribbled on an electric bill from the previous month. He dialed it, and she answered almost right away. They'd spoken before, but always under happier circumstances, while conspiring to plot another rendezvous with Daliya.

"I haven't heard from her since this morning," Rukhsana said. "*Very* early." She sounded peeved about it. "Although I understood why, once she told me where she was. Congratulations." Her tone was scolding. "She was a fool to spend the night. You wouldn't believe the cover story we came up with, but her aunt and uncle haven't called, so they must have gone for it."

"I can't reach her on her cell, and I've been trying all day," Najeeb said. "When I got home my apartment was trashed and the door was open. There was a dead man out front and the police were just arriving, but no sign of Daliya. I was hoping you'd call her uncle's to see if she's there. I sure as hell can't."

Rukhsana's tone changed to one of alarm. "She never turns her cell off. I'll try them now and call you right back."

He waited only three minutes, reshelving books to kill the time.

"She wasn't in. They're worried sick. They're wondering if they should call the police."

Should they? Then the entire story of their relationship would come out, and he would face even more unwanted scrutiny. But where could Daliya be?

"I don't know what to do. But, yes, they should call the police, report her missing." He paused, collecting his thoughts. "Don't mention me, though. Not yet. Not until tomorrow, if you can wait that long."

"But they'll ask where she was last night."

"Use the cover story for now. If you have to tell them about me later, the police will understand why you were covering for her."

But would they? And would Najeeb lie to the police on Rukhsana's behalf?

"Covering for *you*, you mean," Rukhsana said coldly.

"Yes, for me. But if she turns up tonight, there's no sense getting her in deeper trouble."

"But what if she doesn't? What if she's not back by morning?"

"I don't know. I may be on my way to Afghanistan by then."

"Afghanistan?"

Now he detected a note of mistrust.

"Journalistic business. Translating for an American."

"And you can't give up your hundred dollars a day, even for Daliya."

"It's a hundred and fifty. And, no, I can't, because she's part of the reason I'm earning it."

Did he mean that? He thought so. Hoped so. But Rukhsana wasn't buying it.

"Yes, you keep telling yourself that."

She hung up before he could answer.

Najeeb sat on a torn cushion, anxiety building in his chest. He tried to think of any reason Daliya might voluntarily disappear, but he came up empty. Then he remembered the envelope and pulled it from his pocket.

It now seemed malignant. And how could a message carried by a dead *malang* be anything but cursed? He knew that was his childhood speaking, a village superstition flitting around his brain like a bat.

He tore it open, pulling out the folded paper of the same creamy bond, covered with the same cramped writing. This time there were two messages.

"104:1" began the first. "Woe betide every backbiting slanderer who amasses riches and sedulously hoards them, thinking his wealth will render him immortal! By no means! He shall be flung to the

destroying flame. Would that you knew what the Destroying Flame is like. It is God's own kindled fire, which will rise up to the hearts of men. It will close in upon them from every side, in towering columns."

The next passage was prefaced by a brief note in Pashto: "For your American friend." Followed by more Arabic from the Prophet:

"4:78. Wherever you be, death will overtake you; though you put yourselves in lofty towers."

Najeeb crumpled the paper and let it drop to the floor.

# CHAPTER NINE

A RUMBLE OF THUNDER awakened Skelly just after dawn, and he was thrilled to hear raindrops spattering fatly on the balcony. Finally, a downpour to scrub the sky clean, making the air fit for human consumption. He rolled over comfortably in the darkened bed, listening to the trees whipsaw in the gusting squall.

When he threw open the curtains an hour later on the brightness of a clearing sky, it was evident that the storm hadn't been up to the task. Leaves and grass were rinsed of dust, almost shocking in their fresh greenness, but the air smelled like a drowned campfire, and the sky was already filmed over in a sticky whiteness, like Vaseline on a lens.

Maybe it would be better in the hills, and he took heart, remembering that a day of travel lay ahead. Tonight he might well bed down in Afghanistan, without electricity or running water. A regular campout. His gear was piled by the door, and he resolved to check out of his room, even though there was now a waiting list. Jalalabad or bust.

Najeeb was again late for their appointment at the *Frontier Report*, damn him, but it was a short drive to Fawad's house in the heart of the cantonment, next to the local UN headquarters, and when they arrived it was clear no one was leaving anytime soon. Word of the caravan had leaked out overnight, and at least fifty journalists were encamped on the man's lawn. Mounds of luggage and TV equipment sat beneath huge rubber trees. Correspondents and photographers milled loudly, smoking cigarettes and reading the local papers as they stepped around robed old men, bowing silently on prayer rugs.

There was a sign-up sheet going around—in case transportation

ran short, someone said—and by the time Skelly got hold of it he and Najeeb were at spots 53 and 54. So much for being in on the ground floor.

A few minutes later Fawad emerged grandly from the house in a billow of spotless blue garments. He was tall, thin, with a bony irregular head that convinced you he'd led a life of hardship and deprivation. He was at least a decade younger than Razaq, with a trimmed beard and black hair turning silver at the ears and sideburns. He seemed taken aback by the spectacle he'd wrought, shaking his head with a frown of concern.

"We are arranging for more transport," he announced, hands outstretched as if appealing for patience. The mob quieted, drawing closer for the update. "The buses will arrive very soon. Then we will be under way."

The first bus didn't show for another ninety minutes, and it was a creaky red model with a mere thirty seats. *Flying Titanic* was painted in jolly script on the side.

"Now who wants to board *that* one," an Australian said to laughter. The smaller *Cruising Enjoy* arrived moments later, followed by an orange bus from the Nawaz Model School. Skelly wondered how many students would be grumbling about having to walk home this afternoon. By now, at least another fifty hacks had arrived, ants streaming toward the only picnic in town, restive in the broiling sunny haze. Some were already digging into expedition rations as the lunch hour came and went. A tall Swede sat on a cinder block, boiling water on a small propane stove for a pouch of Ramen noodles.

The horde's presence, with its money belts and thick folds of currency, attracted a steady incursion of industrious beggars and urchins. A barefoot boy who looked about ten, his face coated in dust, offered to spit-shine shoes while his companion, a head shorter, played a two-note tune by drumming an empty Pepsi bottle with a stick.

Skelly shooed them away, wishing Najeeb were there to do it. He was probably off in a corner on his cell phone, as he seemed to have been all morning, worse than a stockbroker keeping track of the market. Skelly wondered what had made him so sullen and preoccupied, or maybe he was always like this. Another dusty waif materialized at Skelly's sleeve, bowing with a jerky motion—"How are *you*, sir?"—probably his entire repertoire of English. He lit a tin of incense and fanned the acrid smoke toward Skelly, ashy and sickly sweet, suppos-

edly for good luck, but it was the last thing you wanted to breathe on a hot, soupy day.

"No, get it out of here." Skelly fanned back and turned away. An Italian woman slipped the boy a hundred-rupee note, which would only encourage him.

Out in the narrow street, a man wearing a blue UN cap emerged from between the buses, announcing that they were blocking the UN's driveway. Fawad's minions scurried to accommodate him, and the journalists groaned at the prospect of further delay. Fawad, sensing he was about to lose the audience of a lifetime, then announced impulsively that it was time to board. The protests of the UN man were drowned out by an ungodly rush and clutter, with everyone shouldering cameras, duffels, sleeping bags and satellite phones while shouting in half a dozen languages. Skelly tracked down Najeeb, but by the time they reached the street all three cargo bays were stuffed full, and a sweating face stared from every window.

"Try that one," Skelly shouted, nodding toward the *Flying Titanic*. Not surprisingly, it had the most remaining seats. They barely squeezed aboard, Najeeb near the front and Skelly in the last row, stuffing half his gear onto an overhead shelf and holding his sleeping bag in his lap, wondering if he'd even be able to pull a notebook from his rear pocket. A pencil jabbed his right thigh, which he tried to remedy until discovering that it belonged to the Japanese man seated next to him. By now the aisle was jammed, the standees clamoring after the whereabouts of colleagues and equipment. Skelly mopped his brow. It must be a hundred degrees. He wondered how hard it would be to pry loose a water bottle from overhead, then remembered Najeeb had their water, twenty rows and a million miles forward.

"Fucking great," a familiar voice said. He wrenched left to see Canadian radio reporter Lucy Chatterton across the narrow aisle, peering around the rump of a fat Austrian.

Wonderful. Chatty Lucy, who would have to be endured for who knew how many hours to come. In ten-minute doses she could be wildly entertaining, with a razor wit and easy warmth. Beyond that her conversations turned into monologues, a maddening buzz of insecurities and exaggerations, frenetic lectures to show off her local knowledge and prolific filing habits, laced with anecdotes to demonstrate that she was every inch the macho adventurer, more so than even the most hardened flak-vested blowhard males.

Or maybe Skelly's reaction had more to do with his general discomfiture around female correspondents. One would think he would have gotten used to them by now. There had been a thriving population of women in war zones since the Persian Gulf War in '91, when they flourished despite Saudi restrictions. Most male reporters had taken to it naturally. Skelly never quite made the leap.

It wasn't as if he were Old School, or voted Republican. Nor did he begrudge their chance to be here. Maybe it was just that, at age fifty-three, he'd been born a few years too soon. Or so he told himself, knowing that older colleagues had adjusted fine. Perhaps it was the way some of them tried to turn every journey into a sort of slumber party, sharing secrets of their families and friends until the small hours. Or the knack some had for showing compassion in the field, even grief, but without letting it ruin their copy.

Lucy wore her politics on her sleeve. She'd spout off one minute about the ennobling integrity of an indigenous culture, then rail away in the next about its treatment of women, as if you could fix the latter without harming the former. Yet her prose was as coldly dispassionate as stainless steel, cutting straight to the heart of a nation's woes.

He'd spotted her once outside a sagging refugee tent, taking a family under her wing, doing them favors and bringing treats. Later she'd helped them apply for asylum in North America, shepherding them through the whole horrible system.

Skelly had allowed himself to cozy up to a local family only once, during a two-month swing through Kosovo. He took chocolate to the children and coffee to the parents, and rounded up university applications abroad for the eldest son. The dad built a wooden toy for one of Skelly's daughters, and the mom mailed a sweet card in broken English to his second wife. Two months later Skelly returned to find they'd literally been blown to pieces in a mortar attack, all three children dead and both parents crippled and disconsolate. He'd sworn off fraternization forever, and felt like averting his eyes whenever a colleague started in.

"Looks like we might never leave," Lucy said.

"Think we'll reach the border before dark?" Skelly asked.

"We better. They kick you out of the Tribal Areas at sundown. And we don't want to be on the road to Jalalabad after dark."

"Pretty lawless, I guess. I heard there's a war on."

"We'd make a nice thermal signature on an F-16's radar screen. Be too bad to come all this way only to get vaporized by Uncle Sam."

"You don't think Fawad's got all that worked out?"

"Good point. Safe passage in exchange for a CIA briefing, maybe?"

Or a Transgas briefing, Skelly thought, wondering whether Hartley had been exaggerating about all the competing loyalties and connections. He was of two minds about conspiracy theories in places like this. While it was certainly plausible for some key players to juggle several agendas at once, he also believed that competing interests tended to cancel each other out. The key was finding out which agenda, ideology, or secret motive struck the deepest emotional chord. That's the one that would win every time, long after the money men and gunrunners went home. It was the zealots who had staying power—another reason he'd rather follow Razaq, who carried the unmistakable aura of the true believer. With Fawad one sensed the drab, pale wattage of a ward politician, an opportunist. Even if this expedition pierced the border, it would probably amount to little more than an exotic dateline or two. There would be no grand adventure.

"Shit," Lucy said. "Looks like we're unloading."

It was true. Grumbling and groaning with every step, the journalists were spilling back into the street, sodden with perspiration. Fawad was speaking heatedly with a knot of UN men.

"Will there be an official statement?" Skelly's Japanese seatmate asked no one in particular. "A press conference?" Skelly shook his head, wondering whether Tokyo ever got any news that didn't come from a press conference.

"Who's your fixer?" It was Lucy again, hovering at his shoulder as they stepped off the bus.

"I was just looking for him. Najeeb Azam. Beautiful translation, and supposedly well connected. A bit hard to read, though. So far, anyway."

"Mine's great." (Well, of course he was, Skelly thought. He was Chatty Lucy's.) "And he speaks Dari, which I think we'll need, especially the farther inside the country we get."

"Here's Najeeb," Skelly said. The man looked as hangdog as he had all day.

Lucy introduced herself, then pulled forward her own fixer, whose name was Javed. Skelly didn't catch the last name, but he noticed that Najeeb had gone rigid. If the man had been distant before, he was now positively stony, and Javed seemed to be the reason.

Perhaps the two were journalistic rivals. Javed worked at the *International Daily*. Otherwise there was little about the man to inspire ani-

mosity. If anything he seemed dull, balding and plump with droopy eyes. He looked more like a bureaucrat than a reporter.

"Javed says he doubts they'll let us across the border," Lucy said brightly, testing it on Najeeb. "Even though Fawad seems convinced the skids are greased."

"Maybe Javed has better connections," Najeeb said, not at all warmly.

"His connections are excellent," she said, oblivious to the jab. Javed said nothing. He stared at Najeeb, sleepy eyes unblinking, as if daring him to make another crack.

"Yes, I'm sure they are," Najeeb said. "Excuse me. I have to make a phone call."

"I see what you mean," Lucy said after a pause. "Not the friendliest guy in the world."

Then Javed spoke up. "There are colleagues of mine who are available to serve you, if you are not satisfied with him." He handed Skelly a business card. Nice offer, Skelly supposed, although he wondered if Javed got a referral fee.

"Yes, well. Things are working out for now. But thanks."

The buses revved their engines and were suddenly on the move, momentarily panicking just about everyone who'd left items on board. Fawad appealed for calm.

"We will leave in an hour," he shouted. "Two more buses are coming. We had to make way for the UN. We will reload around the corner."

More grumbling and more dark humor. A few in the crowd set off in search of fresh food and water. Skelly pulled out a notebook and began recording the surroundings. If the day was a bust he might still have to file. But what? A scene-setter? A media story? You never knew what the editors might want, so he kept scribbling.

The delay was an hour, and in the meantime another dozen journalists trickled in. But when the two extra buses finally arrived there were just enough seats for everyone. So, at three o'clock, with at least two hours and thirty miles of traffic, checkpoints and hairpin mountain curves ahead, everyone settled in wearily for the ride. Skelly again trooped to the back, this time grabbing a window seat. Najeeb ended up several rows forward. And with a blast of blue exhaust, the *Flying Titanic* was under way, bound for the Khyber Pass.

It was a cumbersome convoy. At the front was a truck carrying

Fawad and twenty of his men, flags flying. The men were heavily armed, although no one seemed to have noticed them throughout the morning. Next came another truck, similarly fortified, followed by five larger ones loaded to the brim with sacks of flour, lentils, rice and powdered milk. In the spectrum of aid convoys that Skelly had seen over the years, this one was a mere hiccup, carrying barely enough to feed a few hundred people for a week. He suspected that the armed escort carried the more emphatic message—namely, that Fawad intended to be a player in his corner of the new Afghanistan and had the money and the connections for a credible bid. If you ate his groceries you'd be buying into his viability, at least until the lentils ran out.

Skelly concentrated on the view, which as they approached the outskirts of Peshawar gave way first to the Katchagarhi camp, then to a vast sprawl of bazaars and buses, rough-and-tumble shops that were two stories high, stretching down crowded alleys—toy vendors followed by plumbing equipment, then building supplies, then cigarettes, then tea shops. On and on it went.

"What's this place?" he asked, tapping the shoulder of a Brit whose name he couldn't remember.

"Smugglers Bazaar. You can even buy hashish and Kalashnikovs, or a grenade launcher. That's all toward the back, of course. Special escort required. But everything you see comes in illegally. Goes into Afghanistan for about ten minutes, then somebody hauls it back across the border, duty free."

"Even with a war on?"

"Especially with a war on."

A mile or so later, having left the bazaar behind, the buses pulled to the shoulder in a cloud of dust. The drivers climbed out, papers in hand. Skelly saw Fawad disappear into a low guardhouse with two of his men. But the greater attraction was less than a hundred yards farther up the highway. Two round towers of white stone topped by battlements sat astride the pavement, connected by a crenellated arch spanning the highway. Trucks passed beneath it in either direction. On the horizon beyond loomed a huge range of brown mountains against a brilliant blue sky. They'd reached the official entrance to the Khyber Pass. Tired as he was from all of the waiting, Skelly was elated, and as the buses got back under way he gawked like a tourist. They passed the Jamrud fort, chunky and red on a stony knoll. Later, to the right on a bare plain, a forlorn Pashtun graveyard—a leafless forest of thin sticks

poked into the scrabble, each fluttering with a makeshift cloth banner, most of them tattered by the breeze. There was a lonely stillness to the place, yet with every fluttering breeze the site seemed alive with restless souls.

The buses began climbing, engines groaning with effort. But the air here was clean and clear, blessed relief from Peshawar, and he gazed up into the high shadows of the brown crags, unable to resist imagining that tribal warriors were concealed there, training their gun barrels on the intruders as they had done for centuries, leathery creased faces beneath dusty turbans just the way Kipling had described them.

Skelly had been a wanderer for as long as he could remember. Scenery wasn't the attraction. It was sheer newness that drew him. New languages, new villages, new rail routes and forests and hillsides—a craving that had begun in his earliest years. He remembered a long bicycle ride at age ten, a sense of shattering old boundaries and restrictions as he pedaled hard, then harder, down blocks he'd never traveled. It had probably been the blandest sort of suburbia, but even the unfamiliar street names had charged him up, and when he'd gotten home he had furtively pulled a city map from a drawer of his father's desk to retrace the journey, feeling like a junior Marco Polo.

His mother had tried to curb his tendencies, especially after she caught him cycling one day through a neighborhood she never drove through without locking the doors and rolling up the windows. It reminded him of how Janine had become lately, staying ever closer to home. She'd strenuously opposed this latest trip—God, he really *should* have phoned her by now. But that was the trouble with marriage, or had been so far anyway. Every wife eventually turned into his mother, trying to rein him in, ordering him home this instant. Which of course only made him stay out longer, way past bedtime—for so many months on two occasions that he found himself attracted to some other woman altogether. Both had become new Mrs. Skellys, and now he wasn't sure what terrified him more—the prospect he might repeat the pattern yet again, or that he might have finally become so old and undesirable that no woman would ever again offer him the chance.

The bus paused briefly on a hairpin turn, seeming to lurch outward across the yawning canyon. They had reached the literal high point of the ride, and the views were breathtaking. In valleys and glens he saw small tribal villages along muddy streams, the larger houses surrounded by high stone walls and watchtowers. Smuggler barons, he

supposed. Or opium lords. He wondered if any of these places were Najeeb's old haunts, and he sought out his fixer in the forward rows, spotting the black hair of his head as it bobbed with the motion of the bus. But what was this? Najeeb was standing now, inching into the aisle and stepping toward the front, gripping a seat for balance, then leaning low to speak with someone across the aisle. But who?

It was Javed, Chatty Lucy's fixer. So they did know each other, then. Najeeb had turned so his face was in profile, and he wore the glowering expression he'd shown earlier to Javed. It was the most emotion Skelly had yet seen in the man, and Skelly was entranced. Not that he wanted to bond with Najeeb. Chatty Lucy probably knew the name of all Javed's children by now and had already bought them treats. Perhaps Skelly should have her sit next to Najeeb for a while, to pry out all his secrets.

Najeeb was leaning lower now, and both men were speaking rapidly. He saw that Chatty Lucy was watching, too. Skelly thought he heard a heated burst of words in Urdu over the volume of the grinding gears.

"Wonder what that's all about," Skelly proffered.

"An argument?" Lucy suggested.

"Looks that way. Any guesses why?"

Lucy shrugged. She seemed nervous about something, almost embarrassed.

"What? What is it?"

"It's your fixer." She paused dramatically. "Javed says he's ISI."

Skelly felt his stomach drop. "Najeeb?"

She nodded, seeming to make an effort not to gloat.

"And what's he base that on?" Tone rising defensively. Because what clearer verdict could there be for his own poor judgment than being duped by some government snoop?

"He didn't say. But he sounded pretty sure. Says that a few of them get jobs at the local papers, then work as fixers. It's how they keep tabs on us."

It would certainly explain the guarded attitude, and all the furtive phone calls.

"Great. Well, hell. I guess if the *Times* got sucked in, then I shouldn't feel too bad."

"You should fire him. Get a new one. I'd be happy to share Javed today, if you want. If we get across you can always hire a local. Javed has friends in Jalalabad."

Just what he needed, wasting time to find another fixer while everyone else was reporting and filing. Maybe Janine was right. His time for this sort of thing was past.

"Thanks. But I might as well use him while he's here. There won't be much for him to do today anyway, at this rate. Besides, maybe it isn't true."

Lucy shook her head. "Javed knows his stuff." (Translation: And so do I.) "And I don't think anyone on the bus wants an ISI man around, listening to our interviews, tracking our movements. You need to get rid of him."

Others were beginning to eavesdrop. Skelly was furious.

"Look. Let me speak to him first. Preferably before you tell the known world."

She nodded grudgingly, making it clear the agreement was limited. By tomorrow she'd be telling everyone. By now Najeeb had returned to his seat, the back of his head unreadable, and when Skelly turned to look out the window again the romance of the place was gone. Now it was only brown hills and starving peasants—drought, war and famine, in all their sameness. He crossed his arms, angry at Najeeb, at himself and of course at Chatty Lucy. His last great chance for making a splash, and it was falling apart.

Just perfect, he thought, and as the bus rolled deeper into the pass he couldn't help but recall the long roster of foreigners who had come to grief here through similar misjudgments. Dead conquerors, dead explorers and now one dead career.

Just bloody fucking perfect.

## CHAPTER TEN

Najeeb stared straight ahead, rigid with anger, as the bus rounded a curve. He glanced across the aisle, but the Clerk—Najeeb refused to think of him as Javed, too jolly a name for such a cold-blooded creature—was gazing out the window, seemingly bored.

Moments ago Najeeb had finally summoned the nerve to confront him, having brooded ever since the Canadian woman introduced them. Already irritable and frantic over Daliya's whereabouts, he had decided to unburden himself even if every translator on board overheard him. At least the loudness of the bus would provide some cover. So he stepped into the aisle and got straight to the point.

"Why are you here?" he demanded, grabbing a seat back for balance as the bus lurched. The Clerk snapped to attention.

"I might ask you the same. Aren't you supposed to be with Razaq? You won't win any points reporting on this bunch."

"But why are you here?"

"None of your business. And I can't believe you think it is."

"What have you done with Daliya? Where is she?"

The Clerk frowned. "Who the hell is Daliya? I'm working for Lucy."

"So I guess you don't know about the dead man, either."

This at least got a rise out of him, but whether out of embarrassment or bafflement Najeeb couldn't say.

"You're out of your mind. What the hell are you talking about? And do you want everyone to hear you?" The Clerk lowered his voice, forc-

ing Najeeb to lean closer. The nearby foreign journalists seemed mildly curious but mostly annoyed, probably figuring that the locals had brought some petty grudge aboard.

"Do you think I'm the only one on this bus, or this caravan, with something to hide?" The Clerk practically spit out the words, poking a stubby forefinger into Najeeb's chest and hissing into his ear. Najeeb wanted to grab his collar and shove the round head against the window, but with the Clerk now grabbing his shirtfront it was all he could do to keep from collapsing into the seat atop the man. "Do you think I'm the only person here who can do you harm?"

The Clerk then pushed him away. Najeeb, jolted by the parting remark, nearly tripped over a duffel bag in the aisle before sagging past his Swedish seatmate to his spot by the window. And now here he was, still fuming and still afraid, both for himself and for Daliya, waiting for the swirl of angry confusion to calm and settle in his head.

He breathed deeply, his *kameez* sticking to the sweat on his back. Then he tried to take stock of what he knew and where he stood. Daliya was missing and unreachable, almost certainly due to someone who'd been watching them. By now the police would be looking for her, and possibly for him as well, depending on what Rukhsana had decided to say. A nameless *malang*, some religious fanatic from the hills, was dead practically on his doorstep, but only after having penned his direst warning yet. And the ISI still had its hooks in him, which might or might not have something to do with the Clerk's presence on the bus. And who the hell had the Clerk been referring to just now, with the remark about "others" who might do him harm? Then there was Karim, emissary of his uncle Aziz, who'd come all the way to Najeeb's apartment but apparently without a message.

As if all that weren't enough, Najeeb was now trapped in this bus, bound for an unwanted border crossing that might keep him tied down for days, out of touch with everyone who mattered, yet still in harm's way. His world might change completely in his absence, but he wouldn't know until they returned. He pulled out his cell phone, but the signal was gone. It wouldn't be back until they returned to Peshawar.

He considered all the journalists around him. They were tourists, really, even if of a more knowledgeable and inquisitive strain. And so naive. He wondered how they would react if they really knew how far beyond help they already were in case something went wrong. Even

with Fawad's men aboard, and even with the occasional roadside bunker housing soldiers of the Frontier Police, Najeeb knew from experience that with every mile beyond Peshawar the government's influence waned like the signal of a weak radio station, or the signal of his cell phone. By the time you entered the Khyber Pass it was lost altogether in static and whine, an unreachable bandwidth. Lawless was an understatement.

He looked out the window, hoping the view might calm him, but what he saw was a landscape that still haunted and ruled him, and he easily imagined the feel of the stones beneath the thin rubber soles of his sandals. Looking toward the sun, he recalled what it felt like to stand atop a high pass, a moment of calm, bright blueness up where the hawks circled, face raised to the heavens, the air crisp and cool, a clarity that made you gasp for more. He hadn't taken a deep breath like that in years without feeling the stench of the city clutch at his insides.

There were plenty of fond memories locked in these hills, but his current mood seemed to be screening out all but the bad ones. When they'd passed the Smugglers Bazaar a half hour earlier he'd been reminded of one of the worst weeks of his boyhood, a spell of servitude ordered by his father, who had angrily deemed him in need of penance, of toughening. For six awful days he had manned a pushcart for a smuggling baron along the tribal border, an ally of his father's who controlled illicit commerce for dozens of commodities. Najeeb began each circuit at a darkened stone warehouse, piling the cart heavily with cartons of Marlboros and boxes of Surf detergent, then shoved the load at a straining trot a quarter mile down a bumpy path toward the border of the North-West Frontier Province and the crowded stalls of the bazaar, half panicked that a Pakistani customs guard might approach at any moment. If your cart was impounded it wiped out a week's worth of earnings and won you a flogging from the boss. Even if you made it safely to your destination, some pigeonhole shop deep in the bazaar, you gave up half your thirty-rupee reward to the merchant who controlled the transit area.

But the worst part of the week had been the other boys, small-time bullies with their own ideas of turf and tribute, punching and kicking and demanding a cut of his pay, then spitting derisively when he handed it over. They'd been forewarned of the young khan's arrival, the son of the mighty *malik*, knowing he was usually off-limits to such casual abuse. But not this week, they'd been told. The usual rules were

suspended. Treat him as you would any newcomer. Meaning each day brought cuts, bruises and welts along with the few rupees Najeeb managed to hang on to. At times he gave as good as he got, to the point where he was fighting in his dreams. This continued for two weeks after his return home, kicking and scuffling through the night until the blanket came off, then awakening in a fury beneath a sky full of stars.

Such was the lifestyle of these hills, where every division of power had its subdivision, and every line of demarcation was a zone of struggle and torment. There were four major tribes in the Khyber Agency alone, with each divided into *khel*s, and every *khel* into clans, every clan into subclans, and so on, down to the rival gangs of begrimed boys, tangling dawn to dusk for the last remaining scraps of pride and conquest.

Najeeb's father had stood atop one of the loftier levels of this hierarchy. Of course, this was not royalty in the Western sense of the word, as Najeeb would discover whenever he tried to explain his heritage to friends in college. For all its medieval character, it was a knighthood of *kameez* and bandoleer, not ermine and armor; of turbans, not tiaras; Kalashnikovs, not lances. The castles of this realm were stone compounds with wrought-iron gates, mud walls and kitchen smokeholes. Or such had been the case until Najeeb was in his teens, for he had come of age in an era of great changes.

Early in life, his father's status had brought scarcely more than the right to lord it over their village, where most residents barely fed themselves and paid little in tribute or rent. His family ate the same lentils and spinach as the others, his mother pounding barley into flour on a hollowed stone, his sisters churning soft cheeses and curds, buttermilk and *warqa*. They drank black tea by day, green tea by night, boiling the leaves with milk and sugar.

When the villagers brought them anything it was usually tomatoes, which his father shied from, believing they caused impotence, a fear especially acute in a man who had produced only one son. For special meals they might wring the neck of a chicken or dispatch Najeeb and the other local children to help Aziz do some fishing, Pashtun style, not with nets but by cutting a five-rupee stick of dynamite in half, then tying it to a lump of phosphorous wrapped in cloth. Aziz lit the phosphorous, then tossed the bundle into the deepest pool, the flame holding even under water, drawing the fish like a beacon, then exploding with a thud and a bubbling geyser. It was the greatest entertainment

the children might witness for weeks, as stunned fish bobbed to the surface, dead eyes turned to the sky, everyone wading in to skim the catch into woven baskets.

But when Najeeb was only five, war arrived next door in Afghanistan on a wave of Soviet tanks and helicopters, and by the time he was ten the world was a very different place. On came the gunrunners and the quiet men from America with no last names, nodding and smiling with their broken Pashtun, mouths full of promises and briefcases full of cash. Soon in their wake came a strange and sullen breed of holy men, some on horseback, mouths curled in scorn. The men of the village turned ascetic and scornful, yet for all of the new piety the valley's poppy fields bloomed as never before, and the passing caravans were laden with new cargoes—hand-held missile launchers heading west, oozing brown sacks of opium paste heading east. And wedged between them, families of refugees, stumbling through the passes while Najeeb watched from the shadows of the rocks, at rest with his lunch and a flask of tea.

The new commerce quickly pushed his family's standard of living upward, leaping centuries at a time: running water, a telephone in the village, an automobile, even a television. For years its only signal was a screen full of snow with garbled sound, yet it played almost continuously in the *hujera*, like some new totem of authority.

Najeeb's great windfall was to be dispatched across the hills to a school that taught writing and English and mathematics, a three-mile walk that cost him dearly in stones and derision from boys who had learned from their grandfathers exactly what to chant at such presumption:

> *You are learning at the English school,*
> *You are learning for money.*
> *There will be no place in heaven for you,*
> *And for this you will hang in hell.*

To extract payment for these indulgent hours of learning Najeeb's father sent him into the hills every afternoon with an old rifle, on orders to bring home birds for the table, even though by then his family had moved well beyond lentils and barley bread. But the chore proved anything but punishment. Najeeb cherished the old gun, more for its look and feel than for the way it performed. He was never much

of a shot, even when drawing a bead on an imaginary redcoat or a rival Shinwari, and the few times he did bring down a bird he enjoyed it more for the opportunity to study his prey than for the satisfaction of the kill, so much so that he began taking along pencil stubs and scraps of paper so he could sketch them. He began to admire these creatures, to envy their independence and mobility—soaring to far valleys whenever they pleased. But he was discerning in his devotion. Birds that fed and hunted in packs earned only disdain—fluttery sparrows, just like the boys in the village. Vultures, too, were loathsome, with one notable exception—the lammergeier, the only one among them that hunted alone, waiting for the rest to eat their fill because only he knew how to unlock the hidden treasures of the marrow, carrying bones aloft, then dropping them to the stones below, prying the red food from the cracks. Clever, that bird, outwitting them all.

But he hid his drawings, of course, sketching in secret until the day his uncle Aziz came upon him, lost in thought while shading a hawk's spread of tail feathers in grays and blacks. Aziz's shadow fell on the page, and Najeeb braced for a scolding. But Aziz only laughed, then praised the likeness, making it clear that this would be a secret between them. Even then Najeeb was aware that at some level this was a betrayal, but an alliance was formed. It was cemented forever weeks later when Aziz trudged up the hill with a smile almost wicked in its joy, then pulled from his baggy pocket a small bundle wrapped in butcher's paper and tied up with string, stamped with the blue seal of a bookseller in Peshawar. Najeeb tore it open to reveal a flash of colors as brilliant as anything he had ever seen—a set of colored pencils, a small sketch pad and, best of all, *A Field Guide to the Birds of the Indian Subcontinent*. At last he could put a name to everything he shot or spied, even the huge old owl—a Eurasian Eagle Owl, he learned—that haunted the crumbling ruins of the ancient Buddhist stupa.

But the gift, of course, led inevitably to the awful moment of exposure, when his father found his hidden drawings and shredded them in a rage, calling his son a *bedagh*, a whore, and everything he could think of that was womanish or unholy. Yet even his father couldn't bring himself to destroy something as fine and expensive as the guidebook, so he had merely kicked it, then decreed Najeeb's week of penance at Smugglers Bazaar. And Najeeb, emerging tougher yet wiser, had stored up his resentment, letting it silently accrue interest until the pivotal moment in Tariq's office in Islamabad, when he finally paid back his father in full.

"Yes, I know what is in the cave," he had said at last, breaking his silence for the patient professional. And he did know, having found the place on one of his walks. Not a new place at all to him, even if at that particular time it had been filled with all sorts of new equipment— boiling kettles and steel drums, pipes and tubing and pressure gauges. Sacks of opium paste were piled along one wall, their contents being transformed as if by magic into much smaller bags holding the white powder of heroin. Najeeb's father had found the way to eliminate the middleman, and thus became wealthy enough to send his only son off to college, while practically daring federal authorities to do something about it, if they only knew where to look.

Which they eventually did, of course, once the college boy told them. And when Najeeb was then banished from his father's lands the following spring, the worn but glossy bird book had been nestled at the bottom of the small sack of belongings handed over to Najeeb. And now he was back in these hills, staring from the window of the bus, the memories sprinting down the slopes toward him like raiders on horseback.

A SUDDEN SWERVE of the bus lurched him back to the present as his forehead banged the window. The bus was pulling onto the shoulder at a high curve. All the translators and fixers were rising to their feet, filling the aisle to exit. Of course. It was that time of day.

"What the hell are we doing?" he heard Skelly shout from a few rows back.

"Prayers," he said calmly over his shoulder, rising to join the procession. Fawad and his men were already kneeling on the verge, some of them unrolling small rugs. All the fixers were here, too, even the Clerk. Najeeb found an empty patch of ground and whisked away the gravel with his palms. Then he knelt, lowering his forehead to the ground, praying for safety and mercy and peace. He thought of Daliya, wondering yet again where she might be, hoping she was safe. Then he prayed for calm and strength, settling upon a fragment of a sura that had always been a favorite.

"With every hardship there is ease. With every hardship there is ease." Repeating it five more times until it calmed him.

The men around him began to stand, brushing off clothes and hands. For this one moment, he realized, all of them who called this place home had showed their unity and their backsides to the foreign-

ers aboard the bus, and despite his current state of loyalties he momentarily swelled with pride. Faces stared down at them through smudged windows with expressions of boredom and idle curiosity. Najeeb wondered what God must make of this rabble by the road, praying beneath the gaze of the cash-paying infidel. That thought, too, gave him a rebellious sense of pleasure. Then he glimpsed the Clerk, just ahead of him on the left, rubbing dust from his hands, and he relapsed into worry and apprehension.

Just before boarding he saw Skelly eyeing him with what seemed to be disapproval. If he hadn't known better, in fact, he'd have said that the man looked mistrustful, which troubled him more than he would have expected. Hardly the sort of relationship you needed if you were heading into a war zone.

## CHAPTER ELEVEN

H AD THE PESHAWAR POLICE conducted more than their usual cursory examination of the crime scene outside Najeeb's apartment, they might have found a tiny cell phone lodged in a bush some thirty feet beyond the body.

The phone's battery was dead, or else it would soon have attracted the attention of a passerby, beckoning like a cricket from its hideaway. But even in silence it was an important marker, the starting point for an odyssey of panic and indecision that, by the following afternoon, led all the way to Islamabad.

The trail ended at Quaid-i-Azam University, at the office of Professor Rana Bhatti in the Department of International Relations. There, beneath the languid whirl of a ceiling fan, one of the professor's former students sat nervously in a stiff-backed chair by the desk, anxiously awaiting her mentor's arrival. The visitor had been waiting more than an hour. To kill time she scanned the pages of the newspaper *Dawn* for any hint of the troubles she'd left behind. Finding none, she aimlessly surveyed the posters, placards and photos on the office walls for at least the twentieth time since her arrival, wondering yet again what was to become of her. Because for the first time in her life, Daliya Qadeer was on the run and unsure of herself.

From the moment she'd broken free of the man with the knife she'd considered calling her parents. She craved the safety and comfort of their familiar voices, the touch of their hands, the softness of the bed in the room where she had grown up. Under the circumstances, she knew, they would welcome her home in a heartbeat. Yet she also

knew relief would give way to anger and recrimination once her transgressions became known, and she'd had quite enough of anger and
recrimination.

Returning to her aunt and uncle's was out of the question for the
same reason. They would react more as jailers than protectors, outraged to have lost control of their ward. They'd have locked her up,
releasing her only for meals and bathroom breaks until her parents
could be summoned.

She thought next of calling Rukhsana, but when she reached into
her purse she discovered that her cell phone was gone. And by then she
was so accustomed to the shortcuts of speed dial—pound-one for
Rukhsana, pound-two for Najeeb—that she couldn't have told you the
actual number for either if her life had depended on it. And for a while
she thought it might.

Seeking help, she made her way to a PTT call office in the Saddar
Bazaar, an ill-lit shack where the man on duty seemed more interested
in swatting flies than connecting his customers. First she tried Najeeb
at the *Frontier Report*. But by then it was nearly nine o'clock and just
about everyone had gone home. She decided not to leave a message,
worried that it might fall into the wrong hands, especially since Najeeb
might not retrieve it for days. For all she knew he was in Afghanistan
by now, which also meant that returning to his apartment was out of
the question. Too much danger there anyway, and next time she might
not be so lucky.

The vital question then became where to spend the night. In
Peshawar it was especially problematical for a young woman on her
own. Any hotels other than a handful of the best ones would regard a
Pakistani woman traveling alone as virtually a prostitute, subject to
questioning and possibly arrest. All of the finer hotels, however, were
booked solid with foreign journalists.

The police? No thank you. They would only turn her over to her
aunt and uncle.

It was then that she thought of the office at her uncle's computer
store. Her cousins always locked up by eight, and because she occasionally held the fort at lunch she had her own key. There was a small
couch for customers, and a locked washroom just down the alley that
they shared with two other stores. It would be the perfect hideaway
until morning, a haven where she could collect her thoughts and plan
her next move. And perhaps somewhere in the piles of paper atop her
desk she could find Najeeb's or Rukhsana's home phone numbers.

The office was stuffy, creepy. An aging fan that normally ran throughout the day was still, and the becalmed air smelled of cigarette butts, dusty carpeting, unwashed teacups and the warmed plastic of the computer monitors. She considered switching on the fan, but worried—irrationally, she knew—that it might somehow draw attention to the place, as if connected to a sensor at her uncle's house that would bring the whole family running. She flicked on the fluorescent ceiling light just long enough to spot the best way to the couch, then turned it off and negotiated the path in the dark. Exhausted, she sagged onto the dirty cushions. The upholstery was rough, smelling of cigarettes, so she cradled her hands beneath her cheek. By bending her knees slightly she could just fit.

But the moment she shut her eyes the evening's events reeled back, unspooling across her eyelids like a lurid news bulletin. She had tried leaving Najeeb's apartment around lunchtime, only to be spooked by the sound of a door opening on the floor below, the tread of heavy footsteps on the stairs. That convinced her to play it safe, or so she thought, waiting for nightfall when she presumably wouldn't be seen. Perhaps Najeeb would even make it home first.

Darkness came, and Najeeb didn't, so she steeled herself for a quick exit, making as little noise as possible. She made it down the stairs without a hitch, then pushed open the door. No one was around. The night felt fresh and free. There would be a host of explaining to do, and plenty of lying, but with Rukhsana's help she'd make it.

Shortly after reaching the sidewalk, a shadow darted toward her from the left. She barely had time to turn before seeing the glint of metal. But it was the smell that gave the man away, the same as the night before. His breath was a violent emanation of hashish and garlic, and his body reeked of grime.

A callused hand clamped across her mouth, it, too, carrying the distinctive smell, yet also with a dusty hint of rosemary, as if he'd been hiding in a thicket of the stuff. His free hand shoved something hard against the small of her back—the handle of his knife?—pressing her spine as he shoved her forward, stumbling and turning at the same time, as if he was positioning her to make her a more inviting target. The hand at her back fell away, and in turning she saw the blade sweeping toward her in a wide arc. She tried to lunge away, wanting to scream now that the other hand had come loose from her mouth but feeling as if all the air was squeezed from her lungs.

It was then that a second shadow joined them—another hand dart-

ing across her attacker's arm, grabbing the wrist of the knife hand. There was a grunt, a thump, and all three of them piled down like derailed boxcars, heaping onto the dusty bare ground by the sidewalk just beyond the pooled light of the street lamp. Daliya scrambled to her feet, suddenly free of them. Then it was as if they had forgotten her altogether, the two men rolling atop each other, grunting and gasping. No words, only a series of animal noises and a wet, tearing, meaty sound, like the one a butcher makes when hacking into a slab of lamb, followed by a cry as forlorn as any she'd ever heard. She was still briskly backing away, hesitating in flight, feeling she should thank this man for her deliverance.

But what if the wrong man won? Or what if the right man turned out to be even more dangerous? For he, too, was strange to her. So she turned and ran, faster than she had ever run before, fighting off the ridiculous unbidden notion that her mother would strongly disapprove of such unwomanly behavior, her daughter sprinting and sweating like some athlete. She didn't stop for five blocks, despite the stares she drew after reaching the crowds at the fringe of the bazaar. She knew she must be a sight, her eyes blazing with panic, and for once in her life she wished to be covered head to toe. Then she turned a corner and stopped, panting, sweat running between her breasts and down her spine. And she began to walk, trying to control her breathing, looking straight ahead. Thus was Daliya on her way, seeing no possible path that might return her to her former life.

As she lay exhausted on the filthy couch, she inventoried her sins of the past several weeks. The lies and subterfuge were a beginning, and the visits to Najeeb's apartment ranked high. But all those might be covered up or explained away if not for the overnight stay. That was what would damn her in her parents' eyes. It was the point of no return, the unpardonable sin, the irreparable breach. Meaning she would now have to either go it alone or make her way forward with Najeeb, which was like no choice at all. Najeeb was her future, whether he had yet made up his mind or not. So she had better find him as soon as he returned from Afghanistan. In the meantime, she needed a place of temporary refuge, and she thought of one just as she was dropping off to sleep.

She came awake suddenly at the sound of the call to prayer, a loud-speaker squalling plaintively from just down the block. The dim predawn light bathed the office in pale gray. Her mouth was sticky and

dry, her hair a mess, and her clothes smelled just like the couch. She washed up as well as she could at the sink in the bathroom down the alley, spooked by rats that scurried for cover as she approached the door.

When she stepped back into the office she considered making tea, but wanted to leave as little sign of her presence as possible. Besides, it was time she got moving. Her search for phone numbers had been fruitless, but at least now she had the beginnings of a plan. Just before locking the door behind her she considered writing a note for Rukhsana, taping it to the door of the neighboring office, where her friend worked. But there was no telling who might open it first. Besides, Rukhsana was still answerable to parental authority.

One thing Daliya didn't lack was money, and once the banks opened she would have even more. A weekly allowance from her father arrived via wire transfer—a secret they'd kept from her mother—and it had accumulated to a middling sum that might get her by for weeks. She'd supplemented the total by setting aside most of her salary from her uncle. She also had a credit card, yet another offering from her father. He'd made her swear never to use it except in an emergency, but surely this qualified. She decided to hold off using it for as long as possible, however. No sense in furnishing anyone with a map of her movements.

She had decided that her next stop would be Islamabad. Getting there was another matter. Traveling alone by bus wouldn't be impossible, but it would attract unwanted attention. A taxi, then. But not just any taxi, hailed in the streets. Those drivers would be too unreliable, perhaps even too dangerous—or so she believed in her frazzled condition. She knew of only one location where she might do better, and fortunately it was a place where her presence wouldn't necessarily be cause for suspicion. It was the lobby of the Pearl Continental. Najeeb had taken her to the hotel's cafe once, for cake and tea. Wildly expensive, but it had provided a glimpse of how the foreign visitors lived, and she had watched them arranging for cars from a fleet of white Mercedes out front. Better cars, and better drivers.

It went without a hitch. The concierge quickly arranged the trip and took her cash. She was grateful she had dressed well for her trip to Najeeb's apartment, a journey that now seemed a lifetime ago. While waiting for the car she tried calling Najeeb again at the *Frontier Report*, but got only the vague information that he might be away for a while,

and when her inquiries grew more insistent the reporter who'd answered grew curious, prompting her to hang up. There was no way to know whom she could trust.

Yet, with each new move this morning she experienced a burgeoning sense of crossing new boundaries, of breaching the forbidden, and found that this boldness thrilled more than it intimidated. Was this how it was for men? she wondered. This to-hell-with-everyone sense of simply striking out on your own? Or had it become routine for them, a part of their nature? She hoped that the feeling would last, because she was certain she would need it to sustain her through the uncertainty of the days to come.

But as she sat in the office in Islamabad, awaiting the arrival of Professor Bhatti, her doubts again gained the upper hand. It was nearly four o'clock. A full two hours had now passed. Maybe the professor wasn't coming, and maybe she wouldn't help. Calm yourself, she thought. Of course the professor would help. Wouldn't she?

The university was where Daliya, in the ancient days of her previous life, had always felt the most free to speak her mind, and of all her teachers none had been more encouraging than Professor Bhatti. With the professor's encouragement, Daliya went toe to toe with the boys, arguing and bantering, and often as not emerging the winner. The anger that flashed from their eyes announced her triumphs with regularity, as did the professor's nods of approval.

But what she craved most from the professor now were a few kind words, the offer of a hot shower and the refuge of confession. Too much to ask, probably. Perhaps the professor wouldn't even remember her name. If she left now and went to her parents' house it would be awful, but safe. Even the comfortable prison of a disapproving home would be preferable to this cold uncertainty.

And if Professor Bhatti was so exalted, and was indeed the right person to turn to, then how come the university hadn't given her a better office? The woman shared it with another teacher, even though she was supposedly the acting assistant to the department head. The ceilings were high, and there was plenty of shelf space, but the walls needed painting, and the other professor's clutter seemed to be encroaching like some weed that would eventually take over.

Even her father, with his relatively low standing at the ministry, at least had a private office, plus upgraded electrical outlets and his own desktop computer. Professor Bhatti had only a laptop and an old

phone, the sort with push buttons and a rotary dial. And her office was next door to the men's room, with its almost constant comings and goings, the sounds of creaking hinges and flushing coming through the wall. Daliya had pushed the office door shut upon arrival, hoping to be seen by as few people as possible. She hadn't yet decided what to do if the other professor showed up first.

She checked her watch. It was now 4:20, but just as her mood hit bottom she heard an approaching *click-clack* of heels in the corridor, then the rattling of the knob. In walked Professor Bhatti, shocked but seemingly happy to see her visitor, although her expression of concern deepened as Daliya began to tell her story.

DALIYA HAD CHOSEN her audience better than she could have known. Professor Rana Bhatti was a great believer in pushing one's limits, especially when those limits had been imposed by men. When the department's second-in-command had departed the previous fall, she had actively campaigned to be named his replacement, even while knowing that the very insistence which won her the title of "acting" assistant head would ensure that she would be passed over when the job was filled permanently. She knew also, though, that unless she made some noise, they would ignore her altogether.

She was short, another handicap to overcome, but that only seemed to make her more determined. She was also one of the department's most worldly professors, spending two months every few summers in Boston, among American colleagues at Harvard, and after each such trip she returned with another increment in hustle and determination. When she got going on a topic you could hear her voice above all others, even if all you might see was her lustrous head of raven hair, which she covered only for important faculty meetings and trips out of town. In other words, it was hard to imagine anyone in Daliya's world likely to be more sympathetic to her situation.

Yet Professor Bhatti looked anything but overjoyed once Daliya completed her account.

"You really shouldn't be here, you know," the professor finally said, her voice about three decibels lower than normal. She glanced nervously toward the door, as if security police might barge in on them at any moment. "If your parents ever found out." She shook her head. "Your father, he is . . ." Her voiced trailed off, but Daliya knew exactly

what the professor was thinking. If her father were to learn that Professor Bhatti had aided her in her escape, the professor would lose her job, no matter how far down the ladder he was at the ministry. That would forfeit any chance for advancement, all for the whims of a wayward young woman. All those rungs climbed with such tenacity and endurance would be cut from beneath her in one decisive stroke.

But at age forty-three, Professor Bhatti wasn't so far removed from her own youth that she had forgotten what it was like to be staring up from the bottom of that same ladder, dismissed and disregarded.

"Tell me," she said at last, "is this just aimless escape? Wandering around with no real idea of what you're after? Or do you actually have some kind of plan in mind?"

"I'm not sure," Daliya said hesitantly. "That's why I came here. I figured you were the one person who might tolerate a little indecision. I need time more than anything." She noted the beginning of a frown. "Not much. Just enough to catch my breath, figure out what comes next. But I promise you there's nothing random about my intentions. And to be truthful . . ." She spoke slowly. "You might say that I do have at least the beginnings of a plan. It's just that it's so crazy that I couldn't begin to carry it out without first talking it over with someone else. And I can't think of anyone better for that than you."

Professor Bhatti sighed and tutted, twirling a pencil in her right hand. She pulled out a cigarette, lit it, and inhaled deeply as she eyed the phone. The number for the girl's parents was somewhere in a nearby file drawer, she was certain. It would take about ten minutes and this whole drama would be over, or at least her part in it would. She had a lecture to prepare, a career to maintain, a busy week ahead with no room for aggravation and certainly no allowance for foolishness like this. Then she looked across the desktop at Daliya, at those eyes that not only pleaded but demanded. Implored. *Insisted.* Where had she seen such a defiant spirit before? The answer was easy, and the answer disarmed her completely.

"I ran away once, you know," she finally said, in a voice so low that Daliya had to lean forward to hear it.

"You, Professor Bhatti?"

The professor nodded, sighing with a slow stream of smoke.

"I was about three years older than you, of course." Brief frown of disapproval. "And it had nothing to do with any kind of boyfriend. Or banishment. Or anything like what you're up against." A pause, three

seconds that seemed like twenty. "But there was an aunt who took me in. She helped me stay on my feet while I made peace with my family. It was hard, really, and pretty awful for a while. But I came out of it okay. Stronger, even. Or I might not be here at all." She paused again, one last breath before the leap. "Come on, then." She rose to her feet, grabbing her shoulder bag. "The less you're seen here, the better. I've got a sofa bed. We'll talk more when we get there. You can stay the night, or longer if you need to." Then she smiled slyly, smoke snorting from her nostrils in a burst of low laughter. "Just try not to need to."

# CHAPTER TWELVE

S KELLY HAD ALWAYS hated border towns, and in times of war they were even spookier and more disheartening, grimy little outposts where the hopeless and disinherited collected like motes of dust against a screen.

Torkham was no different, although at least the backdrop was spectacular. It was wedged into the last pinch of the Khyber Pass, steep granite cliffs looming to either side. The border fence blocked the ravine like a dam. Beyond it, the valley opened wide and flat, a promising landscape of open skies and far-ranging movement that had lured centuries of travelers and invaders.

The town was small, and its main bazaar was right along the road. Fawad's caravan threaded its way through several hundred men in white robes and skull caps who drifted aimlessly among the shops and stalls, as if awaiting the opening of the gates, or imminent news of peace.

The buses pulled to the shoulder by the last building on the right. It was the customshouse, a white hut atop a small green knoll, bathed in the golden light of late afternoon. A dozen police, clubs at the ready, swarmed in to head off the gawking crowd while the journalists sat tight, hoping against hope that Fawad could deliver on his promise of easy passage. He disappeared inside the customshouse with a handful of transit papers, accompanied by two of his men. Ten minutes later he emerged looking grim and impatient. Then he stepped aboard *Flying Titanic*, the lead bus, to ask for everyone's passports and papers.

A collective groan went up, Skelly loudly joining in. Now they'd be waiting for hours. Any ride to Jalalabad would be made in the dark.

The reporters unloaded, breaking open water bottles and stretching their legs, and the curiosity of it all was too much to bear for the milling men in white, whose excited chatter rose to a wail as they encircled the buses, pushing back the policemen. Skelly guessed they were stranded refugees, although supposedly most of the recent human traffic was headed deeper into Pakistan, fleeing the bombing. Perhaps these fellows knew something nobody else did, but he doubted it. The only thing worse than being stuck in a war was being stuck in the middle of nowhere, without food or family, as these men had doubtless discovered.

The press of the mob made it hard to move, but maybe he could interview a few, pick up a story. He looked for Najeeb, although he hadn't yet decided how to deal with the awkward issue of the man's allegiance. Would a spy for the ISI ever actually admit to it? If not, what proof did Skelly have other than the accusation of Lucy's fixer, who by the look of things had already been arguing with Najeeb?

The crowd surged closer, gaining momentum as it picked up the scent of all those Westerners, the very smell of prosperity. The border police had other ideas. Half a dozen more arrived to hastily form a cordon. One shouted commands through a bullhorn, and the mob complied with shocking ease, as if accustomed to such treatment. Their noise subsided. Yet, to a man the refugees kept gazing at the journalists, eyes pleading, but for what?

The caravan's arrival had also roused the slumbering trade of the pushcart boys, who for a few hundred rupees would cart your luggage through the border gates to taxis and buses waiting on the opposite side. At least that was the idea. A glance across the last hundred yards of Pakistani territory revealed no vehicles on the Afghan side except a battered truck. Probably no one had crossed the border in that direction for weeks. Nor would any of the journalists need their luggage carried if the buses were allowed to pass. This did little to deter the boys, who slipped nimbly past the police and began bidding for business, shoving their rickety carts through the masses as each announced his presence with the ubiquitous "How are *you*, sir."

Skelly inspected the fence. It was topped with razor wire, coiled from one bluff to the other. The huts and stalls behind it were spiked with drooping black flags and tattered banners painted with slogans. There was a large hand-printed signpost to the right, half in Pashto, half in English, but too far away for Skelly to read more than a word or two. The one vehicle, a multicolored truck, was stacked with military

equipment and rocket grenades, racked like bowling pins. Deployed around it were eight grim-looking fellows in long beards, scowling through the fence. They wore white robes and black turbans, and each carried a Kalashnikov or a grenade launcher. Some wore bandoleers.

Skelly made his way closer, pulling free of the crowd and climbing the grassy lawn of the customshouse. This was a better vantage point. Quite pleasant, in fact, the air cool in the shade of a spreading plane tree, although the sounds through the open door of the customshouse weren't encouraging—shrieks and shouts, some self-important official working himself into a frenzy of obstruction—so Skelly concentrated on the view. The opposite bluff glowed like molten copper in the late-afternoon sun, and a breeze from the bazaar blew in the smell of frying kebabs and the fuzzy sound of music playing too loudly on cheap speakers, the whine and sway of desert rhythms. Up here one could easily imagine he was at a government rest house in the 1800s, stopping for tea on his way across the Empire.

A few enterprising boys were now making the rounds among the journalists on the lawn. One, no taller than four feet, stopped in front of Skelly clutching a fistful of Afghan currency. He was peddling it in small, banded stacks, not even pretending to be offering the proper exchange rate, which was about forty thousand afghanis to the dollar. This was strictly a souvenir trade, low-denomination bills that were practically worthless.

"How much?" Skelly asked, figuring this might be the closest he ever got to the place.

"For *you*, sir? Two hundred rupees."

A buck-sixty, then, for a penny's worth of cash, but the boy knew his market—journalists desperate for a piece of Afghanistan. Skelly had seen at least three others making a purchase.

"Fair enough," he said, handing over the rupees, the boy adding them to a shockingly thick stack. Skelly inspected the worn bills, swirls of Dari on pastel reds and greens, with drawings of minarets, fortresses and stout men on horseback.

He supposed that this would be a good time to seek out Najeeb. Confront him about this spying business and get it over with. But first he wanted a better look at the fellows in black turbans standing just across the border. They had moved to the fore of the iron fence, gazing silently toward the journalists. One burst of gunfire would do an awful lot of damage from this range, and he wondered if they were tempted. A man's voice spoke up from over his shoulder.

"Fun-looking bunch, aren't they?"

Skelly turned.

"Roy! Good to see you!"

Roy Canady was a stocky New Zealander who worked as a producer for one of the American networks. He knew his stuff far better than the pretty faces the honchos put before the cameras, and he'd always preferred the company of print reporters, regaling them with tales of buffoonery by the various anchors and up-and-comers he squired around places like this. Skelly liked him immensely but hadn't seen him since Rwanda, where they'd shared a six-pack of awful local beer, flushing out the stench after watching bloated corpses float down the muddy River Kagera.

"Great to see you," Skelly said, shaking hands.

"Just couldn't resist one more war?"

"Manpower shortage."

"Tell me about it. Everyone's budget's in the toilet. Think we'll make it across?"

"By when? Next Tuesday?"

"That's just about their pace. Bloody unbelievable in there." He nodded toward the customshouse. "More cash changing hands than a camel auction, but they're still spending ten minutes a passport, studying every picture like it's Charlie Manson. Typical."

"I take it you've been here before."

"Third time this week. And maybe a dozen more before that, going back twenty years."

"So who's the welcoming committee? Taliban?"

"Definitely."

"How can you tell?"

"Black turbans, for starters. And all those banners. Religious slogans. But this one's my favorite." He pointed right, toward the sign Skelly had noticed earlier with some of the words in English. "Taliban's idea of a touristy welcome."

Skelly was close enough now to make out the words, and he read them aloud:

"Faithful people with strong decision entry Afghanistan. Sacrifice country heartly welcomes you with pleases."

"Lovely translation, isn't it? Makes you want to bring the wife and kids."

Skelly laughed.

"You sound thrilled to be back."

"Gives me the heebie-jeebies just being this close. Lots of bad memories from over there. The longer the border stays closed, the better, far as I'm concerned."

There was a new outburst of shouting from the customshouse, but Canady's attention had been drawn in the opposite direction.

"Uh-oh," he said, shouldering a satchel. "Looks like we've worn out our welcome."

The border police had turned their attention to the journalists and were motioning them back onto the buses. Skelly spotted Najeeb, who seemed to be pleading with one of the officers to lay off. If he was ISI, he ought to get quick results, but the policeman shoved him away.

"Najeeb! Over here!" Skelly had put off their talk long enough. He also wanted to do a few interviews. Work the edge of the crowd. Anything to salvage something out of what was turning into a wasted day—although from a personal standpoint he supposed the ride alone had been worthwhile. How many people could say they'd spent their afternoon breezing through the Khyber Pass?

Najeeb appeared at his shoulder, and they stepped downhill into the street, where more policemen were motioning toward the buses. The refugees, sensing they were no longer the focus, began closing in again from behind. This could get nasty. A few reporters had broken through to the crowd and were hastily doing interviews among tightening knots of the men in white. Skelly spotted Chatty Lucy among them, out there with her fixer.

"A colleague told me that she thinks you're ISI," Skelly shouted above the din into Najeeb's ear. Might as well take the direct approach.

Najeeb looked shocked, even angry. If it was an act, it was a good one.

"It was the Canadian woman's translator, wasn't it?"

"How'd you know?" He looked Najeeb in the eye. Najeeb looked straight back.

"Because *he's* ISI."

A policeman pushed Skelly in the back. He wheeled quickly, ready to shout until he saw the raised billy club.

"Tell him we can't do our jobs."

"I tried," Najeeb said, nudging Skelly out of harm's way. "They're worried because it's almost dark. They want everyone out of here. They say some of the refugees have guns."

"Bullshit."

"Probably. What did her fixer say?"

"That I should fire you. That you can't be trusted."

Najeeb scowled.

"The man had me hauled in two days ago, right after I first met you. Or his boss did."

"Hauled in where?"

"To the ISI. To the office where he works. I can take you to the alley. If you knock, Javed is the one who comes to the door. It's some kind of listening post. His boss is named Tariq, and he was asking for information about Razaq." He paused. "And about you. They're watching everyone, me included."

"And you agreed to help?"

Najeeb shook his head, but this time he didn't look Skelly in the eye.

"Is that what you two were talking about on the bus?"

Najeeb nodded, seeming relieved that Skelly had noticed the confrontation.

"If he really works for the *International Daily*," Najeeb said, "then how come his byline never appears? Ask your friend that."

Good point. But Najeeb could be making it up as he went, Skelly supposed. Knock on the door of the ISI office and maybe Najeeb would answer. He'd already admitted to having been there. But dealing with fixers was a lot like picking them. Gut feelings counted for plenty, and Skelly's gut told him Najeeb was telling the truth. At best he'd now have a little more leverage with the man, maybe even enough to pry loose the tight lid Najeeb kept on everything. It was time they started establishing some sort of rapport.

"Fair enough," Skelly shouted, still fending off the policemen. "But, look, if you really want me to trust you, you're going to have to stop getting so huffy whenever I ask a few questions."

"Yes, okay." Najeeb looked chastened. "I understand." He seemed about to say more, but didn't.

By now the police had pushed all the journalists into a semicircle against the buses, having rounded up the stragglers who'd sneaked into the crowd. The journalists by now were pent up and frustrated with the day's aggravations, and their tempers began to boil over. Some began pushing back, loudly demanding access to the crowd.

"Let us do our job!" several shouted. A few reporters in the middle of the crowd consulted with their fixers about what to do next. Skelly

and Najeeb were just about to join in when they heard Chatty Lucy nominate Javed to take their case to the authorities.

"Watch," Najeeb muttered as Javed sallied forth. "He'll only make sure that we have to leave right away. The less contact these refugees have with Westerners, the better, as far as the ISI is concerned."

Skelly had witnessed such confrontations before—well-paid translators negotiating on behalf of their clients with intractable officials. Sometimes money changed hands, and even then they were usually vigorous standoffs, with waving arms and raised voices, a marketplace haggling that often produced some sort of compromise, especially if the concluding handshake was sweetened with a folded wad of cash.

This one looked altogether different—Javed listening patiently, then nodding, turning his face away from the journalists as he placed a hand lightly on the policeman's shoulder. The policeman leaned closer, listening, then both of them nodded, shaking hands without a smile or frown.

"Christ, it's like they're pals," Roy Canady said, just to Skelly's left. Javed then strolled back to the gathering and calmly announced, "I am sorry, but we must leave immediately. There will be no interviews. No passage. Only Fawad's men and the aid trucks will be allowed across the border."

Lucy looked crestfallen. Her champion had not only fallen, but had seemingly surrendered without a fight. Najeeb and several other translators surged forward to take up the battle, but by now the police again had their sticks out, and more reinforcements were arriving in jeeps.

"Christ, what do we file?" a woman shouted to Skelly's right.

"Color," he answered. "Bullshit and color. Total waste of time."

As if to goad them further, the gates were now opening at the border. The men in black turbans stepped aside to allow the first of Fawad's trucks to pass. The next four soon followed, while the journalists watched longingly in sudden silence, as if their best friends were disappearing over the horizon. The cameramen and photographers, realizing this might be the only newsy moment of the day, scrambled for a shot, pushing more violently than any of the policemen, setting off an angry scrum of elbows and jostling equipment. By the time the cameras were rolling, the last truck was passing through. It was Fawad's, packed full with his armed consort. The warlord must have been miserable leaving behind his adoring audience—he had apparently been too embarrassed to even say good-bye.

"Fuck him," a reporter shouted. "If he can't even deal with a bunch of paper pushers they'll eat him alive over there."

"Good," someone answered. "It'll strengthen the Pashtun gene pool."

The policeman with the bullhorn shouted for everyone to reboard. But there was a snag. A tire had gone flat on *Flying Titanic*, and the driver anxiously blocked the door, waving a wrench as he pleaded with everyone to wait until he could change it.

Skelly could only laugh. The sun was setting on the plains of Afghanistan, his notebook was empty, his fixer might be either a spook or an informant, and his editors were doubtless already reserving space on tomorrow's front page for a Jalalabad dateline that would never materialize.

Najeeb was still off with the other fixers, pleading in vain for more time, so Skelly decided it was an opportune moment to tell Chatty Lucy exactly what he thought of Javed. But as he set off in her direction a bony hand clasped his shoulder, and he turned to see a familiar face. It was the fellow from outside Razaq's house, the one with rheumy eyes who'd made a pest of himself, the leech with onions on his breath and no apparent influence. But if that were so, what was he doing here, among all these Westerners? And how had he made it all the way to the border? Had he been riding with the journalists?

The man smiled crookedly, exposing a bent row of brown teeth as he extended his right hand. Skelly again smelled onions on his breath, but no hashish. He shook hands reluctantly, the grip dry and callused.

"How are *you*, friend?" At least he hadn't said "sir."

"Okay," Skelly answered, already looking for a means of escape.

"I am Idris."

"Hello, Idris. I am Skelly."

The man nodded, still grinning. Apparently that was the extent of his English, which made his presence all the more puzzling.

"Him again?" It was Najeeb, looking none too happy.

"He says his name is Idris. I get the idea he has something to tell me."

Idris spoke in Pashto, Najeeb answering tersely. They went back and forth for a few seconds, Skelly expecting that at any minute they'd raise their voices and he would have to break it up. But their tone was even, their eyes locked.

"He is asking again if you want to accompany Razaq."

"With the so-called rear guard? Same as before? Tell him no thanks."

"I did. He said that he is sure that others will want to come instead, then."

"Good for them," Skelly said, although he couldn't help but experience a pang of doubt at the mention of competition. What if Idris was telling the truth, and others took him up on the offer? For all Skelly knew, the man had been making the rounds for the past half hour, lining up an entire gallery of reporters.

Idris again spoke up as Skelly eased away. But this time it was Najeeb who grabbed Skelly's sleeve.

"You may actually want to hear this," Najeeb said. "He says that the woman, the one over there"—Najeeb pointed at Chatty Lucy—"she wanted to come along, but Idris refused."

"Why?"

"He doesn't trust her translator."

"Is that so?" Idris now had his attention, and Skelly faced him. The smell of onions was stronger than ever, but the man's remark about Javed seemed to indicate he wasn't a complete flake. Assuming Najeeb was telling the truth, of course. With translation, how could you ever know for sure? Idris dropped his voice to a raspy whisper, pointing toward Javed.

"He says that the man there is ISI," Najeeb said, seeming just as stunned as Skelly. "He says he tells you this, but not her, because he knows the man would never translate his answer."

Skelly was still suspicious. "Ask him if he trusts you."

Idris listened to the question, then shrugged, muttering an answer.

"He says he does not know me, but he supposes I can come as long as you vouch for me."

Skelly eyed Najeeb. If the man was lying, why would he have concocted such an ambiguous answer? Najeeb looked back intently, as if realizing this was a moment of truth.

"Tell him I vouch for you. But that I still have questions about him. What is he doing here, for starters."

Idris responded by checking his flanks, as if fearful of eavesdroppers. He motioned them back toward the edge of the crowd, to the rear of the buses where there were no journalists. Then he resumed speaking, keeping his voice low.

"He says he is here for Mahmood Razaq. He says Razaq wanted to know about Fawad's trip, to know whether he made it safely into Afghanistan."

"And his other boss? This rearguard commander. What's his name?"

"He cannot say that here, he is not permitted," Najeeb said. "You can only learn that by meeting with him."

"Then why would this man want to meet with me, or with any reporter, when Razaq doesn't seem to want any of us coming along?"

Idris made a hand motion as if snapping a camera in response to Najeeb's translated question. Then he spoke briefly.

"For publicity, he says. His commander wants publicity. He knows no one will tell his own story if Razaq is the only one who tells it."

A jealous underling, then, greedy for attention. It sounded just stupid enough to be true. Skelly looked at Idris, who beamed goofily back at him, yellow teeth aglow in the amber light. No matter how hamhanded it all seemed, this would hardly be the first time Skelly had encountered such a rank amateur in media relations in a place like this. A Kosovar guerrilla leader had once called Skelly's colleagues together to proudly claim credit for an ambush that had killed five Serbian military police, a blunder that prompted a retaliatory artillery strike within twelve hours that flattened the man's home village.

What the hell, Skelly thought. Why not give it a try.

"I suppose he's still proposing a meeting in Katchagarhi?"

"Yes. In the camp, he says. Away from the authorities. And away from Razaq."

"Ask him if tomorrow morning would work."

Idris shook his head.

"Tomorrow's too late." Najeeb lowered his voice. "He says Razaq is leaving tonight. A few hours after midnight. But I wouldn't take his word for it."

Now it was Skelly's turn to make sure no one was listening. This was news.

"Do you believe him?"

"I don't know. Maybe I underestimated him. He certainly made his way here all right."

"That's what I was thinking. So we would have to meet his boss tonight, then?"

"Yes. And in Katchagarhi."

"What do you think? We could head out there when we get back to Peshawar. Check the lay of the land. If it looks too risky at the camp, we can always say no. And if it works out, we're already packed and ready to go, with all our supplies."

"Only a few days' worth."

"But with plenty of money to buy more, once we're inside."

Najeeb gave him a sharp glance, as if he wished Skelly hadn't mentioned money around Idris, whether the fellow spoke English or not. Not that Skelly's relative wealth wouldn't already be known. The journalists were like walking ATMs, and at any gathering outside Islamabad they were among the wealthiest people you'd find. By Katchagarhi standards Skelly would be a veritable Bill Gates.

Idris spoke again, a note of pleading evident even through the language barrier.

"He is asking again if we are coming."

"Tell him yes," Skelly said, deciding on the spot. If it seemed harebrained later they could always back out. But with Razaq refusing all comers and Fawad gone in a cloud of dust, for the moment Idris was the only game in town.

Idris smiled broadly at Najeeb's answer, then extended his hand to seal the dubious arrangement.

"Thank you, sir," Idris said emphatically, as grateful as a shopkeeper after his first sale of the day. Then he shook his head slightly, as if to say, "Not to worry," and parted by offering what may well have been his only remaining words of English.

"Katchagarhi," he said. "It is not a problem."

"Not a problem," Skelly said. He'd certainly heard that one before.

# CHAPTER THIRTEEN

THE TAXI PARKED on the shoulder, the driver agreeing to wait only after Najeeb promised they'd pay an extra thousand rupees.

Idris was along for the ride, having met them twenty minutes earlier at Skelly's new room at the Hotel Grand, which was anything but. It was nearly ten o'clock. If Razaq's so-called rear guard was indeed leaving at 3:30 in the morning, as Idris had insisted during the drive from the hotel, then Najeeb figured he would be lucky to get four hours' sleep, and presumably at least part of the trek into Afghanistan would be on foot. This was no aid mission that would be barreling down the highway. It was a military infiltration that would be setting out in the dark.

Najeeb hadn't been home since early morning, and wondered what he would find when he finally got there. He had tried again to call Daliya as soon as his cell phone showed a signal, but he got only a recording saying the subscriber was not available.

His greater worry now was how Skelly and he would survive the following hour. He'd been to Katchagarhi just once, with the Swiss TV crew, but that had been in daylight with an armed guard. Now they'd be walking down unlit, unmapped streets and alleys with no assurance of security beyond Idris's promise that everyone would be fine.

"You will follow me," Idris said now. The cabbie rolled up his windows and pressed down the locks, keeping the engine idling despite the muggy closeness of the night air. Skelly stepped in behind Idris, and Najeeb followed Skelly. They set off down an alley that looked like all the others, mud huts to either side, most of them windowless,

some topped with plywood or corrugated sheet metal. Out here on the edge of the camp, where the highway street lamps provided a dingy yellow glow, there were children everywhere, running barefoot through the dust.

But within a block the crowds thinned, and so did the light. They turned left, then right, down an alley barely wide enough to spread your arms in both directions. It smelled of raw sewage, of rotting animals. Idris and Skelly didn't say a word. By now they were beyond the range of the streetlights, and when they turned left into a wider lane a few moments later they entered a world lit only by dung fires. Najeeb heard voices behind the mud walls. He smelled burning kerosene and a heavy, smudgy smoke. From the right, the sudden squall of a colicky baby poured out from a dim hole in the wall. He stepped in something wet and oozy, his nose tickling on a cloud of dust. His eyes stretched wide as the blackness deepened. It was the same way he'd once felt after dropping a flashlight in a cave.

"You still there?" Skelly asked nervously from just ahead.

"Right behind you." He kept his voice low. No telling who might be listening. Any words of English were likely to attract unwanted attention. "This is insane."

"I'm inclined to agree," Skelly said. "But too late now."

There was a sudden jingle of small bells and a heavy clopping from ahead, coming fast, then faster. A leathery animal smell, then a rush of air and a hoof landing heavily only a few feet away, followed by the wisp of what must have been a horse's tail against his right hand.

"Jesus!" Skelly said. "He damn near ran me over."

"Stay closer!" Idris hissed in Pashto. "And stop speaking. It will only bring others."

Too late for that, Najeeb thought, not caring to imagine which "others" Idris was referring to.

A few times he thought he detected the faint shuffle of bare feet behind them, or maybe it was his imagination. No, there it was again. Someone was following them. Probably just children, but even they might not be harmless if there were enough of them. He'd seen a reporter picked clean by just such a pack of thieves in another camp, right out in daylight, although it would never occur to most children here to do anything other than gawk at a foreigner, as if some exotic bird had been blown in on a zephyr. But it was too dark for gawking here.

They rounded another corner, the alley narrowing again as Najeeb nearly stumbled in a rut. He reached out, touching a sleeve as Skelly flinched. If Idris were to suddenly sprint away they might spend their entire night wandering here, trying to find a way out, although he supposed that by climbing onto a rooftop you could locate the row of streetlights on the highway.

Turning again, he saw a kerosene lantern blazing just ahead, hissing and sputtering, a cloud of moths tapping the glass. It hung outside a tea shop, the first building Najeeb had seen yet with a glass window and wooden walls. Idris ushered them inside, pointing to rickety wooden chairs by the door. It was a small shop with a low ceiling of hammered tin, barely large enough for two customers. Behind a rough wooden counter were large glass jars filled with green and black tea, next to an old iron scale, the sort where you piled weights on one side and the goods on the other. Toward the back was a darkened doorway to some other room. Next to it were barrels and burlap sacks of more tea, giving the whole place an aromatic mustiness. The only light came from the lantern out front.

The shop seemed deserted, and neither he nor Skelly said a word while Idris disappeared into the rear. He emerged moments later, pausing on his way out the front door just long enough to say, "Someone else will take you next," as if he had suddenly lost all interest in them. Then he was gone, not even the sound of his departing footsteps audible from inside the shop.

"Well, that was strange," Skelly said, sounding a little peeved. But something about the smell of the tea leaves and the lantern light had calmed Najeeb, who was breathing easier. A small boy ducked inside selling lottery tickets from a thick roll. Najeeb shooed him away. This seemed to attract the attention of someone in the back, who poked a turbanned head through the rear doorway to shout at the boy. Then the head disappeared, and for the next few minutes silence again prevailed.

Nothing happened in the alley outside until a mule cart rolled by a few minutes later. Najeeb saw the metal of gun barrels gleaming in a pile in the back as the wheels creaked past.

"Jesus," Skelly whispered, "did you see that? Must be enough for a small army."

"Probably a gunsmith nearby," Najeeb said. "They make them by hand. Even the automatics."

"And the government lets them?"

"If you worked for the government, would you come here to shut them down?"

"I guess not."

Another five minutes passed in silence, and just as Najeeb was beginning to think they had been abandoned another boy arrived. He looked to be about twelve. "You and the American follow me," he said curtly in Pashto. Najeeb wondered if it was a ruse, but this time the tea merchant stayed in the back, as if he wanted nothing at all to do with the transaction. Najeeb reluctantly stood.

"Come on," he said to Skelly. "I guess he is going to take us there."

OF ALL THE WALKS and journeys and detours Skelly had ever made, there had never been one quite like this—on foot without a flashlight through utter darkness, yet in a densely populated place, past cookfires and mud huts, like a Neolithic village of hunter gatherers, and it gave him the shivers. They passed a dimly lit place where, through square windows, he saw several men in a haze of blue smoke seated before grinding equipment and belted machines, the smell of hot metal in the air. A wizened old man who looked like a storybook sorcerer pushed a hand tool down a gun barrel clamped in a vice. Elves and dwarves, for all he knew. This must be the gunsmith.

They kept going. He stared upward in search of stars but saw only blankness, without even a moon. He checked for perhaps the fifth time to make sure Najeeb was still behind him.

"Yes. Do not worry."

The boy plodded onward. He had taken Skelly's hand at first, his own sticky and dusty, like some little spirit to guide him through to another dimension. A biblical verse flitted unbidden through his brain. "And a child shall lead them . . ."

Were others similarly afflicted with this coursing highway of banalities and clichés, he wondered—quotes and phrases dislodged from deep memory banks and careening aimlessly. Snatches of old ad jingles and glib voices from his childhood. In the bouncing taxi ride out here he had recalled the phrase "Where the rubber meets the road." Firestone? Age ten? Good lord, where did it all come from? And why?

They reached a pool of light cast by another lantern, and on its far edge they came to an open door. Inside were lit candles. The boy held out his hand to signal them to wait, then ducked inside.

Skelly heard a light, rhythmic sound approaching from behind, and turned to see a legless beggar moving past, swinging his arms like crutches and scraping along on his knuckles, which had turned the color of the dirt. It was the third man he'd seen doing that since coming to Peshawar, but somehow it seemed even more desolate here, in this abandoned world on the dark side of the moon.

"Mine victim," Najeeb said. "The camp is full of them. If you think gun smuggling is big, you should see the black market in artificial legs."

The man had turned the corner, but Skelly could still hear the light *thump* and *swish* of his progress. He supposed that if they waited another five minutes he wouldn't be surprised to see a headless horseman gallop past.

The boy reappeared at the doorway, saying something.

"He said to come wait inside," Najeeb translated.

There were dusty cushions on the floor along two walls. The room was cramped, about eight by six. Najeeb took a seat and so did Skelly, wondering what sort of vermin might infest the place. There was a strong smell of candle wax and of something vegetal—hashish, perhaps? A large man emerged from an opening to a rear room. He wore a *kameez* cinched with a canvas military belt, and he carried a Kalashnikov, which he propped in a corner as casually as if it were a walking stick or cane. They stood. He looked first at Skelly, then at Najeeb, still without saying a word. Then he seemed to come to some sort of conclusion, and held out a large hand, grasping Skelly's.

"I am Bashir," he said in English. "Welcome."

Najeeb offered his hand as well, but Bashir ignored it. The message was obvious. To him Najeeb was strictly a servant, a tool and an inferior. He shouted something toward the back, and the boy who had guided them came out with a tea tray, steam rising in the dimness. Perhaps the boy was the man's son. He hoped the tea had been boiled vigorously, but took a warm cup into his hands, blowing across the top and sipping at the sweetness. It seemed to reconnect him to reality, but he ignored the offered slices of round bread that were also on the tray, and the bowl of nuts. This place must be a veritable metropolis for unwanted microbes.

Skelly sized up Bashir. He was not at all like Fawad, whose smooth face and trimmed nails had spoken of privilege and softness, a life in the merchant class and a dilettante warrior. Razaq was a few steps deeper into the warrior class, but obviously out of practice. Bashir,

however, looked like the real thing, as if shaped and hardened at the foundry down the street. He had a dark beard with no hint of gray, and Skelly would guess he was in his thirties. Even in this dim light his eyes seemed clear, and when he spoke it was in a tone that announced that he was entitled to your respect, whether you were so inclined or not. So Skelly remained quiet and still, waiting for Bashir to take the lead.

The man spoke first to Najeeb, sternly, rhythmic and singsong, almost as if addressing a child. Najeeb glared back, but said nothing in reply. Then the fixer turned toward Skelly.

"He is instructing me on how to proceed. He says that I shall speak exactly the words that he says, as if they were coming out of my mouth, not as if I were relaying them second hand. I am not to say 'he says,' or to add any observations or words of my own. I am only to repeat his words verbatim."

"Okay," Skelly said, not sure how to react.

Then Bashir spoke again, and Najeeb complied to the letter, Skelly wondering how the man was supposed to know if Najeeb was doing as told. But why risk disobedience at this point?

So began their odd conversation, carried out with small interim periods of waiting, as if they were on some sort of satellite delay, with Bashir's message issuing from Najeeb's mouth in a monotone.

"You wish to come with us into Afghanistan. Or so Idris says. But Idris is an insect. So I need to hear it from you directly."

Before Skelly could answer Bashir said something more, and the words poured out from Najeeb.

"You will please look at me when I address you. Not at the man who is merely a device, like a telephone box."

Skelly swiveled his head, studying the man again. Such insolence and arrogance, yet also a deep calm. Or maybe it was merely a sense of control, of being on his own turf and knowing they couldn't walk out on him, not if they expected to survive. Yet Skelly didn't feel threatened. He doubted that anyone this haughty would go to such trouble merely to rob and kill them. Why, indeed, would he want to deal with them at all? Especially if they were only going to be tagalong pests who might impede his progress? But he could certainly understand why a man like this would crave publicity.

"Yes, I wish to go to Afghanistan, and I wish to bring my interpreter with me."

Najeeb translated, presumably using the same verbatim method, as

if he were only some sort of filter. Bashir never took his eyes off Skelly, then he nodded and spoke again.

"There will be fighting. I can almost assure you of that."

"I have seen fighting before," Skelly replied, nodding. "But why take us?"

"Because Mahmood Razaq will need witnesses, even if he does not know this yet. He will want the world to know what he accomplishes. But he does not want the nuisance of an entourage traveling with his main body. Nor would the men with him respect him for very long if that were to happen."

"And do you respect him?" Skelly found the pairing odd, to say the least.

"I follow my orders."

"And following orders means you'll bring along a scribbler, even if Razaq might not necessarily know about it?"

"I follow orders," Bashir repeated.

"Why me?" he asked. "And why my newspaper?"

"The others would not come here."

Did Skelly really believe that? Maybe. He recalled his own initial reluctance—and Idris certainly was a poor choice as an advance man. Even Bashir had called him an insect. So maybe it was plausible. Barely. And maybe this was the only way Bashir knew how to do business. It's not like you'd get much practice in media relations here in Katchagarhi.

"You were also chosen because of the people you know," Bashir said, and like an ace from his sleeve he pulled from his pocket a tiny white business card, which he placed face-up on the floor in front of Skelly. It was Sam Hartley's, the name appearing in embossed black letters below the red globe logo of Transgas. Well, now. Wheels within wheels. And an odd sense of delight sprang up within him, as if he had just been admitted to a particularly secretive club where the entertainment promised to be naughty, if harmless enough, provided that everyone behaved and no one revealed the password once the show was over.

"And also this one," Bashir said, producing a second card as his words poured from Najeeb's mouth.

"Arlen Pierce, cultural attaché, U.S. Department of State," Skelly read. There was no embassy listed, no address or phone number. Hartley had said Pierce was in Cairo, but maybe Hartley hadn't known bet-

ter, or the story had been some sort of cover. And what had he called Pierce? The Dark Lord—yes, like he was some sort of conjurer. Well, he'd certainly achieved a kind of alchemy here, a transmutation of Skelly into a media heavyweight, at least in the eyes of the formidable Bashir. Nice to have one's contacts finally paying off.

"You know this man?" Bashir asked, nodding toward Pierce's card.

"Yes. I know him well," Skelly lied, because no journalist knew Pierce well, even the occasional female pursued by him. He was always the sort of fellow you only saw for a moment or two, in some bar or some briefing, smiling faintly at your jokes, then announcing there was some other place he had to be. Then his name would turn up a few days later in some other source's off-the-record conversation, or in the wreckage of some event the locals were still trying to puzzle out. He was reputed to be some sort of diplomatic repairman, one of Uncle Sam's fixer-uppers in the Islamic world.

"Mr. Pierce is helping you? And he is helping Mahmood Razaq?" Skelly asked. "And Mr. Hartley, too?"

But when Bashir's answer emerged from Najeeb's mouth, it was clear he had chosen to ignore all three questions.

"The decision is now yours," was all he said. "You will come with us, or you will stay behind. But I must have your decision now, because we leave in only five hours."

"What do you think, then?" Skelly asked Najeeb, turning his gaze from Bashir, feeling as if he had been gazing for too long at a very bright light, his eyes almost aching with relief.

"I cannot make this decision for you. I can only advise that I think it is very dangerous. But that will be true of any journey into Afghanistan."

Bashir spoke, sounding irritated.

"He says," Najeeb began, then corrected himself, adjusting to the preferred form of delivery while Skelly dutifully turned to face Bashir. "There is no need to consult with him." Meaning Najeeb, of course. "You will either come or not come. It is your decision. And if your answer is no, then do not expect to remain in this country indefinitely. We cannot have these kinds of secrets loose in the streets of Peshawar in our wake."

Was he actually threatening to have Skelly expelled? Or worse? Bashir was either audacious or frighteningly well connected, and the two business cards certainly suggested the latter. But for a moment the

idea seemed to offer a fleeting possibility of escape. Expulsion offered a certain glamour, too, especially for a journalist who wondered deep in his heart if he still had the necessary stuff for taking such risks. For a few seconds Skelly glimpsed green grass and clean skies, a welcoming wife and, yes, also a boulevard of malls and fast-food restaurants, late nights of nodding off before a TV screen with the den gone dark, while fall leaves rustled on the lawn, young Brian asleep at his ankles. Then the vision darkened, and he looked up at Bashir, supposing he was still up to it, after all, if only because it was one last adventure, one last chance to find the big secrets that had always eluded him and wound up in the stories of others.

He swallowed hard.

"All right, then." Steady now. "We'll go."

Bashir nodded.

"You are wise. And courageous."

Bashir as a flatterer somehow didn't work. Or maybe it was that Najeeb's voice had gone shaky. And Skelly supposed that Bashir might even be mocking him.

"Wise? Doubtful. And certainly not courageous. Foolhardy is more like it."

When Najeeb relayed the comment, Bashir nodded, as if Skelly had just spoken words of great wisdom. Perhaps something had been lost in translation. Then he spoke again, more solemn than ever.

"He says . . ." Najeeb began before righting himself. "You will be rewarded for this. A great tale for your newspaper, with great figures of renown."

"Razaq, he means?"

Bashir shook his head, eyes gleaming with either mischief or relish.

"The man who your countrymen seek," came the answer, as if Bashir had suddenly become the teller of riddles from an old book of legends. "The one with the wispy beard. The one who rides a horse and speaks to the world. His path will cross ours. Or so we believe, from what our friends tell us." Najeeb's voice was rushing now to keep pace, almost breathless. "He and his men, all of his Arab guests. It is the real reason for our journey, as you will see for yourself."

"Bin Laden?" Skelly asked, no translation needed for that name. But Bashir acted as if he had uttered a blasphemy, recoiling slightly.

"No names, please," Najeeb relayed. "And no further speaking on this topic, to anyone. But you can be certain that your friends know as

well." And with those words Bashir tapped the two business cards—Hartley and Pierce.

Skelly didn't know what to think. His inclination was to dismiss it altogether as empty boasting. He caught Najeeb's eye, and in the glance that passed between them he could tell that the fixer felt the same. Bashir was bullshitting them, dropping hints of a nonexistent grandeur.

Nonetheless, Skelly suddenly felt more alert now, more attuned to the night, and he knew that when they reached the taxi he would be able to scribble down this entire conversation verbatim. He noticed smells that he hadn't noticed a moment before—a hint of cinnamon, a whiff of cardamom. He spied a lizard crawling on a far wall. And in some part of his brain he was already working out the odds, already building a case for plausibility atop a slender hope that whispered low, "What if it's true?"

But Bashir had moved on to practicalities.

"You will meet us by the highway, where your taxi is now, at three a.m. We'll provide food and water, so don't worry about those." Skelly blanched, making a note to be sure to bring his antibiotics, an entire bottle of Cipro, the same thing Americans were now gulping for anthrax.

"How will we be traveling?" Skelly asked.

"By truck, he says," said Najeeb, finally dropping all pretense of channeling. "Then by horse and mule. Maybe also on foot."

"What's our route?"

"Through the mountains."

"Well, yes. But can he show me where? I have a map."

Bashir seemed to consider this a moment, then nodded slowly. Skelly bent over, rummaging through his satchel before pulling out a large-scale map of Afghanistan and unfolding it on the floor in the dim light.

Bashir snorted, then stood, disappearing into the back.

"He says your map is no good. I guess he must have something better."

Bashir reappeared, already unfolding a white map, large and detailed, with topo lines and spidery dotted routes across tracts where Skelly knew there were no paved roads. Even UN maps weren't usually this good.

"Where did you get this?"

Bashir ignored the question, jabbing a finger at a brown blob marked Katchagarhi. Even on the map it seemed benighted and forlorn. Skelly followed as Bashir traced a path up the main highway for a few inches, then left on a side track that quickly turned to dotted lines, a west-by-southwest bearing roughly parallel to the Afghan border for several miles along the foot of mountains labeled as the Safed Range. Bashir spoke quickly.

"First, we pass through the Tribal Areas," Najeeb translated. "He says the route has been cleared with the chieftains along the way."

Najeeb again sounded a little quavery. Maybe the territory was familiar to him.

The route skirted several possible border crossings—the Sulaiman Pass, the Oghaz Pass, all of them were probably ancient smuggling routes—before joining a larger dirt road near a Pakistani village called Parachinar. It then climbed into the Spin Ghar Range—the White Mountains—before crossing the Afghan border at the Paiwar Pass, just south of a 15,000-foot peak called Sikaram. The topo lines made it all look steep and forbidding, the middle of nowhere, with the route then switching back and forth down the mountain into a small Afghan village, where Bashir now poked his finger.

"Jaji," he pronounced, reading the name.

"That is our first stop." Najeeb said, now looking as if he'd seen a ghost. "Then we travel to Azro, our base of operations, before going onward to Heserak, then all the way to Jalalabad. Where presumably Razaq will be crowned some sort of local king."

"Your words, I suppose."

Najeeb nodded, and this time Bashir didn't object to their conversation. He seemed lost in the map, gazing possessively at the little dots and shadings, finger still lightly touching the smudge marking the outskirts of Jalalabad. When he spoke next, it was with a steady calm, tapping his finger against the smudge.

"He says that is where we are likeliest to meet up with him."

"Razaq?"

"No. The other one. The one he calls 'the Sheik.'"

"Oh," Skelly said. "Him." Too intimidated to utter the name a second time. It was like being promised a glimpse of Sasquatch, or the Loch Ness monster, a personage so heavily freighted with mythology that he seemed to have almost become immortal, a wandering spirit who would never be captured.

"How does he know?" Skelly asked. "How does he know we might see him?"

Najeeb paused.

"Do you really want me to ask that? It's only likely to make him angry. The less said about that, the better, probably."

This time Bashir interrupted, wagging a finger and raising his voice.

"What's he saying now?"

"He wants to know why I wasn't translating what you said. I told him you were worried about having enough to eat, somewhere to sleep. I don't think he believed it. But he assures that you will be well taken care of."

"Yes," Skelly said. "Taken care of. Whatever that means."

Bashir spoke again.

"We must go now," Najeeb translated. "He has to prepare, and he has already told us too much. Be here by three thirty. And if you're not, then he'll have you found and brought here."

"Maybe that's what he meant by 'taking care of me.'"

Najeeb said nothing.

Bashir clapped his hands once, and the boy who had escorted them from the teahouse materialized, this time to lead them back to the taxi at the highway. As Skelly rose to follow, he realized the enormity of the commitment he had just made, and he nearly stumbled. Najeeb supported him from behind with a hand to the small of his back. Heart pounding and legs heavy, Skelly nodded, urging the boy forward.

Skelly turned to say good-bye, but Bashir had already disappeared into the back room, gone without a further word.

CHAPTER FOURTEEN

NAJEEB EXPERIENCED a sort of stage fright as he rode his scooter home, wondering what new drama might await him at the apartment. Two nights ago: a shaken and slashed Daliya. The night before: a dead body, with Karim lurking in the crowd and a trashed apartment upstairs.

Tonight everything at least looked quiet as he rounded the last corner. Windows dark. Shades drawn. No one around.

His mailbox was empty. No messages posted by the entrance. Climbing the empty, fully lit stairwell he began to relax, and to his great relief his door was not only shut but bolted, just as he'd left it.

Perhaps now the war would move on without him. Or so he felt, having decided on a somewhat drastic course of action after the meeting with Bashir. He had come to the decision during the taxi ride back from Katchagarhi.

Skelly had been edgy and elated, talking rapidly:

"I guess if he were just a brigand he would have already cut our throats," sounding as if he was trying to convince himself. "But we'll find out soon enough. I'll need to store my excess gear at the Pearl, which means another cab. Wouldn't trust the Grand to keep it. Christ, and we still don't have a sat phone. Too late now. We'll have to borrow Razaq's."

"Assuming you'll even see him," Najeeb said, breaking a long silence. He wanted to slow down the Skelly express, needing the right opening to break the news of his decision.

"Oh, these things have a way of working out. I've never been any-

where yet where I wasn't able to file. And you heard Bashir. It isn't like Razaq doesn't want the publicity. He just doesn't want the aggravation. He'll keep us out of his hair until he thinks we're needed. Might take a while, but we'll see him."

Now, Najeeb thought.

"You will, maybe. Not me."

Skelly did a predictable double take. "Come again? What do you mean?"

Najeeb employed the old Pashtun stoniness, working to keep his face unreadable.

"I will not be going with you. I will find you someone else. But do not worry, it will not be a problem. I know many good candidates, and they will be happy for the opportunity."

"Don't *worry*? In less than five hours we're crossing into Afghanistan in the dark and you're going to find me somebody *new*? Not a problem? It's a *huge* problem. And why the hell are you doing this?"

Why, indeed?

The main reason was Daliya. Still no word. He had to find out what had become of her, or he might regret it forever. And for all he knew the police were searching for him as well. Disappearing overnight would only arouse further suspicion.

Then there was the matter of the route Bashir had traced on the map. Crossing his father's lands on the Grand Trunk Road, as they had done this afternoon, was one thing. On the highway the government at least maintained a semblance of control. Passage via lesser roads—and at night, no less—was something else altogether. So that was the excuse he offered Skelly first.

"Look," Skelly said, "I'm still not sure what your problem is with going home—you've never really told me. But do you think these guys would be traveling that way if they hadn't cleared it, with your father or whoever? No way Razaq or Bashir would risk not even making it to the border."

A fair point, so Najeeb reluctantly told Skelly about Daliya, her disappearance, and the disturbing silence of her cell phone throughout the day. He left out the part about the messages and the dead body. This, at least, slowed down the Skelly express.

Skelly frowned, grumbling, obviously not wanting to seem cold or insensitive.

"You should call the police," he said curtly. "Let them handle it."

"It's been reported."

Skelly frowned and patted him on the shoulder, an awkward yet affecting gesture of support. Then he sighed. Was he giving in this easily?

"Look, you should do whatever you think you need to do. Get your affairs in order." He sighed again. "Just find me somebody worthy. And soon. Somebody who won't mind roughing it. The next few days aren't going to be easy. Tell you the truth, I'm a little scared. It's a big unknown, what we're getting into. What *I'm* getting into. But this might be my last real shot at a story this big, dumb as it sounds. And if they really are going after who Bashir says they are, well, it might be the one quest worth making." Skelly shrugged, taking his hand off Najeeb's shoulder, then fiddling with his notebook, the taxi suddenly silent except for the thrumming of the tires.

And that was how they left things, Najeeb surprising himself with a stab of regret, as if he might actually begin to miss this man. Or was it the prospect of an adventure he would miss? No. He'd had enough of adventure for a while. Adventure, he decided, was just another word for chaos, for letting runaway events take over your life.

He must have felt guilty, too, because he then insisted that Skelly not pay him for the day, even after at least twenty hours aboard buses and taxis, and trips to the Khyber and into the dark labyrinth of Katchagarhi.

"Nonsense," Skelly said, handing him three fifties, then a fourth. "Just get me somebody good." So that's what Najeeb would do now that he was home. He knew at least four English speakers who would leap at the chance, even on short notice, with only a half hour remaining until midnight. He would brew a pot of tea and give them a call. Then, finally, he would begin to sort out the jumble of his life. And if Bashir decided to have him tracked down when he failed to show up for tonight's expedition, then it was a risk he had to take on Daliya's behalf. Their destinies were now linked, and somehow he was certain she believed that, too. He refused to consider the possibility that she might simply be gone.

He turned the key, pleased to hear the bolt sliding back. Inside it was dark and still, and he set down his satchel with a long, full sigh. Then he flipped on the light, his skin jumping as he saw Tariq seated on the cushions, exactly where Daliya had been two nights earlier. The man smiled primly, hands folded calmly in his lap.

Najeeb bounded forward, reaching for the smirking face. Then a click and a heavy footstep drew his attention to the bedroom doorway, where a bodyguard emerged.

"Why don't you sit, calm yourself," Tariq said. "Usman here was just going to make some tea, if you're interested. Nice place."

Someone had tidied the mess from the day before. The tossed papers were back on his desk, every book reshelved. Even the floors were spotless, as if Tariq and Usman had spent the evening pushing mops and brooms.

"Who cleaned up the mess?" he asked, anger giving way to bewilderment. He wondered if he could ever feel at home here again.

"The mess?"

"The one your men made yesterday, searching the place."

Tariq shook his head, brow furrowed.

"Not our style. I won't deny we've been in your apartment recently. Nor will I confirm it, of course. But we don't make messes. We keep our comings and goings discreet. I doubt even your nosiest neighbor would have noticed. They might see a phone repairman, or some kind of delivery. But a mess? Not in our manual. Maybe you should check with the religious fanatic, the one you claimed was leaving notes for you."

"He's dead."

Tariq raised an eyebrow.

"The body last night?"

Najeeb nodded.

"Well, now."

Tariq eyed him closely, seeming to reappraise.

"Maybe I've underestimated you. Either way, your life seems to get more interesting all the time. The police have been here, you know. Or didn't you? Maybe they trashed the place. Or tidied it. Or both. But they weren't just asking about dead bodies. They're more interested in your friend. Your Daliya has an important father."

Najeeb nodded, fearful of what would come next.

"Is she . . . ?"

"Missing. Has been for more than a day. Last seen with you. An overnight visitor, I'm told." Tariq smiled.

Usman reentered from the kitchen, offering a cup of tea. Najeeb eased onto a cushion opposite Tariq, more confused than ever.

"In fact, if it weren't for me," Tariq said, "the police would have

been here waiting for you instead. They would very much like to arrest you."

"Why?"

"Well, it certainly doesn't look good for you, does it? Spending the night with her—bad start right there. Then she vanishes, and on the same day a man is stabbed to death in front of your apartment. The man who was leaving you love notes from the Koran. Which the police didn't seem to know either, by the way, so I'm wondering how you did? Although maybe I should have guessed it after I heard about the knife. Which reminds me. Usman, would you please show Najeeb what you found in his kitchen?"

Usman snapped open a briefcase and pulled out three large knives of varying lengths and shapes. They looked like the ones from Najeeb's kitchen. In fact, they *were* the ones from Najeeb's kitchen.

"Notice anything missing?" Tariq said.

"There is a fourth one."

"It's in police custody, because it was found beneath the body."

"Did you put it there?" he asked, not that he expected a straight answer. Framing him would be the perfect way to control him.

"Of course not. In fact we've decided to take these other three off your hands for a while, to help you out a bit. Imagine how bad it would have looked if the police had found them. Afraid we can't do anything about fingerprints, however, though we're working on it, of course."

"Of course." He wasn't sure who to believe now.

"But I do wonder how you're so sure that dead fellow was your mystery messenger. Care to explain?"

He didn't. The less he said now, the better, at least until he had time to sort things out, if that was even possible.

"But I didn't kill him, if that's what you're thinking."

"Personally I could care less, although it doesn't strike me as your style, even if the knife suggests otherwise."

"Who was he, then?"

"Nobody we were interested in. Meaning he wasn't with any of the known rabble-rousers. Just some tribal piece of trash. From your part of the Khyber, in fact. Ever heard of a village called Kandao?"

Najeeb nodded. It was only a seven-mile walk from the house where he'd grown up. Rowdy boys quick to throw stones and steal bread. But hardly a hotbed of religious fanatics. There was a small, battered mosque there, but no more than a handful of people who could

read enough Arabic to do anything other than utter a few of the standard prayers.

"Well, that's where he was from. Which doesn't exactly help you out, either. In fact, between him and the missing girl, if things get any worse I might have to cancel our little arrangement altogether."

"Arrangement?"

"Regarding Razaq and his excursion. You're leaving tonight." Tariq glanced at his watch. "In a few hours, in fact."

"I'm not going. Our deal is off. And I have to find a replacement for the American before it gets any later. So if you don't mind."

"Don't mind at all," Tariq said, standing. "And as for those knives, Usman, why don't you put them back in the kitchen where they came from. Then we'll have to wait here until the police come. Couldn't have you destroying possible evidence. Unless of course you decide to change your mind."

Najeeb sighed, then sat back down. Tariq kept his feet, stepping toward Najeeb's desk.

"I thought you might see it my way. Which is why I brought this." He reached into the shadows and pulled out a second briefcase. "It's a satellite phone. Our mutual friend Javed tells me your client didn't have one, and I'm hoping he hasn't come up with one since this afternoon."

Najeeb shook his head.

"Perfect, then. Very easy to use, instructions enclosed. It will be a great way for you to stay in touch with us, and for us to stay in touch with you. We'll be able to listen to any calls you make. Just don't ask me to explain how the technology works, because I can't. Only results interest me."

"So I'm just supposed to leave. Even with Daliya missing."

Tariq shrugged.

"It's not like I haven't done you any favors. The police would like nothing better than to get a crack at you. We're all that's preventing them."

"Oh, yes, you've been very fair. I also appreciate the way you've had me followed."

"Followed? Surveilled, maybe. Once or twice. But followed? I hate to tell you this, but you wouldn't be worth the resources."

"Then why bother to put the Clerk aboard Fawad's press bus?"

"What? Javed? Surely you haven't let roly-poly little Javed rattle you. Just because he went along for the ride?"

"There was no need for it."

"And you think it was because of you?" Tariq laughed, incredulous. "I'm afraid you've overestimated your importance. Javed's as well. Journalists are his little sideline. And because we sometimes like to know what they're up to, we tolerate his moonlighting. Frankly, he likes the extra cash—and who wouldn't? The bastards pay better than we do. And if that happens to also put him in position to view another target, well, even better. But believe me, you're not a target. Just a tool."

Then who *was* the target? Fawad? Skelly, even?

"Then why all the attention, if I'm just a tool?"

"Haven't you heard? There's a war on. We're part of it, like it or not, and there are pieces moving across the board that we have to keep up with, if only to find out who is really making the moves."

"Who besides you, you mean?"

"You really *don't* understand, do you? You're just like all the other dumb bastards who think we secretly run the country, and Afghanistan as well. I'm in the information business, nothing more. What my superiors do with it, or who they sell it to, or whose heads they hold it over, none of that matters. All I care about is acquiring it. From the likes of you and from the likes of Javed."

"So you don't even care who wins."

"If anyone ever won, I might. But name me just one winner you've seen, especially in Afghanistan. The Russians? The Taliban? Maybe for a while, but look at them now. The United States? They'll be gone soon enough, and they won't even leave with the man they came for. He'll either die in a cave or go someplace where they won't be able to follow him. Nobody wins, everyone just plays, and we're the professional spectators."

"So there are no true believers at ISI?"

"Did I say that? You're not listening. Sure there are. And sometimes one of them asks me to believe along with him, so I kneel at his side and pretend for a while. But the true believers don't last. Eventually some new creed comes along and they fall out of fashion, which leaves only the purists like me. Which is why I'm interested only in the product, the information. And that's why I'm interested in you, because you can help me get it. Which reminds me. One other favor, if you don't mind."

As if he could actually say no.

"Keep an eye on Bashir. Let me know what he's up to."

"He's leading the rear guard. That's what he's up to."

"Of course he is. How else do you think we knew you'd be leaving in a few hours?"

"Bashir works for you, too?"

Tariq shrugged.

"For us and for others. Which is why we want to keep an eye on him."

Najeeb remembered the calling cards, the ones Skelly had been so excited about, thinking that they gave the man credibility. He'd forgotten the names but knew that one worked for a pipeline company and the other for the U.S. State Department. He'd seen the same two logos on cards presented to his father, at times, back in the days when promises and dollars were easy commodities. Doubtless they were back in fashion.

"So who am I really supposed to watch, then? Bashir or Razaq?"

"Both. And anyone else who seems interesting. Including your client."

"You sound like you don't have a clue what's going to happen."

Tariq's smile had a malicious twinkle.

"Just about any outcome suits our purposes, as long as I'm kept informed. But one thing about Bashir you should keep in mind, as long as you're still working for Mr. Stanford J. Kelly. Bashir hates Americans. Always has. He even killed a few once. Although that was years ago."

"Then why would he agree to take an American with him?"

"Very good question. Let me know as soon as you have the answer."

"And when I'm done? What happens to those knives in Usman's briefcase? And to the police? Last time you talked about a visa. It won't do me much good if I'm in jail."

"Do a good job and you won't have to worry about anything." He checked his watch again. "But what you need now is sleep."

As if I'd even get a wink, Najeeb thought. Tariq cleared his throat, which brought Usman back out of the kitchen.

"Good luck," Tariq said. "And stay in touch."

The two men left, footsteps echoing down the stairwell. They hadn't bothered to close the door, and Najeeb wondered if it was even worth the effort. Anyone who wanted to seemed able to get in.

Besides, in three more hours he'd be leaving for Afghanistan.

## CHAPTER FIFTEEN

T HE MORE SKELLY THOUGHT about Najeeb's sudden desertion, the angrier he got. Personal problems or not, no previous
fixer had ever similarly abandoned him, and certainly never at such a
crucial moment.

He cursed and fumed in the back of the taxi, loud enough for the
driver to keep glancing back, as if fearful that this madman would tear
apart the upholstery—or worse, stiff him on the fare. The worry beads
clicked against his rearview mirror with fresh urgency at every bump
and curve.

But Skelly paid without complaint, not even arguing when the
driver announced a final price five thousand rupees above what they'd
agreed to. "Too much waiting at the camp," the driver explained nervously, raising his hands as if helpless in the matter. Skelly tossed the
bills onto his lap, wanting only to rid himself of this entire exasperat-
ing day.

He stood curbside a few yards beyond the steps of the Hotel Grand.
While the Pearl Continental was buffered from the highway by a
broad expanse of clipped grass and palm trees, with a guardhouse to
fend off the unworthy, the Grand sat cheek by jowl with the busy highway in the heart of Little Kabul. Even at this hour there was still plenty
of noise and bustle, and the smoke of wood fires was as thick as fog.
The Grand's rooms, at least, faced away from the maelstrom, stacked
in a rectangle six stories high surrounding a gloomy inner courtyard.
Someone had dug a huge pit in the courtyard, at least ten feet deep,
making the whole place smell of damp earth. Perhaps they were build-

ing a pool, or maybe there was a problem with the plumbing. Skelly didn't relish spending the next three hours there, and he lingered by the curb.

When he finally turned, he saw a man climbing into a truck by the hotel's plate-glass doorway, perhaps fifteen yards away. A face appeared at the side window, then quickly turned away, but Skelly could have sworn it was Sam Hartley. Any familiar face at this hour was encouraging, so he waved, calling Hartley's name. But the man didn't look back—was Hartley avoiding him or had he imagined it?—and the truck swerved sharply across the grit. Skelly got a fleeting glimpse of the driver as the truck passed through the glare of the street lamp, and for a moment he was sure it was Arlen Pierce. Impossible. He must have been thinking of the man because of Bashir's business cards. But the truck, he saw now, wasn't of any make or model you ever saw around here. It was a black Chevy Suburban, the sort of big American vehicle you found in embassy motor pools, and it was headed away from Peshawar, in the direction Skelly had just come from. His imagination jumped in five directions at once. Best to have a beer and a shower and try to calm down. Although here there was no beer, of course. Only bottled water or juice. Or Coke, which would only keep him awake.

He climbed the stairs to the third floor, too impatient for the Grand's clanking elevator, the size of a closet and the sort with a door you had to pull open. Strolling the railed walkway to his room, he gazed into the muddy darkness of the hole in the courtyard, which seemed to exhale dankness and decay. Maybe they were digging up the sewerage. Wonderful. But he couldn't shake the image of Hartley and Pierce, if that was indeed who he'd seen, and as soon as he entered his room he picked up the phone, pressed the buttons, and heard the clicks of a rotary dialing signal. Two rings, then an answer.

"Pearl Continental."

"Room 311, please." That was Hartley's. Might as well set his mind at ease, even if it meant waking the man up. Seven rings later the call jumped back to the switchboard.

"I'd like to leave a message for Mr. Hartley in 311."

"One moment, sir. I'll connect you to the front desk."

The desk clerk asked for patience, and Skelly heard papers being shuffled, people talking.

"I am sorry, sir. Mr. Hartley has checked out."

"When?"

Another pause, more shuffling.

"This morning, sir."

"Shit."

"Pardon?"

"Nothing. Thank you—wait! Is there a Mr. Pierce registered?"

"Peace, sir?"

"Pee-erce. P-I-E-R-C-E. First name Arlen."

More shuffling of papers.

"No, sir. No Mr. Peace."

"Pierce. Whatever."

"Yes, sir."

He hung up, then tried Hartley's cell number, getting only a recording, which meant the receiver was either beyond range or turned off. He couldn't help but remember the way the signal on his own phone had died just a few miles west of here.

So had he really seen them? And if so, were they a team? Bashir seemed to think so. But for what purpose? It crossed his mind that he might see them later at the rendezvous point with Bashir. Where else would a pair like that be headed at midnight? Or maybe Hartley had merely driven back to Islamabad, or was flying down to Quetta. Wasn't there a landing strip nearby? Or maybe all Skelly had seen was a pair of foreign hacks. But in a Chevy? Problematic, unless some place around here rented or sold them.

Then he had another idea. He fumbled in his satchel for a typewritten list, looking up the number of the American embassy in Islamabad. All but a few diplomatic personnel had been sent away weeks ago, along with their families, but there would still be a duty officer, even at this hour. He dialed the number.

"United States Embassy." Midwestern accent, flat and non-committal.

"Duty officer, please."

"Speaking."

"Yes, I'm trying to locate Arlen Pierce. Do you have his cell number?"

"Who's speaking, sir?" Wary now. Alert.

Skelly hurriedly mumbled his name and newspaper, hoping to avoid the usual runaround reserved for the press.

"Say that again?"

"Stan Kelly. He knows me."

"With?"

"The *Ledger*. Look, we're old friends."

"You're a reporter?"

"Yes."

"Just a second."

Damn it.

A pause, the receiver thumping on a desktop, then some consultation in the background. Why would there be more than one person of any authority on duty at this hour? Had a bombing occurred, or some other crisis he hadn't heard about? The BBC at eleven had carried only more of the same—stalemated battlefronts and further claims and counterclaims on civilian losses. But whoever answered the phone hadn't rejected the name Arlen Pierce out of hand, and Skelly supposed that was something. They were back on the line now.

"Try this number. Country code 1, area code 202 . . ." Washington, in other words. Then a number that began with 647.

"That's the State Department." It was the old runaround.

"Yes, sir."

"Well, what are you saying, then?"

"I'm saying you can't reach Mr. Pierce at this number."

"Are you saying he's not in-country?"

"Please try the number I gave you, sir."

"But . . ."

Click.

Well, now. Whenever they said nothing, it meant anything but. You'd have thought by now that they'd have learned a smoother way to lie. A bored "Mr. Pierce? Who's he?" would have thrown him off the scent. But in Skelly's experience the State Department's most skilled dissemblers stayed close to home, or maybe it was just that in Washington they never got out of practice.

It almost certainly meant Pierce was in the country, in his world of back channels and unofficial contacts—although it didn't prove he had been the man in the Chevy.

He phoned downstairs to the Grand's front desk, but there was no record of any Pierce or Hartley having checked in or out. If the two men had arranged a meeting they wanted to keep secret, though, it certainly would have made sense to do it here instead of at the Pearl, where half the world's media was gathered. The only hacks staying at

the Grand besides him, Skelly had discovered, were a Dutchman, a Belgian and a couple of Japanese, from publications he'd never heard of. And he could see why. The walls of his narrow room were drab and smudged. Every lightbulb was a dim forty watts. The TV was ancient, the bed a mere three feet wide, and the dirty carpet was currently host to a caravan of ants, winding their way to a sprinkling of crumbs lying next to a crumpled chip bag in the corner.

Skelly set the alarm on his watch for just before 3 a.m., then phoned the desk again for a backup wake-up call, only to learn that no one would be on duty at that hour. He wondered if he would even be able to call for a taxi then—Christ, everything was falling apart—so he spent the next fifteen minutes getting the deskman to arrange for a car to be out front at 2:50. No, better make it 2:40. Less than three hours from now. He should sleep, he supposed, as if such a thing was possible. Hardly even worth getting undressed.

That thought summoned a fresh burst of anger at Najeeb. What if no replacement showed up? Should he even go? Would any of Bashir's men speak English? For that matter, how would he even know he was meeting up with the right group? He might rendezvous by mistake with a gang of smugglers, or a band of religious fanatics heading into town to bomb the embassy.

But at least Razaq spoke the language. Skelly might have to stake everything on meeting up with him at some point, on hoping that the so-called rear guard would eventually join the main body. Then he recalled Bashir's tantalizing allusion to the expedition's supposed true quarry, the world's most wanted man.

If anyone would be able to deliver on something like that, he supposed, it would likely be some fringe player such as Bashir, hidden in a refugee camp yet seemingly well connected. Maybe the man was even a CIA plant. Wheels within wheels, indeed. Skelly momentarily felt the excitement of being near the beating heart of something faceless and powerful, the dread animal crawling at the core of every major event, yet rarely showing its face. Might Skelly get a glance? Could be. Then the moment passed, and he again felt lost, uncertain.

Because there was another possibility, too, equally plausible. Bashir might be a fraud, a con artist, a brigand. He might have saved the calling cards from some earlier chance encounter. Or worse, he'd stolen them from some journalist. But if that was true, why hadn't he already robbed Skelly? Perhaps he was waiting for Skelly to be fully packed

for travel, when he'd be loaded with expensive equipment and all of his cash.

Enough of such worries. Maybe a new fixer would actually appear. For now he supposed he had better check in with the foreign desk.

He got the connection on the fifth try. The foreign editor was out for coffee, so he talked to the assistant, who was thrilled to hear of Skelly's plans, or at least he was until he heard Skelly didn't have a sat phone.

"Don't worry. Razaq has one," Skelly said, letting them assume that he would be traveling near the great man himself. He decided not to mention the possibility of bumping into the leadership of al-Qaeda— partly because he wasn't sure he believed it himself, but partly also because the editor seemed pleased enough as it was. No sense raising their expectations unreasonably when Skelly was already rising on the charts, a star reborn. And for a heady moment he recalled what it had once felt like to have people waiting eagerly for his dispatches, confident that he would deliver the goods. Maybe this time he'd give them the biggest story of all.

"Have you called your wife, by the way? She was checking on you this morning, making sure you were okay."

"Thanks. I'll do that."

He truly was overdue, he supposed, so after hanging up he dialed Janine, this time making it through easily. Fuzz and static, then a few clicks. It was midafternoon where she was, so she was probably picking up in the kitchen.

"Hello?"

"Hi, sweetie."

"Stan?"

"Well, who else?"

"My God, how are you? I've been wondering if you even made it. Then I saw your byline yesterday. Sounded pretty hairy."

"What? Oh, the demo. Just a few hotheads really." And nothing compared to what I'm about to get into, he thought.

"So what's it like over there?"

"The usual chaos and starvation. Anger and shouting. 'Why are you doing this to us?' and that sort of thing. You know the drill."

And she did, having been posted to four different locations around Asia by the Australian economic mission before she'd met up with Skelly in Jakarta. She knew all about the volatile mix of demos and hotheads and starvation.

"Spoke to your editor this morning. He said your stomach was a problem."

"Nothing serious. Just a runny egg."

"You took your Cipro, I hope."

"Popped a couple the other day. Seems okay now."

"They say yogurt's a help."

"They say, but they don't have to eat it. How's Brian?"

"Ear infection, so he's drugged and down for the count. Was up half the night crying, but he's okay now."

"It's what, a little after three?"

"Yes. But you're up late. Been writing?"

"Came up empty today. Wasted trip to the border. Going back again in a few hours. With any luck this time we'll get across."

"Into Afghanistan?"

"Yes."

"Good Lord. With who?"

"Some warlord's rear guard. Well behind any possible action."

"Let's hope so. Did you hear about the Frenchman, the scribbler from *Le Monde*?"

"No." Skelly wasn't sure he wanted to.

"Got caught sneaking across in a burqa. Posing as a woman." Janine laughed.

"What did they do with him?"

"Locked him up overnight, then kicked him out. He was six foot five."

Skelly joined in the laughter. This was Janine at her best, talking the lingo of the field. As a foreign service worker she'd traveled in the same circles as Skelly, swapping the same quirky stories. She knew the survival tricks as well as he did. But after several years of being marooned in the Midwest she had, alas, adapted just as gamely to its vagaries as those of Bangkok or Hong Kong, and she was now an inveterate mall shopper and carpooler, signing Brian up for everything from infant swimming lessons to day school, three years ahead of schedule. This, too, was a demonstration of her flexibility, he supposed, but it somehow lost its appeal when occurring on such familiar ground. Their conversation tonight at least took them back to the subjects they preferred, or that he preferred anyway.

"Oh, I saw the Stephensons the other day at the supermarket. She wished you luck." A pause. "Are you sure about this Afghanistan trip? Sounds chancy. What other hacks are going?"

He'd been hoping she wouldn't ask that.

"Just me and my fixer," he said brightly, knowing that even that wasn't true. "Meaning anything I get will be an exclusive. More brownie points for later."

"Jesus, Stan. I thought you were finished with all that."

With taking undue risks, she meant. As if the trip itself hadn't been one. But she knew, in the way that most people back home didn't, that journeying to a war zone wasn't necessarily a foolhardy venture. The TV types who did stand-ups on the Marriott rooftop would have been taking a greater risk commuting on the D.C. beltway. Joining a possible war party single-handed, however, reeked of uncertainty. Even Skelly suddenly wondered what the hell he'd gotten into. But having told his desk, he now felt locked in. Amazing how quickly your judgment could change after just a few days in-country. He'd arrived as a cautious suburbanite, still spooked from the horrors of Liberia.

"I know," he said, conceding the point. "I thought I was finished with it, too. Then the opportunity presents itself and you figure, well, what the hell am I here for anyway?"

"Yes, well." (He knew she was resisting the urge to say "I told you so.") "You still don't have to do it, you know. You can always tell the desk it fell through."

"I may not have to make that part up. This isn't the most organized bunch in the world. But I have a feeling it will all be pretty tame. And if I spend a couple of weeks across the border the paper will pretty much have to bring me back afterward. They might even treat me a little better afterward."

"Well, don't push it. Coming home sooner would be great. But I don't want it to be in a box."

"Jesus, Janine."

"Sorry. Not trying to jinx you. Just worried."

"Worrying's fine. I'm worried, too. Which means I'll be careful."

They said good-bye a few minutes later, but Skelly was still wondering about the whole idea of being more careful. He remembered the men in black turbans standing at the border. They'd looked willing to shoot just about anyone. He decided that if a new fixer didn't show up, he'd bow out. Bashir might not like that, but it simply wasn't worth the risk. Of course, how would he tell Bashir if no one around them spoke English? Goddammit, Najeeb.

He had better try and get some sleep. He looked at the clock, barely able to read the dial of his watch in this dimness. Even if he nodded off right away he'd only get about two hours, so he decided on a shower. More refreshing, and it might be the last one for days, even weeks.

The shower was terrible, of course, the water spurting everywhere from a cracked valve while a lizard scrambled across the tiles toward a high window. As he dried off he heard a shrill squawk from out back. It sounded just like a peacock, and for the next hour the bird kept up the noise, shrieking every few minutes, usually just as he was dropping off. But he must have finally drifted off anyway because he was suddenly awakened by the beeping alarm. It rescued him from the middle of a vivid dream. Janine had been telling him she was pregnant, while holding the hands of two other small children he didn't recognize. No, it had been Larissa, not Janine. He rubbed his eyes and groggily sat up. The place was still. No more peacock.

He dressed quickly, then grabbed his gear and trooped around the walkway behind the iron railing. The taxi hadn't arrived yet, but it was only 2:38. Five minutes passed, and still nothing. At 2:50 he began to fret, but finally at 2:53 a cab rolled up.

The driver asked for double what he should have, of course, but at this hour Skelly had little choice. They arrived at the rendezvous point fifteen minutes early, which was just as well, giving him a chance to calm down. But there was no fixer there to greet him, and the camp seemed preternaturally still—everyone asleep in the mud huts, finally at peace, a waxing half-moon trying to shine through the haze, orange in the night sky. In a few more weeks it would be Ramadan, he remembered, wondering how that would affect the goings-on.

Ten minutes later a second cab approached—his new fixer, he hoped, wondering if Najeeb would at least have the decency to come along for introductions. It appeared that he did, because Najeeb was the first one out of the back. Skelly would normally have paid their fare, but not under these circumstances. Then he saw that there was no one else. Christ, had the man come up empty? Skelly opened his mouth to begin a tirade, but Najeeb opened both hands in a placating gesture, saying, "It is okay. I am coming with you."

Skelly hadn't felt so relieved in ages. He fairly spluttered, suddenly elated.

"But, I—what happened? What about your girlfriend?"

It sounded funny calling her that—such an offhand reference for

such a serious young man, and it was obvious from Najeeb's expression that matters were still grim, even if he said otherwise.

"It is okay," he said. Then, taking a deep breath, "I think she will be fine."

Hardly convincing, but Skelly wasn't about to try and talk Najeeb out of it.

"And I got a satellite phone." He held aloft the small briefcase.

"You're a miracle worker. That's phenomenal. Oh, wait." He paid for Najeeb's taxi, again feeling generous. He even felt confident enough to send his own cab on its way, now that everything seemed to be coming together. If you kept trying, matters had a way of working out, he reminded himself. Hadn't that always been the case? And suddenly he felt better, figuring that fortune was back on their side.

"Here they come," Najeeb said.

Skelly turned and saw three men with guns slung on their backs walking toward them up the nearest alley through the camp. None was Bashir, but one spoke to Najeeb. It didn't seem as if any of them spoke English, meaning Najeeb had arrived in the nick of time—another serendipitous turn of fortune.

"They said to follow them."

They walked into the camp, this time with a sense of excitement. And when they reached the teahouse, Bashir was waiting. Three trucks were parked nearby, each with about six men loaded in the back.

"You will ride in the last one," Bashir said, not bothering to greet them. Counting the drivers and a few others in the cabs, Skelly figured there were twenty-two men in all. To his relief, there were no other reporters.

It was time to get moving.

## CHAPTER SIXTEEN

THEY BROKE FREE of the haze while climbing a high plateau southwest of the city. The skies opened up to Najeeb like a black velvet blanket, sparkling with starlight. He and Skelly sat with four of Bashir's men on the truck's open flatbed, their backs against the slatted sides, faces bathed by the sudden coolness. The only sound apart from the grind of the engine was the sizzle of gravel in the wheel wells.

Skelly, shoulders jostling to Najeeb's right, asked where they must be by now. Najeeb shrugged, but he knew all too well. Even the smells were familiar—a sharp bite of resin, the duskiness of dry stone. It was pitch-black, but he could have painted the colors of the landscape from memory, forming the shapes of the hills like a sculptor molding clay. He was glad he'd called his office just before leaving the apartment. No one had been in, but he'd left a recorded message, stating his probable destination. If he never returned, at least someone would know where to look for him. Assuming that anyone bothered. Daliya would, that he was sure of. But only if she could. And for a despairing moment Najeeb looked eastward, as if he might spot some sign of her on the blackness of the horizon where the new day would begin. With every mile they grew farther apart. But there was hope, too, mixed with his sense of loss. Somewhere she was still out there, and still on the move. He was certain of it despite all evidence to the contrary. And if at some point he needed her, not even her family would be able to hold her back.

"I think we're stopping," Skelly said.

The engine had shifted to low gear, brakes groaning.

"Probably a checkpoint," Najeeb said. His stomach made a slow roll.

"Border patrol?"

"Private checkpoint. Tribal people."

Skelly said nothing. Perhaps he'd figured it out by now, remembering the route of Bashir's finger on the map at Katchagarhi and Najeeb's audible intake of breath as the dotted track had crossed into his father's lands, right about where they must be now.

A wave of nostalgia breasted his apprehension, taking him by surprise. He nearly shuddered, it was so strong. If he got off here and walked into the night he knew he could find his way home by morning, even in the darkness. Would they turn him away? Shoot him? Welcome him back without a further word? Probably none of those reactions. His father had always had a flair for the unexpected.

The engines stopped, ticking in the night, no one speaking. Pitch-dark, but a fine dust boiling up lazily from the road, tickling their noses. Then a voice called out from the truck just ahead, answered by another on the ground. Bashir spoke up, loudly enough for all to hear.

"Everyone out. This will only take a minute."

If he was lucky, Najeeb thought.

It was too dark to see faces, and Skelly clutched after him like an invalid as they stepped down from the open tailgate, dropping onto rough ground. They trooped forward in a shuffling column as the beam of a tiny flashlight flicked on, illuminating Bashir and a man who was apparently a sentry, a tall bearded fellow in a fat white turban, wearing a brown jacket for warmth.

If the man gave them any trouble they could easily overwhelm him, but that could produce months, even years of trouble ahead for Bashir and everyone with him, not to mention their families. Safety in numbers meant little when pitted against the dangers of a blood feud. That was presumably the code Razaq was counting on to get his men into Afghanistan without harm, although he almost certainly would have sent advance word of his passage.

The sentry had been faced away from them, but now he turned into the light, and his features were familiar.

"Do you know him?" Skelly asked.

"I'm not sure. I think so."

"Is that good or bad?"

Najeeb looked toward Skelly, unable to read his face in the dark.

"Hard to say. I'm not exactly welcome here anymore. I should have told you."

"It's all right. I'd pretty much guessed that. I figured it wasn't every son of a *malik* who moves to the city and starts working for foreigners."

The flashlight made the rounds, held by a second man working with the sentry. He pointed the narrow beam at one face after another, each man reacting with only a squint.

Najeeb wondered about this pair, almost certain that he recognized the tall one giving orders. Perhaps only an hour ago the man had been at his father's *hujera*, smoking and chatting, or listening to the radio. By now perhaps even the TV worked better, with a satellite dish to pull in a proper picture. The music videos from India would be quite a hit.

When the light illuminated Skelly's face, the American's pupils narrowed, but he kept looking straight ahead. To his credit, he didn't look scared. Only excited, as if this was something new, and therefore worthwhile.

"English?" the tall sentry asked.

"American," Najeeb answered, and the beam swiveled to him. There was a pause, as if the sentry were placing his face, followed by low laughter.

"You've returned."

"Yes."

"And now you go."

"Yes." What was this one's name? Of course, now he had it. "You're Rahim."

"You remember. Very good. What shall I tell your father of this?"

"You can tell him nothing, if you wish."

Another pause. Thinking it over. Although Rahim had never been the contemplative type.

"Yes," Rahim said at last, seeming in a jovial mood. "I think that is best. Best for you, anyway. But when you return I hope you have a better story for me. A better excuse. Or at least a better escort."

Najeeb wondered whether he was referring to Skelly or Bashir, and whether the assessment was Rahim's or some secondhand version of his father's. But this wasn't the time to ask.

The light swiveled back to Skelly, whose pupils again narrowed to pinpricks.

"Blue eyes. We don't see so many of those. My cousin thinks they are all the Evil Eye. If he were here he'd want to kill this one."

All this was transpiring in Pashto. Najeeb hoped Skelly didn't demand a translation, or pull out a notebook. Despite the bantering tone, the moment was finely balanced. Any sudden movement might shove it in the wrong direction.

"Would you like to sell him to us, then? An American would bring quite a ransom."

That brought laughter from some of the others. Bashir apparently felt no need to intervene.

"What's he saying?" Skelly asked.

"He is admiring your eyes."

"I'll bet."

Then it was Rahim's turn to wonder about incomprehensible words.

"What is he saying?" Rahim snapped.

"He was admiring your eyes."

Rahim laughed caustically, wheezing into the chilly night.

"He wanted to know what you'd been saying about him," Najeeb continued in Pashto.

"And you told him?" Rahim asked.

"Not exactly."

Rahim seemed to find this uproariously funny, and he slapped Najeeb sharply on the back, then moved on to the rest of the column without another word. After completing his inspection he stopped on his way back down the line, the beam again finding Najeeb's face.

"You were always funny when you had to be," Rahim said. "Even when you were a boy. Making us laugh so hard that we would put down our slingshots. Very clever. But they won't laugh as easily on the other side of the mountains."

Of course. Now he remembered. Rahim had been the tallest of the village boys, and among Najeeb's worst tormentors. Slingshots round their necks, chasing him up the gullies from town like starved mongrels, the stones thudding against his back. When he was inevitably run to ground, his only defense was wit, and fortunately wit had often been enough, partly because Rahim had always been inclined to respond favorably, calling a truce now and then when sufficiently amused by some insult or observation.

The intervening years had been hard on the man. He was weathered and gasping. Perhaps the harsh shadows of the flashlight beam were partly to blame, but Najeeb thought that his face looked more

like that of a man in his forties, even his fifties, than that of a contemporary. Knowing what he did of Rahim, and of his people in general, Najeeb doubted that the man would spread the word of this meeting. Not right away, at least. He would instead use his knowledge for whatever leverage it might provide. And when word finally did reach Najeeb's father, what would everyone think? He had no idea.

Whatever the case, Rahim had again finished with him and moved on. The flashlight was off, the second tribesman obviously hoping to save his batteries, and Bashir's men groped their way back into the trucks. Skelly again clutched lightly at Najeeb's sleeve, feet scuffing in the dirt behind him.

"Is it just my imagination," Skelly whispered, "or was that a close call?"

"You're right," Najeeb said. "It was a close call. Probably for both of us."

He held back a shudder, hoping that would be the last of the checkpoints. The glimmer of nostalgia had given way all too easily to fear. For seven years he had managed to convince himself that the door to home had somehow remained ajar. Now he was certain that it was shut, and had been all along. If and when Bashir's column returned from Afghanistan, Najeeb would have to find some other route back to Peshawar, even if it meant jumping off the back of a truck and hoofing it across the mountains alone. Because Rahim, or whoever was on duty next time, would doubtless be operating under new and stricter orders, a mandate that wouldn't be averted by mere laughter.

"Hurry up," Bashir shouted. "In another hour we'll be across."

"Next stop's the border?" Skelly whispered.

"If we even stop there. The crossing might not be guarded. Not at this hour, on the route we're taking."

"So, then," Skelly said, the excitement evident in his voice, "looks like we might really make it this time."

"Yes," Najeeb said, wishing he was as pleased about it as Skelly.

## CHAPTER SEVENTEEN

THE TRUCKS CLIMBED slowly in the dark with their headlights switched off, picking their way around curves and occasionally sledding the rocky shoulder. Skelly sat with his suitcase between his knees, squeezing his fingernails into the soft cover. He couldn't see more than a few feet. It felt like they were on an amusement park ride in slow motion, weaving and plunging in a way that turned his stomach, although he'd never been prone to motion sickness.

Toward the end of the next hour the sky brightened behind them as they rolled through a small, sleeping village of mud huts and corrugated rooftops, every window dark.

"Parachinar," Najeeb offered.

"I remember it from the map," Skelly said. "We're five miles from the border."

Najeeb must have been right about the lack of sentries at this hour, because ten minutes later they topped a rise past a smattering of darkened signs and a pair of low white buildings with flagpoles—customshouses, no doubt. The trucks didn't even pause, although Skelly heard the hollow sound of radio voices issuing faintly from the cab.

"Welcome to Afghanistan," Najeeb whispered.

"Sacrifice country heartly welcomes you with pleases," Skelly recited to himself, recalling the sign at Torkham. He reached awkwardly behind him to pull out a notebook with a stubby pencil jammed into the binding rings along the top. He checked his watch, pressing the tiny knob to illuminate the dial. It was 6:04. He scribbled the time and date on the first page, followed by the word "Afghanistan" in block

letters. His handwriting was probably crooked and shaky from the motion of the truck, but it was his equivalent of planting the flag at the summit, and he slid the notebook back into his pocket with a sense of a duty fulfilled.

A mile or so later the trucks pulled to the shoulder, such as it was, and the men spilled into the road.

"Are we already in Jaji?" Skelly said, looking around for buildings.

"Morning prayers." Najeeb joined the others while Skelly kept his seat, serenaded by the singsong mutter of the men below, barely visible as they bowed and bobbed. They looked like they were speaking into the ground, casting spells on the land itself. He listened intently for the wail of a muezzin, but empty bluffs ranged high to either side, sealing them off from any village. Looming to their rear was a huge dark peak, probably the mountain he'd seen on the map called Sikaram.

The sky brightened, and the sun finally pierced the horizon with a blazing crescent of orange. After so much bumping around in darkness it had the feel of an all-clear signal, and Skelly's muscles relaxed. The toll of the long hours of watchfulness seemed to finally catch up to him. Already he regarded with nostalgia his last shower, standing beneath the drippy spigot while the peacock shrieked out back at the Grand. Nodding with the motion of the truck, he drifted into dreamless sleep.

A burst of gunfire awoke him. It seemed that only seconds had passed, but his body told him otherwise. He felt awful—groggy, a lump in his throat that made it hard to swallow, his back stiff and sore against the slats of the truck. He blinked against the sunlight, then heard more shots. They weren't close, thank goodness, but the bed of the truck was empty, and he turned with a start, wondering for a panicky moment if he'd been abandoned.

But no, there they all were on a bare brown knoll just ahead—more than twenty men in turbans and skullcaps, peering into the distance over a pile of stones that might have been the ruined battlement of a castle. Bashir stood at the fore with a huge pair of black binoculars. Skelly roused himself, standing woodenly on the tilted bed of the truck. He stretched, feeling a little better, then reached for a water bottle in his satchel, unscrewing the cap for a long swig. Better still. He hopped noisily to the ground, drawing frowns from Bashir's assembly, then stepped behind the truck and unzipped his fly, peeing down the slope, watching the gold stream spatter and trickle down the

rocks, black wetness against the dust. His little contribution to history. Zipping up, he walked toward where the action was. Only Najeeb nodded in acknowledgment. Then more shots sounded from down the mountain.

"What's happening?" he whispered.

"A firefight."

"Razaq?"

"Or maybe just some shepherd boy, shooting at rabbits."

More shots. A long burst, then three single reports in quick succession, drawing the men's attention farther right, although Bashir's binoculars didn't waver. The men began to talk among themselves.

"They're asking how many men he has," Najeeb explained.

"Who, Razaq?"

"Yes."

"Wouldn't they already know?"

"One would think."

Bashir lowered his binoculars and replied in Pashto.

"He says fifteen, maybe sixteen."

"But we've got more than twenty. Why have a rear guard bigger than the main body?"

Bashir looked over sharply, then surprised Skelly by speaking in English.

"Save your questions for Razaq. And do not worry. He will pick up reinforcements in Azro. Or that is his plan."

Skelly tried to mask his surprise.

"What's happening down there?"

"A skirmish. Someone testing him. Nothing serious. Whoever it is has already withdrawn. Probably just a local faction, wondering who he was."

"Probably?"

"Sometimes that is the best you can do here."

"And the town down there. That would be Jaji?"

"Yes. We will be stopping there, once Razaq moves on. From there we proceed on foot. The roads beyond are too narrow for trucks."

"Aren't we lagging back a little far to do Razaq any good?"

Bashir scowled, squinting in the morning sun. This was the first time Skelly had seen the man in full daylight, and there was a definite spark to him. Or maybe it was being out in the field that livened him up. Skelly had met soldiers like that, men who seemed subdued until you placed a weapon in their hands and put them on the march.

"We don't want to run right up his back, now, do we?"

"I guess not."

But if some armed group were to slip in behind Razaq from east of Jaji, Bashir wouldn't be much help up here. Skelly wondered if Najeeb was thinking the same thing, but his fixer's expression had slipped back into unreadable Pashtun blankness.

"So I guess we won't be joining up with Razaq's main force anytime soon, then?"

"On the contrary. Tonight I promise to grant your wish. You will see the man himself."

"Razaq?"

"Of course."

"We'll be joining him in Azro?"

"Please. No more questions You will have what you want tonight."

The men began reboarding.

"By the way," Skelly said, "you speak very good English."

"Yes," Bashir answered, his sparkle more evident than ever even though he hadn't cracked a smile. "I do."

## CHAPTER EIGHTEEN

D ALIYA SLEPT until midmorning, awakening on the couch to find Professor Bhatti gone. There was a note on the kitchen table:

"Water in the kettle. Tea, sugar and bread in cabinet. Milk in fridge. Help yourself. But do NOT leave the apartment until I have returned."

Daliya smiled despite a twinge of guilt. The idea of eating breakfast by herself in this island of peaceful seclusion seemed heavenly right now. She stretched luxuriously. A window was open, and a breeze blew in from the streets. On the sidewalk below, two young women walked past, pushing strollers in the dappled shade.

She'd had a fine night of sleep despite a steel bar running across the middle of the mattress, which rolled against her spine every time she shifted. She and the professor had shared a simple dinner of bread, rice and salad, and Daliya told her mentor all about Najeeb, and the difficulties with her family. Thankfully the professor didn't pry much for further details, and for the balance of the evening Daliya had allowed herself to be a child again, coddled and tolerated as if she were merely winding down from an especially loud tantrum.

But she had awakened with her mind full of ideas and new possibilities. And for all of the uncertainty of her current position, she was sure of one thing—her future would include Najeeb, even if she had to be the one who insisted. Why? There was no other choice, really, not in the way she now viewed the world. Having broken so many other boundaries together, they would simply have to break a few more, even

if it took extraordinary efforts on her part. Najeeb's loyalty to this sort of future was not in question, she felt, whether he knew it yet or not.

Of course, there was one major problem with such assessments, even apart from her own predicament. Where was Najeeb? And if he had made it into Afghanistan, when would he return, if at all? She pondered all this as she folded up the couch, leaving the sheets on, hoping it wasn't too presumptuous of her to expect another night's lodging and refuge.

Professor Bhatti's apartment was furnished plainly, but like many homes in Islamabad the decor was of a more Western style, with couches and easy chairs, the end tables piled with newspapers and magazines. To Daliya's relief, the neighborhood was several miles from her parents', and because the city's quadrants tended to be self-contained there was little chance she would bump into them if she had to make a trip to the market or the bank.

It felt odd being cut off from the rest of the world, although she welcomed the idea of not having to concoct a cover story for a change. She experienced a stab of sympathy for her parents, even for her uncle and aunt, who must be frantic by now. And for the slightest moment she considered the idea of a quick phone call, just to let them know she was safe. Maybe she could even let Rukhsana spread the word. But, no, she finally decided. Matters were too delicate. Even a slight puncture in her bubble of secrecy would let all the air out, and with no word on Najeeb she wasn't yet willing to take that risk. Besides—and here her tougher side showed itself—her family's actions had earned them a little anxiety. Let them stew awhile longer, the way she'd had to stew in her misery in Peshawar all these months.

The kettle was boiling. Daliya brewed her tea sweet and milky, and it felt like perfumed velvet in her mouth, another brief moment of luxury. Then she rinsed the cup and picked up the phone, hoping the professor wouldn't mind the expense of a toll call to Peshawar. Without giving her name she reached a reporter at the *Frontier Report* who told her Najeeb had indeed crossed the border into Afghanistan.

"How do you know?" she asked.

"Because Mahmood Razaq made it across, and Najeeb and the American are with him. Najeeb left us a message." Her heart sank. There would be gun battles and air attacks. Plus fanatics who might do anything if they caught him, especially if he was in the company of an American.

"Who is this, anyway?" the reporter asked. "And where are you calling from? May I please have your name? Hello? Hello?"

Daliya placed the receiver back in its cradle. All the more reason that she now needed a plan of action, she supposed. She jumped as the apartment door opened, but it was only Professor Bhatti. Daliya smiled in greeting. The professor did not smile back. Instead a cloud rolled across her face. She carried a newspaper under one arm, and unfolded it on the table, jabbing a finger at a story on an inside page. It was this morning's edition of *Dawn*, and the professor's sharp painted nails drummed on a small headline in the upper left corner.

"This is exactly the sort of thing I was worried about," the professor said, in the same voice she used on students who hadn't prepared for class. "Take a look." She sighed loudly, taking a seat across the table while Daliya scanned the headline:

"Peshawar Woman Missing after Murder."

The details were grim. Her father was appealing for help in locating his daughter, who had disappeared after the stabbing death of a drifter from the Tribal Areas. Thank God there was no mention of whose apartment building it had occurred at, or what Daliya had been doing there. In fact, there was a comment from Rukhsana establishing that Daliya had last been with her—good old Rukhsana, still protective of her reputation. But if that were so, then how had police made the connection between her and a stabbing at Najeeb's apartment? And why were police also seeking "a young journalist, believed to have fled to Afghanistan." Fled? That was hardly fair. But what could you expect from the newspapers? Or from the police, for that matter. Odd, however, that the story never mentioned Najeeb by name.

"Shouldn't you at least call them?" the professor said. "Your parents, I mean."

On the contrary, Daliya was now more resolved than ever to take independent action, if only because the authorities seemed to be in such a muddle. So she shook her head and said, "I think it would be better to wait awhile longer."

"Better for who? And forgive me if I was also considering the welfare of your host."

"Oh. I'm sorry."

The professor shook her head in exasperation, with an expression darker than anything Daliya had ever seen in the classroom.

"I'll leave, then. Or were you just about to kick me out?"

"I'm not going to kick you out. Not for another day or two, anyway. But tell me, Daliya, did you at least follow my instructions not to leave the apartment?"

Daliya nodded meekly.

"Well, that's something, I guess." She pulled off her head scarf and ran a hand through her thick auburn hair.

"But I do have some errands I need to run," Daliya ventured. "If it's all right with you, I mean. As part of my plan."

"So you have a plan now, do you?" A challenging tone. Would she now expect an outline, with footnotes?

"Yes. The first thing I need to do is buy a burqa. And then . . ."

"Stop!" Professor Bhatti held up an outstretched palm like a traffic policeman.

"But—"

"Stop! Don't tell me anything more. The less I know, the better. For now at least. But I'll take you to buy a burqa. Not on foot, but in my car. And not until after dark, which means not until tomorrow. There's a faculty meeting this evening, so you'll just have to sit tight. I just hope to God no one recognized you as you were coming into the apartment building yesterday. Or while you were on campus. Or waiting in my office." The possibilities seemed to overwhelm her for a moment, and she put a hand to her forehead as if in pain.

It was just as well that the professor had halted her in mid-sentence. Daliya's so-called plan barely existed. She hadn't yet come up with any strategy beyond the vague idea of buying a burqa for safer travel in the Tribal Areas, and if she'd been allowed to continue talking she wasn't sure what she would have said next. Nor was she even certain she would put her plan into action. That would all depend on what became of Najeeb. All that mattered for the moment was that her professor wasn't yet kicking her out.

Perhaps it was this prospect of extra breathing space that freed her mind just long enough to seize on a new thought. It came in a flash, her most unorthodox idea yet—outlandish and fraught with hardship, but exciting all the same. It would require some money, but she had that. It would require courage, but she was discovering she had that, too. Maybe, she told herself, she might even enjoy the next several days, this foray into the rough new wilderness called freedom.

## CHAPTER NINETEEN

BASHIR'S TRUCKS ROLLED into Jaji around noon. It was an outpost of barefoot children and bony dogs, a few dozen mud homes shoved against each other at the edge of the dry valley as if swept aside by a broom.

A rusting signpost on the edge of town said "Drug Free Happy Life" in English, the remnant of some long-gone aid organization. On the wall of a small store a faded mural depicted a variety of land mines above a red warning in Pashto. Someone had recently sprayed it with gunfire.

Within minutes after they stopped, a crowd of curious children zeroed in on Skelly, who waved them away distractedly, too weary to say no. They complied meekly, not nearly as aggressive as the ones at the Khyber, and he almost regretted his brusqueness. But he had nothing to offer except food and cash, both of which he would need in the days ahead.

Bashir conferred with a village elder who had emerged from a doorway down the street. The man pointed up the valley, gesturing as Bashir nodded.

"We will unload here," Najeeb said. "We are going to rest awhile."

"We should try and get some sleep. Maybe I'll do a few interviews later."

The sun had crept above the ridge, and it was warming up, so Skelly found a spot beneath a tree by the browned lawn of a small mosque. He dropped his bags and sprawled against them with the carrying straps looped around his arms in case the local boys got any ideas. He

quickly fell asleep, this time dreaming—jumbled images of long drives through the dust with people he didn't recognize, a sense that he could barely keep his eyes open, and no one saying a word he could understand. A few hours later he again came awake to the sound of gunfire, wondering if this would always be the case here.

There was another sound, too—the throb of a helicopter. He stood stiffly, nearly tripping in the tangle of straps. Some of Bashir's men were pointing and jabbering. The boys he'd seen earlier ducked in and out of doorways, reminding him of prairie dogs at the zoo. A long-ago field trip with his children flashed to mind, taking Carol by the hand as she squealed with delight at the darting, bobbing prairie dogs, poking heads from their dusty caves, her tiny hand sticky from cotton candy, the smell of manure and of popcorn. None of that here. Just a herd of scrawny goats milling in the roadway ahead, oblivious to the fuss and oblivious to Skelly and his memories.

Then he saw the chopper, a small blob of dark green against the sky but moving fast. It was at least a mile away, corkscrewing upward as if trying to get clear of the valley. He heard what he thought was the *whoosh* of a shell, but there was no flash or contrail. Perhaps it had been an echo, some merging of other noises. Then there was a distant explosion, and the chopper reared up and banked away, roaring over the ridgeline and disappearing across the mountains. Skelly hadn't seen any markings, so he couldn't say whether it had been American. He knew colleagues who could have identified the make and model even from this distance, but he had never been good at that. To him every small helicopter was a Cobra and every big one was a Huey.

"We will be leaving soon."

It was Najeeb, approaching from behind. He saw now that the trucks were gone.

"Where's the rest of our stuff?"

"They loaded the generator and sat phone onto horses. We will carry the rest. Bashir has radioed ahead for more horses to meet us on the other side of a gorge."

"We're crossing a gorge on foot? This could take a while."

"Apparently there is a bridge. But we have to hike there first."

And so they did, walking a mile across the valley, then three more miles steadily uphill, the trail narrowing as the switchbacks steepened. Skelly gasped for breath. The air was so dry that the sweat evaporated almost the moment it surfaced, and his back was soon itchy with salt.

He was relieved to finally reach the rim of the gorge until he saw the bridge—a small wooden platform dangling from a steel cable that stretched fifty yards across a barren, yawning ravine, forming a sagging parabola above a thin, muddy river three hundred feet below. The river was so shrunken by drought that it looked more like a series of brown puddles among the chalk-white stones.

"I guess now we know why the horses have to meet us on the other side," Skelly said. "We'll have to cross one at a time on that thing."

"That thing" was a platform attached to the cable by a pulley wheel. The idea was to pull yourself across by tugging on a long rope, attached at either end of the gorge. Gravity would presumably take you halfway, and even a bit beyond if you simply let go. The platform itself—a few splintery planks that had seen better days—was only about four feet by four feet, and there were no rails or restraints except the support posts at each corner. They arched upward to a joint just below the pulley. Otherwise there was nothing to prevent you or your baggage from sliding into the gorge.

Bashir's men didn't seem bothered at all by this, and one by one the first eight of them scrambled aboard and pulled his way across with the ease of alpinists rappelling the face of a cliff. Then it was Skelly's turn. Bashir insisted that he travel across not only with his bag and satchel but also with the generator, which left no room to spare.

He climbed aboard uncertainly while Najeeb held the platform steady, seating himself diagonally with his back pressed against a corner post. He slid his legs around the bags while nudging the generator against the post in the opposite corner.

"Ready?" Najeeb asked, looking concerned.

"Ready as I'll ever be."

Najeeb handed him the rope, and Skelly began to let out length, foot by foot. Some of the men shouted, obviously wanting him to let go, to get moving, but he was having none of that, proceeding hand over hand at a deliberate pace to minimize the swaying. A third of the way across, however, he realized his mistake, and probably the reason for their shouting. If he didn't soon gain more speed on the descent then he'd have a much tougher haul uphill to the finish. So, holding his breath, he let go, feeling the platform give way in a burst of speed while the wheel whined against the cable overhead.

When the platform lost momentum he would have to grab the rope to prevent backsliding, but he must have done the job awkwardly

because the platform tipped violently, swaying with a harsh creak of wood and metal. The generator slid sideways, only worsening the sway, and Skelly had no choice but to lunge forward, grabbing a post with one hand while reaching for the generator with the other. The platform tipped ever more violently, and for one precarious moment the whole contraption seemed to dangle like a trapeze artist, the works creaking overhead.

Skelly held on for all he was worth. The brown pools stared up from below. There wasn't even the hint of a breeze, and from behind he heard a gale of laughter from Bashir's men. His fury overcame his panic, and he slowly pulled himself and the generator into balance while Najeeb offered a shout of encouragement from behind.

"Steady yourself with the towline. Pull it tight."

Skelly complied, letting go of the generator as the platform came level. There was an alarming bit of rocking when he began to pull his way up the incline, but nothing fell into the gorge. From there it was simply a matter of pulling hard until he reached the far side, the rope burning in his palm. He was sweating profusely now, too much even for the dry air to absorb, and when he stepped onto solid ground his rubbery knees nearly gave way. He wanted to shout at the smiling men as they hauled off his gear, but figured he'd earned their derision. Before he could even collect himself Najeeb was at his side, looking none the worse for his own journey across.

"Well, that was entertaining," Skelly said. The worst part was knowing they might have to do it again on the way back.

The horses were waiting as promised—one for each of them plus another half dozen for equipment, tended by an ill-looking pair of men who departed down a side trail after Bashir paid them in American twenties. Skelly had done little riding, but he could handle a trot and a canter, and neither seemed likely in this rough terrain.

"Lean forward going uphill, backward going downhill," Najeeb said.

"That much I know," Skelly replied testily. But he soon discovered just how steeply he'd have to lean. The trail canted wildly up the side of the slope, poorly graded across stones that slid and crumbled with every step. Every few minutes there was a minor slide, and the horses snorted and whinnied, some of them balking. After a nerve-racking half hour Skelly heard a tremendous hissing clatter from behind, like the noise of a giant wave retreating on a shingle beach. He turned

crookedly in the saddle to see a horse on its side, thrashing and pawing in a bed of loose stones some twenty yards below. The rider, thrown clear, was standing shakily, picking up his Kalashnikov as he tried to keep his footing. He sidestepped carefully toward the horse, reaching it a moment later while the rest of the caravan watched in restive silence, saddles creaking. The rider shouted up to Bashir.

"Broken leg," Najeeb translated.

The rider chambered a round in his weapon with a quick tug of his right hand and raised the gun to fire. Bashir halted him with an angry shout.

"'No gunshots,' he's saying." The rider laid down his gun, gently, as if worried that it, too, might slide away. Then he pulled a dagger from a sheath and drew it deftly across the horse's neck. A red fountain of blood burst onto the pale stones, and the animal thrashed briefly, sliding further down the mountain as its whinny turned to a pathetic gurgle, huge eyes rolling back in its head. Skelly turned away, and finally the animal was silent. The rider clambered back to the trail and the column resumed its careful progress, no one saying a word.

A few minutes later Skelly turned back toward Najeeb, whose expression indicated that he wished he were anywhere but here.

"You think this is all part of a trap, don't you?"

Najeeb nodded.

"And not just for Razaq," Najeeb said in a low voice. "Maybe for us, too."

"Not for us. Bashir will still want the story out. The story of Razaq's great failure. Of Bashir's great triumph."

"So he will wait for you to file your story. And then what? You think he will just take us back, safe and sound?"

"Isn't that what you think?"

"Perhaps, *inshallah*. But I have been looking for escape routes, just in case. Everywhere we go, I keep looking for some way out."

"Not a bad idea. Found one yet?"

Najeeb shook his head.

## CHAPTER TWENTY

THE MEN DISMOUNTED an hour later. Najeeb's back and thighs were already stiff, an embarrassment after so little time in the saddle, the city boy gone soft. He tried not to think of Daliya, or of anything but the hours and days ahead, and whatever surprises might be in store.

It was dusk, and they seemed to be in the middle of nowhere—barren hills as far as the eye could see, the sky darkening except for a rim of bright pink in the west. Some of the men set up small kerosene burners to cook dinner. Others pulled rounds of bread and bunches of blackened bananas from sacks lashed to the horses. Najeeb was hungry, too, but before he had time to dig into their supplies, Bashir approached and said to Skelly, "Your time is here. Come with me."

Skelly cast Najeeb a worried glance, and they followed Bashir to the crest of a small hill.

"Azro," Bashir said, pointing below. The town looked about the same size as Jaji, with a few dim lights already twinkling. "Razaq is there. It is a one-mile walk, and once it is dark you will take it. The path is mined, so a guide will show you the way."

Perfect, Najeeb thought. Stumbling past mines in the dark. He'd end up legless and begging in the Saddar Bazaar.

"What about our gear?" Skelly asked.

"I can spare one horse. Provided you do not blow him up."

"We'll try our best."

Bashir grinned. "Wait here. You will eat now. I will send the guide when it is time. And when you reach Razaq, you will give him a mes-

sage. You will tell him that Bashir is here, waiting on the hill." Noting Skelly's dubious expression, he added, "Do not be so worried. After dark, all of the highwaymen and thieves will be asleep. You will have the path to yourselves until you reach the town. As long as no one in Razaq's rear guard panics and opens fire, you should reach him safely."

"I thought *you* were his rear guard?" Skelly asked anxiously.

Bashir shrugged. "Plans change."

"Under whose orders?"

"Those things change as well."

Bashir said nothing more, merely turned and walked back toward his men.

So it was true, then. Razaq's expedition was doomed unless the man could fight his way out, and they would now become the messengers of his betrayal—as long as they weren't shot first. Najeeb looked at Skelly, who seemed dazed as he turned toward his bag of supplies.

"Well, I suppose it's still a good story," Skelly said weakly.

"If you ever get to file it."

"Don't you think Bashir will insist? That *is* why he brought us along." Skelly's tone was hopeful now, almost pleading. Why not give the man the answer he wanted? It came with the job, even if all Najeeb really wanted to do was disappear into the hills.

"Yes, I suppose."

Skelly nodded forlornly but said nothing more.

Najeeb had lost his appetite, but he forced down a little bread and water while Skelly ate beans from a can. For the next several minutes they were silent, resting in a sprawl across stones and dust. Then a thin wailing crept up the hillside from the town. Skelly shifted in alarm until Najeeb reminded him it was only the evening call to prayer. Even in a lost little place like Azro there was an amplified speaker, probably powered by batteries.

"Why don't you pray for us?" Skelly said.

The request took Najeeb by surprise. To date, all of his Western clients had been either Christian or Jew, yet they had been almost uniform in their lack of belief, as if the skepticism required by their profession had overridden even the greatest of life's certainties.

"You could pray, too," Najeeb said. "Do you ever pray?"

"Not often. And usually just for trivial things, or lost causes. 'Please God, let him make this free throw.' 'Please God, don't let me run out of gas.' I doubt my prayers would do us much good. Your god's probably stronger here."

"There is no God but God."

It was the closest Najeeb had ever come to expressing piousness to a foreigner, but he figured Skelly had probably written off his previous displays of devotion as the rote workings of tradition more than faith, an impression that needed correcting. Not that Najeeb was suddenly feeling like some sort of fanatic. But Skelly, like most Americans he'd met, seemed unable to fathom the concept that you could believe every last holy word yet still not be a raving fundamentalist.

"You're right, of course," Skelly answered, fumbling for words. "But maybe you should pray for both of us anyway, since you're the one with actual faith. Pray for our safety and deliverance. Or are Muslims even allowed to ask for that sort of thing?"

"Of course. All of that and more." Then, with a touch of irreverence, "We can even request the vanquishing of our tormentors."

"Then by all means, go for it." Skelly smiled. "Now if we only knew for sure who our tormentors were. Or what we were walking into."

Najeeb surprised himself by returning the smile, dropping the Pashtun mask for a moment as he felt a stirring of kinship for this lonely man. He wondered if he would have allowed himself the luxury if the situation hadn't seemed so hopeless. Whatever the case, he now felt more relaxed, and better prepared for whatever awaited them at the bottom of the hill. Perhaps other rules could work in this terrain as well as the ones he had grown up with, as long as one applied them sparingly.

He stepped away to a more level patch of ground, where he smoothed a spot for his knees. Then he knelt, for once not minding that Skelly was watching so carefully, as if searching for signs of falseness. He bowed his forehead nearly to the ground, then straightened, praying with his hands held upward, palms open to God. He recited a few words just as the loudspeaker from the town went silent with a staticky click, the last threads of the thin, nasal voice trailing off into haunting echoes.

A minute or so later Najeeb stood, brushing off his knees. By now there was quite a chill in the air, and Skelly pulled a fleece jacket from his bag, zipping it to the neck.

"So can you read all of the Koran?" Skelly asked. "A lot of Muslims I've met only knew a few prayers. They didn't have enough Arabic for the rest."

"You have just described my entire family. My entire village, for that matter."

"But not you?"

"I learned Arabic later. In the States."

Skelly chuckled. "Now there's irony."

"Yes. Taught by an infidel, no less. Probably with the wrong accent, too. But I learned to read it pretty well, and the Koran is good practice."

"Is it as beautiful as everyone says? The English translation isn't. I tried reading it once, only got about halfway. Too much smiting and damnation. Very Old Testament, pardon the expression. But I've always wondered how it reads in Arabic."

"It *is* beautiful. Poetry."

"I guess that makes it easier to be devout."

"Maybe. Or maybe it would have if I had learned Arabic here, instead of in America. By then I was already a backslider. I had discovered your country's holy trinity."

Skelly looked astounded. "You converted?"

"Not *that* holy trinity. I meant supermarkets, libraries and women. Three heavens of such plenty that I gave up religion for a while just to worship them."

"That's my kind of backsliding. We're more alike all the time." He settled himself onto a large, flat stone with a nice view, although by now the town of Azro was barely visible in the deepening gloom. In the silence that followed Najeeb expected their easy mood to die away, overwhelmed by their worries. But somehow it lingered, as if Najeeb's prayers—some of them, at least—were being answered.

Najeeb wondered how Skelly must view all of this—all these tribesmen with their Stone Age amenities and their warriors on horseback, living by firelight on bread cooked in clay pits, then cast upon the floor. The American would doubtless use the word "primitive," which was how home had sometimes seemed to Najeeb on his return trips from Chapel Hill or, once, from a post-exam visit to New York, with the city's noises still ringing in his ears, a thrilling symphony that had roared up out of steam grates and down from towering glass summits. Yet here they were now, ever deeper in the world that had produced him, in a valley where the power grid was smashed and water was still hauled from the ground by the bucketful.

"How did you fare with American women?" Skelly asked, breaking the silence. "I bet you were a big hit. The Omar Sharif look. You must have been fighting them off with a stick."

"It was not like that at all. Or maybe I was just never greedy about it. They took some getting used to."

"The way they flirted, you mean? All that Western assertiveness?"

"Not that." Najeeb smiled again, recalling his college years. Two smiles in ten minutes—a new cross-border record for him. "It was the way they talked. All of the questions, like an interrogation. 'What are you thinking, Najeeb?' 'A penny for your thoughts.' I had to stop myself from saying, 'None of your damn business,' the way people from my village did whenever someone asked a nosy question. For a while I was certain I should have been offended, that they were only asking because I was a curiosity, their little brown pet."

"Oh, no. It's what they want from all of us. And it never stops. If you'd stayed any longer you would have learned that. Unless you start telling them what you're really thinking. Then they're usually so appalled they never ask again."

This actually drew a laugh, and Skelly joined in, although they kept it subdued, not wanting to draw attention from farther uphill. And with that unspoken realization threatening to topple the moment's frail structure, Najeeb rushed to steady it.

"So you make up some of your answers, too?" he asked.

"Don't we all, at one time or another? What was your approach?"

"I always thought they were expecting me to be soulful, the sage of the East. So I gave them soulful. Long, contemplative answers about home, about growing up in a rough land of bullies and tyrants. But sometimes I think that is what I really did have on my mind. So maybe they were right to pry."

"Or maybe you were just homesick."

"Maybe I was."

Silence for a few seconds more, but Skelly wasn't finished.

"What about the women here? What did you say your girlfriend's name was?"

"Now *you* are being like a woman, wanting to know too much."

Skelly conceded the point, as if realizing he'd crossed the line. But Najeeb decided to answer anyway, albeit in a quieter voice.

"Her name is Daliya. She seems a million miles from here. She asks questions, too, but always waits for the real answers. So I tell her the truth, maybe because she has earned it. She has had to give up even more than I have for us to be together."

"Must be scary, having to go to all that trouble just to have a date."

"Yes. Sometimes it is."

"Must be nice, too, in a way. I'm not sure any woman would do that for me."

"Not your wife?"

Skelly shrugged. "Maybe. But look at me now. Off on the far side of the world while my wife is stuck at home. Who'd take a risk for someone like that?"

"Your marriage sounds very Pashtun, you know. The man goes where he pleases, the women are stuck in purdah."

"The American Midwest as a sort of purdah." Skelly grunted with amusement. "Works for me. Not sure how they'd feel about it in Illinois, though."

A voice from behind broke the spell. It was Bashir, carrying a lantern, and he wasn't alone. Beside him was a small boy, maybe ten or eleven. Bashir held the reins of a packhorse loaded with the generator and satellite phone.

"It is time," he said. "This one will lead you."

"He's our guide?" Skelly asked.

"He is from Azro. He knows the trails."

"Even where the mines are?"

Bashir muttered something to the boy, who thrust out his right arm to reveal a skinny rounded stump where a hand should have been. He grinned, crooked teeth stained a deep brown. He wore a small white skullcap and a gray wool *kameez* drooping nearly to his ankles.

"As you can see, he has experience with mines. So he will take extra care to avoid them. Give him your flashlight, and you will be on your way."

Skelly complied. Najeeb glanced around, as if some means of escape might suddenly reveal itself. But no further prayers would be answered tonight, it seemed, and when the boy flicked on the beam every route but the one toward Azro was plunged into blackness. The boy made his way forward. It was time to go.

"Remember to deliver my message," Bashir said. "Take it to Razaq personally."

"And will we see you again?" Skelly asked, his voice tightening in the darkness. Najeeb wasn't sure what answer he wanted to hear.

"I cannot say. All is in God's hands now. Tomorrow will tell."

That didn't strike Najeeb as good news, either for them or for Razaq. Escape still sounded like the best option. But even if he had

known which way to go from here, he wouldn't do it now, not on a mined path. And not without Skelly, either, he realized. Another new rule for this landscape, he supposed—looking out for someone else. A foolhardy way to live, but he would have to try. Then he took the reins of the packhorse in hand and faced downhill toward the dim lights of the town. The boy was looking back over his shoulder, waiting for the signal to proceed.

"Okay," Skelly said, in a husky voice. "Let's get going."

They began picking their way down the slope, moving with care, Najeeb straining his eyes in the darkness for anything that looked like a mine or a wire. The going was slow but certain, and the boy's movements exuded a reassuring confidence. Halfway down the hill the boy stopped, directing the flashlight beam at a small green box, which Najeeb recognized right away.

"Mine," the boy said, as matter-of-factly as if he'd just pointed out a flower.

"See it?" Najeeb asked Skelly. "There's a wire coming out of the left side."

Skelly nodded grimly, then stepped left, giving the mine a wide berth. Najeeb stayed close in his wake. Their progress brought an animated cry from the boy.

"No, no!" he squealed, the light dancing back and forth. They stopped dead.

"There!" he hissed. "Another one. You see?"

Najeeb translated the warning for the frozen Skelly, then watched the narrow beam probe like a searchlight before settling on a second green box just ahead. Two more steps and Skelly would have tripped it.

"Jesus!" Skelly hissed, gingerly backing away while Najeeb tried to control the horse, which still wanted to move forward.

"Easy," he cooed, patting the horse on the neck.

"What's that biblical verse about passing a camel through the eye of a needle?" Skelly said. "Now I know what it meant."

Najeeb kept his eyes on the horse's hooves, watching them clop on the stony ground like clumsy hammers. But they managed to get safely past both mines, plus two more during the next hundred yards, the boy pausing to illuminate each as if they were stops on a guided tour. Then he spoke up, delivering good news.

"He says that's the last one," Najeeb said.

"Good. Now we worry about the guns."

They'd come to within a quarter mile of the town, where a few windows were lit dimly by kerosene lamps and cookfires. Najeeb smelled wood smoke, the char of grilled meat. A moment later a voice called out in Pashtun from just ahead, and the boy froze, raising the stump of his left hand in a signal to halt. The mines hadn't frightened him a bit, but now his whole body was rigid. He shouted back in reply, the voice shrill and tight in the cold air.

"What's happening?" Skelly whispered.

"Razaq's sentries. The boy's telling them there are three of us, all unarmed."

After a pause that seemed interminable, the sentry gave the all-clear. The boy dropped his handless arm to his side and continued, and by the time they reached the edge of the village a welcoming party had assembled—five bearded men in skullcaps and turbans, each scowling and holding a gun, indistinguishable from the fellows who'd been traveling with Bashir.

One came forward, and Najeeb recognized him as Razaq's younger brother, Salim, who had greeted them at the warlord's house in Hayatabad. Salim, too, was scowling, but at last he spoke up, keeping everything in Pashto for a few sentences before he turned and stalked away.

"He's gone to tell Razaq," Najeeb said.

"Did you tell him we've come from the rear guard?"

"I think we had better break that news to Razaq himself."

"What do you think he'll do with us? Kick us out? Send us back up the hill? I'm sure as hell not going without a guide."

"He won't kick us out. Not tonight. It wouldn't be permitted."

"By who?"

"By every law he was ever raised with. *Pashtunwali*, the code of the Pashtun. He is obligated by *malmastiya* to show us hospitality, because now we are his guests."

"Uninvited guests."

"Guests all the same. We will be safe here."

"As long as Razaq is safe, you mean."

"Yes."

They said nothing more until Salim returned, nodding for them to follow.

The town of Azro looked just like Jaji, but the presence of Razaq's men seemed to have cleared the streets of the requisite crowds of boys

and animals, and the place was quiet. Salim led them to a brightly lit doorway where a hissing camp lantern hung from a hand-carved wooden pillar. Two sentries slouched at the entrance, barely stirring as Skelly and Najeeb followed Salim into a long room of whitewashed walls. Heavy dark beams were slung across the low ceiling.

Razaq squatted on the floor, legs crossed, at the end of a red rectangular Oriental rug. Six other men were seated around it—some sort of *jirga* must have been in progress. Piled in the middle were the remains of a dinner, platters and bowls of rice, tomatoes, braised chunks of mutton. A stack of bread sat near Razaq. The entire village had probably contributed, even if it meant giving the last scrap from the larder. That, too, was tradition.

There was an empty tea tray with a blackened pot, and Razaq gestured for a refill, then turned to Salim for an explanation, although by now it was obvious that he recognized his visitors. Razaq nodded as he listened, but at the conclusion he did not rise to greet them, nor did anyone else. A bad sign, Najeeb thought, doubting that Skelly realized it. Then Razaq addressed them in English.

"This is quite a surprise, Mr. Kelly, and although you are welcome here as my guest, I cannot say that it is a pleasant surprise. But as long as you are here, please."

He gestured to his right, where two of the men scuttled away on their haunches to make room. Razaq stood, and Skelly approached clumsily with outstretched hand. Razaq seemed reluctant to shake it, but finally did, and when Skelly then placed a hand over his heart Razaq followed suit.

"My apologies, gentlemen," Razaq said in Pashto to the other six. "But I must speak with our guests alone. We will finish our business later." They stood without a word, eyeing Skelly suspiciously as they filed toward the door.

Najeeb settled into place while Skelly took out his notebook.

"I must say, Mr. Kelly, that I seem to have vastly underestimated you. But tell me, if you will, by what route you came, and who was your escort? Or did you simply come alone, with your tribal friend here?" Razaq took a bite of bread, glancing significantly at Najeeb, who suspected that Razaq knew plenty about him and his past. Had the man learned some of the juicier details from Tariq at the ISI, perhaps? Or from his American friends?

"Well, actually . . ." Skelly hesitated. "We came with what we were

*told* was your rear guard. A little more than twenty men. We've been following you since early yesterday."

Razaq stopped chewing. Skelly seemed on the verge of an apology, but Razaq's stony expression stopped him. The man's mood seemed quite grave now that the parlor trick of the journalist's sudden appearance had turned into something more complicated.

"A rear guard, you say. And who is leading these men?"

"Some fellow who calls himself Bashir."

"Bashir? The smuggler who lives in Katchagarhi?"

Skelly didn't have an answer, so Razaq looked to Najeeb, who nodded.

"You knew he was a smuggler?" Skelly asked, sounding hurt.

"It would be his obvious occupation," Najeeb said. "Living in the middle of the camp with all those trucks and weapons."

"And given that he works for Haji Kudrat," Razaq said.

"Who's Haji Kudrat?" Skelly asked.

The name was familiar to Najeeb, but only vaguely, as someone to be reckoned with. He had a dim memory of a face from some long-ago council of his father's. Had Haji Kudrat been some sort of trading partner?

Razaq hadn't answered, so Skelly asked again.

"This Kudrat," he said. "I'm presuming he's not a friend."

"That remains to be seen. But he is an important man in Nangarhār Province, which is our destination tomorrow. And knowing that his man Bashir is on the road behind us, well, that might explain several things."

"Such as."

"This was supposed to be the first of my great rendezvous points, Mr. Kelly. Do you remember all of those visitors you saw at my house?"

"The ones on the lawn?"

"On the lawn. In the kitchen. They were practically everywhere but in the women's quarters. They were from Afghanistan, mostly. From the north and south of here, in Nangarhār and Paktīā provinces, and also from here in Logar Province. For three weeks these men came to pay tribute, village elders and tribal *maliks*. Some of them were old fighters who had been with me against the Russians. One was the elder of this town, of Azro, and he gave me his solemn word that he would greet me here today with a full fifty men, ready to join up."

"To join your army that isn't really an army, you mean?"

"However you wish to put it. Yet I arrived this afternoon to find that he is away on other business, somewhere farther up the valley. A most unfortunate snub. And as a result, do you know how many men have come to join my cause here in Azro?"

Skelly shook his head.

"Seven. Only seven. And now you tell me that twenty others are on the hilltop, looking down on us and our cookfires."

By now Razaq was smoldering. It probably would have been best to let him ride out the moment in silence, but Najeeb could tell that Skelly had no intention of letting up. The man's pencil made a scratching sound as he rapidly took notes, flipping a page as he opened his mouth for another question. He was like a sparrow in pursuit of a crumb, and Najeeb feared for him, remembering that hungry sparrows often didn't notice an approaching predator until it was too late.

"You're saying you've been betrayed, then," Skelly asked with appalling bluntness.

Razaq glowered, shifting on his haunches. "You speak of betrayal as if it is something dishonorable, Mr. Kelly."

"How else would you describe it?" Still scribbling, still forging ahead. Najeeb would have placed a hand on his arm in warning, but he was too far away. Although Razaq, to his credit, seemed to be calming, as if he, too, now sensed the absurdity of this foreigner in their midst, peppering the players with nettlesome questions as they postured and preened for battle.

"It is dishonorable only in the sense that a Westerner might understand it," Razaq said. "Perhaps your friend here, Najeeb Azam, the son of a *malik*, could explain it for you. He can tell you all about betrayal, and what it means in our culture."

The words took him aback. Najeeb was now more certain than ever that Razaq knew chapter and verse of his family dramas. But the insult had gone right over Skelly's head. The American was still in pursuit of his story, pencil poised, eyes imploring. He really seemed to be expecting some sort of cultural explanation, so Najeeb tried to oblige.

"It is complicated," he said. So was their current predicament, he wanted to add, but didn't dare. How to explain, for example, that here it was perfectly acceptable to receive two guests with courtesy and generosity, yet still have them tracked down and killed the moment they left your territory? From here on out, Skelly and he might well be in

danger from anyone they encountered, no matter who emerged victorious from whatever strange storm was brewing. But look at Skelly, eager to learn yet slouched and uncomfortable on the carpet. He was more accustomed to interviews done on chairs and couches, seated upright at desktops and conference tables with men who lied for different reasons, playing by different rules. Deceit here took shapes he never would have dreamed of.

"Betrayal is a skill here," Najeeb said finally. "An art. Even an honorable one, in its way. Maybe because it is always expected of an adversary."

"But who *are* your adversaries?" Skelly asked, turning back toward Razaq. "Beyond the obvious ones, of course. And who are your friends? And what is it you're really after? Surely you can lay it out for me now that we're here?"

Razaq lowered his gaze, as if collecting himself. Then he turned toward Najeeb, who could have sworn he detected a glint of anger in the man's expression.

"Perhaps I can," Razaq said. "But for the moment there are still too many of us in this room for me to feel comfortable."

Skelly stopped writing and looked up, seeming surprised to find Razaq staring at Najeeb.

"All of this must be terribly dull for your interpreter, Mr. Kelly," Razaq said, holding his gaze, "especially since I am speaking in English, making his services unnecessary. So before we continue why don't you send him along. He can arrange the night's lodgings for the two of you."

"Sure," Skelly answered uncertainly. "Go ahead, Najeeb. I'll be along later."

Razaq called for a sentry, who led Najeeb into the night. Now what had all that been about? Najeeb wondered. Perhaps he, too, needed a cultural translation, a refresher course now that he was back in the hills.

Did Razaq's anger have something to do with his father? With a new war in progress, his family's little frontage on the border was again strategically vital, presenting all sorts of new business opportunities. Razaq had crossed without incident, but so had Bashir. Maybe that was the problem.

"Come this way," the sentry said brusquely, and Najeeb followed him down the verandah. It was bitterly cold. Distant campfires now

flickered on the facing hillside—Bashir's men, he supposed, no longer even bothering to hide their presence. Maybe Bashir was watching at this very moment, gazing down through his night-vision binoculars.

So what were their choices now? Stay with Razaq and expect the worst, or try to go back to Bashir and be blasted by a mine. Was there a third way, some route out of this mess altogether? He would pray, asking for guidance, then sleep on it. Perhaps his dreams would bring an answer.

But the sight of the campfires told him that any answer had better come soon.

# CHAPTER TWENTY-ONE

SKELLY SQUATTED in silence, his toes going numb in the cold. The only sound in the room was the hissing of the lantern by the door. Razaq hadn't said a word since Najeeb's departure, and the big fellow suddenly struck Skelly as a pouting Buddha, affronted by this latest twist of the cosmos. The man's best-laid plans were going to hell in a handbasket, and he obviously blamed his visitors. How else to explain Najeeb's abrupt banishment, unless it was some sort of tribal class snub.

"You will excuse me for a moment," Razaq said, breaking the silence, then rising with surprising grace to leave the room, headed God knows where while a baffled Skelly waited.

Skelly decided to stretch his legs, stamping his feet as the blood rushed to his toes. His back was stiff. It must be forty degrees down on that floor. He rubbed his arms for warmth, stepping to the doorway in hopes of another glance at Azro, but the stern glare of a sentry nudged him back inside.

The hiss and pop of the lantern was even louder by the door, and Skelly could smell the burning fuel. It was an oddly comforting sensation, calling him back to boyhood campouts and weekends in the woods, pleasant images that brought warmth—an evening campfire with a column of sparks rising to the treetop blackness, marshmallow impaled on a whittled stick, gentle voice of his father reminding him not to hold it too close to the flame, Skelly ignoring it because what he really wanted was the burst of fire, a tiny conflagration he could blow out, then consume in a gooey crunch of blackened ash.

The sentry stirred, and Skelly stepped back from the doorway, feeling the cold again. In lulls like these he could sometimes detach himself just enough to view the scenery with a fresh outlook, as if borrowing the eyes of some old and distant relative who'd never ventured beyond the seat of a tour bus. It was a fine way of reawakening to all sorts of sights he'd already stopped noticing.

But this time the trick failed him, and he only slipped farther into memory—still warmed by that campfire, his father's presence palpable just over his shoulder. A quarter turn and he would see the man's face, the young version, ambered by firelight. Instead he saw the face as it had looked only a year ago, on a visit to the nursing home. His father lived there alone. Skelly's mother was dead eight years, killed by a stroke while he traipsed across Africa. He'd met his father in the TV room, joining eight other residents in staring at the blaring box. Drawn, translucent faces lit blue and orange by the jolting image, no one saying a word. His old man irretrievable, swimming deeper in his memories than even Skelly could go. Every resident was equipped with either a walker or a wheelchair, and two canes were propped by the door—enough metal to build a B-17, he remembered thinking. His father blinked, turned toward the television, where a news report from Poland was flashing past. Then he blinked again, barely stirring. An agonizing half hour passed without the least sign of recognition before Skelly waved good-bye to the nurses and strolled to his car, crossing a vast empty parking lot by a roaring expressway.

"We will have tea now."

It was Razaq, returning in a regal billow. A servant in tow carried a steaming tea tray. Get back to work, Skelly. Clear your head and take out your notebook. Remember to ask about Najeeb. Remember to ask about Hartley and Pierce, and about Bashir and that whole Bin Laden business.

They settled themselves on the rug, the servant pouring tea, then departing. Skelly realized he was hungry, and took a wedge of bread from the tray, chewing off a bite, then balancing the rest on his knees.

"There is something you should know about your translator," Razaq began. "Several days ago, not long after speaking with my youngest son in the lobby of the Pearl Continental, he was seen coming and going from an unmarked door in the Saddar Bazaar."

"I know," Skelly said. "Local office of the ISI. He told me all about it."

Razaq plowed on.

"And did he also tell you what they asked of him in return for letting him go?"

"No. Why don't you tell me?"

"I am not privy to that. But I would guess they wanted information. They probably wanted to know what my son told him, and they will probably expect a full report from the field."

"Is that so surprising?"

"Not at all. And I would not have given it a second thought if he had not come across the hills in the company of this man Bashir, arriving in my camp like his personal courier."

"We're no friends of Bashir's, and Najeeb would have preferred to have skipped the trip altogether."

"Or so he tells you. But tell me something. This telephone that you brought. The one on your horse. May I see it?"

Skelly shrugged. "Sure."

Razaq's request was only a formality, because when he motioned toward the door the servant immediately reentered carrying the phone, which he had already removed from its carrying bag. He placed it by the tea tray while Skelly took another bite of bread. Razaq made a show of turning the phone this way and that, then placed it back on the rug.

"A very nice model," Razaq said. "Do you not think so?"

"Nice enough. But I'm no expert."

"Ah, but some of my other American friends are. The ones who provided my own telephone, for instance. Which is just like yours. Identical. Do you not find that curious?"

"Maybe it's a popular brand."

"Or maybe it has been acquired through similar channels."

"Or by a similar agency. Is that what you're trying to say?"

"I am trying to say you should ask Najeeb how he came by it. Perhaps he is not in the ISI's permanent employ, but he may have made promises that you are not aware of. I know for myself that he has already betrayed his own father to these people, so why would he not betray you or me just as easily?"

Well, now. That got his attention. Skelly thought this issue had been put to rest, but maybe he should have asked more questions. Was this why Najeeb always bristled at any mention of his family? Or maybe Razaq was exaggerating, or trying to distract him. Don't forget the story, Skelly.

"Okay, then. I'll ask him. But I have questions for you, too."

Razaq spread his hands to show he had nothing to hide, but he couldn't resist another goading glance at the phone, as if it might be recording their every word. Skelly ignored it and got straight to the point.

"What exactly are you trying to accomplish with this expedition of yours, anyway? And no more of this peace and brotherhood bullshit, if you don't mind. Convening the elders to discuss a better tomorrow is great, but if you were hoping to pick up fifty recruits here in Azro, then obviously you're raising a war party."

"Perhaps I am. Or was. Not because I thought I could win any great victories, and certainly I never expected anything so grand as capturing Kabul. My only wish is to establish a base of operations, a stronghold for myself and my people, so we will still have a voice in our own affairs on that inevitable day when the Taliban retreats and the Northern Alliance arrives."

"And so you'll have a top seat in any new government?"

"You find that objectionable?"

"I find it enterprising. And I'd guess that your American backers—the ones who gave you the nice phone—do, too."

"They did until recently. In the past week they seem to have changed their minds."

"The Americans?"

Razaq nodded.

"Maybe they decided to put their money on Karzai in the south," Skelly said.

Razaq smiled, patronizing him. "If their true interest was in the future of Afghanistan, perhaps I would believe that, too. But their plans for me have nothing to do with my interests, or my country's. They want to put me in place as a sheriff, a posse. Someone to seal the border once they begin chasing their prime suspect. The one everyone here calls the Sheik."

"Bin Laden?"

"Whatever you wish to call him."

"But the border's long, and your part of it is small. Even if you succeed."

"Unless they know of someone on the other side who is willing to welcome him, once he has worn out his welcome here. Perhaps that part of the border is also small, small enough even for someone like me to block it, or to influence where any crossing should occur."

"Making you the gatekeeper."

Razaq said nothing, but nodded slightly, as if conceding the point.

"Bashir mentioned Bin Laden," Skelly said. "He seemed to be convinced that we might 'cross paths,' or something like that, with a few Arabs. All very cryptic. Then to sell it he showed me a few business cards from a couple of Americans. Friends of mine. One of them, anyway. Sam Hartley and Arlen Pierce. Heard of them?"

At last it was Razaq's turn to look surprised. He even seemed to sag a bit, covering his reaction with a sip of tea.

"Mr. Hartley. Of course," he said finally, recovering his composure. "The man from the pipeline company. I would guess that half the men in Peshawar have one of his business cards by now. And most of them have probably been promised one thing or another."

There was no mention of Arlen Pierce, however, and when it seemed that this might be all Razaq had to say on the subject, Skelly offered a prod.

"I ran into Hartley in Peshawar. Over at the Pearl. Your name came up."

"Did it indeed?" Razaq lowered his gaze, again raising his teacup but not sipping this time. "I am curious, Mr. Kelly. What sort of thing does Mr. Hartley say to a fellow Westerner about someone like me?"

"He wasn't very optimistic about your chances. I think the words he used were, 'The fix is in.' Then he advised me not to get mixed up with you."

"Perhaps it is because he finds me frustrating. Mr. Hartley would prefer that I show a little more zeal where his commercial interests are concerned. I have made it clear that my own agenda comes first. But I think he knows I will be receptive to his overtures when the proper time comes."

"So who's this friend of Bashir's you're worried about farther up the road? This Haji Kudrat."

"A friend of the Taliban. Who tomorrow will no longer be a friend of the Taliban, if that is what suits him."

"Very flexible of him. And no friend of yours, I take it."

"Our families have a history, as you might put it. But I would not worry so much about Haji Kudrat. Not with the backing I have."

"And you still believe in this backing? Even with Bashir on your tail and a poor turnout by the locals?"

"Considering the role they want me to play, why shouldn't I believe

in it? Bashir is a complication, a dangerous one. But I have dealt with complications before, and so have the Americans."

Razaq either truly believed it or was putting up a brave front. Either way, he was in too deep now to do anything but continue, and either way Skelly now had a fine story to tell. Ideas began taking shape in his head in the form of headlines, circling his mind like impatient petitioners in a waiting room: "Pro-West Warlord Crosses Border, But Support Mysteriously Fizzles." "Warlord Enters Afghanistan; Has a Rival Preempted His Plans?"

Razaq stood. Obviously the interview was over.

Skelly also stood, his toes again numb. He reached for the telephone, but Razaq's voice cut him short.

"I must request that you not yet file any dispatches."

Skelly straightened, prepared to argue his case. "Why? Obviously your enemies know you're here. A day-old report in my paper won't make any difference."

"All the same, I will keep your phone awhile longer. It will be returned, of course, when we reach our destination."

Skelly bit his tongue, lest he say something intemperate. So much for his exclusive, he thought furiously, and so much for his plans to check in with Janine tonight. Another fine beginning, and God only knew what tomorrow would bring.

Razaq was on his way out the door, phone in hand, but Skelly had one more question.

"You never told me where we're headed," he said. "Tomorrow, I mean."

"North. Onward to Nangarhār Province. Twenty-five kilometers in all, and a full day in the saddle. In the evening there will be another *jirga* in the town of Heserak, where others will join me."

"And if there's another poor turnout?"

"Then we will never reach Heserak without a fight. It is Haji Kudrat's road we will be traveling, and the valley leading to Heserak passes through the Ali Khel Gorge. If he intends to stop us, that is where he will try."

"You sound like you're speaking from experience."

"It was always a lucky place for me against the Russians. A few rounds of RPGs and you could stop an entire tank column. One day we got three."

"Three tanks?"

"Haji Kudrat and I, fighting together."

"How quickly they forget."

"As you said. He is a flexible man. And he may yet change his loyalties, once he sees the sort of backing I have."

If you still have it, Skelly thought, wondering what Hartley and Pierce were up to.

"Tell me this, then. If you really don't want the story out, why talk to me at all? I mean, hell, I might find a carrier pigeon and send it out in longhand."

Razaq smiled for the first time, although it was the pained smile of a man with too many worries.

"Perhaps I have decided that you may have your uses, after all. If for some unforeseen reason I fail, Mr. Kelly, I want someone who will be able to hold others accountable."

Meaning the Americans? Perhaps the man had a few doubts, after all. But Skelly didn't like being thought of as some sort of insurance policy.

"Be ready to leave at sunrise," Razaq said. "You and your translator." He spoke the last word with a sneer, then disappeared through the door.

Skelly would be ready, all right. He wouldn't miss this one for the world.

# CHAPTER TWENTY-TWO

NAJEEB LAY AWAKE under his blankets in the dark. The only sound from the town was an occasional passing conversation, and he didn't like what he was hearing. For the past half hour he had been trying to dream up a way out of this mess, and he was pretty sure he had come up with one.

A flashlight beam shone through the slatted door, and the next voice he heard was Skelly's.

"Damned dark out here, isn't it?" Skelly stepped inside, clipping his light to a dead electrical wire dangling from the ceiling. "Jesus, it's filthy in here."

"I don't think this *hujera* is used much anymore, except by boys and animals."

"Are we the former or the latter? After two days without a shower I'm not sure." Skelly groped for his sleeping bag.

"They came and took our phone while you were gone. The generator, too."

"Heard about the phone," Skelly said, tossing aside the bag, then looking straight at Najeeb. "Razaq had it. He was asking where you got it. Said I should ask you, but he seemed to have a pretty good idea."

So that was why Razaq had been upset. Najeeb wondered whose informants had been talking to whom and what they had been saying about him. Whatever the case, it was time to level with Skelly. Otherwise they were finished, and he found himself deeply regretting the possibility.

"The ISI gave it to me," he said, holding Skelly's gaze. "One of their supervisors, a man named Tariq."

"You might have told me. What else have you been holding back?"

"What else do you want to know?"

"Razaq seemed to think you have a history of this."

"Of what?"

"Being an informant. Ratting people out."

"Like my father, you mean. That was the only other time."

"Razaq said you betrayed him to the ISI."

"Another case of coercion. Not that I can defend it. My father was in the opium trade. Tariq wanted information, and like a fool I gave it to him. That was seven years ago. I have not been home since."

"I'm sorry." Skelly seemed to mean it. "Guess that explains the reception you got at the checkpoint. The one where they got us out of the truck. That one guy was eyeing you like a trophy. He work for your dad?"

"Yes. I knew him growing up."

"Well, whatever the reason, Razaq is convinced you're now some kind of spy for Bashir."

"No. Just for Tariq. He wanted a full report. On Bashir as well as Razaq."

"Sounds like they don't trust anybody. Either that or the Americans have shut them out of the loop on Razaq. Anything else I should know?"

Najeeb hesitated, then decided why not. "Yes. Daliya—my girl-friend, as you call her—she is still missing. I never found her, and I would not have come with you except Tariq ordered me to. That is when he gave me the phone."

"Ordered you?"

"He would have handed me to the police, who wanted to question me about Daliya's disappearance. And, well . . . also about a body at my apartment building. They found him lying next to a knife from my kitchen. He had been putting religious messages under my door."

"You didn't . . . ?"

"No. I did not. But someone made it look like I did. And now Tariq has me doing whatever he wants, so here I am."

"In one hell of a mess."

"We both are."

"By being with Razaq, you mean."

Najeeb nodded. "I have been listening to his men as they walk by. They are scared, expecting the worst. When Razaq sets out tomorrow, he will find that a few more of them have disappeared."

"He's heading north all the same. Right at the crack of dawn."

"To Heserak?"

Skelly nodded.

"The Ali Khel Gorge," Najeeb said. Just as he had feared.

"He mentioned that. Said it might be trouble."

"Which is why we should avoid it."

"As if we had a choice."

"We do. We can stay behind."

"For you that might work. Razaq might prefer it. But he wants me along as a witness. To tell the world in case somebody does him wrong."

"It doesn't matter. We can still hide you. Right now, if you wanted."

"What about the sentries?"

"We bribe them. Fifty dollars and they will do whatever you want. From what I have been hearing it might not take that much."

"Then where would we go?"

"Into some family's house. Another bribe. A year's worth of income in one of these homes. They will keep us in the back until Razaq's gone. He may want you along, but no way he wastes time searching house to house."

"Then a few hours later Bashir rolls into town and we're right back where we started."

"So we wait a few extra hours. Maybe an extra day. Then Bashir leaves and we work our way back to Peshawar. With the money you have we can hire all of the horses and guides we need."

"Unless someone decides it's more profitable just to rob us and kill us."

"Yes, that is possible, too."

"Look, Najeeb. I know I'm paying you a hundred-fifty a day. But if you want to pack it in, I wouldn't blame you. Razaq's English is good enough that I can make do as long as he's around, so I'm going. Stupid, maybe. But it's my job, not to mention a hell of a story, the biggest I've ever had. I'm no cowboy. Never have been. But if I bail out now then I might as well never have gone into this business. Understand? Besides, if Razaq has the backing he claims, he should make it fine, even if Haji Kudrat's waiting up ahead."

"American backing, you mean. Do you really believe in that?"

Skelly shrugged. "Sometimes. If I don't think about it too hard."

For a moment Najeeb considered arguing the point. With a little more persuasiveness he might even have won it. Skelly's insistence on

proceeding was, at best, foolhardy. Yet there was something ennobling about it as well, as if the man were laying claim to his small niche of history, like every other foreigner who had made a name in these hills—spies and soldiers and scouts, toiling for the greater glory of distant monarchs and ministers—all had traipsed naively into the dust. And now here was Skelly, scribe of the West, trying to make sense of these imponderable rustics for the enlightenment of the plain folk back home. It was a strange business the two of them were up to, a dynamic he wouldn't have diagrammed in a millenium of imaginings. Yet here they sat, trying to convince themselves they still controlled their destinies, even as one warlord slept just down the hallway and another was camped on the mountaintop just over their shoulders.

Skelly would need him tomorrow, and also on the day after that. And soon enough, he hoped, Daliya would need him as well. In the world of his boyhood he would have been expected only to save his own skin, to cut and run. But in the world he was trying to fashion for himself now, he supposed, it was time to show some staying power, some trust and reliability. Besides, even if he were to return to Peshawar tomorrow, Tariq would likely throw him in jail, and then where would they all be? For now, at least, the best means of escape was to keep moving forward, deeper into uncertainty.

So, rather than argue, Najeeb simply nodded.

"All right, then," he said. "I will go north with you in the morning. But we should sleep now. It will be a long day."

Skelly seemed almost disappointed, as if he'd secretly wanted to be talked out of his venture. Then he, too, nodded and crawled into his sleeping bag. A moment later he shut off his flashlight, and the only sound in the room was the mutter of a sentry, well down the corridor. Talking sedition, no doubt. Sedition and desertion. Maybe Najeeb should have argued after all. Too late now, either way. In six more hours they would be on the march.

## CHAPTER TWENTY-THREE

S KELLY AWOKE covered in sweat, clammy and shivering against the slippery liner of his sleeping bag.

"Great," he muttered, groping for his duffel in the dim light, wondering where the Cipro might be. The call to prayer blared through the town, the amplification as harsh and fuzzy as on a cheap car stereo. It sounded like the mosque was right next door.

Najeeb stirred, groaning beneath his wool blankets, nothing of the man visible but black hair. Skelly swallowed a dry lump in his throat, but his greater worry was his stomach and the regions below, gurgling warmly, a thermal spring of bubbling mud. He reeled slightly as he stood on bare feet, reaching for a water bottle. He felt wrung out, brittle.

"Where's the shitter?"

"The what?" Najeeb sat up, propped on his elbows.

"The toilet. The WC."

"Next door."

It was another open doorway beneath the verandah of the guest house, a small, gloomy room that looked as if it hadn't been washed for weeks. There was a ceramic hole in the middle of the floor, with a bucket of water parked nearby for manual flushing. Skelly grubbed himself into place, forehead beading with sweat as a violent chill seized him like a spirit. Thank God he had his Cipro. He'd take two now for maximum wallop, then a third at midday. His belly clenched, issuing forth a gush like molten lead. Then another shudder, goose bumps on his arms and legs. He cleaned up as best he could and stepped outside,

opening the water bottle to rinse his hands, dripping dark blotches onto the dusty street. The prayer droned on, piercing his eardrums.

Skelly had expected to find the streets empty, but at least a dozen men were already out, shooing goats as they tightened straps on horses and pack mules. Every man but one had a gun on his back, and that was Razaq, giving orders and pointing this way and that.

Najeeb materialized at Skelly's side, a scrap of bread in his hand. Skelly didn't want to even think about food, but it was probably a good idea to force some down even if it carried a fresh load of microbes. His belly gurgled as if arguing against the plan. He wondered whether their satellite phone was strapped to one of the mules. Their ISI sat phone, he reminded himself.

"Looks like we better get moving," he said. "Why don't you get our stuff together. I'll try to get a word with Razaq."

In his weakened state, Skelly felt as if he was walking on stilts, and he was nearly spent by the time he reached Razaq. The warlord had paused in his preparations and was gazing up at the hillside where Bashir must be. Skelly could faintly make out the path Najeeb and he must have taken last night. Razaq, he saw, was wearing the old sword, the one from his ancestors. It was sheathed at his side and hanging from a belt.

"For luck?" Skelly said, pointing.

"And for memories. We leave in ten minutes."

Then he turned away, shouting more orders in Pashto. Skelly's stomach rumbled, and he headed off to find his pills. Maybe nerves were part of the problem. Whatever the case, it was time to saddle up.

Ten minutes later, right on schedule, they rode out of Azro single file, clopping and clanking in the morning stillness. Not even the children came into the streets to see them off, and the only two women in sight began arguing loudly with each other from facing rooftops, shouting across a narrow alley past fluttering gray banners of drying laundry. Najeeb's prediction of further desertions proved correct; despite the addition of a few new recruits from Azro, Razaq was departing the town with about as many men as he'd brought.

Skelly soon grew used to the nauseous motion of the horse, the bump and sway nearly lulling him to sleep as his saddle creaked like a rocking chair. Najeeb kept his thoughts to himself, for the most part. Small talk would have seemed out of place, and there was nothing to translate or describe—nothing but the brown-gray monotony of the encircling hills.

After the first few miles the sun crept over a ridge, finally bringing a little light and warmth to the gloom, but Skelly felt no better than when he'd awakened, alternately shivering and burning, sweat beading on his forehead and running down his back. Najeeb pulled alongside, a concerned look on his face.

"You don't look well," he said. "It is good that I came."

"Yes," Skelly said, although he was beginning to wonder if they'd done the right thing. "I think we'll be all right." Every few minutes he checked the hills behind them for sign of Bashir's party, but there was nothing, not even a glint of sunlight on metal.

Toward noon they rounded a wide bend and halted. Just ahead the valley narrowed, with steep rock walls towering on either side and huge stones piled in a sloping tumble on both sides of the road. The passage ahead looked narrow enough in some places to resemble a tunnel with the roof removed, a hardscrabble of coruscated brown and gray that went on and on, the blueness of the sky tempered only by a faint corona of dust that seemed to rise on every breeze. At the head of the column, Razaq pulled binoculars from a saddlebag. Some of his men dismounted and began kneeling by the side of the road.

"The Ali Khel Gorge," Najeeb whispered from behind. "A good place to stop."

Skelly dismounted, and his stomach folded back in on itself. He took the opportunity to stumble into the boulders a few yards, where he again unloaded his bowels, hands gripping the dusty stones while the men muttered in prayer just beyond. Another bout of nerves, he told himself. Reaching his saddlebag, he took a long draught of water, rinsing his mouth and swallowing deeply.

"Next time shit in the road," Najeeb said firmly. "I did not see you'd gone there until it was too late."

"Mines?" Skelly asked.

Najeeb nodded.

As they remounted a few moments later Skelly peered farther down the formidable gorge, trying to imagine what it must have been like piloting tanks down the narrow road—the big green craft beetling along like alien creatures, turrets swiveling, treads ringing and whining. Then some barefoot Mujahedeen in a turban rising up from a boulder to fire a tube from his shoulder, a shell whooshing into the treads as warriors swarmed suddenly from the rocks, darting flares of blue and white gowns. He held that vision as he watched Razaq unsheathe his sword and raise it high, pointing it forward from the

saddle as the column prepared to resume its progress. Skelly yanked out his notebook to record the moment, oddly charmed by the gesture—Razaq's massive bulk astride the big roan and all his men at the ready. There was no one but them in the valley, it seemed, them and the big clean sky where only a hawk was on patrol, spiraling on an updraft as it disappeared over the ridge.

Razaq sheathed his sword and they were under way, Skelly's horse setting off before he had time to pocket his notebook. A bloom of heat flushed his face and chest, followed by a shudder of cold.

For the first hour he flinched at every new sound, at every clank and mutter from the column, scanning the stones for signs of movement. Gradually he fell back into his earlier rhythm, nodding and swaying, but just as his eyelids began to droop there was a white flash of light from ahead on the right, followed by a second flash, even brighter, and his stomach clenched. A rider four horses ahead slumped left, blood geysering from his side just as the sound of the gunshot reached them, a sharp boom that echoed up the sides of the gorge.

"Jesus!" Skelly cried, struggling to free his feet from the stirrups while keeping his head down.

From high on the slope to the right a voice shouted maniacally in some foreign tongue, seeming to carry Skelly's heart with it as it reverberated up the opposite hillside.

Then all hell broke loose.

Gunshots seemed to come from everywhere at once, *cracks* and *zips* and *thunks* as the slugs found stone and flesh, echoes doubling the effect. Skelly finally wrenched his feet free and dropped awkwardly to the ground, certain that at any moment a bullet would tear into him. The better riders were pulling their horses to the ground with them, but Skelly could only watch and listen as a slug struck his own mount with an ugly *thwack*. A hole in the saddle spurted blood, and Skelly had to scramble crablike out of the way of the red stream. The beast groaned and sagged to its front knees, slumping left and nearly falling on him. He crawled between a pair of boulders, his mind seeming to scatter in a hundred directions at once. Thankfully, the same aspects of the terrain that made it prime ambush country also made it easy to take cover.

Skelly jerked his head left and right, looking for Najeeb, feeling that his eyes were rolling in his head like those of a wild animal, bulging with panic and adrenaline. He finally glimpsed Najeeb, pressed to the ground behind him, sheltering in the same rocks.

"You okay?" Skelly shouted, his voice emerging in an unsteady croak.

"Yes. The man behind me was hit."

By now some of Razaq's men were returning fire, aiming toward muzzle flashes and puffs of smoke. Echoes roared up the canyon, then for a moment the shooting seemed to abate. Skelly eyed the road behind them for any sign of Bashir, but for the moment their escape route seemed clear. Up ahead Razaq was crouched among boulders on the opposite side of the road, speaking with some of his men. There was shouting back and forth between the stones.

"They're saying we should fall back," Najeeb said. "Work our way back down the road. The attackers won't be able to move as quickly as we can. The footing is very bad. Very steep. In some places all you can do is go up or down. But we've already lost four men, maybe half the horses, so be ready to move soon."

"Is it Bashir?" Skelly asked. "Just harassing us, maybe."

"Not possible. There is no way he could have moved ahead of us without us knowing. Not last night, and not in the gorge."

"So is it Kudrat, then?"

"Maybe. Him or bandits. Or some other person who thinks the gorge belongs to him. Look, we are moving. Ready?"

Skelly would have preferred staying put for the moment. At least here he knew he was under cover. And what he really needed now was water. His mouth was so dry he could barely speak, and even breathing was difficult. But the men around him were indeed on the move, so Skelly got going as well, crabbing his way back down the road from behind the boulders, keeping his head low, palms and knees already scoured by the rough ground. A few gunshots pinged in the rocks like the remnants of a hailstorm. One popped the dust a foot ahead of him, and he had to fight back an urge to rise up and run. Then came an even stronger impulse to freeze, to press his face into the dust and wait for it all to end.

"Move," Najeeb urged from behind. "Keep going."

Other men scrambled nimbly past, staying just off the roadway, weaving through stones and boulders. A horse trotted past, a miracle it was still standing. Did Skelly have his notebook? Yes. That was something, he supposed. And his satchel was where it almost always was, strapped across his shoulder. What about his bag, with all his clothes? Forget it. Just get out of here. Maybe the attackers wouldn't pursue them. Even if they were caught, maybe he'd be spared—after all, he

was nothing but a hack. But for the moment he was a target like all the others, a head and torso to aim at.

"Keep moving!" Najeeb shouted. "If we fall behind they'll cut us off!"

"I'm going, I'm going." His voice had begun to return. Better, he told himself. Just stay calm. Stay low.

Their movement meant that only one or two of Razaq's men were bothering to return fire, and for a few moments the shooting from the hills intensified, although so far there had been nothing heavier than automatic-weapons fire.

He wondered momentarily about the satellite phone. It was probably gone by now, shot full of holes or crushed beneath a horse. Across the narrow road to his left a man raised up on his knees and fired a burst from his Kalashnikov, then immediately dropped. As far as Skelly could tell, the man hadn't even aimed. Was this how they'd done it for twenty-three years here in all the nonstop fighting since the Soviet invasion? Ambushes and wild firing among the ravines, lobbing the occasional shell into cities and towns. Or maybe this was the way gun battles went the world over, no matter what the army. If so, he could hardly blame them for shooting wildly. For all his experience in war zones this was the first time he'd been caught in the middle of a firefight, and he'd be damned if he'd have taken aim either in the middle of this chaos.

Twenty minutes of scrambling took them a few hundred yards, past a sharp bend in the road, and once they cleared it the gunfire practically disappeared. Najeeb must have been right about the ambushers' lack of mobility. None had apparently been able to keep pace. The route behind them remained clear. Perhaps they really would make it out of here.

Skelly saw Razaq dare to stand for a moment, cool as could be but still scanning the hills for muzzle flashes or signs of movement. This emboldened several of his men to stand, as if competing to prove their worth. Skelly waited a moment longer—nothing to prove as far as he was concerned—then he, too, rose to his feet, brushing the dust from his pants and shirt. He was spent, limp and feverish with a new flush of heat. Suddenly light-headed, he sat back down a moment, then rose unsteadily again and shouted to Razaq.

"Where to? Back to Azro?"

"It is our only option."

Provided that Bashir had left the option open, that is, although neither man dared say so.

"Do they know?" Skelly asked Razaq, gesturing toward the other men. "About your so-called rear guard, I mean."

"I told my brother and my son. Not the others."

Skelly nodded, not sure what he thought of that. Then he turned to Najeeb. "Maybe you were right. Maybe we should have stayed in Azro."

"It is not to question now," Najeeb said. "What is to happen will happen."

"Maybe. But you were right all the same. I'm sorry."

Najeeb didn't reply, but he didn't seem angry either. Good for him, then, because from here on out they would need each other's help more than ever.

Razaq took stock of his caravan. Five of his men had been hit. One was dead for certain—Skelly had seen the man's face, or lack of it. So was the man who'd been shot in the chest at the beginning of the ambush. Three others were wounded but still on their feet. One with a bloody left leg groaned loudly as he wrapped the wound with his *kameez* and struggled back into the saddle, shirtless atop one of the seven remaining horses. The other two men had wrapped their arms with shreds of their filthy garments. Both were expressionless, as seemingly unmoved by their misfortune as seasoned commuters confronting another traffic jam.

Once regrouped, they set out again for Azro, moving quickly but warily, taking care not to bunch up or string out too far. No one spoke. From time to time Skelly glanced over his shoulder, expecting the worst, but he saw only the same brown tableau that had been there all day. It almost seemed that the ambush had been a mirage, a daydream. His stomach, surprisingly, had met the challenge, sealing every sluice gate, and for the moment his fever seemed in retreat. The antibiotics must have finally slammed into effect, or maybe his nerves had shut down all systems in a biological state of emergency.

They rounded the next bend to find five horses gathered skittishly. Skelly spotted the telephone strapped to one. It looked unscathed. Amazing. And somehow reassuring, even though filing a story was the last thing on his mind. Two more horses loomed just ahead, bobbing their heads and prancing, nervously keeping their distance.

But as the caravan approached the head of the next bend a half hour

later, the renegade horses returned at a gallop, whinnying and snorting. Everyone stopped to watch.

"Something spooked them," Najeeb said.

"Bashir," Skelly said. "He's sealing off our retreat."

"That would be my guess."

They looked at each other, neither needing to say a word this time.
Always trust the advice of the local on his home turf, Skelly thought.
But too late now. What is to happen will happen, just like Najeeb said.

Razaq must have reached the same conclusion about what was lurking around the bend, because he ordered everyone on horseback to
dismount, and the column slowed its pace. They then halted, and he
sent two scouts ahead while everyone waited. A few men chambered
rounds in their Kalashnikovs while others changed clips, a sudden jamming and clicking that started Skelly's pulse hammering anew.

"Jesus," he muttered. "I don't know if I can take another one."

The next five minutes passed in silence. Then they heard footsteps
crunching toward them, everyone lowering to a crouch only to see the
two scouts emerge around the bend. One shrugged, which Skelly took
to mean they'd seen nothing. They conferred with Razaq, who gave
the order to advance in a low voice, barely audible.

The caravan cleared the bend without incident, and five minutes
later Skelly was beginning to think they'd overreacted to the horses.
Perhaps Bashir had decided to wait in Azro. Anything would be preferable to another ambush along this remote road, hemmed in by the
hills. In another mile or so they'd be out of the gorge altogether.
Twenty minutes tops.

A gunshot ended those calculations, and Skelly's stomach leapt back
toward his throat. Two more shots followed, bursting with flashes from
both slopes, and everyone dropped to the ground, scrambling behind
rocks and pulling their animals down. A horse shrieked, a whistling cry
of pain through flaring nostrils, and Skelly heard a man gasp and curse
from the rocks just ahead.

Razaq shouted, trying to rally his men, but the gunfire was too
intense. The only way back to Azro would be by fighting their way
there. Skelly bent lower to the ground as the shots pocked and pinged
around him. He felt the sun hot on his back just as his fever returned,
blooming high in his torso. Somewhere among the rocks a shot found
its target, and a man screamed, high-pitched and sudden, oddly like
that of a joyous child at play. Skelly squeezed his eyes shut, sweat beading on his forehead, and a memory from long ago swam before him

unbidden—another hot afternoon with the sun at his back, beneath leafy trees on a suburban sidewalk in Illinois. He was with his daughter Carol, years ago. She was six and setting off on a bicycle, her small round shoulders in his hands as he ran alongside to hold her steady, then let go, watching her wobble, all that heat on his back as he slowed his pace, Carol heading down the walkway toward the corner, ponytail swaying as she pedaled, indecisive as the corner approached, Skelly running hard to reach her but too late, watching her clatter to the pavement with an anguished cry. He leaned low, reaching to brush away the tears.

"Skelly!" It was Najeeb, who had crawled alongside him, placing a hand on his sweaty back, bending closer now. "Are you hit? Are you all right?"

"Fine. I'm fine."

It was the fever, he told himself, the fever and the madness of the fighting. All that metal flying barely overhead, whizzing into stone and flesh. He had never realized that the air he breathed could be so alive with menace, as if he were trapped in some test chamber in a lab, an artificial universe dense with subatomic particles, every one of them tracing vectors toward his skull.

"Stay down," Najeeb urged, easing away.

Skelly checked his watch. It was around two o'clock, leaving four hours of full daylight, plus an hour of dusk. If they could hold out that long they might be able to slip away through the rocks. But of course the attackers would be able to move undetected as well.

The firing turned scattershot as everyone sat tight, and after a while Skelly's nerves began to calm. So this was how one grew accustomed to battle, he supposed. No wonder it induced nightmares—all that fear to be stored away and buried, time after time.

The fighting settled into an uneasy stalemate. Whenever anyone above or below showed a head or tried to move, someone on the other side fired, usually prompting an answering shot. A few of these tit-for-tats escalated into longer exchanges, frantic bursts followed by the eerie trickle of spent casings against stone.

Skelly wondered how much ammunition Razaq's men had. He heard clips being exchanged and rammed into position from time to time. Perhaps there was a shortage on both sides, which would explain the virtual silence that fell on the scene an hour later, when at least twenty minutes passed without a shot.

But as it turned out, Bashir's men were only waiting for the first

group of attackers to close in from behind Razaq's caravan. This group announced its return to the action with a long burst from the far bend, in the direction back toward Heserak. Skelly pulled tighter up into the rocks, feeling suddenly exposed now that there was shooting from both front and rear.

By now it was four o'clock. The day was moving much too slowly. Skelly reached into his satchel for his pills and water bottle, swallowing another Cipro. No matter how much water he drank, his mouth seemed to immediately go dry. He pulled out his notebook and tried to take a few notes, but everything seemed like nonsense. At this point he couldn't even say who had been shot, or in what order. Everything blended into a continuous blur of noise and hazard.

One of the men just ahead had rescued some bread from one of the horses and was passing it through the rocks. Skelly tore off a piece and handed the rest to Najeeb. It was dry but tasted wonderful, anything to soak up the pool of bile at the base of his stomach. He heard someone sidling up behind a rock just above, and he reached for a stone, clenching one in his right hand and raising it to strike. But when a face emerged, it was Razaq, who shoved forward Skelly's phone.

"Mine was destroyed in the fighting," he said without preamble. "This one is our only hope for getting a message out. You said you are a friend of Sam Hartley?"

"I suppose he'd agree with that."

"Do you have his number?"

Skelly nodded. All the phone numbers were in his satchel.

"But last time I tried him he'd checked out of the Pearl. If he's out here somewhere his cell will be useless. Even if I get him, I'm not sure what he can do for us."

"It is his connections we need. To the U.S. Army. Helicopters, missiles. Whatever he can manage."

"And you think Sam Hartley can call in an air strike? I don't think you really know the way America works."

"And I am quite sure that you do not know the way Afghanistan works. So if you will try and reach him, please."

What could it hurt? If anything, Hartley could also call Skelly's editors, his family, let them know what was up. Skelly could do that himself, of course, now that he had the phone, and for a moment he toyed with the idea of filing a story, some exotic dateline like "Under Fire near Heserak," but the urge passed. The idea of filing seemed well

down on his list of priorities right now, and without the generator handy the phone's batteries might have only enough power for half an hour.

The phone was roughly the size and weight of a laptop computer, with the antenna built into the top cover, which Skelly unfolded, pushing the Start button on the side. He had tried it out once on the rooftop of the Pearl, with perfect results. He eased back from the nearest boulder to allow for a clearer path to the sky, taking care to keep his head down. He noticed Najeeb watching from a crouch. There was another burst of gunfire, but the shots pinged off some rocks well above them. The phone was showing a strong signal, and Skelly punched in the numbers, deciding to try Hartley's cell phone first. It took only a few seconds for the connection to go through.

"It's ringing," he said, handing the receiver to Razaq.

Razaq shook his head. "It is best if you speak with him first."

"Me?"

Skelly was about to protest, then it dawned on him what the man was up to. Of course. Let Hartley know that not only was Razaq in a jam but the press was here to record it. Let me go down, Razaq was saying, and the whole world will know it. But that was assuming there was anything Hartley could do to help, which Skelly doubted.

"Hello? Hello?"

It was Hartley, faint but unmistakable, and to Skelly the connection seemed no less miraculous than the one between Alexander Graham Bell and Watson.

There was a fresh burst of gunfire just as Skelly answered, so he shouted.

"Sam? It's Skelly. Can you hear me?"

"Barely. Lot of noise. Where the hell are you?"

"Afghanistan. With Razaq. His column is under attack. In some gorge just north of Azro."

There was a pause. Had Hartley sighed, or was it just static?

"Unwise, Skelly. I tried to tell you not to do that."

So where had the old chumminess gone? The backslapping compadre with a job offer in one hand and a cold beer in the other?

"Actually your advice was that he'd never take me. But someone else did. A guy named Bashir, who had your business card. Yours and Arlen Pierce's."

Silence again. Was the connection dead?

"Hello?"

"I'm here. Just trying to add everything up. Bashir from Katcha-garhi?"

"You know him?"

"Know *of* him. And don't you go saying otherwise."

"Can we worry about that later? We're just trying to get out of here alive."

There was another burst of gunfire, this time closer to the mark, as if someone was zeroing in on his voice.

"One word of advice, Skelly. If you do get out of there in one piece, first chance you get, bolt."

"Bolt where?"

"Anywhere. Just bolt. Too many black turbans headed your way, from what I've heard. Plus assorted others you don't want to run into. So get the hell out of there, for your sake and mine. Now where's Razaq?"

"Right here. I'll hand you over."

"Wait. First give me your GPS coordinates."

"My what?"

"From the phone. They'll be on the display."

Skelly scanned the screen. There were the numbers, just as Hartley had said. Skelly slowly read them aloud.

"Great. Now pass me to the old man."

He rolled awkwardly onto his back to hand the receiver to Razaq, taking care not to jostle the phone and throw off the signal. Let the warlord handle the matter now. These two were clearly out of his league.

Razaq also had to shout, but he turned his head away as if not wanting to be overheard. Some of the conversation was in English, but later it turned to Pashto. Skelly supposed he shouldn't be surprised to learn that Hartley spoke a little of the native tongue. Or had Hartley, too, handed the phone to someone else? Whatever the case, the conversation lasted only a few minutes more, and when Razaq handed back the receiver the connection was dead. Skelly had wanted to ask Hartley to phone his family and his editor, but now it was too late.

"What's going to happen?" Skelly asked Razaq.

"He will do what he can."

"Which is what?"

"We will find out, *inshallah*."

Skelly thought about that for a moment, but by the time he thought of a reply Razaq was crawling back toward the front of the column.

"Do you think it will do any good?" Najeeb asked.

"Like he said. I guess we'll find out."

"*Inshallah.*"

"Yeah. *Inshallah.*"

"I suppose the ISI heard all that. I wonder what they will make of it."

"More than I could, I hope. The more people who heard us, the better. Christ, what a mess."

His last words were drowned out in another burst of gunfire. Maybe it was the sound of English that enraged them. He resolved to keep quiet for a while.

BY DUSK they were still in the same fix, with no sign of any sort of help. The sun had long ago disappeared over the ridge behind the opposite side of the road, replaced by a deepening blue that grew dimmer by the minute. As the temperature dropped, so did the appetite for fighting. Gunfire was sporadic and halfhearted.

Maybe Bashir really was waiting them out. Skelly hoped so. But having eagerly anticipated nightfall throughout the afternoon, he now found himself dreading it, figuring it would only bring matters to a head. The idea of a sudden assault and a groping firefight in the darkness was terrifying.

Then there was a new noise, coming up from the south—a throbbing, as if the rocks themselves had begun to pulse. Skelly realized with elation that it was a helicopter, moving closer every second, the sound of its blades like the bugle shout of a cavalry charge. So Hartley had done it, then. He or Pierce or whoever else must have called in their coordinates and rallied the troops. Amazing.

A minute later the noise of the chopper filled the sky, and Skelly heard incredulous shouts from the slope just above, a rapid chatter going back and forth in a tone that he hoped was panic.

The chopper came in low from the direction of Heserak, straight up the pipeline of the ravine and no more than a hundred feet off the ground. It shrieked past overhead, the dust curling up toward it in great swirls, as if vacuumed. A desert zephyr, right out of legend. Then it climbed steeply and rounded back on them, as if scouting the dim-

ness of the scene below. Without warning something came whistling and whooshing from guns mounted on the chopper's sides. A pair of rockets spiraled slightly before slamming into the hillside well above them in a thunderous roar, followed by a brimstone rain of slag and dust. Skelly squeezed his eyes shut but got a mouthful of grit, then reopened his eyes just in time to see the chopper rearing up again, now circling near the top of the ravine. Then came a second *whoosh*, this one from down on the ground, and Skelly saw the bright trail of some shell tracing toward the aircraft, accompanied by the glowing streaks of automatic-weapons fire. Bashir's men were striking back, but missing badly. The shell, most likely an RPG round, exploded against the far wall of the ravine. This token resistance nonetheless had an effect, and the chopper swung outward in a wider arc, heading farther down the ravine. Then, with another burst of speed, it rose and tore across the ridgeline, vanishing from sight.

The valley was suddenly quiet, the thrumming noise receding as quickly as it had arrived.

"Is that it?" Najeeb asked.

"No," Skelly said. "They'll be back."

He believed it at first, and for the next five minutes he kept expecting the helicopter's return, watching for it to come roaring back over the ridge with missiles firing and all coordinates locked in. The last of the day's light was bleeding into the hills, but surely the chopper had some sort of infrared targeting that could spot the attackers on the slopes above. He listened closely for the throbbing blades, but there was nothing. No sound but the wind. Then, a bumping noise, but it was just one of Razaq's men, shifting position, moving among the rocks like a snake sliding off to bed. Skelly knew then that the moment had passed, that the chopper wouldn't be returning.

"So I guess that's it, then," he said. "For now at least."

Najeeb said nothing, and Skelly heard him smoothing out a place to rest, lying down. Skelly sagged against a boulder, spent, and reached for his water bottle. The temperature seemed to drop farther as darkness settled into the valley for the night, and he yawned, suddenly worn out now that rescue seemed out of the question. He rested his head on the ground, brushing away a few stones with his hand, and within minutes he was breathing deeply, asleep.

Only seconds later, it seemed, Najeeb was tugging at his shoulder, speaking softly into his ear.

"Wake up. Something's happening."

Not yet fully conscious, Skelly pushed himself up with one hand, then thought better of it and tried to stay low. Then he realized it was pitch-black, and no one could have possibly seen him. A pale half-moon sat on the opposite ridge like a white blade poised to drop into the gorge.

"Where are you?" he rasped, suddenly panicked, his heart going a mile a minute.

"Right here. Razaq's on the move. I think he and his sons are trying for some kind of breakout."

"What time is it?"

"Almost eight. Listen."

Now he heard it, a slight clank and scuffle. Were they mounting their horses? And if so, why wasn't everyone doing it—or would that have been too foolhardy to even consider? Skelly also remembered that there were no longer enough mounts for everyone. Perhaps the entire fight would now swing down the highway, leaving Najeeb and him safely to the rear. Somehow he doubted it.

"Here," Najeeb said. "Take this. You might need it. I have one, too."

It was too dark to see what Najeeb was handing him, but the feel was unmistakable, the cold steel barrel and the wooden stock.

"Where the hell did you get this?"

"From one of Razaq's men who was hit. While you were asleep. I got one for me, too."

Skelly had handled a Kalashnikov only one other time in his life, while traveling through Bosnia with a hard-drinking Finn. The Finn had been on his last tour of duty in the Balkans and had gotten fixated on the idea of testing the worthiness of his bulletproof vest before heading home. He'd propped it up in a trench and taken a shot, borrowing the weapon from a bored Muslim militiaman. Then he'd invited Skelly to have a go at it, showing him how the thing worked. Skelly still remembered the bruise the stock had left from bucking against his shoulder, and he felt odd about taking the weapon now.

"Careful," Najeeb muttered. "I've chambered a round and the safety is off."

"Where'd you learn to use one?"

"Where do you think? Where I grew up you don't make it to your tenth birthday without firing one of these. I would rather not have to use it now, but you never know."

True enough, Skelly supposed. But it was a strange sensation for him, going against every professional instinct. The scribbler was supposed to be the one passive observer, fading into the scenery to wait for

the shooting to stop, then emerging unarmed to interview the survivors and tally up the dead. But if a final round of fighting were to commence now, he supposed no one would bother to check his press credentials, especially not in the dark.

"Okay, then, I guess I'm ready. But damned if I'll know who to shoot."

"Listen. They're moving again."

Skelly strained his eyes forward, and for the slightest moment he thought he saw a slender glint of moonlight on the blade of a sword—or maybe it was just some romantic shred of his imagination, wanting Razaq to be the warrior he once had been, ready to ride off into the pages of an old book, some illuminated manuscript of silver spear points and galloping sultans. Was it the feel of the gun in his hands that gave him these delusions?

Then he heard the creak of leather, the jolting of hoofbeats, and shouts, followed by gunfire, muzzle flashes erupting brightly on either slope. Red tracers arcing wildly down the hillsides. Skelly flinched, gripping the gun tightly, still not accustomed to the sights and sounds. But he couldn't help but be mesmerized by the beauty of the scene, like some fireworks display gone horribly awry.

Up ahead there was more shouting and a terrible crashing collision of some sort, like the sound of a great beast going down, followed by more gunfire, the bursts of light strobing and sparking—total sensory commotion for a few seconds, followed just as abruptly by a moment of silence, when all he could hear was Najeeb's breathing, barely a foot to his right. It was cold, he suddenly realized. Bitingly cold. The ground beneath his knees felt like a grainy slab of ice.

A few voices tentatively called out. Then came the sound of footsteps, heading their way from farther up the road, too many of them for it to be anything but bad news.

"What are they saying?" Skelly whispered. "What's happening?"

"They have him," Najeeb said. "They have Razaq, his brother, and his son. It is Bashir speaking, in the road just ahead."

Skelly laid down the gun and heard Najeeb doing the same.

It was over, then. For all of them.

"So what now?"

"We surrender. And hope for the best."

## CHAPTER TWENTY-FOUR

IT WAS DALIYA'S first time in a burqa shop. A university friend had once wanted to visit one on a lark, but at the last minute they thought better of it, figuring their scornful giggles would have been asking for trouble.

The place gave her the creeps. Burqa shops were monuments to conformity, every wall and rack draped in the same pastels, most of them blue—garment after garment with the same baggy shape and the same shuttlecock top, like a gathering of burial shrouds. So the quicker this transaction went, the better, she decided, darting inside while Professor Bhatti hovered at the entrance, as watchful as a bodyguard.

The saleswoman appeared immediately. She struck Daliya as the prudish sort. You sensed this even though she didn't wear a burqa herself. She didn't need to, since no man ever set foot in the place. She had, however, ostentatiously parked a burqa near the door for when she ventured into the streets. She spoke up just as Daliya found what seemed to be a likely fit.

"Here," she said, picking up a second one. "You might want to try this size as well. One of them will probably be perfect."

Her voice was surprisingly warm. Perhaps Daliya had judged her too quickly.

Daliya slipped the garment on over her clothes. It was horribly claustrophobic. The front draped against the tip of her nose and brushed against her lips when she moved her mouth to speak. Her first inclination was to take it off right away, to drop it on the floor and stroll briskly from the shop, never to return.

Yet there was also a shuttered sense of privacy, which had its appeal. It was like watching the world from a hiding place behind a grated vent, anonymous and unreachable. It would take patience to wear one of these for long, but Daliya supposed that after a while you'd forget it was there. This one fit fine, so she pulled it off and said, "This will do."

"You are probably right," the saleswoman said, "but why don't you try this one as well?"

Daliya obliged her, slipping into the next one but finding that it was so long that the lower hem brushed against her shoe tops with a slight break. When she took a step she felt in danger of tripping on the garment. A few blocks of walking in this and the thing would be filthy.

"No," she said, lifting the larger one back over her head. "This one is too long."

The saleswoman wore a pained expression. She seemed to be fairly bursting with the urge to speak.

"Yes?" Daliya asked.

"I am pleased that you are choosing the path of modesty, my dear. But am I to assume you will be using this garment for travel?"

"Yes, I will be." Daliya blushed. If her intentions were this easy to spot, perhaps she'd better rethink her plans.

"And if it isn't too much of an intrusion, may I ask where will you be traveling?"

"To the North-West Frontier Province."

"Beyond Peshawar?"

Such coyness. Why did neither of them just come out and say, "to the Tribal Areas," which even before the war had seemed exotic and foreign to anyone who didn't live there. A land of kidnappers and smugglers. Now, more than in any other benighted corner of Pakistan, the inhabitants were also seen as a land of wild-eyed holy men and armed uprisings, of jihad and frenzy. Or such was the popular perception in Islamabad.

"Yes. Well beyond Peshawar."

"Then choose the larger one, my dear. You'll travel more safely, *inshallah*."

"Ah, yes. I see."

The woman was right, of course. Everyone had heard the horrible tales of women rapped sharply on the ankles if they showed the slightest bit of flesh when boarding buses or climbing stairs. Most such stories came from the dominions of the Taliban, inside Afghanistan, but

not all. And while every tribal area wasn't alike, who knew what the rules would be in her destination. So Daliya thanked the woman, paid for her purchase and was on her way.

Professor Bhatti seemed immensely relieved once they were safely back in the car, and Daliya again felt a stab of sympathy. Was this what it meant to be a successful woman, to have every minor pitfall loom as a potential disaster? She looked over at the professor, but her eyes were locked on the road, and for the rest of the drive she seemed oddly preoccupied, as if working something over in her mind.

By the time they reached the apartment the mood was more relaxed, and they talked for a while upstairs. Shortly before midnight the professor stood, saying, "I'll brew us a last pot of tea."

Daliya heard her switch on a radio in the kitchen, the jangly music accompanied by the comforting domestic clatter of teaspoons and clinking china. A few minutes later the radio clicked off, and the professor emerged with two steaming cups. But her face was ashen, her expression grave.

"They just came on with a bulletin," she said. "Razaq has been captured, with all his men. The Taliban have them."

"And Najeeb, too, then," Daliya said, lowering her gaze. The professor slid a teacup to her across the end table. Daliya raised it mechanically to her lips, but she was unable to swallow. She set the cup down and pushed it away, breathing deeply to maintain control. Poor Najeeb. Surely they wouldn't keep him? The American, maybe, for some sort of ransom. But not the son of an influential tribal *malik*. And wouldn't that mean he would end up on his father's lands, back in his home village of Bagwali, just as he'd feared? Retrieved, but not released. All the more reason she must put her plan into action, and soon, if only to keep from going insane with worry and all the waiting.

"You're going to go there, aren't you?" the professor asked quietly, eyeing Daliya with an expression of intense concentration and concern. "And I'll confess that I overheard you in the burqa shop, saying you're going to be traveling to the Tribal Areas."

"Yes, I suppose I am."

Professor Bhatti nodded, seeming to accept it. Then she gently set down her teacup and leaned closer, speaking in a tone that suggested a confidante more than a mentor.

"If I were a sane person, a responsible person, I would pick up the phone right now and contact your parents, or even the police. But of course if all I had was responsibility and sanity I never would have reached the place I am in today. I've only become cautious in trying to protect what I have. I've become a politician, a stagnant and careful politician."

"No. That's not fair. You've—"

"Please. Let me have my say."

Daliya nodded respectfully.

"You'll need to take some of the same kind of chances if you're going to rise above this place, but you shouldn't try doing it alone. So I'll help you—and God help *me*, please—in any way that I can. I have the name of someone who might do you some good out there. But before I give it to you, you should know that even in a burqa you're not going to get very far. Not by yourself. Once you're west of Peshawar, you'll need a male escort. Even two women dressed properly can't get very far unless a man is with them. It's simply the way things are."

"I know," Daliya said, her voice sounding very small. "I know all of that. Which is why, as I told you before, I have a plan. A strange one, maybe. But a plan."

"So tell it to me, then. And I will try to admire it, instead of being appalled."

Daliya smiled, picking up her teacup. For the first time this evening she felt a stirring of confidence in what she was about to attempt. She would need luck, for sure, but she knew now that she would at least have the necessary resolve.

"All right, then," she said. "But I hope you can stay up later once I have, because there's a lot of work to do. And I'll be leaving in the morning."

"For your great adventure," the professor said, smiling uncertainly.

"Yes," Daliya said. "Great, and probably foolish. But an adventure for sure."

So Daliya told her, and the professor was very admiring.

But also quite appalled.

## CHAPTER TWENTY-FIVE

BASHIR'S MEN MARCHED them at gunpoint to Heserak, then loaded everyone into six pickup trucks in the dark. That was when Najeeb spotted Haji Kudrat, who stood at the middle of the action in a dirty gray *kameez* and a thick woolen vest, shouting orders.

A nearby lantern lit his long, weathered face and bushy auburn beard. A swirled black turban sat regally on his head, like a layer cake with licorice frosting. He was obviously Pashtun, yet his crinkling almond eyes betrayed a touch of Hazara, the beleaguered peoples supposedly descended from the hordes of Ghengis Khan.

When Kudrat wasn't speaking he was scowling, an expression both imperious and impressive. Strapped to his neck was a large pair of binoculars, which around here was as clear a symbol of authority as a jeweled mace. A holstered pistol was suspended from a canvas military belt.

A man poked Najeeb in the back with a gun barrel, letting him know it was time to stop staring and get on board. But he'd seen enough to recognize Kudrat as a long-ago visitor to his father's house. The man had made quite an impression even then, sprawled on the cushions of the *hujera* and inhaling deeply from the hubble-bubble, his voice never losing its tone of command even as his eyes glazed over. Unlike others who were subjected to his father's lavish hospitality— most of whom wound up being treated more as hostages than as guests—Kudrat had seemed to come and go as he pleased, a mark of his stature. A week after his departure a convoy of trucks had arrived from Peshawar with crates of grenade launchers, escorted by a pale and

talkative American. So even then the man had known how to use connections, and now he was directing everyone like a imperious traffic cop. When others approached for orders they kept a respectful distance, as if further permission were required to move closer.

For all his apprehensions, both for himself and for Skelly, who'd hardly spoken since their capture, Najeeb found the atmosphere of this place oddly comfortable. He couldn't say it was to his liking, but there was a distant familiarity from his boyhood. There was an almost holiday feel in the air, an electric charge of men in motion, fueled by the ripe promise of coming violence. It was a mood that seemed to have its own smell, like that of an approaching storm. All the more reason to keep Skelly nearby.

They now sat next to each other in the back of the pickup, a white Toyota. Skelly's shoulders were bunched against his own. Skelly was taking notes, which he'd been doing almost continuously for the past hour, as if finally emerging from the stuporous roar of the firefight. Four of Razaq's men were in the truck with them, one of them oozing blood from his left thigh, his pants glistening darkly.

The engines revved, and the first of the trucks pulled out. Theirs was next in line, but just as they were getting under way Bashir ran up, signaling the driver to halt. He glanced into the back, flashing a thumbs-up to Najeeb. Then he leered with triumph when he saw that Skelly had a notebook out, and waved the driver on. It really was beginning to seem that the man had invited them along simply to have a personal scribe, someone to document his name for the world at large. He'd obviously also enjoyed sending Skelly ahead to taunt Razaq. There was some currency in that sort of notoriety, Najeeb supposed, but he wondered if the businesslike Kudrat would approve. And it hadn't seemed to alter their status as captives. If Skelly and he were truly special, shouldn't Bashir be letting them ride up front? Najeeb supposed he should feel anger toward the man, but he felt weariness instead. It would be like throwing a tantrum over the doings of a hawk, or a vulture. It was simply the man's nature, his fool's way of living and surviving.

"Think we'll be okay?" It was Skelly, finally speaking up. His eyes were glassy. From what Najeeb could see of the scribbling in his notebook the words were barely legible, more the result of compulsion than careful observation. He reached up to feel Skelly's forehead. Hot and dry.

"You should take more of your pills. They may not feed us for a while. And if we ever get a chance to leave, we will need to move right away."

"Think we'll really get one?"

Najeeb didn't know, so he didn't say. Skelly nodded, as if he understood.

The trucks trailed out of town in a dusty convoy. By now the moon was high in the sky, providing just enough light to see the faint outline of the hills. Since they had crossed the border into Afghanistan two days earlier, their journey had traced a crude upward crescent, which was now bending northeast, a route that brought them to the lower reaches of the wide, fertile valley spilling westward from the Khyber Pass. Jalalabad, Kudrat's reputed base of operations, sat in the middle of that valley, some thirty miles east-northeast of Heserak. If that was their destination, the roads from here on out should be relatively straight and flat.

They weren't smooth, however, and as the trucks bounced forward Najeeb noticed a dark liquid pooling at the base of the closed tailgate. It seemed to be coming from the wounded man, whose face was no longer visible in the night. A mile or so later Najeeb noticed someone next to the man leaning closer. Then, over the noise of the engine, a voice announced, "He's dead." Najeeb translated the news for Skelly, who dutifully recorded it after consulting his watch. The five survivors shifted and realigned, giving the dead man more room now that he no longer needed it.

"Do you know his name?" Skelly asked.

Najeeb relayed the question to the others. One grunted in reply.

"No one knew him."

Skelly scribbled a few moments more, then put down his pencil. Najeeb wondered if the dead man had a family, any children. If he was like most fighters, he had probably been at war for years, since his teens, carrying a gun for one warlord or another since before he was old enough to shave, forgetting not only his age but any skills he might have learned for earning a living. Other than fighting, of course. If peace came anytime soon, as everyone hoped, what would these men do, other than return home to fields of dust and drought? And now Najeeb and Skelly had been washed into this stream of the aimless warrior class, bumping from one forlorn destination to the next. He could get angry over that, too, he supposed wearily. If not for Skelly's

headstrong pursuit of a story they would be making their way back across the border by now, toward Tariq and the ISI. So keep moving forward, wherever that led. And keep trying to conserve energy for the first chance of escape. He would be drawing upon reserves he hadn't needed in years.

The night was cold and getting colder, and once or twice he heard Skelly's teeth chattering. The notebook was back in his pocket. A half hour later they saw the twinkling lights of Jalalabad. The town's electricity was the strongest testimony yet to Kudrat's prestige. The fealty of various gangs and factions meant little for very long unless you controlled the ones who kept the water and power flowing.

But when they reached the town the convoy drove through the outskirts, passing quickly into orange groves that sheltered the road, speeding past low, darkened homes and a lonely checkpoint or two where campfires were burning, then another mile or so into the countryside before turning left, bouncing across a dirt track alongside a bare field. The route continued in a jostling series of turns across more farmland, beneath long promenades of drooping eucalyptus, the menthol smell heavy in the night air. When the trucks finally stopped, no one spoke a word. There was only the sound of doors slamming and tailgates dropping. During one lull he heard Skelly's pencil scratching anew, an insistent mouse gnawing at the baseboard. Then a deep voice came up from behind as their tailgate bounced open.

"Everyone out."

"Where are we?" a captive asked.

"Rishkoor."

It was a small military base just outside Jalalabad, and for the moment it appeared to have no lights. Either that or it was operating under blackout orders. The silhouettes of a few low buildings were barely visible. Beyond them was a moonlit field littered with hulking dark shapes. Trucks? Tanks? He couldn't be sure.

Someone switched on a flashlight, and the beam lit Skelly's face. Then one of Bashir's men grabbed Skelly by the arm. Najeeb stepped quickly to keep pace, passing a huddle of men muttering to themselves in a foreign tongue. Najeeb thought it was Arabic but couldn't tell for sure.

"Wait here," the man told Skelly, then departed.

Someone nearby pull-started a generator, the engine beating noisily to life, and a short time later a string of dim lights flared overhead.

Najeeb stole a glance at the knot of strange men, squinting into the glare. They were sullen, a tough-looking bunch, and definitely not locals. Each of them was armed to the teeth.

Skelly nudged him, as if trying not to attract too much attention, then nodded toward the men.

"Taliban?" Skelly said under his breath.

"*Guests* of the Taliban."

"Guests," Skelly repeated, sounding exhausted. "You mean some of the retreating forces from the north? Or is this a way station for visitors?"

He said it almost dreamily, as if he might be half expecting a cameo appearance by his friend Sam Hartley, the wheeler-dealer, blowing in on the next breeze to set things right with assurances of commerce for all.

"*Arab* guests," Najeeb clarified. "From Syria, Saudi, Yemen. Or countries like that. They're the ones your government calls al-Qaeda, although I doubt that's what they'd call themselves."

Skelly reached for his notebook, then seemed to think better of it and let his hands fall to his sides.

"I guess we'll either have one hell of a story, or we'll soon be very unwelcome."

Najeeb supposed he was right.

A few minutes later one of Kudrat's guards tugged them toward a line of captives walking single file toward a long cinder-block building. Then Bashir seemed to materialize out of nowhere, remonstrating with the guard.

"They're arguing," Najeeb translated for Skelly. "Bashir's saying we belong to him. He's trying to separate us from the others."

Bashir eventually got his way, which Najeeb took as a good sign. At least he was a known quantity, and for all his deceit the man seemed to have a vested interest in keeping them alive. But he'd had to raise his voice to win the argument, and that had attracted the attention of the Arabs, who didn't seem to approve. The farther they got from Azro, the more the man's authority seemed to diminish.

Bashir led them toward another low building and ushered them into a small room at one end. He turned on his flashlight to help them get their bearings. It looked like their room in Azro, dirty plaster walls and a few thin mattresses on the floor.

"Where's the rest of my stuff?" Skelly asked.

Najeeb thought he looked a little better, but perhaps it was wishful thinking.

"Tomorrow," Bashir said.

"And my phone?"

"Tomorrow. Patience."

Then he flicked off the light and departed, shutting the door and leaving them in darkness. Najeeb groped his way toward one of the mattresses, supposing they wouldn't be getting any food tonight. I can do this, he told himself again. I can live this way for as long as I have to. Now if only Skelly can do the same.

"He didn't lock the door," Skelly said.

"They don't have to. I heard one of the guards saying the Americans had dropped cluster bombs. There are apparently hundreds still in the fields, unexploded. Try to sneak away and you'll probably set one off."

"Not that we'd know where to go anyway."

"We should sleep while we can. Who knows what they'll want out of us tomorrow."

"Do you know where they took Razaq? Him and his sons?"

"I couldn't tell. They were in the first truck. It was empty by the time the lights came on."

"But I guess they won't harm him, right?"

"Unless they give him to the Arabs."

"Or whoever's with the Arabs. Or leading them."

"Yes." Najeeb didn't want to say the man's name. "That could change everything. For us, too."

Skelly said nothing more on the subject, as if he, too, feared it might jinx them.


NAJEEB FELL ASLEEP quickly. There were no prayers calling through the night here, no sound except the shuffle and mutter of a few men outside the door. At some point in the night a few of the trucks drove away, but it was impossible to say how many.

Hours later he was awakened by a flash and an explosion, the ground shaking, and for a terrifying moment the oxygen seemed to be sucked from the air. A rain of dirt and stones showered the roof. Then a jet shrieked overhead, leaving in a hurry. He heard Skelly moving in the darkness, throwing back his blankets.

"What the . . . ?"

"Stay here," Najeeb cautioned.

"Just getting my bearings," Skelly said, sounding shaken. "Wonder how much more of that is coming."

There were three more explosions, but each was progressively distant, like a cloudburst moving down the valley. Someone was moaning outside, then there was a flurry of footsteps followed by silence. Najeeb must have fallen back asleep shortly afterward, because the next thing he knew Bashir was standing over him, his face lit by flashlight, jostling his shoulder.

"What is it?" Skelly said groggily from the other side of the room. "Who's there?"

"Come," Bashir said. "You must both see this."

His tone was urgent, and he must have been excited because he wasn't bothering to speak English for his scribe. Najeeb translated Bashir's orders, but Skelly barely mumbled in reply, and when Bashir turned his beam toward the reporter Najeeb saw that Skelly's brow was bathed in sweat, his hair matted and askew. He reached across. The man's forehead was steaming.

"I need another pill," Skelly mumbled. "And I need another shit."

"He's sick," Najeeb said.

"You must come anyway. Now."

Najeeb translated quickly, and Skelly, for all his troubles, reached first for his notebook, then began pulling on his pants. He, too, had untapped reserves, Najeeb observed, grateful for the knowledge.

"What is it he wants us to see?" Skelly asked, and this time Bashir answered in English.

"Justice," he said. "Justice for Mahmood Razaq. He is to be tried for treason, with his brother and son. Then they will be hanged."

Skelly looked over at Najeeb, then muttered a short sentence, barely audible.

"What?" Bashir asked. "What is he saying?"

Najeeb recognized the words well enough, having heard an American professor use them long ago in response to some legal outrage or another. It was a line that had intrigued him enough to go and look it up, finding to his surprise that it came from a children's book, an imaginary world where animals and playing cards had walked and talked, a place where logic and order were turned upside down.

"What he said was, 'First the sentence, then the trial.'"

Bashir nodded. He seemed to find the concept to his liking.

"Come," he said again, eyes blazing. "You must see it."

# CHAPTER TWENTY-SIX

T HE TRIAL WAS unlike anything Skelly had ever seen, made all the more surreal by the recurring waves of fever.

Bashir had chivvied them into a low plaster building where at least fifty men squatted on a concrete floor beneath a dangling forty-watt bulb, barely brighter than a candle. Razaq stood defiantly at the front along with his son, Haji din Razaq, his brother, Salim, and two other men from his caravan, one of whom was wrapped around the middle with bloody bandages, hunching forward with his face in a permanent grimace. Every time he sagged farther, or tried to sit, a man with a long switch would rise from the front row to swat at his ankles, to the delight of the crowd, which didn't so much laugh or cheer as huzzah, heads nodding, as if he'd had it coming.

Opposite the defendants—that was the word Skelly put in his notebook, unable to come up with anything better—was a tall elderly man with a graying beard and a soiled white turban, clutching a brown blanket around his chest like a shawl. Kudrat stood nearby with a watchful eye, seeming firmly in control of the proceedings.

When the older man began to speak the crowd went silent, Skelly scribbled a description of the place while trying not to notice how bad he felt. He'd swallowed another pill with the last of his water just before leaving their room.

"What time is it, anyway?" Skelly whispered, causing a few heads to turn toward him with scowls of disapproval.

The floor was stone cold, like sitting on an ice rink, and there wasn't a rug or cushion in sight. The whitewashed walls—or what you

could see of them—were scuffed and pocked. A chill breeze wafted through an open window, the remnants of the panes swept into a pile of broken glass.

"Almost four in the morning," Najeeb said, leaning closer, again placing a palm on Skelly's forehead, a look of concern creasing his brow. "We have to find you some food and water."

"Just tell me what they're saying."

"Blather mostly."

More heads turned, the scowls deepening, and Najeeb lowered his voice to a whisper, causing Skelly to cup a hand to his ear. "He is calling them traitors. Spies for America. He asked them what they had to say for themselves but he kept on talking. He is preaching a sermon, really."

"Some sort of imam?"

"No. Just a blowhard. A political."

Skelly looked at Razaq, the only one of the defendants who seemed to have held on to his pride. The others were downcast, looking at the floor, but Razaq glared at anyone who caught his eye, first at the speaker and then at the crowd. For a moment his gaze seemed to settle on Skelly at the back, although it was doubtful the man could have picked him out of the crowd in the dimness. The overhead bulb flickered once, then twice, making it seem even more like candlelight, but the crowd took it in stride as the speaker droned on, now raising his right arm and shouting.

"He is saying that the penalty for treason is death. That they must pay with their lives as a lesson to others."

Razaq suddenly spoke up in a booming voice. Skelly remembered the big sword and saw that it was gone. He wondered who had taken it as a trophy. Kudrat, perhaps. He tugged at Najeeb, wanting words, but Najeeb shook him off, attentive to the unfolding scene. The judge, if the man indeed called himself that, was now shouting back at Razaq, and for a moment their voices canceled each other out in a blur of noise, the foreign words buzzing past Skelly's head like bad music. He felt dreamy, weakened, and he stopped writing for a moment to steady his posture, placing a palm on the chilly floor. He wished he had a blanket to pull around himself, and he didn't like the concerned look on Najeeb's face whenever he looked Skelly's way. The man's quiet and careful translations seemed as much in deference to his fragile condition as to keep from offending Kudrat, who had flinched and frowned

at the first of Najeeb's interludes, but now seemed to tolerate them as one would the buzzing of a fly.

The man with the stick, sitting in the front row, rose again, this time to lash Razaq across the side, the big man fending the blows off with his left hand. He didn't look proud anymore.

"Razaq said he is a Pashtun, a Durrani of the Lokhali tribe, and that all of them should be ashamed, taking orders from an Arab slave. You saw what happened next."

Skelly told himself he would write it down later. It was good stuff, but he was suddenly too weary to move. Then the crowd began to stand, bursting into excited chatter. Before Skelly could even get to his feet, men were pushing past him, the smell of sweat and onions and tobacco everywhere. His knees felt creaky, and Najeeb took his arm, pulling him along, the young man's grip strong.

The voice in his ear said, "Come on. Try to keep moving."

Skelly's head swam, then he steadied. He panicked for a moment, thinking he'd dropped his notebook, then realized it was still clutched in his left hand, the pages sweaty.

"I feel awful. Where are we going? Is it over?"

"They are going to be hanged now. All of them. Everyone is going to watch."

Skelly shuddered, whether from his fever or from the thought of witnessing an execution he wasn't sure, but he suddenly felt more attuned to the proceedings, and horrified at what he was about to witness.

They were among the last ones out the door, the crowd shoving ahead at an eager pace. In Skelly's clouded state of mind he couldn't help but think of store openings and giveaways he'd had to cover in the United States. Free gift to first fifty customers. Free hanging to first fifty Pashtuns. He experienced a wavery déjà vu from the grand opening of a Warren County Wal-Mart, overweight women pushing past him through a bank of doors toward a counter beneath a sign with a yellow smiley face. He stopped, if only to shake the weirdness of the image, Najeeb still trying to tug him along.

"Just give me a second. I'm about to pass out." Then a rush of panic seized him. "Have you seen the Arabs again?"

"No. Come on."

Skelly checked again for his notebook. Still there. Still in his left hand, which clutched it like a claw. He thought again of the Wal-Mart,

a woman in flowered capri pants nearly knocking him to the ground by the drink machines out front. Cokes for thirty-five cents. He would do some damage for one of those right now, a cold and fizzy swallow of sugar. The thought seemed to clear his head, and he was moving again, out the door into the night, following the crowd by its smell and shuffle.

The gallows was as crude as the courtroom, and the process just as peremptory and raucous. Someone had taken a twenty-foot pole—the kind often used as a checkpoint barrier—and lashed it between two eucalyptus trees, about twelve feet high. A camp lantern hung from one of the trees, and the mob swarmed toward the light like a mating frenzy of night bugs, shouting and raising their arms, sharp cries to Allah and deep, throaty rasps. Razaq and the other four had disappeared into this maelstrom, and Skelly was struggling at the rear, grasping at Najeeb's sleeve but feeling steadier now that he was back in fresh air. He looked upward. The stars were out, no hint of dawn yet visible in the east. A rope soared into the air up front, tossed as crisply as a lasso, but it struck the pole, then fell to the ground. A second attempt put it across. Then four more ropes followed in succession, spaced evenly down the pole. This was their gallows, then, a crude make-do affair, but it certainly seemed up to the task at hand. The ropes jiggled for a second, charmed snakes all in a row, and Skelly raised on his toes just high enough to see men below fashioning nooses.

"Jesus," he gasped, causing Najeeb to turn his way, clutching him as if Skelly might be about to fall. "No. I'm all right. I just can't believe this."

He looked at Najeeb, whose eyes were wide, glazed in the light of the lantern. These were his people, Skelly suddenly realized, in a way he never had before. What must he think of all this?

The two Razaq men whom Skelly hadn't recognized were the first to be hanged, and they went in a hurry. Their mouths were open and moving, and you could see the crazed look in their eyes, but the din of the mob was too loud to hear a thing they were saying as men rushed to either side of the tableau for a better view. Najeeb took advantage of the surge to push forward a good fifteen feet or so. Skelly pulled out his notebook, his head still clearing.

"Shouldn't someone be selling popcorn?" he croaked, the dark joke ringing hollow even to his own ear as the first two bodies twitched into

view, eyes bulging, tongues lolling and the baying of the crowd rose to a roar.

He looked again toward Najeeb, who was expressionless now, watching his people swarm and surge around the bodies while two volunteers tugged again at the ropes, as stout as seamen reefing sails in a storm. Then Skelly looked around at the faces of the crowd, their teeth showing as they shouted and bounced, and he realized he'd seen them all before in one place or another across the world, his own country included. At wars and demos and sporting events, calling for blood and victory. These were Skelly's brothers, too.

Skelly's fever suddenly blasted him with a wave of cold, a chill that threatened to drop him to his knees, so he grasped Najeeb's shoulder, nearly letting go of his notebook. Najeeb gripped him around the waist and held on until the moment passed, Skelly nodding to let him know it was all right, the crowd surging around them once again.

Razaq's brother and son were next, handled clumsily as attendants thrust them toward the ropes. One was stoic, the other shouting, which caused the spectators at the front to spit—lunging motions that produced trailing gobs of brown liquid from the hash and tobacco they'd been chewing. Other men leapt forward in ones and twos to slap at the victims' heads and kick at their calves, the shouts coming in great bursts now.

Nooses slipped over their heads, then tightened, and the attendants stepped back. The two men then rose next to the previous victims, twitching and kicking as they lurched upward, heave by heave, toward the branches of the eucalyptus. Skelly now recognized Salim as the one on the right, the one who'd been shouting defiantly. He remembered him from Razaq's house, gracious and quiet, and he felt sick to his stomach, no trick of fever this time. Someone bumped him from behind and he shoved defiantly back, the brief surge of strength departing as suddenly as it had come, so that he nearly fell. Najeeb caught him, pulling him forward. Skelly looked again toward the gallows and saw Salim still kicking, baggy garments fluttering as his knees pumped, face turning purple. One knee, then the other, like a beetle on its back. Then slower. Then nothing, head sagging but still with a face the color of raw meat.

A man standing near the front, the old fellow from the courtroom who had wielded the switch, raised both arms, and the crowd began to go quiet, because now it was time for the main event. The shouting

died quickly, and every head turned toward the right, because there he was, the one they'd all come to see.

Razaq merited three escorts to the gallows, not that he was struggling in the least. His mouth was shut, drawn in a prim line. There was a purplish bruise across his left cheek where someone must have struck him on the way out of the courtroom, but if the man was in pain he did a fine job of hiding it. Skelly touched his notebook, then thought better of it. He would have no trouble remembering a single detail of this. The problem would be in forgetting it, and a shudder momentarily gripped him as if his body were already trying.

The last of the crowd's noises vanished as the noose went round Razaq's neck. The atmosphere was almost one of reverence now, or perhaps it had finally hit home to everyone exactly what they were doing, killing this man who could claim hundreds, perhaps thousands, of followers. This moment would either make their names or mark them for life.

The tugs now came, with audible grunts and heaves, two men pulling together. Razaq's answer was a gargling cry, as if he'd at last thought of something to say but had waited too late, the words trapped below the knot. You could actually hear the rustle of his *kameez*, the scuffle of sandals in the crowd, then a lonely cough. Razaq made one feeble kick, then another. Then his face went dark and the light left his eyes. Skelly sighed loudly, Najeeb's grip tightening around his waist.

The crowd stirred, still transfixed by the body that now swayed gently above them, high toward the leaves. Then Kudrat stepped before them. Where was Bashir for all this, Skelly wondered, feeling sickened and angry. Was the man gloating? Accepting congratulations? Counting up the payment for his services?

Then Skelly spotted him over to the right, nearly as much in the margins as Skelly and Najeeb, almost as if he were trying to melt into the surroundings. He no longer looked either triumphant or eager, and it dawned on Skelly that some strange new dynamic might now be in motion. But as far as Skelly was concerned, Bashir's place in this tiny moment of history was ensured—he was the blackguard, the betrayer, the Taliban henchman who had delivered Razaq to the mob. The thought seemed finally to stir his professional instincts, and Skelly sensed the story beginning to percolate in his mind—an exotic and horrifying morality play, even though he wasn't yet sure of some of the

roles. Was Sam Hartley really a player? And if so, for whom? To what end? And where were the Arabs he had seen earlier?

The extra thinking took energy, and it cost him. A new blaze of fever took hold, consuming all the questions he'd been mulling. He looked back up at Razaq, the big man's body now still in the glow of the lantern. It felt as if he were viewing the scene through thick glass, while a weary heaviness settled in his bowels.

Looking left to the fringes of the crowd, there they were once again, he realized. It was the Arabs he'd seen earlier, plus about half a dozen more, seemingly having materialized from nowhere. Perhaps they had arrived in the middle of the proceedings, while his attention had been turned toward the front. Some were on horseback, and now he could smell the animals. Manure and hay, the sweat of their hides. The longer he looked, the more of them he saw, although it was back toward the limits of the lantern's lighting, so he couldn't be sure of their numbers. Toward the rear of the scene, fainter still, was a new arrival on horseback, this one tall and lanky, almost abnormally high in the saddle. He wore a green camouflage jacket around a white *kameez*. Salt-and-pepper scraggle of a beard, and the long face everyone knew so well, topped by the white pillbox that he wore in every poster in every bazaar. Skelly shivered, feeling that even his illness had suddenly turned melodramatic. He didn't dare take out his notebook now, not wanting to be seen scribbling any description of these men, but he furtively squinted toward them, wondering if he could really be seeing what he thought he was. Then the horse turned, and the tall rider drifted into shadow. Skelly looked to Najeeb for confirmation of the sighting, but the young man's eyes were still locked on Razaq, a forlorn gaze bereft of hope.

"Najeeb," he said breathlessly, tugging at a sleeve. "Who are they back there? Do you see them?"

Najeeb turned slowly, then shook his head, seemingly unimpressed at first, then turning quickly back toward the gallows, as if prodded by a new sense of urgency.

"The Arabs," he said. "Don't look at them. Don't let them see you."

Somewhere nearby a generator roared to life. A string of lightbulbs switched on, garishly lighting the scene, throwing long shadows from the five bodies into the field behind the trees. Skelly glanced left. No sign now of the Arabs, or of anyone on horseback. Shouldn't he have heard them galloping away?

Then Kudrat spoke, his voice pealing loudly over the heads of the mob, turning every face toward his. His message was brief, presented sternly. Najeeb translated without prompting.

"You see before you the fate of traitors."

Skelly would have expected something better, a touch of the poetic, or a quote from the Prophet. Some rhetorical flourish to give his account a punchy ending. But on further reflection he supposed that it fit. Blunt and businesslike, just like the executions. A chilling man who killed, then strode onward to the next transaction.

Then another man stepped forward by the lights, older than Kudrat but wearing an identical black turban.

"The local imam," Najeeb muttered. "He is quoting the Koran. 'Let evil be rewarded with evil.' Plus a few other lines."

"That one will do fine," Skelly said, taking out his notebook and jotting it down.

The rest of the man's speech was as predictable as that of an evangelist at a tent revival, he supposed; standard fire and brimstone. Damn them all and pass the plate. He realized that the adrenaline of the previous moments was flagging, and now all he wished to do was to crawl back into his bed. Let the pills do their work, then when daylight arrived he would try to track down the satellite phone. He was certain that Bashir would want to oblige, provided Kudrat would let him.

When the imam finished, some of the crowd began to drift away. Their earlier joy was drained. Perhaps they had begun to consider the possible consequences. Or maybe they were already bored.

Then Kudrat stepped forward with raised arms, and everyone halted. So there was more still to come, then. As Kudrat began to speak, Skelly sensed the crowd perking up, as if some new twist had reclaimed its attention.

"What is it?" he whispered to Najeeb. "What's happening?"

Najeeb held up a hand, intent on hearing, which Kudrat didn't make any easier by slipping into a low tone, not gentle or calm but stern and foreboding, no longer king of the rally but still its master and executioner.

"There are two more," Najeeb said in a low voice. "Two more traitors to be hanged."

For a few harrowing seconds Skelly was sure the two would be Najeeb and himself. But no one came to grab them, and everyone looked to the right, where there were the sounds of a struggle, then a

shout. He was appalled to see Bashir being hauled forward along with one of his top men. Bashir yanked and struggled, and for an astonishing moment he broke free, only to be grabbed by men up front who seemed only too eager to assist Kudrat. Bashir reacted with an outraged shout in Pashto—no more English from him now—and as he continued he disappeared in a hail of punches and kicks, the muffled sounds of the blows creating a ripple of amusement in the crowd, appreciative of this encore performance after so little drama during the first five killings.

By the time Bashir's face surfaced again he was nearly to the gallows, with a streak of blood on his right cheek. His mouth opened and he cried out.

"Traitors," Najeeb said. "He is calling everyone traitors."

"Why are they doing this?" Skelly asked. Everything was dissolving—his story, their means of escape, perhaps their very chance for survival—all of it being led to execution along with Bashir, and for the life of him he couldn't figure out why.

"I suspect it is because either he or Kudrat has ambitions we don't know about," Najeeb said, leaning to speak into Skelly's ear. "And I suspect that they may have something to do with your friend."

"Sam Hartley?"

"I would not say his name again in present company." Najeeb's manner was as grave as his own.

The rope went around Bashir's neck. He was still shouting—incoherently now, the pale pink mouth flashing like the belly of a landed fish. Then he stopped issuing sound altogether as the noose tightened and the volunteers hauled at the line. Bashir jolted upward. A foot. Then a yard. Then another. For a few moments he kicked like an angry child, then he went still, his tongue lolling.

The men around them began to drift away now that this last bit of entertainment had ended with such a whimper. Najeeb took Skelly's arm, and they turned to go as well, both of them too stunned to speak. Then Kudrat approached from the left on a course to intercept them, red beard bobbing with every step. He spoke, and a few of his men turned to listen, although most paid it no mind, perhaps because the action was done for the night. Kudrat's message was in Pashto, and Skelly tried to glean the gist of it by watching Najeeb's face. The results weren't promising. His fixer's mouth went tight in a grim line, and his eyes seemed bottomless. Maybe they'd been expelled, told to

scram even before it was light, and they'd have to spend the next few hours picking their way through the fields of unexploded bombs.

Kudrat was finished now. He turned away without another glance at them, which Skelly hoped was a good sign. If they were so unimportant, then why go to the trouble of doing something unpleasant to them?

"What did he say?"

Najeeb wouldn't look at him. "You do not want to know all of it."

"I do. Every word."

Najeeb sighed and looked him in the eye.

"He asks that you think of this moment in your dreams tonight, because tomorrow there will be another trial. Yours."

Skelly supposed that he should feel a bolt of fear, or terror, but his mind had seen and heard all it could hold for one evening, and the idea of a tomorrow seemed remote, far across a weary chasm of fever and sleep. A gurgle from his stomach told him that he must have absorbed the blow somewhere, but for the moment all he could do was offer the phrase that had leapt to mind earlier, when Bashir—was the man really *dead* now?—had burst into their room with his flashlight. Then he spoke it, in the barest of whispers.

"First the sentence, then the trial."

"I will do what I can," Najeeb said, placing a hand on his shoulder like a brother, or a father, a strength of grip that in Skelly's weakened state was nearly overpowering. "I am very sorry. I will do what I can."

## CHAPTER TWENTY-SEVEN

NAJEEB LAY AWAKE in the dark listening to Skelly's ragged breathing, amazed that the man could sleep. He supposed it had more to do with exhaustion and illness than with the ability to relax under threat of a death sentence. Perhaps the humane thing to do would be to withhold his medicine, for what could be worse than awakening fine and recovered only to be harangued and hanged, strung up by people whose shouting he wouldn't even comprehend. Najeeb wondered how much he should even translate, appalled at the idea of deciphering their hatred to the bitter end. Far better if Skelly were to remain delirious, barely cognizant.

Or perhaps other options remained. The door was still unlocked. But when he had opened it a few minutes earlier he had found two burly men posted outside, eyes and gun barrels glittering in the lantern light. In another hour the sky would begin to lighten. He wondered if any of Bashir's men were disillusioned enough to help him try something. He doubted it. They seemed to have taken their leader's execution in stride. Another day, another boss.

He must have drifted off to sleep because the next thing he knew someone was beating on the door. He sat up with a start, blinking. There was pale light at the crack beneath the door, then a full wash of misty brightness as the door swung inward, the opening filled by two dark shapes, one of which reached toward him. A painfully strong grip took hold of his shoulder.

"Come with us."

Najeeb barely had time to put his sandals on as the men pulled him toward the door.

"Just wait. Hold on."

"Come. Now."

"Hold it."

Skelly was still asleep, breathing quietly now. Najeeb hated the thought of the man awakening alone. No breakfast and nothing to look forward to but an execution, surrounded by babble.

"I have to stay."

"Come!"

The second man kicked him in the backside, driving him out the door like a goat. He began to wonder if this wasn't the prelude to yet another trial. Or perhaps with him they'd skip the preliminaries altogether. He was merely the American's paid minion, who could be dispatched with no audience other than the two ruffians who'd spent the night outside his door.

But once he came along they loosened their grip. They walked him to a little grove of eucalyptus where the remains of a campfire sighed and whined. A small man crouching next to it placed a teapot on the coals, then piled sticks at the other end, blowing at the reddening bundle.

"Wait here," a guard said, then both men left.

Najeeb squatted by the fire to warm himself. By now the little man had coaxed a flame, which built as he added sticks, hissing and crackling, the sound of morning itself, with the air redolent of smoke. The man ignored him, so Najeeb said nothing. Then he heard footsteps approaching from behind and turned to see an oddly familiar bulk against the eastern brightness. Or was it the smell he recognized, an aromatic sharpness of someone who has been striding through open countryside just before dawn, a dewdrop bouquet of rosemary, goat dung, sweat and sandal leather.

"Najeeb, my son. Rise."

It was an order he knew from long ago, from naps in the hills and overnight hunting expeditions. The man might as well have been his father, though by all rights he might also have been a rival.

"Aziz?" Najeeb stood, fully awake now.

"Tracking you down again, just like the time when you were twelve, following those eagles over the passes until you stumbled into Shinwari country. They'd have cut your balls off, and these fellows will do the same if they get half a chance. Fortunately the two outside your door were a little more agreeable. Let's get you out of here."

The man had aged—hardly a surprise—but the old light in his eyes

looked different. It was as if someone had knocked the glass from a lantern. The flame still burned strongly, but the gleam on the surface was gone, the spark that had once shone from dawn to dusk.

Aziz seemed to be appraising him as well.

"You're a man now."

"I was a man when I left."

"No. You were still a boy, or you never would have opened your mouth to the government."

For a moment Najeeb thought Aziz was going to lecture him, and the flame in his eyes flared briefly, only to subside, making Najeeb wonder exactly what price Aziz must have paid for his indiscretion seven years ago.

"I learned my lesson," he felt compelled to offer. "No more betrayals."

"Not much of a lesson," Aziz said gruffly. "Not if you're going to survive out here."

The teapot began to steam, and Aziz picked it up, oblivious to the little man who had stoked the flame. Instead of taking offense, the man produced two cups. Aziz had always had that effect on people—a natural leader even if he'd had no sons nor any clan to rule.

"As soon as we drink this, we go. There's bread in my saddlebags. You can eat as we ride."

Would it really be so easy? Then he thought of Skelly, perhaps awake by now, alone and bewildered.

"I can't leave. Not yet."

"The American?"

So Aziz knew that as well.

"Yes."

"Has he already paid you for today?"

"It's not that."

"So he hasn't, then. Meaning you owe him nothing. He brought you here, and I'm getting you out. Consider yourself lucky. He'll be free of his troubles soon enough."

"I can't just leave him."

Aziz sighed, tossing the last of his tea to the ground in apparent anger.

"He belongs to Kudrat. As will I, if we stay any longer."

"Bribe them," Najeeb said, the solution suddenly seeming clear. "Bribe the guards."

"With what? This tea? My promises? Both would be worthless to them."

"The American has money. It's in his satchel."

The way Aziz's eyes widened Najeeb wondered if he should have mentioned it at all. He seemed to be calculating the odds, and his decision was quick.

"All right. But the guards will want to come with us. At least for a few miles."

Najeeb realized what he meant. The moment you let someone outbid you for Kudrat's services, he supposed, was the moment when you knew you had better make tracks.

They walked quickly back toward the room, which fortunately was at the far end of Kudrat's encampment. After all the festivities of the night before, everyone was sleeping late. Except, of course, the seven men who'd remained up throughout the night—the ones still dangling from the gallows, faces drained of blood and garments sagging with dew. Najeeb shuddered as he caught sight of them, just across the compound.

"We have horses," Aziz said. "We'll have to ride across the fields, straight into the sun for a while."

"There are supposedly bombs in the fields."

"Then they'll be less likely to follow us. But at the first sign that they are, we leave your friend behind. It will be him they want, not us."

"But . . ."

"My rules. It's the only way I'll risk it."

Even after several days among these men, Najeeb was just beginning to realize how out of practice he was at this way of life, how unfamiliar he'd grown with its sudden brutal turns and the disarmingly simple factors that could determine whether you lived or died.

"Let me worry about him, then. He's sick. I'll take him on my horse."

Aziz said nothing more, which Najeeb knew was his form of grudging assent. He went inside to deal with Skelly while Aziz began negotiations with the guards, who'd seemed surprised to see them return.

Skelly still slept. Najeeb felt his forehead—warm but dry, the fever apparently under control if not yet gone.

"Skelly," he hissed. "Stan." It was the first time he'd used the man's Christian name.

The eyes blinked open, bloodshot.

"Where are they? What's happening?"

"Where is your money? We have to bribe the guards."

"Bribe?" He seemed to collect himself for a moment, rising up on his elbows. "Are we getting out of here?"

"My uncle has come for us." No sense telling him that his uncle would rather have ditched him altogether.

"How much?" Skelly fumbled for his satchel, coming awake all at once. "How much do we need?"

"I will check."

He grimly wondered what to tell Skelly if Aziz hadn't been able to cut a deal. Perhaps they wouldn't relent at any price, having seen what had become of Bashir.

Najeeb poked his head out the door, catching Aziz's eye. The guards looked around nervously, which Najeeb took as a good sign. A few moments later Aziz came through the door. He seemed taken aback by the sight of Skelly, who was rubbing water on his face.

"Can he even ride?"

"I told you. I'll take him. I'll tie him to the saddle if I have to. How much do they want?"

"A hundred apiece. But I said fifty."

"We'll pay the hundred," Najeeb said, "just to make sure."

"They agreed to fifty, so we'll pay fifty. You've gone softer than I thought."

"It's his money, and his life."

"Then he won't mind paying me the leftover hundred, for my services."

Skelly was shakily on his feet now, and Najeeb told him the plan. The American reached into his satchel, unzipping an inside pocket and emerging with two crisp fifties, which Aziz eyed with wonder.

"How much more does he have in there?"

"Enough," Najeeb said. "Enough to get us all the way to Peshawar if we have to."

Aziz shook his head.

"No need. Our destination is much closer."

Najeeb wondered what Aziz meant, but they were running out of time.

"Bring him to just beyond the trees, next to the campfire," Aziz said. "Karim is there, waiting with the horses." So Karim was along as well. Najeeb's guardian angel, back on the job, or so he liked to believe,

more certain than ever that the man must have saved him from the *malang*, doubtless at Aziz's bidding. The thought summoned a fleeting memory of Daliya. Where was she now? Out there somewhere. He was sure of it, and now he'd be riding to join her.

Skelly was still weak, but he managed a few swallows of water before slinging his satchel across his shoulder.

"I hope I'm up to this," he said.

"You will be. Just hang on tight."

Skelly nodded gamely.

When they reached the trees there was no time for greetings. Karim and Aziz were already mounted. Getting Skelly aboard was a struggle, but it didn't look as if he would have to tie the man down. Najeeb felt the American's arms locked tightly around his waist as they swung into motion, keeping the horses at a walk to avoid attracting attention. Most of the camp was still sleeping. Najeeb wondered where the guards had gone.

Aziz nodded eastward, toward a broad field where the red rim of the sun was just peeping over a low ridge.

"Let's go," he said. "We've made enough noise already."

THE FIELD WAS BROWN, fallow, the ground a chalky powder after three years of drought. To their left rose the Kashmund Mountains, higher than anything they'd yet crossed, the distant peaks dusted with snow. To the right, still farther, were the jagged peaks of Tora Bora and the Safed Range. Somewhere in that general direction was their eventual destination, depending on the route Aziz had chosen. But for now they would move due east across the fields.

They rode slowly for the first minute, Najeeb still expecting the guards to join up with them any second. Ahead in the dirt he saw small yellow and white blossoms and wondered what could have sprouted in this dryness. Coming closer, he saw that the flowers were small cylindrical canisters tethered to tiny white parachutes.

"Cluster bombs," Skelly muttered in his ear. "Hit one of those and we're dead."

Najeeb passed the word to Aziz and Karim, who nodded, then wove through the strange crop of bomblets, which now seemed everywhere, as if the entire load had failed to go off, although a few small craters suggested otherwise. Along a line of trees at one end of the field

Najeeb saw a shepherd boy who had risen early, waving a stick toward about a dozen dirty sheep that seemed intent on crossing the field, heedless of the explosives.

Then from behind came the sudden pounding of hooves. Najeeb glanced over his shoulder to see two horses at full gallop—the guards, no doubt, foolish in their noisy haste. A gunshot crackled from the direction of the camp, which was now about five hundred yards to the rear.

Aziz cursed.

"Idiots," he muttered. "Asses! Keep your heads low."

He and Karim squeezed their heels into the flanks of their horses, and Najeeb followed suit as a second gunshot crackled through the morning stillness. Then came a burst of firing, followed by a sharp cry.

"He's hit!" Skelly shouted.

Najeeb assumed he meant one of the guards, but didn't dare turn to look. One of the yellow canisters passed just beneath them, making his heart leap to his throat, but they were still moving forward, the ground passing rapidly beneath them even though Aziz and Karim were pulling farther ahead.

Skelly was hunched closer than ever, his fevered breath on Najeeb's neck as they nestled like lovers, staying low for survival. Then more shots, and this time the unmistakable whiz of lead streaking past, smacking into the trees just ahead. Najeeb wondered if anyone was in pursuit.

"Are they coming?" he shouted. He felt Skelly twisting for a look, then going loose, nearly falling. A desperate grab clutched Najeeb's side as the man gasped and grunted.

"Jesus! Nearly lost it. No, no one's coming. Just the other guard."

Najeeb heard a small explosion, the air trembling, and glanced over his shoulder in time to see the last of a puff of smoke and a small shower of dirt, perhaps a hundred yards to their rear.

"The other guard," Skelly said. "Must have hit a bomb."

Aziz saw it, too, and shouted back to Najeeb. "And you wanted to pay them a hundred. You see?"

The gunfire abated when they reached the line of trees, and in the field beyond there were no bombs. Najeeb rose in the saddle to take his bearings. Far to the right was the field he had noticed on arrival the night before, the one where all the dark shapes had been. It was a graveyard of military armor—tanks with their treads unraveled and

artillery pieces blown in half. A turret lay on the ground next to one tank. Another was canted crazily on its side, a gash torn down the middle, as if it had been split open by a knife. There must have been twenty vehicles in all, none unscathed.

"That's where the air strike must have hit," Skelly said. "A bunch of Russian junk, by the look of it."

"Are they following us?" Aziz shouted, slowing to a canter. Najeeb supposed this would be the moment of truth for Skelly, and he looked back half expecting to see a wave of horsemen, or a fleet of the Toyota trucks, fishtailing through the dust. But there was nothing, only the shepherd boy and his flock.

"No," he said with relief. "They're not."

"Then they've decided we're not worth it," Aziz said, reining in. "Or Kudrat has radioed ahead for someone else to take care of us. Which is why we'll turn south as soon as possible. Avoid the villages and try to get to the fringe of his control as soon as we can."

"So have you made an enemy of Kudrat?"

"He wasn't a friend to begin with. But he's not your father's friend either, and that is what is more important. As you will soon see."

Najeeb wondered at the ramifications of that remark. Aziz had never spoken quite so openly of this rift in previous years. Perhaps times had changed. There were layers to all this that Najeeb supposed he might never understand. But he could live with that, as long as he made it back to Peshawar. Then the American would have his story and he would have his life back, once he tracked down Daliya.

"How's he holding up?" Aziz asked, nodding toward Skelly.

"He'll make it. We need to get some food in him."

"There will be time for that in a few hours, when we've reached the hills. How much will he be paying me?"

The crudeness of Aziz's pragmatism was still jarring to Najeeb, who realized he'd allowed himself to romanticize the man's role in his life in the intervening years. Aziz had indeed taught him much, and done much for him, but Najeeb was reminded that no one from his village did anything unless it served some purpose. It was not selfishness, or callousness. It was simply the way of life's daily commerce, part of the barter of survival. It seemed unduly harsh only if you had been away from it for a long time. Perhaps Skelly would find it amusing.

"I'm sure you will be able to name your price if you get him safely out of here," Najeeb said. "I'll even help you negotiate."

"Just tell me how much he has to work with. That would be a start."

"Probably at least—" Najeeb was about to say a thousand, because he believed that was the case. Then he checked himself, remembering he was playing under new rules. "At least four hundred," he said. "But he'll need some of that to get to Peshawar."

"Like I said, we won't be going there. You're going nowhere but home."

"Home?"

The word froze him. He glanced over to see if Aziz was joking, but the man was looking straight ahead, eyes on the mountainous horizon, perhaps calculating how many bills he would be thumbing by day's end.

"Home?" Najeeb said again, almost ashamed to have the word tumble out so weakly.

"I'll tell you more later. Just keep riding."

## CHAPTER TWENTY-EIGHT

SKELLY AWAKENED to the buzzing of a bee, only to discover it wasn't a bee at all but a whining ember sizzling in the remains of a campfire. Then it popped, spouting a tiny parabola of sparks, a private firework into the night chill.

No one else seemed to be awake. He was flat on his back. He remembered little of the day except for the almost constant jostling on horseback, holding his balance by pressing his face to Najeeb's back even when the heat and chill of fever had been almost unbearable. He felt wrung out, but dry and cool, as if whatever had gotten hold of him during the past several days had at last relinquished its grip.

He put a hand to his forehead to make sure, which only reminded him of the many caring hands of others over the past years—doctors, his mother, wives and daughters, a village laundress in Monrovia, and now Najeeb. Awakening briefly the night before in Kudrat's compound, he had seen his fixer watching over him with concern, while Skelly in his delirium had begun believing he could actually handle death, could prepare to meet it gracefully. And what would his late mother have said to that? For that matter, what would she say now, seeing him like this? He remembered how she had cared for him when he was sick, stretched on a bed or sofa, usually with the TV on and a half-eaten bowl of soup on a folding table. Even in Monrovia, during his Liberian misadventure, he'd at least had a cot. All that Afghanistan could offer tonight was a wool blanket on hard ground. But at the moment he didn't mind. His stomach was finally tranquil, and in the skies a bright plasma of stars rolled silently across the blackness, so wondrously deep and dense it seemed that you could plunge into it.

He shifted on the ground, and someone nearby moved as well, startling him, his body aching with the sudden movement. But he felt well enough to sit up for a look around.

Under a nearby blanket was the unfamiliar bulk of Najeeb's uncle, Aziz, who had unwrapped his turban to reveal a bushy black mane and was now breathing deeply with his mouth open. Just beyond was Najeeb, and on the far side of the campfire was the uncle's assistant, Karim—awake, he now saw—probably as the appointed sentry for the wee hours. Wise move, he supposed, although something about Karim had made him uneasy from the beginning. Even through the haze of illness the man had struck him as overly smug and watchful. Najeeb and Aziz had treated him as an obvious subordinate, paying him no mind. But Karim had noticed them, all right—or so it had seemed to Skelly.

He pushed the button to illuminate his watch. Nearly four o'clock. Looking across the embers again he saw Karim watching intently.

"Where are we?" Skelly asked in a low voice.

Some small creature in the rocks stirred in response, but Karim said nothing, and from his blank stare Skelly realized the man probably hadn't understood a word he'd said.

Skelly had come across many a person in his foreign travels who, under the same circumstances, would have tried answering in sign language, by frown or gesture or drawing symbols in the dirt, eager to communicate even when language failed, especially at such a lonely hour. Not Karim. He just stared back, impassive as a house cat, then swiveled his head to look down the mountain, off into the darkness.

Skelly spotted a water bottle within reach and suddenly was thirsty. He unscrewed the cap for a long, cool swallow, not caring if it was pure. By now the Cipro must have so thoroughly purged his system of microbes that he would be impervious. The coolness was like elixir, coating his throat and stomach, and he gently lay back down, content to have the rest of the night for further recovery.

So Najeeb had done it, he thought, awash in relief and gratitude. The young man had saved them both, even when it would have been easier to leave Skelly behind. He wondered what he might do to thank Najeeb, to reward him. Surely he would have to pay something extra, although the thought of recompense merely by dollars seemed coarse, even tawdry. All the same, it was probably what Najeeb needed most. He and his girlfriend, wherever she might be. If they had time once

they reached Peshawar, Skelly hoped to meet her, although he now seemed to remember something from the haze of his fever about a detour suggested by Aziz.

Skelly then turned on his side, curling up under the thin blanket, the ground more comfortable than he would have expected. And as he drifted toward sleep he again recalled the journey's most vivid memory—that of the tall man on horseback, with his white pillbox and the salt-and-pepper beard, soulful eyes aglitter in the dim light as he watched the hanging. Skelly had seen him, he was sure of it now. There was also the overland journey with Razaq, the firefight, the capture, the hanging—so much in his notebook and his head. The story within his grasp was huge, the biggest yet to be written here. But saying what? He recalled what Razaq had told him, something about being the force who was supposed to push the Arabs and their charismatic leader out of their Afghan refuge, presumably into some sort of trap. But with Razaq gone, who would do that now? Kudrat? Someone else? And why had the Americans let Razaq go down the tubes if he was supposed to play such a crucial role? Or had that lone helicopter with its feeble missiles been all they could scare up on such short notice? Then there was Bashir, perhaps the key to the puzzle, now dead like Razaq. But Skelly was certain he was close to the heart of it, and he clutched that knowledge to him like a pillow as he drifted toward his dreams.

THE SUN WAS UP when he next opened his eyes, a dusty orange ball that had roused everyone but him. He still felt fine, even better than last night, and he immediately reached for more water. There was only bread to eat, but for now that seemed like enough.

Najeeb smiled when he saw Skelly up and about. Skelly smiled back, finding it interesting that Najeeb wasn't shy about showing emotion now, even in front of his gruff uncle. Good for him.

Najeeb walked over and placed a hand on Skelly's forehead. He was obviously pleased with the result.

"Thanks," Skelly said. "Thanks for getting us out. For not leaving me."

Najeeb nodded solemnly, perhaps even a little embarrassed, so Skelly said nothing more.

"It was my duty," he said.

Skelly noticed now that Aziz was watching. Karim, too.

"Where to today?" Skelly asked brightly, trying to lighten the atmosphere, which suddenly seemed strained. Not that he needed to lighten his own mood. In the freshness of morning he was as excited as he had been as a boy before setting out on an epic car journey across America, knowing his father would be stopping only for gasoline and historical markers until they reached their destination.

"Aziz has a truck waiting a few hours from here. We'll take that the rest of the way."

"Won't we be crossing the border first?"

"We did that last night. We're camped a mile or so inside Pakistan."

Skelly was mildly disappointed to have missed the moment. Or maybe he figured he should have known the difference.

"All looks the same, I guess."

"Up here the border does not matter," Najeeb said. "Tribes matter. Tribes and clans, and whoever is in charge."

At that moment the idea of borders struck Skelly in the way it must have always been clear to the locals: a construct of foreigners, some marking made long ago by a British geographer in a drawing room, or out on a verandah, gin and tonic at the ready and a mosquito net overhead, wiping his brow as he traced the contour lines. Then, later, some lord or earl presenting the handiwork to the chieftains and *maliks*, who nodded, then went about their business exactly as before.

"What time will we reach Peshawar?"

Skelly relished the idea of a hot shower. But even more, he craved having someplace to get down to work. His laptop was gone, but he could borrow one. Or he would write in longhand if he had to, then fax it from the hotel. Once he nailed down the details, he'd have a story that would be quoted on the BBC, CNN and every major newspaper—the sensation of the month, perhaps of the year—and he would have an adventure for the ages in his memory banks. He was now glad they were across the border, out of danger and heading for the home stretch.

"We are not going to Peshawar," Najeeb said. "Not today, anyway."

Najeeb's somber tone worried Skelly as much as the message.

"What's going on?" He eyed Aziz, hoping the man didn't speak English.

"I am not sure myself."

"But it's Aziz's idea? Or Karim's?"

"Not Karim's." Najeeb seemed amused by the idea of Karim calling the shots. "Aziz insists we have to see my father. Partly because we would not be welcome on any other passage. Bandits and rivals. We would be at their mercy. You especially. We would need an armed escort like Bashir's to make it across."

"I thought you weren't exactly welcome at your father's anymore."

"It is true, what you say."

"But they'll let us pass?"

"They will receive us, for certain. Your presence ensures that."

"Mine?"

"As a Westerner, an American. In my company you will be viewed as a guest, subject to *malmastiya*. And because you are on the run from Kudrat and his Arabs there will also be *nanawatay* to consider."

"Nana*what*? And what was the first one?"

"*Malmastiya*. And *nanawatay*. They are part of *pashtunwali*, the closest thing we have to law, or a constitution. It is our code of behavior. *Malmastiya* obligates us to provide hospitality. Even to our enemies, as long as they come in peace."

"And *nanawatay*?"

"Refuge. Asylum. You will have an honored lodging in the *hujera* for as long as you care to stay."

"But I don't want a lodging. I want passage. This story won't hold forever."

"Tell that to my father. He will be your host. But do not push him. And do not refuse his hospitality, unless you want to stay even longer. If he offers too much food, eat it anyway. If the bed is too soft, sleep there anyway."

"Sounds more like hostage-taking than hospitality."

"You think there is a difference?"

"In most places."

"Not here. The more generous the hospitality, the more controlling the host. If you go for any walks, you will be sure to have an escort."

"What about you? Will you have a problem?"

"Not as long as I remain in your company. I am afraid that now it may be your turn to protect me."

He owed Najeeb at least that much, story or no story. Perhaps he could even pay for Najeeb's freedom. But now didn't seem like the proper time to bring that up. Not with Aziz and Karim around.

"Don't worry," he said. "I'll do what I can."

Najeeb nodded grimly. "There is one other thing I should explain. Aziz has been my father's rival for years, while pretending to be his ally. It may work to our advantage, or it may work against us. But keep it in mind, whatever happens."

Skelly wondered what must have been discussed around the campfire in the hours before he awakened, or yesterday during their long journey on horseback, when he was barely cognizant of what was going on. Already he could sense that Najeeb was withdrawing, marshaling his thoughts and energies for whatever lay ahead, retreating behind his Pashtun mask of blankness.

THE TRUCK WAS WAITING, as advertised, and it felt good to dismount. Skelly's rump was bruised, and his thighs ached. The fever, however, showed no sign of returning, and the simple but filling breakfast had boosted his strength.

Less than an hour of driving brought them to the crest of a ridge, where a narrow road twisted below in a series of unpaved switchbacks. Beyond was a village by a sparse grove of green trees. A stream ran through it, glinting in the sunlight.

"Bagwali," Najeeb said. "My village."

Halfway down the slope they passed a pair of barefoot boys wearing slingshots around their necks. A mottled dog, rib cage outlined on its fur, sauntered past with a hungry look, its tongue dangling close to the ground. The boys stared openmouthed at the truck, oblivious to the rolling cloud of dust and exhaust. Najeeb's expression seemed almost mournful.

In the village below, Skelly now saw two red mini-trucks streaming toward them on a dirt track, leaving a long brown contrail. Two men sat in the open bed of each, guns at their sides. The trucks could only have been responding to their arrival. They must have easily stood out on the side of the mountain.

"Here they come," Najeeb said in a flat voice. "Our welcoming committee, preparing to say hello."

"Let's just hope they also know how to say good-bye," Skelly said, watching the trucks with growing apprehension.

Najeeb had no answer for that.

# CHAPTER TWENTY-NINE

A T A CRUMBLING aid agency outpost atop a crumbling hill, Karen Wilkins sat at a borrowed desk shaking her head, certain now that she really had seen everything. Seated before her was a new twist on an old ruse—a woman disguised as a man—and if Wilkins hadn't seen it with her own eyes she wouldn't have believed it possible, not here, not in this wild countryside where no stranger went unchallenged and no woman on her own went unmolested.

Yet there was a certain logic to it, she supposed, especially if you were as bold and desperate as the young woman who now sat before her, clearly exhausted but just as clearly relieved to be on safe ground. And clearly, as well, the woman had done a convincing job of making herself resemble a callow young man. Wilkins's first reaction had been to order her from the building, because a male face within these walls always set her wards aflutter, tossing their chadors and burqas back into place like schoolgirls who'd been caught skinny-dipping.

"I'm sorry," Wilkins had announced sternly in a burst of Pashto, "but this area is for women only, and you should know that."

She'd wondered if this one would even understand her, because he'd looked Punjabi. No beard and no turban. Just a white pillbox skullcap, plus those luminous brown eyes that she envied among all these people, men and women alike—placid pools that invited empathy even when concealing treachery. Quite an asset, such eyes, not least when your own were as blue and easy to read as the skies, betraying every shift in mood and emotion.

Yet, when the face finally spoke, the voice emerged softly, wearily, even timidly, halting Wilkins in her tracks.

"Please, I need your help. And I am a woman, not a man."

And so she was—an attractive young woman at that, once you got past the severe haircut and the clothes, hanging upon her frame like dirty sails. Wilkins had heard outlandish tales that this sometimes happened in the slums of Peshawar—young women frustrated with their lack of opportunity dressed for a while as boys, taking odd jobs that they would never have a shot at as females. But never out here. Not in the Tribals.

"So tell me . . . Daliya, was it?"

"Yes. Daliya Qadeer."

"You've been on the run for how long now?"

It was the very question Daliya had just been asking herself, because it seemed like weeks. Yet she had set out from Islamabad only that morning, trying to reach the village where she was hoping Najeeb would end up.

She had considered contacting the place first by telephone, just as Najeeb had advised on a night that now seemed ages ago. He had given her the number for a PTT office in his home village of Bagwali, and told her to ask for his mother, Shereen. But even if the message got through, Daliya told herself, how would a mother react to the idea of some strange woman pursuing her son? Especially in that culture. Not well, she decided. So instead she formed a plan of independent action, knowing only that she must somehow reach the village of Bagwali and hope for the best.

It was a long shot, she knew. But far preferable to the alternative of returning home. At worst, she would have an adventure before heading back to her parents in defeat. And when she'd heard the news on the radio that afternoon at Professor Bhatti's, plus later updates stating that the captured Mahmood Razaq had been hanged—or so the Taliban was claiming—she was sure she was on the right track, even though none of the reports said anything about an American journalist or his young Pashtun translator.

So on she traveled, intent on reaching this very woman, Karen Wilkins, at this office, within a mile of the famous Jamrud fort at the eastern entrance of the Khyber Pass, just off the Grand Trunk Road. The destination had been the idea of Professor Bhatti, who'd pegged Wilkins as a likely and able confederate, having met her at a conference a few months earlier.

"She's got contacts out there," the professor had said, speaking of

the tribal frontier as if it were Siberia. "And she's an Englishwoman, with access to her own trucks and bodyguards, so she can actually move around a little. Mention my name."

Daliya did just that, and the response was impressive. Wilkins smiled, eyes twinkling, and seemed to lower her guard just a bit. Then she frowned, the eyes crinkling with a hint of disapproval.

"Did Professor Bhatti advise you to dress up like this?"

"Well, no . . ."

The professor, in fact, had found the whole idea outrageous, even dangerous, although in the end she offered her grudging assistance as Daliya clipped her hair in great clumps upon the floor. Daliya had then bound her breasts with an Ace bandage and donned a baggy new *kameez*, feeling she was stepping into a realm of freedom she had always yearned for on the streets. Now she would be able to board any bus she pleased, speak her mind to strangers, stroll any avenue at any time of day, and demand her money's worth from every merchant.

But the moment she walked into the streets in her new getup she tensed, certain that she would be unmasked within seconds or that her voice would betray her even as she cast it an octave lower, straining like a singer for the proper projection while awkwardly adopting the rough vernacular of men. She had hoped that a few hours of practice would make it second nature, but it never happened, if only because every few minutes seemed to bring a fresh threat of exposure.

The worst such moments still loomed vividly. There was the man on the bus from Islamabad to Peshawar who'd eyed her intently the whole way, a smile playing about his eyes as if he were reading her thoughts and could see through her garments. Or the fat, hairy one, all sweat and stomach, who'd pressed against her when boarding the microvan to Jamrud, pushing just hard enough to feel the yielding softness beneath the wrapping around her chest. He'd shot her a look of surprise, as if she might be some sort of freak, then the look had turned to a knowing leer, but he'd mercifully disembarked at Hayatabad without a word to anyone.

There had been at least a dozen close calls, and during each of them she had been fearfully certain she was about to be revealed or, worse, denounced and attacked, stripped of her *kameez* and exposed as the freak she was. The anxiety had destroyed her appetite, and she had foresworn food and spoken only when necessary, her voice sounding contrived and falsely throaty.

Yet she had survived, and now here she was, seated at the very refuge her professor had recommended. And as she told her story to Wilkins she realized that she could finally relax. The revelation came upon her so suddenly that she felt light-headed, and began to slide from the chair, unfolding like a creased sheet of cardboard returning to its original shape. Tears of relief brimmed but did not spill—one last reserve of discipline hanging tough—but her descent to the floor continued inexorably until she reached her knees.

Wilkins came quickly round the desk to catch Daliya beneath the armpits, rough, strong hands and a milk-white brow furrowed with concern.

"Jamila, bring a glass of water! Quickly!"

The sound of scurrying in the corridor, then a hand appearing to Daliya's left with a sweating glass. She sat up, sipped, then gulped, feeling better already. She'd reached bottom and was now swimming for the surface, racing past the bubbles.

"There now," Wilkins cooed, squatting on the floor next to her. "Are you all right?"

Daliya eased from her knees onto her rump. Wilkins stayed within reach, as if Daliya might yet shatter.

"Why don't you lie down for a while? I'll get you a cushion."

"No, thank you. I really am okay. But tea would be nice. And maybe some biscuits."

Wilkins nodded to her assistant, who hurried off to comply. To make the rally complete Daliya stood, if a bit unsteadily, then sat back down in the chair. Yes, much better now. She picked up the glass from the floor and drained it. A few moments later the tea arrived, steaming and sweet. There was bread on a plate, and she tore off a piece.

Wilkins waited a few minutes, not returning to her desk until she was sure Daliya wouldn't slide right back to the floor. Brow still furrowed, she began tapping a pencil on her chin, seeming to realize for the first time exactly what sort of responsibility she was about to accept.

"So Professor Bhatti sent you here, then."

"Yes."

Wilkins thought that over some more, the pencil still tapping.

"How old are you, Daliya?"

"Twenty."

The pencil froze in midbeat.

"And your parents, do they know you're here?"

Daliya shook her head.

"They live in Islamabad?"

Daliya nodded.

"My father works for the government."

Wilkins set down the pencil with the greatest of care, as if it had suddenly turned into a stick of dynamite.

"Doing what, if I might ask?"

"He's an assistant to the deputy minister for commerce."

Wilkins paused, perhaps calculating just how much she might stand to lose either by helping Daliya or by sending her away. In either course of action there was no telling where the young woman might go next. The only safe solution was a phone call straight to the parents. She supposed she could ferret out the number easily enough.

But what was her mission here, if not to help women, even if this one happened to have lived a life of privilege and wealth? You could tell that from her skin, and from the way she'd nearly dissolved after a mere day of traveling. Yet why be so quick to return her to the crutch of patriarchy when she was just beginning to steady her legs?

Wilkins had been in Pakistan ten months now, and she hadn't yet tired of writing her friends back home about how backward the place was in its attitudes toward females. But she also wrote them about how rewarding the work could be, assisting these tribal women who were stretched to the limit by the strict codes of purdah. And if Daliya wasn't as needy as they were, well, she was at least willing to make leaps that Wilkins's other wards would never dare. So why not help her, too? Risk be damned.

"So where are you trying to go from here?"

"Bagwali. There are . . . people there, who I have to see. It's personal."

"Yes, I know the place."

Daliya brightened, the sugar from the tea spreading through her system.

"You'll never get there dressed like that, though. They'll eat you alive before you even make the next five miles."

"What about traveling in a burqa? I brought one."

"In a group it might work. I could send you out with a few others. Or how about this—I can take you myself. Not to Bagwali—I'm not really welcome there, I'm afraid. I'm a bit too brash for the taste of the

elders—but to Alzara, the next best thing. We have a district office there, a small clinic for mothers and babies. I can drive you there. Not tonight, it's too late. But you could stay at my place, then I'll run you by in the morning. Or by midafternoon at the latest. Too many appointments in the morning, I'm afraid. From there, of course, you'll be on your own."

"How far is Alzara from Bagwali?"

"No more than five miles. But distance isn't the problem. Bagwali is an Afridi village. Alzara is Shinwari, right near the tribal boundary. Which means it's not usually the happiest of places, and sometimes it's a jumping-off point for little wars and disputes. The good side is that you can actually move around Alzara as a woman, because everyone's so poor. Nobody with enough airs to make a fuss. The bad part is that there's no way you're traveling over to Bagwali from there, not by yourself and not with me. And even if by some miracle you found a way to slip across the tribal boundaries without any trouble, you wouldn't want to be seen alone in the streets. Not in Bagwali."

"Without another woman, you mean?"

"I mean not at all. Bagwali is something of an aristocratic town. By local standards, of course. Poor but elevated, or that's the way they see themselves. Meaning unless there's a wedding or a funeral you'd better keep your pretty little burqa'd head indoors if you know what's good for you."

"There have to be some exceptions."

Wilkins shook her head.

"Tell me, have you ever heard of osteomalacia?"

Daliya shook her head. "It sounds like some kind of bone disease."

"It is. It's also called rickets, and in most places only children get it. Not enough vitamin D, so their bones go soft. Well, out here, especially in places like Bagwali, there are adult women who get it. It's because they're indoors all day. Every day. Especially in families too poor to have a walled courtyard. No sunlight, so no vitamin D. Appalling, isn't it? And that's the culture you're up against. Still interested in going?"

It sounded horrible. But having come this far, it would have seemed absurd not to take one more step. At the least she might pick up some news in Alzara, if such news ever traveled beyond the boundaries. With luck she might find a way to send a message.

"Yes, I'm still interested. I'll ride to Alzara with you."

"Well, you've got spirit, which is more than I can say for nine out of every ten women who walk through that door."

"Thanks."

"Don't thank me. Just don't blame me later if it all goes to hell. You're about to step back into the past about five hundred years. Try not to get stuck there."

CHAPTER THIRTY

HIS FATHER still looked regal, Najeeb gave him that. And in the past seven years Malik Mumtaz Azam Khan seemed to have aged hardly at all.

"My son," his father said, in level, rasping tones, the voice strong but as dry and sandpapery as the air of the valley. He stepped forward with arms outstretched, leaning from the waist and placing his arms around Najeeb. It was a light, perfunctory hug with a ceremonial feel, a reserved sort of greeting normally bestowed upon visiting government authorities and rival *maliks*. So Najeeb held back as well, not wanting to surpass the display in either warmth or exuberance, of which there was none. Then they broke apart, his father kissing him lightly with dry lips upon either cheek. There were no repeat hugs, such as old friends would offer each other even when meeting on a village path. Najeeb saw and felt that it was mere formality.

But the memories came anyway, and not all of them were bad. He recalled their days of hunting, and the morning of his first kill at the age of eight, a single shot fired from a rifle he could barely hoist to his shoulder that had brought down a quail, flushed near a Buddhist ruin. A burst of feathers, a sharp echo from the bluff, then silence while his father stepped forward like a stalker, as if certain the bird might yet rise and flee. Upon confirmation of success his father had not smiled, but his eyes had danced, and his hands rested warmly upon Najeeb's shoulders like a blessing.

But the eyes were not dancing now, and without that liveliness his father's face was otherwise unremarkable. Handsome for his age,

Najeeb supposed, despite the tall forehead where the skin seemed stretched too tightly, and his towering white turban was, as always, immaculate.

The man's most noticeable aspect had always been his stillness, his bearing. Najeeb's father had never been one to fidget or grow restless, even after long spells of sitting or standing, well after everyone else had begun squirming like a nest of worms. When he stepped into bright sunlight, he did not squint. In the cold he did not shiver or rub his arms or call for an extra blanket. Nor did he sag or wilt in the most sweltering heat. It was as if he wanted to show he could defy the elements as easily as he defied other men.

And certainly he had never bent or yielded when it came to accommodating his son, which was Najeeb's chief memory as he stood there, trying to give as good as he got, offering a gaze that was almost a glare even while knowing he would be the first to look away. He turned toward Skelly to begin introductions.

"This is my friend and colleague," he said, the order of words intentional. "Stan Kelly, whom you may call Skelly."

"Mr. Skelly," the *malik* said evenly. Then, in Pashto: "You are welcome here for as long as you like."

Skelly nodded in response to the translation.

"Thank you, sir. That's very gracious of you."

Najeeb translated for his father, while wondering how much English he had picked up through the years.

The *malik* had not come out to meet them, of course. They had come to him, escorted to the great room of the *hujera*. Doing otherwise would have been considered bad form for the *malik*, considering his son's current status, no matter how long they'd been apart.

The two red trucks had brought the four of them downhill to the town, Najeeb and Skelly riding in one while Aziz and Karim remained in their own, tucked between the other vehicles lest anyone have second thoughts about completing the journey.

The armed men had announced the importance of their arriving cargo by firing Kalashnikovs into the sky, rapid bursts that startled Skelly, who turned abruptly to see if Aziz might have come under fire.

"It is all right. It is because they are happy," Najeeb said, knowing that wasn't entirely true. He placed a calming hand on Skelly's arm, but maintained the expressionless gaze he had been practicing all morning. "They are showing pride of possession," he said, closer to the truth.

"Their pride in you?"

Poor Skelly. He said it so hopefully.

"Their pride in *possessing* me. And you as well, if I had to guess. They do not get many American visitors."

"So what's this going to be like for you? Emotionally, I mean."

It would likely be the last time in a long while that anyone asked about his feelings, and it was such an American question, seeking innermost thoughts with an almost offhand expectation of an honest answer. All the questions soon to come from his father would be engineered for more practical results. Not that knowing someone's emotional state wasn't useful. But you never found it out here simply by asking. Even a query as basic as "Why?" often drew only a response of "Asai," meaning "None of your business," a sort of bland Pashtun "Fuck you," to remind others that in a land of few possessions, thoughts were proprietary.

"It is going to be difficult," Najeeb said flatly, "but I will deal with it."

Allowing himself a final show of feeling, Najeeb squeezed Skelly's upper arm in kinship and reassurance. "Do not worry for either of us. I will not forget your interests. You must remember that, no matter what it seems like I am up to. I will not be able to translate everything once we are with my father and his lieutenants. So be patient, and try not to smile too much. And whatever you do, do not ask if you can leave. Doing so today would be rude. Doing so tomorrow might be acceptable, which would only be worse. Because the moment they let you cross into other lands will be the last moment anyone sees you alive, unless you leave with me. So wait for my cue. Trust only me."

"And if something happens to you?"

"Then God help you."

But the more Najeeb tried to bottle up his emotions as they approached the village, the more they boiled up within him—a geyser of nervousness, anticipation, dread and excitement. It would be a struggle, his greatest in ages.

There was nostalgia to deal with, too, especially as they passed through the village, where everybody seemed to be staring back at him from an earlier era. Old men leaned toward the windows with grizzled faces and missing teeth. Underfed curs snarled and barked. There were no women, of course, although he thought he glimpsed a face or two in second-story windows and rooftop parapets.

His home lay just beyond the town in a prime location, literally a stone's throw from the stream. It was a small compound of mud-and-stone buildings behind a twelve-foot-high wall, with a stout watchtower at one corner. Somewhere inside was his mother. He peered through the grating of the big iron gate as they passed, but saw no one. He doubted he would be able to see her before tomorrow, if then, for the meeting with his father would take place at the *hujera*, the men's guest house outside the compound walls.

As the trucks skidded to a halt on the gravel, he looked behind them for Aziz, but only Karim remained. Aziz had vanished, as if he'd never been with them at all. Najeeb could have sworn that none of the vehicles had stopped on their way down the mountain, but he must have been wrong. It was unsettling. He had hoped Aziz would offer an extra measure of protection. Now he would be facing his father alone.

The engines stopped. Truck doors slammed, and the armed men fell in single file behind Skelly and him. He knew his father would be waiting just inside, standing in the long, immaculate room with brightly embroidered cushions arranged at the base of whitewashed walls, just as it had looked during counsels and *jirga*s he had attended as a boy. Except then he had sat quietly to one side, observing and supposedly learning. Now he would be one of those men he had always pitied, subject to his father's inquisition.

Which is where he stood now, seeing the familiar face, hearing the voice, and watching the way the man's hands moved, also familiar, remembering now how the gestures once reminded him amusingly of a nightjar as it settled onto its nest, ruffling and preening. The recollection calmed him, and he felt certain he could make it through the day. Age and experience had begun to serve him. Without realizing it, he supposed, he had grown from dove to eagle just as his father had always admonished, and in some hidden place perhaps he had even grown claws, if not yet bared them. With any luck, his father would underestimate him.

The *malik* soon made it clear he was saving the day's most important business for later, because shortly after introductions he ordered others to show Najeeb and Skelly to their lodgings. Dinner, he said, would be in two hours.

"It will be my honor to serve you both," his father said, face impassive.

"And in the meantime," Najeeb said, "I will visit with my mother."

"Patience. There will be time for that tomorrow. For now, it would be best if you rested. Both of you."

Don't move beyond my sight, in other words. And your mother is off-limits. Najeeb's heart sank. That part of his life seemed to fall away from him, the last survivor of his childhood, now gone.

"Yes, Father. That would of course be best."

"As you wish. We will meet again this evening."

How odd to play such a part opposite your father, a stilted role in which you still weren't sure what the next act would bring. Perhaps his father hadn't decided either. But the *malik* had never been one to make up a script as he went along. He was an inveterate planner, and Najeeb figured he was saving the dramatics for dinner. So after translating this first exchange for Skelly, Najeeb would rest while he could.

But when he turned, someone had already whisked Skelly away to his room. Every possible ally was disappearing, everyone but Karim, who lingered at the entrance, Najeeb's designated escort. Perhaps that was a victory of sorts. His guardian angel.

"So maybe you can get me a visit with my mother," Najeeb said, allowing a brighter tone to creep into his voice.

It was a mistake.

"You heard the *malik*. No visits."

Najeeb scrutinized Karim to see what was up, but could read nothing. Karim turned, and Najeeb followed.


HIS ROOM WAS well furnished, far more nicely appointed than he'd remembered from years ago. It was clear that his father's position had continued to rise, and his wealth to accumulate, even from the days when he had enjoyed the windfall of the weapons trade and his entry into the heroin market. Never mind the government raid on the production facility, the one that Najeeb's indiscretions had helped bring about. His father had easily rebounded, with the sort of aggressive diversification that would be the envy of any Western tycoon.

The summons to dinner came with a knock at the door from Karim. They strolled together to the great room, where twenty men were already seated on cushions around a bright and elaborate red carpet, stained here and there by the banquets of twenty years, and threadbare in places. But you wouldn't have wanted it looking too new, not in this room where so much important business was transacted. That might imply newly minted power, of unproven durability.

Najeeb had a sudden urge to explain all these nuances to Skelly, but he was seated on the opposite side of the circle, looking bewildered and out of place between two men who probably didn't speak a word of English. Najeeb would try to steal a moment with Skelly after dinner, even if he had to bribe Karim, a prospect that made him indignant.

Aziz was conspicuous in his continuing absence. It was one thing not showing your face during a routine evening at the *hujera*, when your known presence elsewhere might be construed as a minor but forgivable snub. Failing to show for an occasion such as this seemed tailored for insult. Perhaps the rift between Aziz and Najeeb's father was old news around here, but he noticed many of the men glancing around, as if looking for someone.

The other surprise in the arrangements was the continuing presence of Karim, who instead of standing at the margins as befitted his status had joined the circle, seated only a few men from the *malik*.

Serving boys carried in the food, which was sumptuous, a nonstop caravan of lamb, roast chicken, bread, eggplant, tomatoes and sauces. After the thin, rude fare of the past several days it was more than welcome. Najeeb ate heartily and saw Skelly doing the same. He hoped the man's stomach would be up to the challenge.

Most of the meal passed with small talk. His father made no major pronouncements and didn't bother to announce either Najeeb's presence or Skelly's to the company at large, which was mildly unsettling. As trays of fruit and sweets began to appear, the conversation ebbed, and Najeeb glanced up to see his father looking toward him, the high forehead jutting like the prow of an arriving warship. It seemed that the real festivities were about to begin.

Instead, someone brought forth the hubble-bubble hookah, the pipes already loaded with the mild blend of hashish and tobacco known as *naswar*, which Najeeb hoped wasn't too potent tonight. As the instrument went round the room he took a few puffs, deciding that a little relaxation might actually help. Poor Skelly, obviously heeding Najeeb's advice from earlier in the day, also inhaled, seeming to turn a little green as the smoke hit home. Then Najeeb's father cleared his throat, and everyone went silent.

"Tell me, Najeeb," he said loudly, "do you still think of your uncle Aziz as your friend? Your protector, even?"

There were no gasps or awkward looks, as there might have been in the dining rooms of New York or London, although Najeeb couldn't help but notice sidelong glances flickering from face to face, even as

heads remained fixed, trained on their lordly *malik*. He realized then that his father must have planned a grander spectacle than Najeeb had anticipated. He only wished he could relay the news to Skelly, because he was now certain that some perilous moments of theater were ahead.

Najeeb decided on a bold approach, meeting the issue head-on.

"I don't think he is my protector. I know he is." Then, remembering the dead *malang* outside his apartment building, and certain that his father somehow knew of that event as well, he added, "The *malang* also knows he is."

"Then why do you think he is not here tonight at my *hujera*? And why did he not even bother to ride with you into the village this afternoon? For that matter, what makes you so certain that it was he who had anything to do with the *malang*?"

"Because Karim was there that night."

"This very same Karim who sits with us here, you mean?"

"Yes," Najeeb said, nodding even as he began to feel confused, and embarrassed. He worried that his father might have just manipulated him into exposing some sort of duplicity on Karim's part. Perhaps this would be the evening's first humiliation—the exposure of Karim as a plotter against the *malik*. It might be the sole reason the man had been welcomed into the circle of his betters. But if that were so, why was Karim still seated so calmly, without a care to crease his brow?

"Ah, so now you begin to see things more clearly, perhaps," his father said, doubtless having read the confusion on Najeeb's face. "You see that Karim does not run from this room in fear, so how can he be a spy for his master Aziz? But you are right about one thing. I did know about the *malang*. And I knew as well about the messages you received at times from your mother. I knew as well, even though you may not, about Aziz's little visits with your mother. About their long history with one another."

The last statement floored Najeeb. His mouth fell open, and he shut it too late. The *naswar* had relaxed him far too much, which he supposed his father must have counted on. The *malik* had always had a flair for pursuing an attack on a wavering enemy, and Najeeb expected him to do so now.

"I would have supposed that a man of the world such as yourself, one who takes a mistress before he even takes a wife—a bachelor with a concubine, now that is something new for our family—I would have expected someone like that to have figured all of this out by now. But I

can tell from your face that it is news to you. Staying in touch with you was what your mother needed to do, I suppose, as were her dalliances with Aziz, if only as a way of getting back at me for my own infidelities. Aziz, of course, only participated to humiliate me.

"But that is a secondary matter. It was you he was always courting the most. I saw that from your earliest days. I always wondered what Aziz would do to oppose me, once his wives were unable to produce a son. Then when I found all those drawing books, those bird sketches beneath your bed, then I knew. He'd taken you for his own. Hunting together, smuggling supplies to you for your little insurrections. Taking my own son and turning him against me. You became his wedge, his weapon, and with every passing year he honed your edge against me. But of course he made the edge too sharp, too fine. In trying to make you someone other than my son, he made you something other than a Pashtun, and so I pushed you even further, to ensure that you wouldn't belong to him, either. Which is why I sent you away, off to university. So arrogant and haughty you became there, with your libraries so far above us, and with all of your women—yes, I heard about them, all those American girls. Then our government friend, Tariq, came along to show us what you had truly become. You wrecked my little factory for a while, but not for so long that we couldn't recoup our losses. And others, of course, paid the greater price. But I don't suppose your uncle Aziz ever told you what happened to him."

Najeeb slowly shook his head. The world was reshaping before his eyes, and collapsing on his head. He felt buried, emotions at a boil. He swallowed hard and set his jaw, determined not to flinch or look away.

"I heard he might have gone away for a while," Najeeb said. "To lie low."

"Lying low. That's one way to put it. Imprisonment would be even better. Nothing of the official variety, like they have in Peshawar or Islamabad. But your friend Tariq insisted that someone, preferably with higher standing, had to pay a price or else things just wouldn't look right. I offered him Aziz, and arranged it so the state would be spared the expense of his incarceration, which Tariq liked even better. So the next time Aziz was off in Afghanistan supervising a caravan from an opium supplier, I arranged for our Taliban brothers to happen upon him, and all his wares. Karim, why don't you fill him in on the rest?"

Karim proceeded to do so in lurid detail; an expressionless mono-

tone rehash of the way Aziz had been subjected to a peculiarly effective brand of Taliban punishment reserved for drug runners—two years of beatings interspersed by hours at a time in chambers of frigid water. No wonder Aziz hadn't wanted to linger around Kudrat and his Arabs once he'd rounded up Najeeb. One more slip among those people and he'd doubtless have been up on the gibbet next to Bashir. Or perhaps Karim had made a secret deal to prevent that. Any alliance seemed possible now, and that would explain the ease of their escape.

Whatever the case, Najeeb felt devastated. Even if his uncle's affections had been calculated all those years, the help Aziz had offered had been invaluable. It was crushing to learn he'd been responsible for so much pain. But there was no use giving his father more satisfaction from it, so Najeeb held himself in check—blinking once did the trick—and stared back toward his father.

"Of course, by the time he returned you were an outcast," his father continued, "and he wasn't quite sure what to do with you, or more to the point, what to do *to* you. So he simply stayed in touch, pretending he was still your friend until he decided on a course of action."

Najeeb felt suddenly defeated, humiliated before the entire assemblage. He looked across the room to see that even the uncomprehending Skelly now looked worried, and tried to signal with his eyes, telling him that the news was only getting worse. Najeeb shook his head slowly. There was no sense in any further pretense about a mask. His father, sensing that the son must have finally figured it out, let him speak next.

"The *malang*. He . . ."

"Was sent to kill you, by your uncle. Only he was no mere assassin. Your uncle always thought of himself as too clever for such bluntness. Everything had to be artful, elaborate. Thirty years of trying to outwit his older brother made him too enamored of details. So he found this *malang*, this mendicant from the hills, and all he had to do was tell him of the life you were leading, show him the things you'd written in the newspaper, the people you spent time with, the beverages you drank, and he knew that would be enough."

"So the *malang* sent me the notes."

"Yes. As a warning. As an opportunity for you to mend your ways and save your soul. But you didn't heed them, of course, as Aziz knew you wouldn't. He had no doubt that plans would move to a rapid conclusion."

"He was going to let him kill me."

"It would have been a humiliation for me, once word got around what had happened and how it had transpired. It was to have been a demonstration of Aziz's new powers. But it was a humiliation I wasn't willing to endure."

"How compassionate of you."

"Your only concern should be that I saved your skin. Thanks to the actions of Karim here."

"Yes, Karim, who killed the *malang* with a knife from my kitchen."

"It was that or have Karim compromise himself. And what better way for me to keep control of you than for you to land in the Peshawar jail. But of course your old friend Tariq interfered once again."

It was hard getting used to the idea of Tariq as an ally. Or perhaps he was only the lesser of many evils.

"Then, of course, Aziz heard you'd gone off with Razaq."

"And when I was in trouble, he came and got me," Najeeb said, spotting a weak point in his father's rationale and eagerly prodding it. "He got both of us. If all this is true, why not let them kill me?"

"Because he had found a better use for you here. He brought you back as a trophy. You gave him something to rub in my eye, to blind me with just as he was preparing to make his final strike, in order to disrupt my most ambitious venture yet."

"More heroin factories?"

"Please, my son. I do not repeat mistakes. But it is fitting that you mention that, because the very cave that you told the authorities about will now be put to much more advantageous use. As a home for new guests, ones who prefer to avoid notice in the village."

"Guests from where?" Najeeb asked, although he knew the answer.

"From a foreign land. A little like your Mr. Skelly. Only far more devout than him, I would wager."

"And bearing gifts, I would suppose."

"It will be up to them, of course, to determine the value of my hospitality."

No one had to tell Najeeb that it wasn't a good sign that his father was confiding in him. A son guilty of betrayal would never again be trusted with such information, unless the father had devised a means of ensuring the son's silence.

"So what will you do with me now?"

"Give you back to Aziz. He will come for you, and I'll let him have

you. Not without pretending to put up a fight, of course. He will then deliver you to his backers as a great victory, a sign of his new powers that will ensure their support."

"He will deliver me how? Dead? Alive?"

"I am afraid I am not privy to *all* his plans, Karim's efforts notwithstanding. But I am sure that with patience you will find out soon enough."

"Who are his backers?"

"Our usual rivals. The Shinwari, right across the hill in Alzara. Aziz has been trying to interest them in joining in an uprising for years, but they've never been convinced he had the necessary strength. You'll be the evidence he needs. But we'll be waiting, of course, with certain new arrivals of our own, which will spell the end of them, and the end of Aziz. So you see? Your arrival was fortunate. And worthy of this dinner, and this evening among friends and honored guests."

Najeeb nodded toward Skelly.

"And what will you do with him?"

Skelly, sensing that the conversation was now about him, perked up accordingly.

"He is my guest. So even though it troubles me greatly to hear of all that he saw across the mountains, what else can I do except show him our hospitality? And if there are those among my new visitors who seek to do him harm, I will of course protect him. As is only right."

"And when he decides to leave? When he crosses the boundary of your lands?"

"Then he will no longer be my guest."

This told Najeeb everything he needed to know.

"When will Aziz come for me?"

The *malik* turned toward Karim, who answered.

"Tonight. I am the one who will let him inside the compound, him and a few others. There will be shots. Perhaps we will even kill one of his men, just to make him believe more deeply in what he has accomplished. And I will fall, too, of course. Or pretend to."

Presumably so Karim could stay behind, and join in the final plot for Aziz's destruction. But in all that confusion, might Najeeb find his own way to safety? His father seemed to read his thoughts.

"I would discourage any idea you might have of foiling those plans through your own initiative, my son. Should you remain upon

the grounds once Aziz has departed, Karim will know how to deal with you."

The same way that he dealt with the *malang*, Najeeb supposed. All in all, he would rather take his chances with Aziz. But that would mean the end for Skelly, who would be left alone and unprotected. And eventually it would mean the end for him as well.

So had the dove really matured into the eagle after all? It sure didn't feel like it. But if somehow he had, then this eagle had better soon discover its claws.

## CHAPTER THIRTY-ONE

IT HAD BEEN HOURS since Skelly had heard a word of English. He had never felt so isolated. He tried to reach Najeeb after the dinner, but two men escorted him away before he could catch Najeeb's eye. As he was leaving the great hall he saw Karim leading Najeeb away by the arm.

Skelly spent the next hour being squired around by the nudges and grunts of a pair of unsmiling bearded men. He ended up on the verandah of the *hujera*, seated on a cot to watch the moon rise as it cast a pale light on the walls of the family compound. After half an hour in silence, one of his escorts drifted away, but the other maintained the vigil, working through a pack of cigarettes by lighting each from the burning stub of the previous one. Skelly gave up any hope of seeing Najeeb until morning and rose to take his leave, shadowed all the way to his door.

Now he lay in bed—a decent mattress stretched across a rope frame, his most comfortable berth in days. He'd stripped to his underwear and already imagined he could feel lice crawling from the thin blanket onto his chest. But anything was preferable to another night in his clothes, which he hadn't changed since Azro. His beard bristled and itched after three days without a shave, and he would have paid hundreds for a shower, or even clean underwear.

The dinner, at least, had been restorative, if heavy on his stomach. He must have drunk a gallon of hot tea, in preference to the questionable water. Late in the meal someone had surprised him with a warm Pepsi, the bottle looking like something from a vending machine in

the 1950s. He gulped it down, and the sugar and caffeine still sang in his veins. The smoke from the odd-looking hookah had scorched his throat despite the water filter, but it had at least seemed to relax him. He had no idea what had transpired this evening, although the stunned look on Najeeb's face at the end of the dinner had worried him, especially when Najeeb began frequently glancing his way during a lengthy pronouncement by the *malik*. But Skelly had been unable to decipher any message beyond a general impression that things were going poorly.

He had forgotten how bewildering life in a foreign land could be without a translator, and it was doubly frustrating knowing his fixer was right across the room, separated by familial duty and centuries of tradition. So he had kept eating the food as it was offered, just as Najeeb had advised. And now, stretched out on the bed, he replayed the night's events as if they might hold some clue for what would happen tomorrow.

Skelly had been surprised to see Karim at the dinner, and even more surprised when the man spoke up, delivering a short speech of apparent importance, judging by everyone's rapt attention. And where had Aziz gone? If he was now out of the picture, Skelly supposed that was further bad news.

Yet for the first time all week he felt relaxed. Maybe the food had done the trick, or the hookah. More likely it was that he felt protected here, despite all the restrictions on his movement. As long as he did as he was told he would be sealed from harm. Tomorrow he would lie low and work on his story. Too tired to think about it now, he soon drifted off. With no fever to warp his dreams he slept soundly, slipping into a blank realm where his body seemed to be counting time. So it was that when he finally awakened it was as if he was emerging from the bottom of a pool, surfacing to the jarring sound of gunfire and an angry commotion outside his door.

He groped for his clothes, tumbling out of the low bed with a painful thud, his own stench rising to his nostrils as he stooped to pull on his shoes. His back ached from the day on horseback. Stepping groggily onto the verandah, he heard shouting and rushing feet from the nearby compound. Then came two gunshots and what sounded like hoofbeats. A burst of machine-gun fire followed, a few rounds striking the wall overhead and sending down a shower of mud and plaster. For a horrible moment he wondered if Kudrat's men had come

for him, bursting into the village after an overnight ride, and he edged back into the doorframe.

Then the shooting stopped and the hoofbeats receded. He stepped off the porch, looking up to see turbanned heads in the moonlight atop the parapets of the compound wall. To the right a man passed on horseback in no apparent hurry, the beast nickering, tail flicking. A man on the wall shouted, eliciting rough laughter from someone below. A hand grasped Skelly's arm from behind, and he nearly jumped out of his skin. One of his escorts had returned and was tugging him back toward his room. But Skelly wasn't going without trying to find out what was happening. All he could think to do was shout out the name of the one person who he knew could help.

"Najeeb!"

Silence. Another burst of laughter.

"Najeeb?"

The escort again tugged his arm, then croaked out the first words of English anyone seemed to have said in ages:

"Najeeb gone. Gone."

"Gone where?"

"Gone." The man waved dismissively with one hand as he pulled with the other. Skelly finally relented and went with him.

"Gone." A key word, but with so many possible meanings. Departed? Dead? Gone to the compound, or to some other place, perhaps on horseback? For all Skelly knew, the escort's English was so limited that he might even be referring to Najeeb's previous seven years. Gone, but now returned.

"What do you mean, 'gone'?" he asked, desperate for more. He suddenly felt quite alone. The desolation of abandonment seemed all too near.

"Yes, gone. Najeeb gone."

No use, he supposed, and by now the compound was again quiet. Perhaps there would be some answers in the morning, but for the rest of the night the word "gone" troubled his sleep.

THE MORNING OFFERED nothing clearer.

Skelly wandered outdoors into the early sunlight, only to be chivvied toward breakfast. They brought him yogurt and bread along with a pot of tea and a bunch of small, blackened bananas. He tore off

three of the sweet, mushy fruits and wolfed them down. The tea was milky and hot, and he swallowed enough to burst his bladder, figuring that unless someone offered another Pepsi it might be the only liquid he could trust until he got back to Peshawar.

There was still no sign of Najeeb, and his questions now were answered only with blank stares. But for all his worries, his story was now preying on his mind. He would have killed for a phone, but he didn't see any lines coming into the *hujera* or the compound. The only cables were electrical wires. Maybe the village had a public telephone office, where he could pay enough dollars to make an international call. "I've seen him," he wanted to shout across the miles to his editor. "I've seen the man himself, and there is some sort of plot, either for his capture or for his protection." Details to follow, of course, as soon as Skelly discovered what those details might be.

Perhaps he could find someone who spoke a little English. He thought of trying to work on his story in longhand—a few potential lead paragraphs had darted through his mind as he awakened, all of them featuring prominent references to al-Qaeda Arabs and a colossal betrayal of Razaq. The puzzle was where the Americans fit in, and why.

He walked back to his room, and with nothing else to do he pulled his notebooks from his satchel, covering everything from his jottings about his beers with Sam Hartley to the hangings back near Jalalabad. He arranged them in chronological order, then began flipping through the pages, adding things up as best he could, inching toward conclusions that had previously eluded him. It felt good to be back at work, arranging the pieces of this puzzle and beginning to discern a shape. Feeling thirsty, he got up for some tea, which by now had gone cold in the pot. He saw by his watch that hours had passed, but there was more yet to do.

Skelly worked a few hours more, sketching a detailed outline and a few conclusions, all of it in longhand on the broad yellow pages of a legal pad. His top remaining questions were on the last page, starred and underlined. He was so close. Then he pocketed his pencil and packed away the notebooks, slinging his satchel across his shoulder and strolling out the door.

By now it was midafternoon. There was still no sign of Najeeb, and with each minute the man's absence seemed more ominous. There was also no sign of Najeeb's father, or his uncle Aziz, or even the shadowy

Karim. In fact, no one seemed to be around either the compound or the town but a few old men and small boys.

The place was almost spooky in its silence, oddly reminiscent of a Sudanese town where Skelly had once sat around with a hut full of women and children, anxiously awaiting the return of a raiding party. There was the same air of impending judgment, as if everyone of importance was off somewhere else, determining the future.

But here even the old fellows carried guns. It was apparently part of their wardrobe—*kameez*, sandals, blanket, turban and Kalashnikov.

Skelly realized that he craved news. He hadn't listened to the BBC in days, ever since losing his portable shortwave along with his laptop and the rest of his luggage in the ambush. For all he knew, the Taliban was already on the run. He wondered if the Razaq story had gotten out, and how it was playing. Anything might have happened.

He decided to again test his escort's English—the man was lurking just down the corridor of the *hujera*—and he tore out a page from his legal pad and scribbled the word "Najeeb." Then he realized that if the man read at all, his letters would be in Pashto, or Urdu, which to Skelly looked just like Arabic. So he crumpled the paper and tried a few words aloud, but got only stares in response.

This was hopeless. He decided simply to begin walking, to see what would happen. He left the verandah without a problem, strolling beneath the wall of the housing compound. As he approached the compound's iron gate, his escort drew near, taking hold of his arm and firmly but not belligerently steering him away. Perhaps they feared he would stumble into a group of uncovered women. Fair enough.

Next, Skelly turned onto the path leading toward the village, scanning the streets ahead for signs of telephone wires. Twenty feet along the hand grasped him again.

Skelly turned, smiling, but drew only an impassive nod. His escort looked to be in his seventies, although from experience with other Pashtun men Skelly realized the man might actually be a contemporary, wrinkled and dried by hard living and the relentless sun. These hills were not engineered for graceful aging, nor was the lifestyle.

He tried another path with some success until it, too, turned toward the village, and the arm steered him away. He felt like a sheep being herded by a border collie, nudged this way and that. But finally he found a footpath heading away from town toward a small rise that might at least offer a vantage point for the surrounding countryside.

The old man didn't seem to mind, and Skelly began to worry more that his guard would simply disappear. He recalled Najeeb's advice that he not try to leave the clan's territory on his own. Perhaps he would unwittingly cross some nearby boundary, prompting the old fellow to shoot him. But it seemed safe to at least go up the hill, which looked like a climb of only a few hundred yards.

Looks were deceiving. It was a half mile or more to the summit, and Skelly was panting and thirsty by the time they got there, skirting a dust devil as it swirled down the slope. But the view was worth it. He sat on a large stone, taking in the sights while the old escort kept his feet.

Judging by the path of the sun, he supposed that Peshawar lay off to the right, well beyond a series of low hills. Straight ahead across a widening plain he could just make out a narrow track, where a truck inched along before a tiny contrail of dust. Behind Skelly was an even higher bluff, which would probably require a half day's climb and a full canteen.

The most interesting view was down to the left, back toward the village. From his current elevation he could see past Bagwali, across rolling countryside to a second village that was now just visible beyond yet another stony hill. He figured the other town was no more than five miles away.

It was too distant to hear any noises from the place. In fact, there were no sounds up here except the distant bleating of sheep and the rasp of his breathing. His old escort seemed to have hardly broken a sweat.

Ten minutes later Skelly decided he had seen all he wanted. It was time to head back to the *hujera* and round up another pot of tea. Then a crackling noise like distant fireworks rolled across the plains. His escort snapped to attention, and together they gazed into the distance. The old man pointed toward the far village, muttering something in Pashtun. "Alzara," he said. "Alzara." Perhaps that was the name of the place.

It now sounded as if a full-fledged battle was in progress, small-arms fire punctuated by deep thumps from what must have been RPG rounds. On a hunch, Skelly tugged at his escort's sleeve. The man seem transfixed by the noise, as if it might be encoded with a message. When Skelly finally got the man's attention he pointed toward the sounds and said, "Najeeb?"

The old fellow nodded eagerly, as if Skelly had just provided the answer to an important riddle.

"Najeeb. Yes!"

Then the escort pointed toward the town, and as another deep thump echoed through the hills, said evenly, "Najeeb gone. Najeeb gone."

## CHAPTER THIRTY-TWO

A FEW HOURS EARLIER, Daliya was sitting in yet another office, getting nowhere fast. A nervous woman named Allison didn't seem to even want her there, much less out on the streets of Alzara.

"You just don't do that here," she insisted.

"Karen Wilkins said I could."

"Karen doesn't have to live here." And Karen, who at midafternoon had driven Daliya from Jamrud on a rutted lane barely wider than a goat path, had just departed. That left Allison Clymer in charge, and she was making it clear that Karen's opinion didn't count for much here at the Pakistan Women's Network's Alzara clinic for women and children. But that didn't stop Daliya from invoking the name one last time.

"Karen said it wasn't as restrictive here for women as it is in Bagwali."

"Please," Allison said, holding out a hand in warning and practically coming out of her chair. "Don't say the name of that village so loud here. There's a lot of trouble between the two places. A lot of rumors lately. Saying it aloud will only make people suspicious of you."

Daliya had indeed noticed a few heads turn her way when she'd said "Bagwali," although she couldn't say whether they were shocked or angered, because even indoors nearly every head remained covered by a veil or a burqa. There were perhaps a dozen women in all, seated on benches with babes in arms and infants underfoot. The men who'd brought them waited outside the open door, where loud music blared from a shop on one side, and the air was heavy with the scent of popcorn and frying meat.

Daliya had thought she knew what to expect in a place like Alzara. She had traveled by taxi through some of the poorest and most clogged streets of Rawalpindi, where she'd always turned up her nose to the reigning squalor, noise and confusion. And if her months in Peshawar had taught her anything it was to stop being such a snob about people who got a little grimy by having to claw their way through life.

But this place was the roughest and most unseemly she'd seen yet, and not only because of the dirt, the mounds of garbage and the general frontier scruffiness. The men carried enough weaponry to start a small war, and they'd stared through the truck window at Karen and her with icy, offended glares.

Daliya had also expected that it wouldn't be too difficult to arrange some sort of transport to neighboring Bagwali, rivalry or not. Her unlikely run of success during the past several days had taught her—incorrectly, as it turned out—that persistence and ingenuity could overcome all obstacles, cultural or otherwise. But as far as this testy woman Allison was concerned, Daliya would have had more luck planning an afternoon stroll up Mount Everest than a five-mile ride to Bagwali.

"Look, it just can't be done. Maybe on some days you could take a little walk in that direction, with an armed guide from one of the neutral clans, and by sticking to the side trails. But today you'd be lucky to even make it around the block. Even fat old Malik Jamil has been lying low, and that's never a good sign."

"Who?"

"The local warlord, Jamil Rafik-Khan, a Shinwari clan leader. Lives outside the village but keeps a *hujera* at one end of town. He usually puts in at least one appearance a day, a sort of grand tour every afternoon to allow the great unwashed to gaze upon his regal bearing."

"You don't sound impressed."

"He's a thief and a scoundrel. Skims half our supplies and generally makes my life miserable. He's the main reason none of these women you see here came without an escort. Him and his thugs. And none of these ladies would even dare go anywhere near"—she paused, lowering her voice—"Bagwali. Didn't you see all the men out in the streets with guns?"

"Aren't they always like that?"

"They are. But there are more of them than ever. They've been trickling in for the last two days from farms and other villages. Only a

few dozen more than usual, but here that means something. A feud. A battle. Something bad, and soon, and you don't want to be caught in the middle of it."

"Something to do with Bagwali?"

"Please." She again raised her hand like a Stop sign. "None of the women seem to know for sure. But they've been gossiping about it. There's a *jirga* tonight, some sort of war council. A lot of them are keeping their children indoors. Believe me, the streets are usually filthy with the creatures."

Such a nice way to describe the people she was supposed to be helping. Daliya couldn't help wondering if she, too, had ever sounded like that, nattering among her friends in Islamabad. It would probably be easy to burn out here, amid all this need and despair.

"Well, risky or not, you can't stop me from going out that door," Daliya said, speaking more bravely than she felt.

"I can't, but they can. All those men with guns. Once you're in the streets you're at their mercy, and I'm taking no responsibility for you. Understood?"

"But Karen said . . ."

"Karen." Allison spat the name like a cherry pit, the weary disdain of someone whose decisions had been countermanded one too many times. "Karen doesn't know the half of it. *Karen* considers Jamrud hazard duty, and she's what, three hundred yards from the main highway? Eleven miles from Peshawar? Jamrud's a stroll through Knightsbridge compared to this place. If Karen thinks you can go for a nice little walk in Alzara, maybe she'd like to be your escort. If this were just any day, I might even squire you around in mufti. But as you can see I've got eleven women with babies to treat and only two hours left to do it."

"Then I'll just get out of your hair."

"Wait." The hand went up again, this time in supplication. Allison quickly scanned the room while flipping a strand of hair off her forehead, a harried gesture that made Daliya regretful for the intrusion.

"Go in our truck, then," Allison said finally, heaving a great sigh. "I'll send Muhammad with you. He won't like it. It's beneath his manhood playing nursemaid. But the truck's got our logo on the side, which still counts for something, thank God. And he'll just have to get used to it if he wants to earn his rupees."

"Where will he take me?"

Allison shrugged.

"Around the block. Through the bazaar. Up one end of town and down the other. Which will last all of a half hour if he drives slowly enough. Not much of a tour. But since I don't really know what you're looking for other than a way out of town, it will at least give you a feel for the place, and show you what you're up against. Maybe it will even convince you to just go back home."

Back home. The words dropped heavily to the base of Daliya's stomach, and despite having been on the verge of doing just that, she resolved to keep trying, even if it meant a little more wandering, and even if she wasn't yet sure what she would be looking for. A vantage point, perhaps? Someplace where she could scan the horizon for roads and paths that might lead to Bagwali? She realized with despair that she didn't even know which direction to look in, and she felt too embarrassed to ask. Truth be told, what Daliya needed most right now was luck, but she knew you almost never got lucky by sitting around waiting. Luck had to be ambushed, taken by surprise, and for the moment this offer of a driver was her only hope for doing so.

"All right, then. I'll ride with Muhammad."

MUHAMMAD GRUMBLED from the moment Daliya stepped into the cab of the small white truck. He wasn't used to ferrying around women in local dress unless they were seated in the back, on the open flatbed. But Allison had ordered him, and Allison paid him every Friday. So, this woman in the blue burqa whose name he didn't even wish to know had eased onto the seat, forcing him to prop his Kalashnikov in the middle, right next to the stick shift and hand brake. If any of his friends saw him and disapproved, he'd tell them it was for a huge bonus, a number that would make their heads spin.

Daliya was appalled anew by Alzara's poverty. The children caught the worst of it—and if a lot of them were being held indoors then Allison was right, because there were swarms of them nonetheless. They were grimy and barefoot, garments in tatters and hair matted. Occasionally she spied a woman's face in a high window, up near the rooftops where wood smoke poured into the endless blue sky. Otherwise there were no females to be seen older than the age of ten. Men with guns stood at every corner, some with grenade launchers, extra shells dangling from their other hands like soft drinks, swaying as they gestured in conversation.

After fifteen minutes of what seemed to be the same one-block circuit, repeated three times, Daliya demanded some variety.

"Where's this *hujera*?" she asked. "This place where Jamil Rafik-Khan lives."

"Busy place," Muhammad said, dismissing it with a wave of his hand. "Too many people there."

"Can't be any busier than this." A donkey cart had halted in front of them. Waves of men poured around it like a stream around a boulder. "Take me there."

"It is too busy there. Too much happening." Did she detect a note of fear?

"Allison said I should see it. Just once."

Muhammad cursed, waving his hand again as if shooing a pigeon. But invoking the magic name of his paymaster seemed to have done the trick, and half a block later he turned up a side street that angled toward the end of town. The crowd thinned until they approached a cluster of low buildings beneath eucalyptus trees near the end of the lane. On one side were a few shops. On the other was a ramshackle house, where Daliya again saw blue-covered faces in an upstairs window, gazing out upon the world below. And there was much to gaze at here, because right next door was a large, low building surrounded by a mud fence. Six armed men stood out front near an iron gate. A line of vehicles along the curb included a long black truck with an enclosed rear, of a make she had never noticed before.

"The *hujera*," Muhammad said quickly, flicking a hand toward the fenced-off building. He seemed to want to get out of here as fast as possible. The armed men were glowering, stooping for a better look inside the aid agency's truck. But just as it seemed they were in the clear, two red trucks rounded a curve toward them on the narrow lane ahead. Muhammad, who had driven aggressively among the children and the horse carts, now pulled meekly to the shoulder to let them pass. It made Daliya wonder if the local *malik*—what had his name been? Jamil Rafik-Khan, that was it—was inside one of them.

"Wait," she said, as Muhammad prepared to ease back onto the road. She wanted to see the show, too, just like the women in the house next door, but Muhammad kept rolling. "Wait!" she repeated. "One minute, that's all. Or I tell Allison."

He mumbled something under his breath, but stopped the truck. Daliya looked back to see that the red trucks had pulled up in front of

the *hujera*. The six men who'd been eyeing Muhammad and her were now fully absorbed in welcoming the arrivals with hugs and hand-shakes. Leading the newcomers was a tall turbanned man who, judging by the reception, must be Jamil Rafik-Khan.

"Now?" Muhammad said, easing off on the brake.

"Just wait!" she said. "One second more." The hairs on the back of her neck prickled beneath the burqa, and she found herself glancing sidelong through the mesh so it wouldn't be obvious she was staring. Such was the malignant nature of the man's power, she supposed, or maybe some of Muhammad's fear had rubbed off.

A second man in a white turban, big and loud, and with a bushy brown beard, also got a warm reception. The next pair to emerge from the trucks—two men pressed together, as if one were holding on to the other—moved quickly through the welcoming party without word or gesture. But that wasn't what caught her eye. The fellow who seemed to be in tow turned slightly as the pair edged through the crowd, and the flash of his profile in the sunlight of early afternoon was electrify-ing. The giveaway, however, was his eyes, as familiar as old friends, and even in the brief glance they seemed sadder than she had ever seen them. But why would Najeeb be here, in the heart of what was suppos-edly enemy country? Surely she was mistaken, but she had to find out.

"Wait here," she said, a foolhardy plan of action taking shape. She knew that if she paused to reconsider she would never go through with it, so she quickly unlatched the door, stepping into the street as the incredulous Muhammad turned toward her.

"What are you doing?" he hissed, still too frightened to shout. "Are you crazy?"

"Yes," she said, shutting the door in his face.

She crossed the street diagonally, rushing straight for the house next to the *hujera*, the one where she'd seen the women upstairs. She had to restrain herself from breaking into a run, and she didn't dare glance back at Muhammad, although she hoped he wouldn't drive away. Two of the armed guards perked up, frowning at her, and she watched them through the burqa out of the corner of her eye. If they made a move, she would run.

But the distraction of the arriving guests, and perhaps also the aid agency logo on the truck, must have set their mind at ease just enough for them to let things slide, especially once Daliya disappeared into the front doorway of the neighboring house. Luckily for her, the menfolk

weren't home. Perhaps they were even next door, having a smoke inside the *hujera*. She headed straight for the steps in case anyone was following, and her pulse didn't slacken until she reached the upstairs room, where the three women still huddled by the window.

They'd heard her coming, of course, and had seen her exit the truck. But they were only curious, not frightened. What could possibly be frightening about the sudden appearance of a woman dressed just like them, who for all they knew was a friend? In this town it was men who caused the problems, especially the ones next door. And at their sparse end of the village there weren't even any female neighbors to shout at from the rooftop. So, if anything, Daliya was greeted as a welcome distraction, another bit of spice for an afternoon that had already provided more than the usual dose of stimulation, with the excitement of a *jirga* still to come.

Daliya didn't really know what to say, so she mumbled a hello in her terrible Pashto, hoping it would suffice. But of course it didn't.

"Who are you?" said an older voice. Then the woman, the shortest of the three, came away from the window and pulled off the top of her burqa, leaving Daliya to feel obligated to do the same.

"My name is Daliya. I've come from Islamabad." It sounded idiotic to her own ears, but was apparently exotic to her audience. The other two, she saw now, as they also pulled off their burqas, were young women around her age. The older one must be the matriarch.

"Why are you here in our house?"

"I am sorry, but I am in danger." She was again groping for a footing, but this statement too seemed to be a hit with the younger ones.

"In danger from those men out there?"

The woman's tone seemed to signal that an answer in the affirmative would result in a quick banishment, so she said, "No. From the Afridi. From the men of Bagwali."

The young ones were again impressed, but the old one saw right through it.

"Then you have no need to be frightened in Alzara. You can go back to your truck, and I am sure everything will be all right as long as your driver leaves soon."

"Yes, I'm sure you're right." What to say next? "But there is one person I must see first. Before I return. And this may be my last chance ever to see him."

She gestured toward the window that they'd been gazing out of. This time, at least, she was telling the truth, and for whatever reason—compassion for Daliya's agitation, the temporary absence of males in the house, or perhaps nothing more than the thrilling prospect of taking independent and even risky action in the midst of a hard and numbing life—the woman agreed to help, a decision eagerly endorsed by the two others.

So they gathered by the window, their four heads bunched as closely as space would allow. The house was old, and sat at a slight angle to the street, and from the window they could see perfectly what was happening on the grounds of the *hujera*. The new arrivals were now headed inside, presumably into the great room, leaving only one man on guard outside.

"And who is this man you seek?" the older woman asked.

"His name is Najeeb. He's my brother." Daliya was certain the old woman knew she was lying. She thought it best to withhold the vital information that Najeeb was Afridi.

Suddenly they were distracted by the sounds of shouting from next door—whether in triumph or anger wasn't clear. Then there was a sort of collective huzzah, as if a rally were beginning, and a few minutes later Najeeb himself emerged—there was no doubting it this time—followed closely by a man with a Kalashnikov.

"That's him," Daliya said, her heart leaping. "That's . . . my brother."

The armed man led Najeeb to a doorway near the closest end of the *hujera*, ushering him inside, then shutting—but apparently not locking—the door. It was a helpful reminder. These weren't armies, Daliya told herself, nor was this a jail. It was a guest house, and these were tribes, clans, glorified ruffians, only slightly more organized than a pickup team of cricketers, even if much better armed.

"This man—your brother, you say?" The old woman's expression suggested she knew the real nature of their relationship. "He doesn't seem too welcome there."

"No, I don't think he is." Here was the moment of truth, she supposed. Then one of the younger women intervened.

"Look. The *malik*! He is leaving."

He was indeed.

Perhaps now he would take the so-called grand tour about the town that Allison had mentioned. Next to Daliya, the old woman tutted, a

look of disgust on her face. She then seemed to ponder something a moment, as if coming to a decision. When she finally spoke, her voice was tinged by bitterness.

"Yes. The great and powerful *malik*. Wastrel of young men. Come with us to the kitchen, Daliya. I think we may be able to help you."

## CHAPTER THIRTY-THREE

NAJEEB SAT EXHAUSTED on a cot in the musty darkness, fretting like an actor awaiting reviews after an anxious opening night. He'd played his part as promised, dodging gunfire in the dark and doing as he was told right through dawn. But of all the day's scenes, the last had been the most difficult and disheartening.

Aziz had bundled him into the back of a truck and brought him here, to the *hujera* of Jamil Rafik-Khan, a pompous, rail-thin man who upon introduction had barely acknowledged Najeeb, obviously as a show of disdain for Najeeb's father. Yet the man hadn't shied from trotting him out as a prized centerpiece a moment ago, when rallying the troops for action.

But Najeeb had been more upset by the actions of Aziz, whom Rafik-Khan had introduced to the rabble as a sort of holy convert, a new brother in arms. Aziz returned the favor by talking down to Najeeb before the assemblage, then putting words in his mouth—words of betrayal and upheaval, and of undying devotion to Rafik-Khan. Najeeb took his cue and nodded compliantly, mumbling a few halfhearted words of assent as the men cheered his disloyalty. It was then that he had spotted the two Americans standing at the back of the room, or so he guessed, judging by their looks and their manner of dress. They were somber and unsmiling, as if merely there to observe, but they weren't taking notes, so they must not have been journalists. He'd never seen them before, either at the Pearl or at the embassy, but he figured Skelly might know them. And for whatever reason their presence only disconcerted him more. Aziz, sensing that his costar

might be about to crumble, had then ordered Najeeb sent away for "rest and preparation." So here he sat, his performance over unless he could dream up some other way to make himself useful.

Throughout the morning Najeeb had considered telling Aziz everything he knew—all about Karim, and his father's plan to turn the tables on this little revolt. But Aziz would only have seen the confession as yet another ruse, a desperate pack of lies cooked up by Najeeb to save his skin. Also, for whatever it was worth now, Najeeb had vowed not to betray his father a second time, even if his father had used him as casually as he might have used a hammer from a workbench, and only to further another of his dubious schemes—trafficking this time in humans rather than in opium, timber or weapons. But given the choice between his father and Aziz, he now thought his father was the lesser of two evils.

Neither man would need or want Najeeb's loyalty now, however. Through pratfall and pride, he had achieved this landscape's most hazardous status. He was alone, unarmed and expendable, with an imperiled foreign journalist as his only ally.

There was Daliya, too, of course, yet another well-meaning if ineffectual innocent. For all he knew, by now she was either dead or back with her parents, virtually imprisoned. The mere thought of her brought his frustrations to a peak. But instead of anger there was only the emptiness born of exhaustion.

Feeling that he had to do something, he stood up with a sigh and tried the door. Unlocked. There was still a guard just along the wall, and another was posted at the front gate. But even if he could vault the walls before being shot—a slim chance at best—where would he go for refuge in Alzara? He supposed it was yet another sign of his obsolescence that he no longer merited close attention, so he shut himself back inside, determined to think matters through. He figured that his father's attempt to turn the tables would take place before nightfall, because that was when Rafik-Khan's men intended to strike. That left Najeeb no more than a few hours to come up with a means of escape, unless Aziz disposed of him first.

He was startled by a knock at the door. Perhaps his time was already up. But it was only a boy, who looked around twelve but of course had a Kalashnikov slung on his back. He was giggling, as rare a sight here as a waterfall.

"There is a *duma* here for you. Sent by the Malik Rafik-Khan. As a gift."

A dancer, in other words, or more commonly, a whore, usually the wife of the village barber, if for no other reason than tradition, so far as Najeeb knew. This must be someone's idea of a joke, possibly Aziz, seeing if his nephew could still get it up even when robbed of his future.

"I don't want a *duma*."

"Well, you can't refuse one," the boy said, obviously enjoying his empowerment. "Not when she is a gift of the *malik*." He shouldered his weapon provocatively, as if signaling that further resistance would produce sterner consequences.

"Whatever you say, urchin. Send her in."

The *duma* was covered head to toe, already a departure from tradition, which held that the *duma* was the one woman in town who might walk uncovered in the streets, showing her face to men. Because what was she, after all, but damaged goods and the property of many? This one at least smelled better than the usual selection.

When Najeeb was a boy he had looked forward to such visits, not that they occurred frequently. They were initiation rites arranged by his father, to assure the patriarch that his heir's vital parts were in working order and would someday be up to the task of propagation. But Najeeb had long since outgrown that level of curiosity, and at the moment the thought of being entertained by a strange woman only seemed tiresome.

"Well, do your dance if you have one," he said, sitting on the cot. "Then go. I'm not interested in anything else."

"Are you certain of that?"

The voice took him aback, as did the accent. He knew only one woman who spoke Pashto so poorly, but surely it was a trick of his weariness. Then she pulled back the top of her burqa, and he saw that it was really her.

"Daliya!" He stood, reaching for her.

"Quiet. We don't have much time."

"How did you . . . ?"

"Later. I'll tell you all of it later. The longer I stay, the bigger the risk."

But by then she was in his arms, and his despair was replaced by the warmth of relief. Having held himself in check for hours he could now let go, and for a moment neither said a word as they savored each other's touch and smell, eyes brimming with the emotion not only of reunion but of all they had endured.

"All hell is going to break loose in an hour or two," Najeeb finally said, still holding on tight. He had at least a dozen questions, but urgency shoved them aside. "You'll need to get as far from the town as you can. So however you got in, I hope you can still get out." He stroked a hand across her cheek, pushing back a strand of hair. "I just wish I could go with you."

"You can," she said. "That's why we have to hurry. Look what I brought."

She opened a small plastic bag. Folded tightly inside it was her farewell gift from the three women next door, a blue burqa just like the one she was wearing, only several sizes larger. It had belonged to the taller of the younger women.

"Put it on," she said, then saw his look of disbelief. "I don't care what you think, just put it on. The boy outside has been bribed. His grandmother hates the *malik* because he has already cost her a son. So hurry."

THEY WEREN'T SPOTTED going out the door. Najeeb shuffled his feet awkwardly, finding that the garment bound his knees. You could never run in one of these things, he thought, and the rectangle of mesh across the front of the hood kept drooping below eye level. He hoped no one would see his sandals, clearly those of a man. A guard noticed as they rounded the corner of the *hujera* and shouted, doubtless believing he'd discovered a pair of skulking whores, who'd been known to use the rear entrance.

But he didn't pursue them, and the boy threw open the rear gate as promised, still wearing his impish grin. Within seconds they were in the alley. Najeeb had trouble keeping up with Daliya, who was fairly skipping toward a small lane that cut back toward the main street. He wondered how one ever got used to these things. Thinking that he heard footsteps pursuing them, he turned to glance over his shoulder, but the sliding hood blocked his view and he nearly tripped. Daliya had disappeared around the corner and he redoubled his efforts to keep up.

"He's gone," she hissed angrily, head turning both ways as she scanned the street. "No. He only moved, the coward. It's my driver. Come on."

Najeeb got his first look at Muhammad, who was slouched behind

the wheel of an aid agency truck a full block down the street from the *hujera*. He leaned his head out the window, waving uncertainly, as if unable to tell if this was Daliya headed his way.

"It's me," she said. "We have a passenger. Let's get out of here."

Muhammad didn't seem happy about the extra rider, and Najeeb kept his mouth shut, letting Daliya take the seat in the middle. They crowded together three abreast, not even leaving enough room for Muhammad to wedge his Kalashnikov against the hand brake, so he placed it on the narrow ledge behind him, against the rear window of the truck's cab. When Muhammad turned the wheel back toward the office, Daliya spoke up.

"Not that way. Just get us out of town."

"No," he said firmly, his sense of aggrievement boiling over. "The truck cannot leave the town. It is not permitted."

"Oh, come on. I'm sure you must take it to Jamrud sometimes."

"Only with Miss Karen. Not with you." Digging in his heels. "It is *not permitted.*"

"It's permitted now," Najeeb said.

From Muhammad's expression it was hard to tell what shocked him more—a man's voice issuing from a burqa or the barrel of his own gun aimed at his face. Najeeb loudly chambered a round to show he meant business, and Daliya flinched. But Muhammad was already turning the wheel in the preferred direction.

"Okay, then," Muhammad said weakly. "We go to Jamrud. Just this time."

"No," Najeeb said. "We go south. Turn up here and head for those hills."

"They will fire me," Muhammad squeaked, one last chirp of protest before he fell silent altogether.

Najeeb had never set foot in Alzara before today, but it was easy enough to figure which way to go by the lay of the land, the angle of the sun, and the set of the hills—and because he was only five miles from home. He looked back over his shoulder to make sure they weren't being followed, wondering how long it would be before someone sounded the alarm at the *hujera*, but the road was empty.

"I guess you can take that off now," Daliya said, with the hint of a giggle. But Najeeb knew that the danger was only just beginning.

"Not where we're going."

"Peshawar?"

"Eventually. With one stop on the way."

She didn't need to ask where.


Halfway up the slope of the high ridge that separated the two villages they saw a glint of sunlight off the windshield of an approaching truck on a high curve. Then a second truck came into view, then a third, followed by more. It was an entire convoy, and each bristled with men and guns. Muhammad lifted his foot from the accelerator.

"Keep going," Najeeb shouted. "Go right on past them. Don't look at them and don't slow down. And if they stop you, we're just two women coming from the clinic. We live in a tent on the far side of the hill. We're not going to Bagwali, just to the other side."

"But their guns . . ."

"You only need to worry about *this* gun. Drive."

The first truck was approaching, the driver frowning through the windshield and hitting his brakes but not giving any ground. Najeeb lowered the Kalashnikov out of sight, knowing it would be useless to try and shoot their way past this much firepower. He slid it beneath Muhammad's feet and under the seat as the man whimpered. By pulling the truck onto the shoulder they were able to squeeze past the first of the approaching vehicles, and then the second, but the third one swerved outward to block their way.

Muhammad groaned, slamming on the brakes as they slid to a halt in the dirt, and Najeeb saw his father step from the cab of the facing truck, an imperious look on his face and a gun in his hand.

Najeeb recognized every one of the five men on the back of the vehicle. They all carried loaded RPGs, bulbous green shells sprouting from the barrels like some exotic fruit. The quivering Muhammad could barely roll down his window.

"What are you doing up here?" his father asked, leaning inside and inspecting the cab. "There shouldn't be anyone on this road."

"Health clinic," Muhammad said. "Medical emergency."

God, he was an idiot, Najeeb thought.

Najeeb's father slowly swiveled his head, looking closely toward the eye shields of both burqas. Fortunately, women were supposed to hold their tongues in this situation, although Najeeb felt certain that at any moment the man's hand would reach in to snatch his hood away. Surely his father would see his eyes through the mesh, or recognize his

smell, or even his fear—the one emotion his father had always zeroed in on, in the way that an eagle can sense the heat of any living thing, even from a hundred yards in the sky. He heard Daliya's steady breathing, could feel her next to him, pressed warmly to his side.

Then his father leaned back, thumping a hand impatiently on the door as Muhammad flinched.

"Get them out of here. And don't try to go back to Alzara, not before morning. Go now!"

"Yes, sir," Muhammad said, so eager to comply that he nearly hit Najeeb's father's truck before it could move out of the way. Several of the men in the back laughed, shaking their heads. Theirs was the swagger of warriors on the way to battle, bandoleered and ready. Muhammad passed eleven trucks in all, each fully loaded, and as they reached the end of the column Najeeb turned for a better look at the sinuous line as it disappeared into the rising dust, working its way down the slope.

It wasn't hard to envision how events would unfold from here. The invaders would take the village by surprise, and the ensuing fight would be not so much a battle as a scrum—a few wild exchanges of gunfire punctuated by the occasional grenade. Each side would lose a man or two, and Rafik-Khan would hold out just long enough to salvage a measure of pride before coming to terms by handing over the prize—not his village, but Aziz. Then the two warlords would go back to the uneasy arrangement of old, with his father having secured the necessary stability for pursuing his latest ambitions.

For a moment Najeeb felt a pang of sympathy for Aziz, who must have believed that his entire life had been leading up to this moment of glorious defiance. Instead, he would be dead by nightfall. They might even hoist his head as a warning. By dawn he would be just like the men on the gallows, stiff and dewy, his face drained of blood.

But the pang passed, because Najeeb had other, more pressing matters to attend to, and for once he was not someone else's tool, or employee. He was working now for himself, and for Daliya, with a final favor still to carry out for a friend and ally. And he felt good about their chances, because if all those trucks and all those men meant imminent trouble for Alzara, they meant something entirely different for Bagwali. For a rare and fleeting moment, the village and his family compound would be virtually unguarded, left in the hands of a few old men. Najeeb intended to seize the opportunity.

First things first, however. When they were a good half mile past the convoy and somewhere near the tribal boundary, Najeeb told Muhammad to stop.

"Out," he said. It wouldn't do to have a coward at the wheel, not with the business ahead.

"No," Muhammad pleaded. "I must stay with the truck."

"You want to spend the rest of your life in Bagwali, then? Okay. Drive on."

Muhammad opened the door with a sigh. He stepped into the road and began walking without another word. Najeeb climbed across Daliya, then took a moment to awkwardly pull off the burqa, tossing it to the floor. He turned toward her, smiling, then threw the truck into gear.

Just before rounding the next curve he glanced in the rearview mirror for a last look at Muhammad. The man was shuffling forlornly toward Alzara, where, judging from the rising sounds of gunfire, the battle was just beginning.

## CHAPTER THIRTY-FOUR

T HE SOUNDS OF BATTLE still crackled from far away as Skelly walked disconsolately down the hill. No sense baking in the sun, he supposed, especially when he felt so marooned.

He considered again the words spoken by his escort, both last night and a moment earlier—"Najeeb gone." It was still Skelly's only clue concerning the whereabouts of his fixer, and the possibilities seemed more bleak by the minute. He felt responsible, having coaxed the young man along on this trip that was ending so badly.

The gunfire from the distant town—Alzara, he presumed—would at least seem to explain why Bagwali was deserted. Everyone must have gone off to fight. It probably also explained the tension at last night's dinner.

But was Najeeb involved in the fighting? Might that be where he had "gone" to? Or had he been disposed of beforehand, meaning he was already gone, and for good?

Walking down the path, Skelly couldn't help but marvel at all the tangled threads of power out here in the tribal territories, on both sides of the border. Unravel them and you might solve a century's worth of riddles that had vexed everyone from the Russians to the CIA. He doubted if even the visiting Arabs had a real handle on the dynamic. People here were motivated by something far more complicated than religious zeal. Or perhaps that was just the sunbaked fancy of a tired old hack in need of a cup of tea and a few bites of bread.

He quickened his pace toward the *hujera*, the silent escort in his wake. The old man had still barely broken a sweat. Then a flash of sun-

light caught his eye in the near distance. A truck was out there, headed their way along the serpentine road from the ridge separating Bagwali and Alzara.

Was someone already returning from the battle? A truckload of the wounded, perhaps. But it seemed too soon, unless the attackers were already in retreat.

The sight of the truck seemed to agitate his escort, who slung the gun off his shoulder and chambered a round with a harsh clatter.

"Easy," Skelly said, palm outward, as if calming a growling mastiff. "Easy now."

The truck drew closer, still about half a mile away as they neared the *hujera*. They paused to watch as it looped around the village, still coming toward them, the escort now bringing the gun to his waist. On the truck came, finally skidding to a halt a hundred yards away. Someone was moving around inside the cab, although it was hard to tell through the glare of the windshield.

Skelly's escort shouted, perhaps in warning, and when there was no reply he raised the gun to his shoulder, shouting again. A head poked from the window, then the barrel of a gun. Skelly dove to the ground, heart jolting, satchel flying.

His escort fired a deafening blast, and there was an answering shot from the truck. Skelly heard glass splintering, then a short, piercing scream. The old man grunted and fell to his knees, blood spattering Skelly's pants. He reached over trying to help the man, who was clutching his right thigh. The truck revved its engine, and when Skelly saw it moving closer he grabbed the escort's gun. Blood was still spurting from the wound, but the man wouldn't let go.

"Christ, give it to me!"

The truck was nearly upon them. But as Skelly finally wrested the weapon free, a voice called out his name.

"Skelly, hurry! Get in!"

Not believing his ears, he looked up to see Najeeb looking across the cab. The truck's windshield was gone, shattered by the old man's shot. A young man in blue was at the passenger window. Neither of them seemed hurt.

"Leave him," Najeeb said. "Others will be coming soon. But bring his gun."

Skelly ran to the truck, gun in hand, satchel bouncing on his back. The second man—who Skelly now realized was a woman with a

severely short haircut—slid over to make room, and as he climbed in
he saw that the shot had plowed through the middle of the front seat,
leaving a tangle of shredded foam and vinyl.

The doors slammed. Skelly was safe. He was elated, incredulous.

"Where were you? What was happening over there?" he asked,
meaning the far village.

But Najeeb was distracted, glancing sharply toward Bagwali and
the family compound. Skelly turned to see the escort's reinforcements
moving toward them. Two were young boys, and two were older men,
one of them missing a leg yet traveling with surprising speed with
the aid of a crutch—a ragtag foursome, but well armed, and Skelly
watched with amazed horror as the amputee dropped the crutch and
shouldered his weapon while balancing on one leg like a grizzled
flamingo.

"Get down!" he yelled as the gun boomed, the shot going wide.

Najeeb floored the gas pedal, the truck fishtailing in a spray of
gravel before surging forward. More shots sounded, one of them slamming into the tailgate. From a slope just ahead of them on the right
another boy seemed to materialize from nowhere, darting toward
them and throwing a stone. Najeeb swerved, and the rock sailed
through the open windshield, just missing the woman before crashing
into the window, then dropping harmlessly in Skelly's lap. She was a
lucky one, Skelly thought, wondering where the hell Najeeb had
found her.

Two more shots missed as they topped a small rise. Then the truck
dropped mercifully below the crest, swerving around a rocky outcrop
and out of immediate danger.

Najeeb slowed, checking the mirror.

"Gone," he said. "And all the trucks from the village are off in
Alzara. They won't catch us now."

"Close one," Skelly said.

"The whole day has been a close one."

"But now we're going to make it. Right?"

There was a pause, as if everyone was waiting for someone to con-
tradict Skelly's hopeful assessment. Najeeb broke the silence. "Yes, I
think we are going to make it." Then he turned to the woman in the
middle. "Daliya, this is Skelly. Skelly, please meet Daliya."

"Honored and amazed," Skelly said, grinning and baffled all at
once, not sure whether it would be proper to shake her hand and still
wondering about the haircut, yet so immensely relieved by their turn

of fortune that he wanted to burst out laughing, whooping to the skies in triumph. Then for a panicky few seconds he remembered his notes, thinking he'd left them behind. But, no, they were safe in the satchel, still slung clumsily across his back. He wrenched the bag around front, zipping it open for a reassuring glance inside. It was all there, everything but a few key ingredients. And now they were headed for Peshawar, where he could loose it upon the world.

THEY TOLD EACH OTHER about the events of the day. Daliya's tale may have been the most admirable, but Najeeb's was the most intriguing. Najeeb deciphered for Skelly the details of the previous night's dinner, and the ruse cooked up by his uncle Aziz, then trumped by his father. He rushed through an account of the war council in Alzara and described the beginnings of the firefight, which he and Daliya had been able to see from the overlooking ridge. It had been clear that his father's forces would quickly carry the day. Then he wondered aloud what must have become of Aziz.

More pieces of the puzzle, Skelly thought, already trying to envision where they fit, his excitement building.

"I've sketched out a lot of the story on a legal pad," he said. "It's going to be a hell of a tale."

They were all smiles now, though for different reasons, even if Najeeb seemed a little subdued since things were calming down. He had chosen a route that avoided Alzara, but said they had already crossed into Shinwari territory. He figured that the number of men in the town meant they should encounter little if any resistance all the way to the Grand Trunk Road, which would give them an unobstructed route to Peshawar. They drove east by northeast as the sun lowered in the western sky, and judging by the clear view across the rolling countryside it seemed that their luck would hold.

They topped the next rise to see a blessedly empty plain. But a few moments later a lone dark vehicle poked into view from a crease in the hills to their left, angling toward them in a great hurry. Skelly figured it was too far away to do them any harm, but Najeeb kept glancing in that direction, and soon it was apparent that they were on a collision course.

"I saw that truck in Alzara," Daliya said, as the huge black vehicle loomed closer.

"It's a Chevy Suburban," Skelly said. "I think I know who's in it."

The vehicles slowed, approaching each other cautiously—two predators off their turf, each probing the mettle of the other.

"Hell, what am I thinking?" Skelly said, and he leaned out the window, raising his torso and waving both arms while Najeeb brought the truck to a halt.

"Sam!" Skelly shouted, still waving, and for a moment he worried he'd guessed wrong about the truck's occupants. Then to his relief one of the smoked-glass windows rolled down and a familiar face emerged. Pale skin, sunglasses and a button-down collar. It was Sam Hartley, all right.

"Skelly?" Hartley pulled off his sunglasses. Now the Suburban had stopped, too. They were still about forty yards apart.

"Who else?" Skelly shouted back. "Fancy meeting you here."

Hartley shook his head with an incredulous smile, then the Suburban lumbered forward halfway across the breach before stopping again, rocking on its springs. Hartley opened the door and hopped out. He wore khaki pants and a blue work shirt, the top buttons undone. It was a jarring sight after days of seeing nothing but *kameez*, giving Skelly an inkling of how odd Westerners must look here—himself included—not just their pasty skin but all their accoutrements, which now seemed so ill suited for the landscape.

The driver's side window rolled down, and a second head poked out, also with reflector sunglasses, but the face was familiar enough for Skelly to tell that Arlen Pierce was at the wheel. So he had been right. Hartley and Pierce had indeed been together on that late night in Peshawar, outside the Hotel Grand.

But what did it mean? Was Hartley's job merely cover, or were he and Pierce actually mixing pipeline business with a security mission? Either way, both men probably would have been unhappy about Skelly knowing the whole story. All the more reason to keep pursuing it.

Now Pierce was out of the truck, so Skelly opened the door and clambered out, too. Najeeb and Daliya exited on the driver's side. Everyone standing now, but still wary—or was that Skelly's imagination?

"They were in Alzara, at the *malik*'s war council," Najeeb muttered across the roof of the truck, trying not to be overhead. It was interesting news, worth bringing up right away.

"So you escaped the firefight in Alzara?" Skelly shouted to Hartley,

unable to resist a little needling and half hoping for an intemperate but revealing answer.

Hartley seemed taken aback. He looked at Pierce, apparently in consultation, but the other man said nothing.

"Yes," Hartley finally answered. "Got out in the nick of time. The idiots. I've had it with these stupid people."

Skelly flushed in embarrassment.

Then Pierce spoke up. "Sam told me you were with Razaq. You're lucky to be here at all."

Skelly nodded. "I've had an interesting couple of days." He probably should have left it at that. But journalists who've struck gold can almost never resist offering others a glimpse at their fortune, and Skelly was no exception. "I was at the hanging. A lot of Arabs were there. Some pretty important ones."

Pierce seemed to mull that over for a moment.

"Impressive. Your desk must've loved it."

"They don't know yet. The bastards stole my sat phone, so I haven't had a chance to file. Just as well, I guess, since I'm still trying to figure where all the pieces fit. I thought you two might be able to help me with that."

Pierce turned toward Hartley, saying something Skelly couldn't hear, then shouted back, "Maybe we can. But you're not going to get very far going in that direction. That way's not safe. Sam knows another route, so why don't you follow us? You can ride with us, Skelly. More room. You guys look a little cramped."

"Stay with us," Daliya hissed, surprising both Skelly and Najeeb. Given her luck so far, it seemed like sound advice.

"That's okay," Skelly shouted back. "We'll follow you."

There was further consultation on the other side, the sun moving lower in the sky.

Najeeb whispered, "He is not right about the way back. *This* is the best way."

"Don't worry. We can peel off once we're moving," Skelly said. "If they don't like it, that's their problem. I can catch up with them back in Peshawar."

"Look, Skelly." Another shout, this time from Sam Hartley, whose tone was plaintive. "We really can't let you go on your own like this. Not until we've had a chance to explain."

"I'm all ears," he answered.

Then Pierce pulled out a handgun. Skelly could scarcely believe it.

"I'll lay it all out for you in the car," Hartley said. "So come on."

Najeeb edged toward the open door of the truck, where one of the Kalashnikovs lay on the seat.

"Stay away from there," Pierce shouted, turning the gun on Najeeb. "You're coming with us, too. All three of you. Come on. We're wasting time."

But Pierce hadn't counted on resistance from Skelly, so when the reporter reached into the truck for the second gun it surprised the man, although not half as much as Skelly surprised himself—chambering a round before anyone could blink, grateful for the little refresher course Najeeb had given him back in the Ali Khel Gorge.

At first Pierce looked shocked. Then he began to laugh.

"Good God, would you look at this." He lowered the handgun. "A hack with a weapon." He was smiling now, as if to say it had all been a bluff.

But just as Skelly was convinced they'd won the point, two more trucks emerged over a nearby rise in a scatter of gravel, trailing billows of dust. Everyone watched transfixed as the trucks made a beeline for their tense little huddle, braking to a halt just behind the Suburban, flanking it at angles like the horns of a bull. Each was filled with several men armed to the teeth, dusty and sweating. Straight from battle, Skelly supposed, and it was pretty clear whose side they were on now.

"Looks like we have a standoff," Pierce shouted, still smiling. "Your move."

Skelly considered their options, most of which seemed to involve bloodshed. Perhaps Pierce had been bluffing before, but these new arrivals probably didn't know the meaning of the word.

"All right," he said. "I'll come with you. Only if Najeeb and the girl can leave." He didn't want them to know Daliya's name. "But first send your army away."

"The army stays until you're in the car. But your friends can go."

Skelly briefly considered the terms, then nodded.

"No," Daliya hissed. "Do not do it!"

Skelly cast a glance at her. Amazing eyes, and enough spirit for all three of them. No wonder Najeeb had fallen for her.

"Fair enough," he shouted back.

Pierce nodded, then spoke in a muffled burst of Pashto to the men in the trucks, who lowered their guns, engines still idling.

"Okay," Pierce said. "Your turn again."

"Get out of here now," Skelly said to Najeeb. "Just toss me my bag first."

Najeeb hesitated.

"C'mon. He won't keep 'em leashed all day. And while you're at it, reach in and get the money. Bottom pocket. You've earned it. Just leave me a few hundred. We'll settle up the rest in Peshawar."

Najeeb seemed to be complying by the sound of it, although Skelly kept his eyes on Pierce and the men in the trucks. The satchel then sailed across the roof of the truck, landing at his feet with a puff of dust.

"We'll wait for you at the highway," Najeeb muttered. "Or I can double back and try to follow."

Skelly shook his head, then looked Najeeb in the eye with all the gratitude he could muster. "Look, you saved my ass. Twice. Let me return the favor. Do it for her."

He nodded toward Daliya, who reached out a hand as if she might be able to touch him from across the roof.

"Now go."

The two complied without a further word. The engine started, and the truck rolled away, the others watching without a sound until all that was visible was its dust contrail, tracing a thin brown line along the dimming horizon.

"Well, come on, then," Hartley said, relaxed now, trying to sound cheerful. "Climb in and we'll get started."

Skelly sagged, feeling alone in the sudden silence, his protector gone, along with the lucky Daliya. He wondered how long it would be before he saw them again.

## CHAPTER THIRTY-FIVE

PIERCE ORDERED the other trucks away, and they headed back toward Alzara as Skelly climbed into the Suburban. It was air-conditioned, as chilled as a Houston shopping mall in July. Neither Pierce nor Hartley had said a word to him since he'd put down the Kalashnikov and walked to their vehicle. But at least Pierce had put away his handgun.

Skelly slid across the cool vinyl seat, trying to get comfortable.

"Here," Pierce said. "Maybe this will make you feel better."

He held the handgun, offering it to Skelly across the front seat.

"I took out the clip. Consider it a peace offering. But there was no way we were letting you out of here without being sure you heard our side. Off the record, of course."

"Of course," Skelly said, still tense from the standoff.

Pierce's gesture was reassuring, all the same, and Skelly sensed his inner alarms subsiding, although his adrenaline was still surging. If Hartley and Pierce would go to these lengths to control him, then they must have really screwed up. The question was whether Transgas interests had anything to do with it. The only thing worse than letting the world's most wanted criminal slip through your fingers would be doing it while trying to turn some sort of corporate profit. And while betraying a supposed ally, no less.

The potential repercussions of such news simmered heavily in Skelly's stomach, like something molten, and in his lingering anger at Pierce he felt the urge to spew it in the man's face, flaunting it, taking his vengeance by displaying his knowledge of their cunning and their foul-ups, their callous blundering among these hills and tribesmen.

But there was danger in that, too, he knew, and a cautious voice deep within told him to hold on, keep it in check. Don't spill any secrets until they spilled theirs. For the moment, at least, he held a certain advantage, because they probably wanted information from him even more than he wanted it from them. But, truth be told, there were still gaps in his story, and Hartley and Pierce might be the only people who could fill them.

Pierce started the engine, then took off his sunglasses for a moment, rubbing the weariness out of his face. He glanced back at Skelly, grinning tightly, although the blue eyes still offered only admonishment, the small-bore glower of the cheated. Then, as if he'd already revealed too much, he put the glasses back on, like someone in a limousine rolling up the smoked window, and threw the car into gear.

"You're probably wondering exactly what it is you saw over there, aren't you?" Hartley chirped from the passenger's side.

Sam didn't seem so tense now, another good sign. Skelly could live with a delay, he supposed, as long as he got something in return. He just hoped they didn't intend to stay overnight out here.

"I guess you could say that," Skelly answered. "Got some great stuff, though."

"How'd you like to know the rest of the story, then?" Hartley said, easing into sales mode. "All off the record, of course." A furtive glance at Pierce. "But usable as far as helping you shape it."

"I can live with that."

"Great." Hartley smiled. All that was missing was the mug of beer. "Then why don't we swap a few war stories. And Arlen here can tell you which end is up. The theory being that if you're going to spill the beans you might as well spill the right ones. We'll have you back in Peshawar in time for dinner. My treat, even, as long as you give me that debriefing you promised. After you've filed, of course."

They were going to spin him, in other words, just as he'd expected. No problem. In fact, Hartley's words were music to his ears. Everything about the preceding moments—Pierce pulling his gun, the armed men in the trucks—had seemed to spell doom and danger, but Skelly was now beginning to believe that things would be fine. He was almost ashamed at his growing sense of relief, because he knew that it came partly from being back among his own people, his own tribe, returned to a world where everyone not only spoke his language but knew the same cues, the slang, the rules of the game.

He pulled out a notebook, propping it on his knee, with the whole

backseat to himself. The cushioning of the black vinyl seats felt like a mattress at the Ritz after the places he'd been sleeping lately. And in a Chevy, no less. They might just as easily have been rambling down Pennsylvania Avenue toward Capitol Hill. Just three fellows bearing secrets with a scandal to manage, probing each other for weaknesses while the clock ticked.

"You really can't mention us in this piece, you know," Pierce cut in. Nothing warm in his voice. "Not just by, but by position. None of this coy 'unnamed pipeline company official' or 'Western diplomat' bullshit. Got it?"

"No problem."

Pierce raised up for a glance at him in the rearview mirror, and Skelly felt like he'd just been hooked up to a polygraph.

"But maybe you could tell me for my own benefit exactly what roles you two have been playing out here?"

"Well, my ID is from the State Department," Pierce said. "It says I'm a contract security officer, escorting our friend here, who's an official representative of the commercial interests section."

"And unofficially?"

"None of your damn business."

"Look," Hartley chirped, playing the peacemaker, "why don't we figure out what it is you need explained?"

"You could start by telling me what you were doing in Alzara. And what it had to do with Razaq, or with the possibility that some Arabs might still be on the loose, including the big man himself."

"Let's just say that some of our interests were in play in Alzara," Hartley said. "And for the moment they happened to coincide with the interests of some of the tribesmen."

"Tribesmen who didn't fare too well, from what I've heard."

Hartley and Pierce looked at each other, and Pierce spoke up, turning in the seat. His voice was tense, almost a snarl.

"Hey, Skelly, look at me. And look at your friend Sam here. Tell me, do we look happy? Satisfied?"

"Hard to tell with those shades on."

Pierce yanked them off as the Suburban slurried into a curve. Pierce was agitated, all right, deep creases of hard-won dissatisfaction. And those eyes again.

"So what do you think now?"

"I think you're pissed off. Meaning somebody must have fucked up."

"And you figure we'll just spell it out for you, huh?" Pierce was shouting now. Hartley looked down at his lap, face reddening. "What you're seeing in our faces is damage control. Covering our ass. But we're also trying to rally and get back into the game. And if you come along and lob some bomb of a story into this mess, full of half-truths and speculation about things you saw, or *think* you saw, then you'll just be making it tougher for all of us. For your friends, and for your country. Understood?"

"So you're appealing to my patriotism."

"I'm appealing to your pragmatism. I'm saying wait for the dust to clear and you'll have an even better story. With our full cooperation."

"Meaning, give you enough time and you'll be able to come up with a good-enough cover story so it won't look like the profit motive cost us Bin Laden, or killed Razaq. Is that what you're trying to say?"

It was a shot in the dark, and Skelly almost immediately regretted having let Pierce goad him into it. But it must have scored a direct hit, because Pierce slammed on the brakes.

The truck skidded to a halt, dust clouds boiling past the windows. Pierce got out, snatching the keys from the ignition and slamming the door behind him. Hartley watched with mouth agape as Pierce stalked forward, fuming, then jamming his hands in his pockets. Skelly instinctively looked for the handgun, which was still on the seat. He nudged it into his open satchel, hoping Hartley hadn't noticed.

"Jesus, Skelly," Hartley said with a tired sigh. "What'd you have to set him off like that for?" Hartley then opened the passenger door and climbed glumly from the Suburban, the wife trying to calm her enraged husband on behalf of an unruly child. He shut the door behind him, and the two men walked away from the car, Hartley with his hands out in a pleading gesture, Pierce shaking his head vigorously, his mouth moving.

With all the windows shut, Skelly couldn't hear a word. He tried opening his, but they were power windows, of course, and with the keys gone the button was useless. Now their voices were raised, but the words were muffled and indistinct. Pierce looked back toward Skelly, his face under control once again. Hartley was the one shaking his head now. Then Pierce leaned into Hartley's face, mouth in motion, voices no longer audible. A minute or so later they climbed back in, keys jangling as Pierce shoved them into the ignition and cranked the engine.

Hartley said nothing, looking straight ahead, ashen. Perhaps Pierce

had decided to give the man up to Skelly, a burnt offering to save his own skin, or Uncle Sam's. Poor Hartley. But better for Skelly's story if the result was that both men turned against each other. Much better than if they'd simply clammed up.

Then Pierce spoke up, his voice calmer now.

"Okay, Skelly. A proposition."

"I'm listening."

"What would you say to the idea of us setting you up with someone who knows even more than we do—somebody connected, who not only knows where the pieces fit, but would also speak to you on the record? With a name and everything?"

So Pierce was going to let someone else do the dirty work. Someone who would no doubt pin the blame on Hartley and Transgas, while glossing over any official U.S. involvement.

"As long as it's no later than tomorrow." No way was he letting Pierce maneuver him into a delay.

"Is an hour from now soon enough?"

"Sure, but . . ."

"What the hell are you talking about?" Hartley said, sounding rattled.

"You know him, Sam. Our friend across the hills?" An unreadable look passed between them.

"Jesus, Arlen. I dunno." Hartley shook his head, looking out the window toward nothing in particular.

"You don't trust the guy?" Skelly asked.

"It's not that," Hartley said. "It's just . . ."

"Just what?"

"Yeah, just what?" Pierce said, the edge creeping back into his voice. "Don't worry, Sam. We'll still have you back in town before the Gulbar closes."

"So who is this source anyway?" Skelly asked.

"Just that," Hartley said weakly. "A source. All of us use him sometimes." He shrugged. "Maybe Arlen's right."

"Damn right I am. But only if you're game, Skelly."

Skelly checked his watch, already plotting how the next twenty-four hours might proceed. They'd get back to Peshawar later than expected, but still in plenty of time for a long shower and a good meal—not that he'd be likely to get his room back at the Pearl. He could live with the Grand just fine, though. By midday tomorrow he'd

have culled and consolidated his best stuff, and by nightfall he'd have filed his story and would be negotiating with his editors for space. Although for once he was certain he would get all he needed.

"Sure," he said finally. "I'm game."

Pierce nodded, saying nothing, and a few miles later he turned left onto a track even bumpier than the road they'd been on, pointing the big truck west toward the lowering sun.

THEY DROVE for nearly an hour, saying little and climbing steadily as the sky darkened. Hartley seemed to have gone pale, looking sickly in the green glow of the dashboard lights, as if realizing at last that there was no way to stop the story from coming out. So much for that job offer, Skelly supposed. But he hoped they'd be stopping soon.

"We must be getting pretty close to the border by now," he said.

"Pretty much," Pierce said.

"We're not crossing it, are we?"

"Relax."

But Skelly couldn't help remembering how he'd already crossed it once without knowing it.

"I'd be interested to see where we are on the map," he said.

"Sam will show you once we're back at the hotel, I'm sure."

Hartley barely grunted in reply, still gazing out his window into the evening. A short time later Pierce picked up a radio handset lying beside him on the seat and spoke into it in Pashto. Skelly wondered if he had used it to summon the two trucks earlier, the ones that had arrived before Najeeb and Daliya drove off. He wondered where the two of them were now, and hoped they were in Najeeb's bed, enjoying themselves. He felt a stab of jealousy, of longing for some companionship of his own. But home seemed like a million miles away.

After a short delay someone answered in a crackle of static. Pierce replied, then set the radio down, nodding.

"Good," he said. "The gang's all here." A mile or so later, the road growing bumpier, they rounded a downhill curve to see a grizzled fellow with half his teeth missing and a gun blocking the way, squinting into the headlight beams. Pierce pulled alongside him, speaking out his open window in Pashto.

The man nodded, expressionless. Then he pulled out a radio just like Pierce's and mumbled into it.

"How's your Pashto, Skelly?" Pierce said, turning in the seat.

"Nonexistent."

"Then I'll see if he's got anybody who can interpret."

"I guess you'd do in a pinch."

Pierce snorted.

"It would have to be more than a pinch." He spoke again to the sentry, who got back on his radio, then spoke to Pierce.

Pierce turned in his seat toward Skelly.

"Okay, fella. You're on. Straight down the hill and right around the corner."

"You're not coming?"

"No need. They've got an English speaker."

"I meant for introductions."

Pierce shook his head.

"Like I said, no need. Only make him nervous if all three of us went."

Skelly hesitated. Hartley didn't make a sound.

"Well, do you want the lay of the land or not?" Pierce asked. "Your choice, but we're on a timetable. The less time we're stuck out here in the dark, the better."

So Skelly got out, making sure he had a pencil, a notebook and his satchel. Then he headed down the hill, the sentry falling into step behind him. After about twenty yards he heard Pierce's radio crackle again. He wondered how Hartley put up with the man, but supposed that was another reason Hartley made the big money. Hard to believe that only days ago he'd been feeling burned out enough to seriously consider a career like Sam's. All it had taken to recharge Skelly's battery had been this story, and the excitement again stirred inside him. Frankly he needed it just now, to help tamp down a darkening bubble of apprehension. He wished Najeeb was still with him, someone who would have been the better judge of what moves to make, not to mention a better translator than whoever this source was likely to offer.

As they came around the rocky bend he saw about twenty men seated around a cookfire, surrounded by darkness. Their apparent leader stood a few feet away from them with his back to Skelly, barely illuminated as he consulted with two others. A white turban topped his head, neat as a layer cake. As Skelly approached he saw that a pair of binoculars hung from the man's neck. In one hand he held a radio, in the other a gnawed bone of whatever they'd cooked for dinner.

Several faces around the campfire turned to watch Skelly. The encampment stank of sweat and wood smoke, and of overcooked meat. Skelly thought he heard the spin of tires on gravel. Just Pierce positioning the car for an easy exit, he supposed.

The leader turned to face him, and Skelly recognized him right away, although the last time the man's turban had been black. It was Haji Kudrat. Was he really the source, or was this some awful practical joke?

"So which one of you speaks English?" Skelly said, his voice sounding too high.

No one answered.

"English?" he offered again. This time Kudrat replied in a raspy burst of Pashto, pocketing the radio and nibbling the bone a final time before dropping it to the ground. He stepped closer, inspecting Skelly from head to toe as the rest of the men watched. Then he asked something in Pashto.

"I don't understand," Skelly said, wondering what the hell Pierce had gotten him into. Kudrat spoke again, only a few words, but several of his men laughed roughly, heads bobbing around the fire.

"I'll get Pierce," Skelly said. "He speaks Pashto."

"Pee-erce," Kudrat said with a nod, having finally heard a word he could understand. But when Skelly turned to go, two hands seized his shoulders from behind and shoved him back toward Kudrat, who was reaching to his waist, right hand gripping the hilt of a sword. And not just any sword. It was Razaq's. Kudrat raised it aloft. Skelly couldn't move, still held firmly in place by the hands on his shoulders. Watching the sword rise he could faintly make out the inscription on the blade, remembering Najeeb's translation. "No Return."

The sword wavered, catching a glint of firelight. Then, to Skelly's horror and astonishment, Kudrat swept the blade downward in one great motion that seemed to last forever. Skelly raised his hands in defense, but far too slowly, the blade whisking away a finger like a shaft of celery, then still coming, now slicing into his cotton shirtfront and the butterfat of his skin as it began a diagonal trace, furrowing his chest from neck to waist, screaming through him in a wide deep valley, a red canyon opening across his torso. If he was making a sound he did not hear it, for it was shouted down by the sudden agonies of his nervous system, all systems in retreat and disarray. He felt his legs sag but still couldn't bear to look as he landed on his knees, then flopped to the

side, feeling the warmth that now covered him like a slick of burning oil as a sort of dreaminess overtook him, everything in his field of vision gone gummy and indistinct. Then darkness, and all was still, clarity at last emerging in a long moment in which he saw them all, everyone who had ever been important to him—his children, his wives, his editors and colleagues, and yes, Najeeb too, all of them clean and sensibly dressed, and peering down at him from a high surrounding circle, as if from the rim of a well, every face frowning with worry and concern. But most disheartening of all was that no one spoke a word. His oldest daughter, Carol, over there to the left, moved forward, the only one to do so, almost reaching him now as she extended a hand in care and in sorrow. But her hand never found him, for he was falling, below them all into a shaft without end. Good-bye, he'd wanted to say. But he never got the chance, and now, in his last flickering instant of awareness, he knew it was too late. Too late.

## CHAPTER THIRTY-SIX

## Regional Briefs

### By Our Correspondent

**FOUR KILLED:** Three men were killed and seven others injured in a clash between Afridi and Shinwari factions in the village of Alzara this week in the Khyber Tribal Agency, in an apparent dispute over timber rights and motor lorry transport. The warring groups attacked each other with automatic weapons and grenade launchers. Three men were taken to hospital for treatment. Police rushed to the fighting and controlled the situation.

**WOMAN MURDERED:** A married woman was axed to death yesterday by her cousin, allegedly due to an old family feud in the village of Manduri in the Kurram Tribal Agency. Mustafa Zahoori barged into the house of his cousin Shamayla and killed her with repeated blows of the axe. The deceased was the mother of four children.

**BODY IDENTIFIED:** A man killed during a robbery in the Khyber Tribal Agency has been identified as missing American journalist Stanford J. Kelly. Mr. Kelly had not been heard from since entering Afghanistan the previous week. Identifying the body was industrialist Sam Hartley, a friend of the deceased. The remains will be transported to the United States under arrangement of the American consulate. Mr. Kelly's colleagues plan a memorial service for 3 p.m. today at the Pearl Continental Hotel.

NAJEEB AND DALIYA took seats near the back. Hotel employees had set up folding chairs in a small conference room with a coffee urn on a side table, and if not for a huge floral arrangement near

the podium it would have looked as if a business seminar was about to begin.

About thirty people showed up, not a bad turnout, Najeeb thought, although it was a slow news day in Peshawar. All the action now was in Afghanistan, where after weeks of stalemate the Northern Alliance had finally broken through and the Taliban seemed to be on the run. Already there was a rising clamor among the foreign journalists for travel passes to Torkham, in case the border should open up. The moment Kabul fell there would doubtless be a headlong rush, whether the authorities were ready or not. But for now there was still the sense of a calm before the storm, so in a way it was the perfect time for Skelly's colleagues to pay their respects.

Najeeb recognized several faces from the earlier bus ride to Torkham, including the woman Skelly had called Chatty Lucy. Her face was already blotchy, and she was dabbing her cheeks with a handkerchief before the first speaker opened his mouth. She was one of the few journalists accompanied by her fixer, and Najeeb was pleased to see she'd hired a new one. Skelly would have liked it, too, he thought.

None of this had prevented the Clerk from showing up, who in an extreme show of bad taste sat by himself in the back row, furtively taking notes in a small brown pad that he slipped beneath his thigh.

Neither Sam Hartley nor Arlen Pierce came. Nor had they returned Najeeb's phone calls during the past several days. He doubted he would see either of them again.

For three days running Najeeb had tried to write his own version of events for the *Frontier Report*, only to have each attempt spiked by his usually inattentive editor, who argued with uncharacteristic zeal that the account of Razaq's hanging was old news, even if the apparent details regarding the men who'd betrayed him weren't.

Najeeb had at first attributed the sudden timidity to the stresses of wartime, figuring he might get a more favorable reception once the Taliban was defeated. But he'd changed his opinion earlier in the day, when he'd again been plucked from traffic on his scooter and escorted in an unmarked jeep to the battered gray door in the alley off Saddar Bazaar.

He arrived once again at Tariq's desk, where he found the man reading a printout of his latest stillborn dispatch.

"Interesting stuff," Tariq said. Najeeb kept his feet. "But how much of it is true?"

Najeeb didn't want to tell him a damn thing, of course. He had purposely avoided reporting back to Tariq since his return, especially once Skelly failed to appear. When his worst fears were confirmed, he continued his silence, out of grief, anger and, to be frank, out of fear of further meddling in his life.

Tariq, seated before a half-finished dinner, seemed relaxed in the extreme.

"Well, are you going to answer my question or not? And sit down."

Najeeb sat, but maintained his silence. Tariq reached into a desk drawer and pulled out a few sheets of official-looking paper with the letterhead of the Peshawar police.

"Here's some reading material that might loosen your lips."

It was a charging document, citing Najeeb for murder. He was alarmed, certain that he was about to be framed for Skelly's death, which he supposed would be easy enough since no one had yet come up with any details, other than a half-baked story about a robbery by rogue elements of some warlord, who wasn't named in the dispatch.

Skelly's American friends themselves had supposedly only barely escaped, but Najeeb was skeptical, and when neither Pierce nor Hartley returned his calls he took that as confirmation of their complicity.

But as he scanned the document now before him he realized from the dates and other particulars that it concerned the *malang* killed outside his apartment.

"The girl turning up safe helped you," Tariq said, "but it didn't clear the decks. There's still this little matter."

Najeeb opened his mouth to protest, to tell him about Karim, but Tariq stilled him with an upraised hand.

"I couldn't care less what really happened that night. All that matters to me is what happened afterward. In Afghanistan and beyond. Everything you saw, right up until now. I want a full debriefing, whatever you can remember, including what you saw of the Arabs *and* of the Americans."

"And what about this?" Najeeb said, holding up the police papers.

"We have a suspect in custody. A drug runner and timber smuggler."

"Name?"

"Does it matter? It's not Karim, if that's what you're thinking. And, yes, I know about him. I know about some other things as well. But not everything. Which is why you had better start talking. And if I can't

interest you in saving your own skin, you can be sure there are still some things we can charge your little friend Daliya with. Flight from a murder scene, for starters."

Najeeb scowled, but did as he was told. He spent the next three hours going over what had happened. Tariq didn't take a single note, probably because somewhere in the room there was a microphone recording it for him. Afterward he placed a phone call to the police while Najeeb sat and listened.

After a few introductory remarks, Tariq said little other than an occasional "yes" or "no." Then he hung up.

"There," Tariq said. "Nothing more for you to worry about. Provided, of course, that you cease in your attempt to publish this." He dropped the printout of Najeeb's story into the trash.

"But what about Skelly's death?" Najeeb protested. "Do you really think it was a robbery?"

Tariq held up his hands.

"That's above my pay grade. Although I would imagine there will eventually be arrests."

"More drug runners and timber smugglers?"

"It's out of my hands. Apparently there is some question whether the death even occurred in Pakistani territory, so the Americans are taking it over. This Mr. Pierce you've spoken of, I believe it is now his affair."

Which didn't surprise Najeeb a bit.

"So what were they doing there?" he asked.

"The two Americans?" Tariq shrugged. "They were in over their heads. I think someone had convinced them that they were about to corner the market on both pipeline routes and stray Arabs, with the help of a few warlord friends. But you know how it goes out there. No one corners the market on anything in the Khyber except the tribesmen. People like your father. And even their fortunes change with the wind. The bad part for me, of course, is that now the Americans will expect me to do something about it. Maybe even to go and find their Arabs for them, including the one they covet most. But you've seen how much influence we have there. So I will give them a copy of my report and hope that they will feel better for a while. And when someone else comes along in some other country who interests them more, I expect they'll forget all about me."

But in trying to sort out recent events, Najeeb had an advantage

that Tariq didn't. It was a lengthy and well-conceived summary including all the players, with everyone's role sketched out on a yellow legal pad. At first the handwriting had been difficult to read, but once he'd gotten the hang of it Najeeb had concluded that Skelly really knew how to tell a story, and it made him oddly proud.

At the moment of their parting in the hills of Khyber, Najeeb had taken the man's notebook instead of his money, less for its value than to ensure its preservation. And earlier this morning, just before he'd been rounded up off the streets, Najeeb had sealed the notebook in a large envelope and passed it along to another foreign journalist at the Pearl, who promised to make sure it got back to Skelly's editors in America.

Would they publish his final dispatch? Perhaps. Perhaps not. Najeeb knew little about the workings of American newspapers. But he had done all he could for the man, and for the moment that was enough.

"So I'm free to go, then?" he asked Tariq, rising to take his leave.

"There is one other thing. Something I still owe you."

For a brief, heady moment Najeeb was sure Tariq was about to slide open a drawer and produce two visas to the United States. All he got instead was an explanation.

"I tried," Tariq said, "but the U.S. is out of the question. They're in total shutdown—even the usual unofficial channels—especially for fellows like you. But Britain's another matter. Apparently the door's still ajar, so I'm working on it."

Najeeb nodded. Better than no hope at all, he supposed.

"One word of advice," Tariq continued, standing now to escort him from the office. "Things would probably move faster if you and your friend were . . . more legally connected?"

"We're working on it," Najeeb said.

And they were.

Daliya was back on her own, sort of. She'd enjoyed a tearful reunion with her family, all transgressions momentarily forgiven in the glow of her miraculous reappearance. Once they calmed down, they of course wanted to lock her up in a Punjabi version of purdah. Her father even made noises about resuming the search for a suitable husband, his clumsy stab at a conciliatory gesture.

But she insisted on returning to Peshawar, where Professor Bhatti had promised to help her find lodgings with female students from the local university, and for the moment none of her relatives felt strong

enough to object. She had returned to them as a strange and unreadable creature, like some exotic bird blown in on a freak storm, and no one yet had the nerve to cage her.

So now there they sat, side by side at Skelly's memorial service, two strange birds in tandem, paying respects to their fallen friend.

Three speakers were scheduled—a Frenchman, a Brit and an American—and between them they seemed to have traveled alongside Skelly at every one of the world's wars during the past twenty years. Each was a gifted storyteller, both poignant and irreverent, and after one particularly nice moment Daliya glanced at Najeeb and almost gasped to see tears rolling down the cheek of her stern Pashtun lover.

She reached up to brush them away, but Najeeb stopped her with a calm but firm gesture.

"Leave them," he whispered, his brown eyes dry even as his face was shining. "I want to feel them for a while."

Daliya nodded. Having been to the Khyber, she understood.

## ACKNOWLEDGMENTS

No, I am not Skelly. My wife and children will attest to that, although without their attractions I might have become some pale version of him, forever restless in search of the far-flung story. But I do proudly claim membership in the esteemed tribe of the foreign correspondent, whose members have taught me a lifetime of lessons with unflagging humor, expertise, professionalism and esprit de corps. Dozens come to mind whom I should thank, but for space reasons I'll limit it here to Barry Bearak, Bill Glauber, Michael Hedges, Tom Hundley, Stephanie Nolen and Doug Struck. I also wish to honor the memory of Azizullah Haidari, Harry Burton, Maria Grazia Cutuli and Julio Fuentes, who were killed on the road to Kabul; and also of Michael Kelly and Elizabeth Neuffer, former colleagues and traveling companions, who lost their lives while reporting from Iraq. Their determined work will outlast us all.

None of our tribe's accomplishments would be possible without all the world's fixers, some of whom would even put Najeeb in the shade, such as Rafi Sayad in Jalalabad, Mahmood Khattak in Peshawar, Muhammad Azfar Karim in Islamabad and Aimal Khan in Quetta. Thanks also to driver Mohammed Hassan, whose quick thinking and lead foot saved five lives.

For insight and advice on various matters on which I am probably still at sea—no blame to them, and all to me—many thanks to Dr. Rukhsana Siddiqui at Quaid-i-Azam University in Islamabad, Dr. Mumtaz A. Bangash of Peshawar University and Dr. Charles T. Lindholm of Boston University, particularly with regard to Dr. Lindholm's

*Generosity and Jealousy* (Columbia University Press, 1982), his excellent study of daily life among the tribal Pashtuns of northern Pakistan.

Thanks also to Ahmed and Shah Wali Karzai, for the time and hospitality they offered in Quetta, affording me a glimpse inside the Afghan diaspora even while their brother, Hamid, was risking his life across the border, succeeding where others failed. May their country someday heal its wounds and finally live in peace.

To my knowledgeable and supportive foreign editors at *The Baltimore Sun*, Jeff Price in the old days and Robert Ruby in the new, many thanks for all the opportunities, but especially for the trust. And much gratitude to my outstanding editors, Sonny Mehta in New York and Selina Walker in London, for their encouragement and unerring guidance. Thanks as well to peerless agent Jane Chelius, there from the beginning.

But as always I reserve the highest praise and affection for the people at home, the best destination of all: parents Bill and Ginny, my sister, Laverne, my wife, Liz, and my children Emma and Will, who inspire more loyalty and devotion than any lordly *malik*.

Westminster Public Library
3705 W. 112th Ave.
Westminster, CO  80031
www.westminsterlibrary.org

"Enlightening and entertaining. . . . A riveting and sometimes frightening read. . . . Fesperman sheds light on the tribal culture in such a way that a murky idea momentarily crystallizes into a vivid picture."　—*The Charlotte Observer*

"[Fesperman] exhibits a keen eye for the landscape's details. . . . He excels at drawing characters."
　　　　　　　　　　　　　　　　　—*Pittsburgh Tribune-Review*

"[This] veteran reporter . . . depicts politics, geography and the tradecraft of reporters, smugglers, warriors and spies with rare insight."　　　　　—*San Jose Mercury News*

"*The Warlord's Son* is a story of humanity, of how primal instincts come to the forefront in dangerous situations. But it's also about friendship and loyalty and redemption, either achieved or disappointed. . . . One of the must-read novels of the year."　　　　　　　　　　　—*January Magazine*

(8) 4/18 KG

H

*Acclaim for Dan Fesperman's*

# THE WARLORD'S SON

"A novel ripped from the headlines. . . . Better than any news dispatch and . . . far more entertaining. . . . Fesperman amazes [with his] searing insights into human nature."
—*The Baltimore Sun*

"A convincing, accurate thriller. . . . This book is worth reading if only for the passage where the hero, Skelly, glimpses Osama bin Laden at a public hanging; the scene both convinces and frightens."
—*The Economist*

"Thoroughly gripping, intelligent and wholly believable. . . . There will be other novels written about the last days of the Taliban . . . but few will match the verisimilitude, drama and compelling characters found in *The Warlord's Son*. . . . The conclusion . . . has the impact of a stun gun."
—*The Flint Journal*

"A first-rate geopolitical yarn. . . . Fesperman combines his strong eye for detail with bleak film-noir cynicism."
—*Entertainment Weekly*

"Fesperman's experience as a war correspondent, together with his powers of description and characterization, produce an utterly compelling thriller and quite simply the best I've read all year."   —Susanna Yager, *The Sunday Telegraph*

Westminster Public Library
3705 W. 112th Ave.
Westminster, CO 80031
www.westminsterlibrary.org